'Mama, please

Now Jane

Holly!'

Holly ran into the kitchen from the yard. The screen door banged behind her. She looked from her mother to her sister and said nothing. Rose had come from the parlour and was standing in the doorway. She, too, silently watched. Jane was working her hands together. Lily, head bent, tears falling, stared down into her lap.

'Holly, go get your Daddy,' Jane commanded.

'Mama, I'll go,' Rose volunteered.

'No.' Jane did not even turn towards Rose. Her eyes were fastened on the little dark girl who stood with her back to the door. Dementedly, she demanded, 'Holly. I said for Holly to go.'

Holly didn't move.

'Go. Go get your Daddy. Bring him here. Tell him that his whore-daughter Lily has something to say to him.'

'Mama, please, I'll go,' Rose said again.

'No!' Jane screamed. 'You, Holly, go!'

This book is dedicated to
my mother and my grandmother,
their sisters, and my own.

PART ONE

❋

JASMINE

❀

Chapter One

❀

An arid river valley in New Mexico, Easter Sunday, 1929 . . .

"How many whores?" she screamed out to him. It was a pierc-
ing howl that he could not answer.

For a moment there were no words. The stillness was total
and terrible, in the room where they were, in the house, and
beyond. Their house, that single dwelling rising up from the
desert, only deepened and did not relieve the isolation of the
place. If it had been left to nature, all of an implacable piece, the
vast waste would not have been so strikingly painful, but that
lone human construction tore through the desolate landscape
leaving a vision of absolute aloneness. As a train whistle slices
through a night and makes the silence heard, so this roof raised
here made this alkalescent wild appear more forsaken even than
it was. To the east there was a great mountain, its scarped peak
shrouded in cloud, and there lived, the Indians believed, Wind
Woman who brought the spring dust storms to the desert. Now
the wind came stirring, whipped by her deific hand. It was a
spot of unspeakable solitude, but from the house the howling
voice came again. And the terrible stillness was shattered into
more terrible pieces.

"How many?" she demanded to know of him. Within her screamed question there was a surer and louder accusation.

"I've told you, Jane," he said finally. "I've told you over and over again . . ."

She, not waiting, but shrilling over his words: "Yes! Yes, you've told me. I remember everything you've told me. All your lies! I'll always remember what you've said . . . and what you haven't said. I'll always . . ."

Now he forced his shouts down upon hers. "I've always told you the truth."

"The truth! You've never told me the truth!"

He stared at her. Her eyes were enormous and pale, the irises so light a blue they looked white and the pupils contracted to tiny black pinpoints. "I've told you the truth but you've never heard it," he said, and his voice quieted, deadened. "You hear only what you want to hear."

She sensed his waning anger. "You don't know what the truth is!" She could not let him drain away from her in weariness and pity. "How many were there? Are there? How many whores have you had? Are you having? How many will you have to have before you've had enough? Or will you ever have enough?" She was shrieking, beyond control, beyond reason, and beyond answering, caught up in her own insane snare. She flailed in her hysteria.

He wanted to reach her, to touch and stop her, but he could only join her. He felt he was the cause, the root of her aberrancy, and that was impelling. He began to speak, a cracked and rising speech.

"Yes, they give me pleasure, whores do!"

"You are a whore. You can only love what's cheap and easy. You can only love what you can leave behind before it's light, leave behind lying wet in a filthy bed!"

Their tangled violent voices came clearly through the closed door and out into the largest room of the house where the six Calder sisters were. They all wore white. They sat silently, very careful not to spoil or crease their new Easter dresses. They waited for the words to cease, and listened to them, too. Their mother and father had been arguing for hours and for all their lives. It was always the same, a cruel continuum. It did not seem possible that the inseparable sharp-edged sounds were made by

two human voices, two human beings who had once in shining
faith, but now incredibly, promised to love and cherish one
another. The closed door was meant to contain the virulence but
that had long ago infected the little girls in white.

The oldest, fourteen-year-old Lily, was the most familiar with
the ongoing battle. She, of all the sisters, with the possible excep-
tion of the baby Poppy, heard the least now. She had ingested it
and it was within her. She appeared emotionless and without
response, but hers was a practiced, a hard-won, impassivity. Her
hands gripped her arms, not to comfort but to constrain herself.
She pressed hard against her large and lately swollen breasts as
if to force them back into her body. Lily had lightish hair of no
distinct color and cloudy close-set eyes. In the narrow face her
full and perfectly molded mouth was a rebellious incongruity.
She habitually bit back her lower lip, hiding and punishing it at
the same time. Her dress was pinched at the waist by a blue
ribbon sash. Lily had taken blue as her own, her acquisitive instinct allowed and encouraged by her mother. The younger
sisters never wore Lily's color, not any shade of it. Only she did.
Lily, jealously, possessively, and tightly bound in blue, not the
best or the brightest or the most beautiful Calder sister, but
the first.

In a far corner, apart, but intently watchful, was Jasmine. She
rocked back and forth in a delicate, nearly indiscernible motion,
prayerlike. Her fine and straight silvern-white hair shimmered
and betrayed her movement. Jasmine's was a genuine detachment,
a real and fluid escape, unlike Lily's heavy withdrawal into herself. There were two years and an eternity between these two
sisters. Solid sunlight passed through an open window near
Jasmine, but she stayed back in shadow, expression and emotion
flashing across her face, her moods changing swiftly. She was
both absorbed and absent, a blonde, black-eyed, ancient child.
The words from the other room touched her and did not, like a
stone skimmed across a pool of water, seconds of contact and
moments of flight. Jasmine's sash was purple, glossy on its
surface and dark in the folds.

Rose contorted her freckled face, trying to make little Poppy
smile. When she succeeded, she grinned widely, satisfied. Rose
was desperate to be happy, and if she had to lie or practice deceit
for happiness, she would. Her eyes were slanted upward and the

corners of her mouth too tilted up. Rose had an unpretty plastic
face, mobile, styled for easy laughter. Her short hair, curly orange
tufts, stuck out all over her head. In a family of few jokes Rose
was naturally the source of most, beginning with her birth. It
was said that Jasmine was such a silent baby they forgot they had
one and so Rose was born barely a year after her. Rose was
boisterous enough for herself and Jasmine and two or three
others. Her eyes darted around the room, from face to face. Then
she stopped and listened for a moment to the shouting from the
other room. Even in sad and staring abstraction she seemed to
smile. Rose was a clown, destined and doomed for clowning. Her
sash was a bright green.

Holly's eyes were fixed upon the closed door. She heard only
her father. She unconsciously twisted the red ribbon tied too
highly upon her, wrinkling it, and risking her mother's ready
wrath. Eight years old, the only dark sister, a small feminine
replica of her father, born in winter while all the others had
come in the sweet green seasons of spring and summer, Holly
felt the intense emotions that she sparked in both her mother and
her father without knowing why she sparked them. Clay and
Jane Calder had tried to end their marriage after Rose was born.
They had lived apart for nearly two years, but in a blind, unwilling flare, a hot and driven reunion, Holly was conceived.
The trap was set and sprung, and who was trapped and who had
trapped became lost and confused. What was plain and un-
deniable was the baby, the dark irrevocable proof that they would
never be free of one another, that they would live on in tortured
alliance and bitter passion. Of this Holly knew nothing. Her
mother dressed her in red, a color she despised. While her heavy
black brows and olive angular face were innately alienating,
Holly felt that red further marked her and made her different
from her fair sisters. Red was the blame her pale mother placed
upon her for being born, red in the wrongly tied sash, and red
in the thick welts that rose on the thin backs of her legs from
her mother's blows. Holly was more than physically like her
father. She, too, like him, could be impenetrable and unreach-
able. She incited her mother's pure white fury as her father did,
but there was no mitigating residual love for the child as there
was for the man. Jane could not forgive Holly who had grown
within her body and was born a total stranger with nothing of

herself to recognize. Jane had loved her husband once, even loved him still, but never his daughter Holly.

Iris was a honeyed beauty, a shining six-year-old. She wore a yellow sash and two yellow ribbons in her hair. She played with one of her thick blond curls, twining it around her fingers. She was fascinated and enthralled by the silken threads. Iris knew vaguely of the trouble between her parents but was unaffected by it. She felt that anyone, everyone, had only to look at her to love her. There could be no trouble for her that would not melt away by looking at her and loving her. But no one could love Iris as much as she loved herself, and she loved only herself, adored and golden, completely selfish, Iris.

The baby, Poppy, in pink and white, impatiently swung her short fat legs. Her face was pallid and pouting, but she stayed in her place, aping the others' obedience, fearful of displeasure. Poppy was pliant yet.

The door opened and Clay Calder walked out. He passed through the room, rushing by the gathered little girls in white as if they were invisible. Jane stood in the doorway and shouted after him.

"Don't you leave this house! I'm warning you! Don't leave. If you go now, don't come back! If you go, don't . . . don't go! If you go now, don't . . . Come back! Come back! Clay! Clay!"

"Jane, I'll be back," he said sadly. He hopelessly left.

At the sound of the closing door Jane's eyes snapped from it to Holly, a direct line from the escaping father to his wayward child. She saw the wrinkled red sash. She rushed at Holly.

"Look at you. Look what you've done. Look at the others. Why can't you be like the others?" she said. Her voice had gone from harsh screaming to a more ominous whisper.

"I'm sorry, Mama," Holly said.

"You're not. You're not sorry."

She slapped Holly hard across the face. The child fell backward from the force of it, but quickly righted herself and stared unflinchingly, and without tears, at her mother. That steady gaze further infuriated Jane.

"Why don't you cry! Don't you have any tears?" She was beginning to scream again. "You'd better find some tears!"

Holly continued to look at her, not answering, unmoving. Then, from perfect stillness, she darted up and ran for the door.

The suddenness of her movement gave her the time she needed. She was out of the house and across the porch before she heard Jane's chasing steps. They were close, the sound of them, too close. She called out to him.

"Daddy! Daddy! Wait for me, Daddy!"

He had not yet driven away. The engine was running, idling fast, but he was bent, still, over the wheel. Holly shouted at him again, but he seemed not to hear her. And all that she could hear were her mother's footsteps. They were louder now, nearer and nearer to her. She could see the car beginning to move. She rushed toward it, headlong, off balance, running and falling desperately together.

"Daddy! Wait! Daddy!" she cried.

"Holly! Stop! Holly!" Jane's voice was raging and strangely fearful, too. "Holly! Stop!"

Clay glanced into his rearview mirror and saw the little figure in white running toward him, a cloud of fine sandy dust rising around her. And beyond he saw Jane. He braked and reached for his door handle. His first thought was to get out of the car and confront the scene behind him, but he was too tired. He paused for only a moment and then leaned over and opened the passenger's side. Holly flung herself inside and swung the door shut after her. He shifted into gear as the little girl whispered between heaving breaths, "Hurry. Don't let her catch us, Daddy."

He accelerated. They felt a jolt. Jane had run close enough to the car to strike the metal trunk with her bare fist. Clay could see her in the mirror, her face horribly distorted with the soundless words she was hurling after them, but Holly did not turn around. She stared straight ahead. She could see her mother clearly without looking back. She touched her hot tingling cheek to the glass of the window, but it offered no coolness to soothe. She rolled down her window. Clay rolled down his. The air rushed through the stifling car. Holly brought her knees up to her chest and felt the rutted road bounce beneath the wheels. She wished that they could leave the ground, fly, and never land. She didn't care where they were going, only that it was away from that house where her mother was.

"Holly," he said. He took one hand from the steering wheel and put it under her chin, turning her face toward him. He looked from the road to her. "She slapped you, didn't she?" he asked.

Holly did not answer immediately. She looked at her father and the joy of being beside him made it not matter, none of it. Nothing mattered as long as she could be with him.

"Holly?" he said again, more insistently questioning.

"Yes," she answered. "She was angry about my sash." She started to remove the red ribbon from her waist. "I wrinkled it," she said. Now she held it balled tightly in her fist.

"She wanted to hurt me. Not you. Can you understand that, Holly?"

"No. Why does she? Why does she want to hurt us?"

"Not us. It's me, not you. Because I hurt her."

"No, you don't, Daddy."

"I do, and most of the time I don't even know that I do. She wants all of me, everything that's in me, and I can't give that to anyone—" He stopped himself. He had said the words not thinking to whom he spoke. "Someday, Holly, you'll know what I mean. You will."

"I love you, Daddy."

His arm went around her thin shoulders and he drew her next to him. She nestled against him, burrowed, like a small fond animal. She could not get close enough to him and he could not have her close enough. They remained like that for a long stretch of road until Clay Calder began to feel disturbed by their nearness. He gently pushed her from him.

She responded easily to him and moved back to her window. "It's warm," she said, giving the excuse he needed. She was aware of the line of anxiety on his forehead and his clenched hands on the wheel. She saw all of him, but not yet could she give reasons for what she saw. She did not understand her restive father, she only loved him. She was able to wait and watch until he brought her close to him again as he always did.

"We'll go to the dam site. Would you like to see where we're going to build, Holly? It's finally decided."

"Yes, Daddy. Did you tell them where the best place would be?"

"I tried."

"And your dam will make all the desert a garden, won't it?"

"Yes, Holly, I hope so," he said.

"Will there be men working?"

"No, not on Easter Sunday."

They rode in silence for a time.

"We'll have it all to ourselves?" she asked.

"Yes. Today the canyon will be all ours."

Holly smiled. She trailed her hand out the window. Slowly she let the red ribbon sash slip from her fingers. The wind caught it and then it fell to the ground, coiled in the center of the road like a bright snake.

Jasmine had slipped away from the house unnoticed. In the midst of her mother's madness and her father's flight, she had gone, but they were not what moved her. She had a definite course and it was her own. She was not driven by them. She did not stay to stare after her father's speeding automobile. She caught a brief sight of him and Holly, the sun reflected on the car's windows, and knew that he had fled again, knew that her sister had joined him. She did not listen long to her mother's screams, but heard them dying and knew that she stood like an effigy in stone and hatred before the house.

Jasmine was tracing a path backward, back where she had been two days ago. She wanted to be there as swiftly as she possibly could. She did not want to explain, to be apprehended by questions and slowed by answers. She wished that she could be magically transported there and not have to rely on the poor force of her legs to take her, but even so she traveled quickly. She wanted to see him again, wanted to stand on the rise and look down to the low sun-dried structure that held him. Jasmine had to know if he was alive or dead, whether he breathed still or if they had truly killed him in their ritual. She needed to know more of him, he who had carried the rough cross on his back in the sacred mockery that she had accidentally witnessed last Friday, Good Friday.

She threaded lightly south, through the rabbit brush and greasewood, the mesquite, all the sprawling, enormously tenacious, sand-gray growth that covered the ground. She passed over the rusted network of roots, barely hidden, spread in ubiquitous search for life, water, both elusive and illusive. She crossed the desert with ease and grace. This vivid colorless expanse, this vivid colorless girl, so enigmatic and misunderstood, so oblivious to their shared distortions.

Last Friday Jasmine had been out searching for lizards. She often roamed the desert looking for them, tracking for miles, her patience and the horizon boundless. She was as quick and could hide as well as her quarry, waiting for them, and finding them always alone as she was. She would deftly catch them, one by one, and put them together, train them, teach them things that others might have called tricks but she never did. As soon as they had learned what she taught, she freed them, and went out seeking new, wary, and solitary ones. On Friday, instead of finding lizards, Jasmine had come upon a crucifixion in the desert. She could not stop seeing what she had seen. At night she dreamed of it, and she had begun to wonder if that was really all it was, another strange dream of hers. Today she looked for a resurrection, from the dead, from the dream.

Two days ago, late in the morning, after hours of fruitless search, trailing her empty lizard sack, she had climbed a high and stony slope, closely watching the ground for the shy creatures she sought. Reaching the top, she had looked below her and had seen a crowd of people. They had startled her, so certain was she that she was alone. They were gathered around a windowless adobe house. She had never seen the house before but the faces she had. These were the villagers that her mother forbade her and her sisters to speak with. She had been warned not even to look at them, but she had and she did. She recognized some of them, those who returned her stare with bottomless black eyes when she had passed through their village of Moracoma in her father's car. It had seemed that these people were waiting for something or for someone. So she, Jasmine, above and apart from them, as isolated on this slope as she had been insulated in the automobile, not knowing their passion or their faith, had joined in their wait with them. She had crouched down and watched. After a long time a man had come from within the house. He was very dark-skinned, his face and body thin and elongated, almost grotesquely so. He was bent beneath the weight of his burden, his cross. Others had followed him outside. They were barefoot as he was, but they wore long black hooded robes while he was naked except for a pair of loosely fitted white trunks and a crown of ebony-yellow opuntia flowers crushed low upon his brow. A cart was pulled from the house. Within it rode a carved wood skeleton, Death, an image of death conceived by man. The

villagers, men, women, and children, fifty or more, kneeled down
and appeared to pray, but Jasmine had been unable to hear their
vocal oblations.

They had risen from their supplication and the procession was
begun. The Christ-man led the way up toward her. They had
come slowly, tortuously, to the stony rise where she was. She had
moved off from their sight but remained close enough to see
them. The dark one had fallen several times under his cross. His
hands and legs were raw and bleeding. Others bled, too, those
who beat themselves with whips and scourges. On the crest of
the rise they had stopped. They laid their Christ supine upon his
cross and bound him to it with cloth bands. They had lifted the
cross, raised his suffering to the desert sky. They went to their
knees and in orison, in unison, wailed a word that Jasmine heard
but could not understand. *Pecado. Pecado.* The strange word was
repeated time after time. The Christ-man's body had begun to
turn blue. Those in the black robes had lowered the cross and
had carried him away. The villagers had drifted off, no longer
melded by agonizing belief, no more a cult or procession, but
alone and doubtful. One of them had run back up and had
placed the cross upright.

Jasmine had waited until it was totally deserted. An hour had
passed since they had all gone. She had let another hour go by
before she finally approached the cross that stood like a barren
tree; came close enough to see his dried blood upon it. She had
looked down to the house where they had taken him. She had
turned from the sight of it and run but she could not outdistance
her memory of him, and today she came to the stony rise with
aversion but captivated.

She found the cross still standing, a testament. Below, the clay
house without windows sat blindly and alone. She could feel that
he was there, within. Either he or his corpse awaited her. She
started down. The sun was bright but the wind off the Sandia
Mountain was cold. Her thin white dress was little protection
against it. Jasmine shivered. She was very near the house. It
seemed a sacred place to her and she went forward with fearful
reverence. If there had been even one small window she would
have gone to it and looked inside, but there was none. She was
forced directly to the plain wooden door, compelled to open it,
and to enter.

The light allowed in did little to dispel the deep gloom. It smelled of the earth, like a newly dug grave. It was a room of denial, one of suffering and pain, the walls steeped in screams and prayers. Standing on the threshold, Jasmine felt rather than saw this. Slowly her eyes adjusted to the darkness and she began to discern strange outlines and objects. She saw the cart from the procession and the skeleton propped against one side, at awkward rest, its mouth gaping. There was a large wood carving of Christ upon the cross, bleached and lifeless, but with bright painted blood streaming all down it. On the walls hung whips and chains, spattered with blood not painted, and flails of leather studded with cactus thorns. Near a stark altar, on a bench, she saw him lying. He might have been asleep or dead but for his burning eyes that met hers. She felt the icy wind at her back and the deeper cold within this shelter. She could not move. She stood in the doorway, transfixed.

He saw her standing in the shaft of light, her long fair hair and white dress wavering. He thought she was an apparition, a figure from his delirium, so still and insubstantial she seemed, but then she moved, walked, floated, toward him. He thought then that she might be some heavenly visitation. She was kneeling beside him. He reached out and touched her hand, grazing a fold of her dress. At the textured reality of her flesh and the cloth he drew back.

"What do you desire here?" he asked her. His speech was slow and halting. He had been taught to read word by word by his mother. Now he read only the Bible and religious tracts copied word by word by monks. He rarely ever used his voice. His prayers were silent. And so when he did speak it was with a kind of stilted beauty that misfit him for the age and the world into which he had been born. "What is it that you desire?"

"I came to see you," she answered. She watched a muscle twitch in his jaw. "You."

"No. You cannot stay here," he told her.

"Why?"

"It is forbidden. You must . . ." he broke off painfully. ". . . go."

"Why didn't you tell me to go when you first saw me at the door?" she asked.

"I believed . . ." He stopped.

"What?"

"I believed you to be an angel," he said.

Jasmine smiled. "I'm Jasmine Calder. I live near here. No, not near, but not far."

"You should not have come here."

"Is this a church?" she asked him.

"This is a *morada*."

She did not take her eyes from his and barely shook her head. "I don't understand. What is a *morada*?"

With effort he spoke. "This is the house of my brotherhood."

"You're priests?"

"No." He paused, building strength for his next words. "We are the Penitent Brothers."

"The ones in the black robes, are they your brothers?"

Powered by surprise, he questioned her. "How do you know of them?"

She watched the twitching of his jaw for a moment. "I saw them on Friday."

"You saw? What did you see?" he asked her fearfully.

"I saw everything," she said, thinking that she had. "I saw you coming from here with the cross and I saw what they did on the hill. Why did your brothers and the villagers punish you?"

"Not punished," he said and shifted on the bench. He had to tell her. "I was honored."

"Even if you'd died?" she asked.

"Especially if I had died."

"You were Christ for them. Why were you their Jesus? Why? Why did the others beat themselves? What did it all mean?" she asked and asked, her questions overflowing.

He did not answer. He looked at her and wondered a hundred things about her, but he was too weary and hurt to begin to ask. He managed to form two questions. "How did you come to be here on Friday? Why have you come again?"

"On Friday I was looking for lizards," she said. She smiled slightly at his tired confusion. "I catch them and teach them things," she explained, not making him ask. She realized how weak he was. She touched the dark effloresced blood on his scarred back. He stirred and pulled away. "I was afraid that you were dead," she said.

"There was no reason to be afraid."

"Aren't you afraid to die?" she asked him.

"No."

"You weren't afraid on Friday?"

"No."

"You're really not afraid?"

"Not since I came to the Brothers have I been afraid," he told her.

"Never?" She could not quite believe him.

He breathed shallowly. "In the Brotherhood I learned that evil dwells in the flesh. My flesh has been scourged of evil. I have no fear of death." Even as he said it he wanted again to touch the fine thin cloth of her dress and he was afraid of her and, too, of death that would deprive him of her. "You must go."

"No, don't make me go. I want to know what the Brothers told you. I'm afraid and I don't want to be."

"These things are not for you . . ." he faltered. ". . . to know," he finished.

"Did the Brothers cut your back?" she asked.

He stared at her, not speaking.

"There are so many scars," she said.

"You see too much," he said. He felt a desire to tell her what he should not. He could hardly speak above a whisper and he hoped she would bend closer to hear him. "When I came here I was cut by the *sangrador* with the obsidian knife. This was done after I had been sworn to secrecy. Now I have told you. I have broken my vows. Why do you ask these things of me? And why must I tell you?" he asked her and himself together, but neither answered.

Jasmine stared at the caked black blood and the old white scars on his skin. She thought of the sheets on the bed that she shared with Lily. She could see again the thick wet stains and Lily frantically cleaning them away. She thought of her sister lying beside her, neither sleeping, both silent, Lily shamed and she afraid. She knew that soon she must grow soft and full of bloody secrets like Lily. Jasmine looked at the man, this hard, ascetic, godlike man who was unafraid and she hoped that he could drive out her fear. She could not know how fearful she made him.

"You must go from here," he told her again.

"What does it mean when they cry out the word *pecado*?" she asked.

"Do not. Do not ask me this," he said. He looked away from

her, helpless to make her go, wanting her to stay, and despising his desire. He tried to move from her and groaned involuntarily.

She leaned over him, peering into his averted face.

He had wished for her nearness. Now he had it, and he loved and hated it.

"What does it mean? *Pecado*?" she asked him again.

"I have sinned," he said. "It means I have sinned. It is a Spanish word."

"*Pecado*. I have sinned. *Pecado*." It was easy for her to say. "*Pecado*."

It was hard for him to hear it from her.

"Have you sinned?" she asked him.

"All flesh sins. It is the nature of flesh to sin."

"Have you sinned with whores?" she asked.

"How do you know that word?" he wanted to know. Again she had shocked him into inquiry. "How do you know it?"

"I've heard it," she answered.

"Do you know what a whore is?"

"I think I do. I've heard my mother say that my father sins with whores. Do all men? Do you?"

"There are many ways to sin."

"I think it's a sin to hurt someone."

"I believe that too."

"Then your brothers have sinned against you. They hurt you badly, very badly."

"No, you do not know."

"Help me to know," she said. "Help me to understand."

"I cannot."

"What would they have done if you'd died on the cross?"

"They would have buried me and taken my shoes to the door of my mother's house. I would have been blessed and honored in my village. I wish that I had died," he said. He was trying to believe that he did still want this and that his path had not been turned by the appearance of this angelic child. "Death is not to be feared. When a child dies in my village, the funeral is a happy occasion. Everyone dresses in white and wears flowers. There is dancing and singing, and fandangos played on all the violins. There is great rejoicing because the child, innocent and untouched by life, has left this world for heaven."

"Yes, I see," she said, and she looked as if she had glimpsed something that she had never seen before. "What is your name?"

"Estevanico."

"Estevanico," she repeated after him, perfectly reproducing his inflection.

They stared for a long moment at one another. Only the sound of a distant voice calling unlocked them.

"Jasmine! Jasmine!" The voice penetrated the thick adobe walls. It was closer than it sounded.

"It's my sister Lily," she told him.

"Have you other sisters?"

"Yes. There's Lily and myself and four others."

"Now I know. You are one of the six little white girls whose father has come to build the dam on the land of the Zuni."

"Yes, Daddy's come to build a dam, but who are the Zuni?"

"An Indian tribe. The land that your father has chosen for his dam belongs . . . belonged to them."

"Jasmine! Jasmine!" the calls came again.

"Go to her," he said. "Do not tell her of this place."

"I won't. Don't be afraid. I don't talk much to Lily or to anyone. May I come again?"

"No, Jasmine." It was the first time that he had spoken her name. He had used it to strengthen his refusal. "Jasmine," he said again, this time purely for the sweet sound of it.

"Jasmine!" Lily called.

"This place is not for you," he whispered.

"Only if I were an angel. If I were an angel then you'd want me."

"You are not that."

"Please let me come again."

"No," he said, and that was all that he intended to say, but he added, "not here."

"Somewhere else," she said quickly.

"On the rise."

"By your cross. It's still standing," she told him.

"It will stand for a year."

"We'll meet there tomorrow."

"Jasmine," he said.

"Yes, tomorrow . . ."—she would not be denied—". . . and every day until your cross comes down."

"And then?" he asked of her.

"And then every day after that," she answered him.

"Tomorrow," he agreed, succumbing to her. "Now go, Jasmine."

"Estevanico," she said. That was all that she said, and she was gone, gone as swiftly and as strangely as she had come.

He lay in the dim room, turned uneasily on the hard wood bench, and thought of her and of the light that she had brought and taken away with her.

Jasmine stumbled out into the glittering brightness. She wanted the darkness of the *morada* around her, wished herself already back in the tomb where he lived. She could see Lily not far away. The wind still gusted, and stronger now. The dust swirling in the air with the sun shining through it gave a beautiful luminous glow to all. Even the short thick figure of Lily was somehow made extraordinary. Jasmine went to her but her thoughts were of tomorrow.

Chapter Two

The scalloped white clouds passed swiftly overhead, driven by the wind. The fluid sky reflected down and made the earth appear to shimmer. Colors mingled. These were desert days of rare beauty, a brief, blossoming passage that came only once in a hundred years. Seeds that had been buried long in the dry cracked ground, deeply dormant, were brought close to the surface by rushing rainstorms. After the cloudbursts the sun blazed down upon the freshet-veined desert and these seeds flared into fleeting, stunning flower. It was during this exquisite vernal visitation that the twelve-year-old white girl and the dark man formed a friendship much like the lovely and ephemeral days themselves.

It had been nearly a month since the Easter day Jasmine had gone looking for Estevanico and found him in his *morada*. Now they went for daily walks in the desert. They talked of all things, near and far, large and small things. Sometimes the mighty were diminished, the dwarfed made great, and significances shifted like the blowing sand.

Today the heat was especially intense. It was late April. Estevanico knew that the short-lived season they had shared would soon be over, spring gone to summer, and the desert returned to its scorched and barren, bloodless existence. He knew this but attempted to stave off the knowledge. The wind was wrapping Jasmine's face and neck in the silver strands of her hair. He ran a hand through his own coarse hair and wished that it was hers he was touching. His wishes sprang up like the desert flowers that would shortly die.

"There is a tree that is like you, Jasmine," he told her. "It grows only here and nowhere else."

"What tree is it?" she asked him.

"It has two names, a very important-sounding one and the one that it is known by."

"Tell me both, Estevanico."

"*Dalea spinosa.* The smoke tree."

"Will you show me one?" she asked. She looked around her, past the willows and the cottonwoods that she knew, for this smoke tree that she did not know. Her eyes traveled up to the tall and timbered mountain that curved in powerful ascension over the valley. "Is it up on the mountain?" she guessed. "Is it too far for us to go?"

"No."

"There's one near here? Will you take me to it?" she asked.

"Yes," he said. "We will go there now."

Though much smaller than the tall man, Jasmine matched his stride easily. She could walk the land as he did, with the same surety and sense of it. They shared it. It was their home.

"I couldn't live anywhere but here," she told him.

"But you have and you will," he said, voicing his own fears that she would someday leave.

"Did you know that I was born on the desert?" she asked him, and continued before he answered. "In New Mexico, but north of here, near Colorado. Daddy was there to look for a place to build a dam. He picks the places. That's his job. He picked this place."

"He has chosen wrongly," Estevanico said.

"Has he? I love it here."

"A dam will change it."

"Daddy says that dams do change the face of things, change people's lives even. I think he likes that, but we never stay long enough to see the changes."

"He will not stay for the building of the dam?"

"No," she answered. "It's his job to say where the dams will be and then he goes on to other places. We've gone with Daddy everywhere. I can't remember all the places that we've lived, but I know that I love it here best. It's like I've been waiting to come here and I didn't even know that I was, but we never stay anywhere. I never minded leaving before, but I do now. I don't want to leave here."

And he did not want her to leave, but he could not say that to her. He said instead, "It will not be as it is now, not after the dam is built."

"The dam will make things better. Daddy says it will."

"No."

"No? Why?" she asked him.

"It is difficult to tell you." Now he gazed out as she had when she looked for the smoke tree. He was not seeking any one thing, but trying to hold it all in his eyes, imprint it on his memory, knowing that it must live within him or not at all.

Jasmine was watching him, waiting for him to speak. When he did not, she said, "The people are very poor here because the land is so hard. If there were water it would be easier to farm. The dam will bring water. How could that be bad?"

"The land is hard but it is beautiful, yes?" he asked her.

"Yes, but there's been rain," she said.

"Rain. A miracle. God's pure water, not from the dams made by men."

"But water is water, and it's good. It's needed here."

"It is what comes with the water of the dam that is bad, Jasmine."

"What?"

"Many things. Men come. Strangers. Not farmers but men of business. And taxes come, taxes that cannot be paid by the poor farmers, so their land is lost to the men of business who can pay. The dams, they change things, but not to the good."

"The dams have come, Estevanico. There's no going back."

"No, there is only wishing to go back."

"Do you think that my father is a bad man? Do you hate him?"

"I only hate his dam," Estevanico said.

They walked for a while in silence, making a path through the glorious plain of flowers. There were gilias, white, pink, and yellow; lupines, asters, and phacelias. A long ocotillo tree rose up before them, green, with bell-like blossoms flaming red. And al-

ways in the distance was the mountain, austere and sternly menacing, looming so coldly permanent over the hot beds of transi-
tory splendor that surrounded them.

"I could never leave this place, Estevanico," she said.

He seemed not to hear her. "The smoke tree will be in bloom."

"Everything is."

"Yes," he agreed.

"All my life I'll remember the desert as it is now. I'll want it
to be this way again and it probably never will. I'll have only this
one time."

"Will not the memory be enough for you, Jasmine?"

"I don't know. I don't know if I want any memories. I think
that they're sad things, memories are. I don't want to be forever
remembering this spring and have no other ever match it. I don't
want to look back and think that I had the best, the most beautiful, and it's gone and will never come back."

He knew that she was thinking of him as she spoke. "Like me?"
he asked her. "Like me wanting to stop the waters of the dam
with my bare hands, wanting the old times to return when they
are dead, were long dead before I was born."

"Estevanico, how old are you?"

"Thirty-two years," he answered.

"You seem older."

"You too are older than your years."

Her gray eyes darkened, pierced him. "Do you remember telling me about the children's funerals in your village?"

He responded reluctantly to her thoughts, slowly to her words.
"I remember."

"I see it," she cried suddenly. "That's the smoke tree, isn't it? It
must be."

"It is."

She ran ahead of him. He saw how her hair streamed, flying in
the air like the jets of crystalline water from the fountain at
Santuario de Chimayo. He remembered holding his father in the
holy waters of the fountain, praying for a cure. He and his father
had made the pilgrimage, walking the many miles from their
village, but he had returned alone. His father had died and his
faith was shaken. It had taken the Brothers to restore it. Now he
suffered new doubts. They sprang from his feelings for Jasmine.
He hurried to catch her. She had stopped beneath the gorgeous

tree and thrown her head back, staring awestruck up into the branches. Her white skin was turned vaguely lavender by the reflecting profusion of purple flowers, thousands of them, hundreds to a single spinule.

She did not face him, but feeling he was beside her, spoke. "I could live in this tree."

"I know."

"It's not always like this?" she asked, knowing that it couldn't possibly be.

"No."

"When it's not in bloom how does it look?" she asked him.

He had been certain that she would ask him this and he carefully answered. "Even more beautiful and more like you than it is now, Jasmine."

Now she turned to him. "More beautiful," she said. "How like me?"

"The smoke tree when it is not in bloom is a dream. It appears like a cloud of smoke rising with the sunlight passing whitely through its gray branches."

"It's very beautiful today."

"Today it is real."

"Yes," she said, understanding him. "So strong and bright."

"Soon it will be again the dream of smoke," he said.

Bending down, she picked up some of the fallen purple blooms. "Already it's beginning."

"Even as some open, others fall."

He looked down into her pale face surrounded by the soft silvery hair and she was frighteningly beautiful to him. He knew little of women, but this girl he loved. Jasmine was his dream, a fragile innocent, a smoke-white, spiny virgin. He knew, in time, she would explode into gaudy flower, potent and purple allure. She would never return to bud, to dream, as the smoke tree would. He was knowing the last of her purity. He feared he would be the destroyer of it, of her as she was at this moment.

"I must go now," he said.

"I think I'll stay a little longer."

"Can you find your way alone?" he asked her.

She smiled, a dreamy smile. "Yes."

They said nothing about meeting tomorrow. That was accepted between them. They never made plans or arrangements. She left

or he left and they came together again inevasibly. He walked
away from her. For more than a hundred yards he fought his
desire to have one last look of her. Then he stopped and turned.
He saw that she had lain down on her back beneath the tree. She
seemed to him like one more fallen bloom lying there. He started
back to her, but stopped. He stood watching her, knowing that
he had introduced her to the beauties of death. He had shown
her the fatal fascination of it.

After hours beneath its branches Jasmine reluctantly left the
smoke tree. As she had assured Estevanico, she had no trouble
finding her way home. Her difficulty came in believing that the
house she entered by its back door was her home. She felt that she
belonged out under the tree and not confined within these walls
with her sisters and her mother. They sat at the kitchen table and
silently ate their supper. Jasmine could almost hear her mother
listening for her father's arrival and the heavy sense of waiting
troubled her, made it hard for her to swallow her food or even
breathe the thick air.

Clay Calder drove up to the house. It was not yet dark. Usually
he arrived home later in the evening. He was never tired from his
day's work. The labor at the dam site exhilarated him. He didn't
feel weary until he faced this door. It was then that his energy
drained from him. The sight of his wife exhausted him. The day's
accumulation of accomplishment and satisfaction was depleted
by her. He didn't know what it was, as other men did, to want
to come home. There must have been a time when he anticipated
with pleasure coming home to Jane, he thought, but he could not
remember. It was a nightly battle, his return to her was, but return he did, time and again.

He walked into the kitchen and briefly greeted Jane and the
girls, but he did not join them at the table. He went to the front
room and sat down in the gathering darkness. He heard footsteps.
He hoped it wasn't Jane coming to demand explanations that he
would try to give her and hear them turn to excuses. Holly
climbed onto his lap. He cradled her close to him. He was glad
that it was Holly. She was so often asleep when he came home.
He sacrificed his daughter to avoid contact with his wife and he
regretted that. Jane's voice came from the kitchen.

"Holly! Holly, come and finish your supper."

Holly smiled up at her father. "I'm not hungry, Mama!" she called out. "I want to see Daddy," she said softly to him.

"You come back in here and finish your supper," Jane's voice insisted stridently.

"Jane, she's not hungry!" Clay called to her now.

They heard a chair push back, scrape gratingly across the kitchen floor, and then Jane's sharp steps. In a moment she stood before them with her arms crossed tightly, her hands clenched, glaring.

"I suppose you're not hungry either?" she asked her husband.

"Not now. Maybe a little later, Jane. I want to sit here for a while," he answered, not looking at her.

"Everything will be cold later," she told him.

He glanced up at her over Holly's dark head.

"That's all right," he said.

"Holly should finish her supper."

"She doesn't want any more."

"Well, it's her night to do dishes," Jane said.

Holly felt the anger between her mother and father. She seemed to be the reason for it, but not really. It was as if she had disappeared and left only dissension behind. To bring herself back to them, she spoke.

"Mama, today's Wednesday."

"I know very well what day it is, Holly."

"But Tuesday's my night. I did the dishes last night."

"She's right, Jane."

"How would you know? You weren't here. You're never . . ."

"Jane," he broke in on her.

"Clay, I want to speak with you alone," she said.

"Later, Jane."

She stood staring for a moment. Then she turned. She snapped on a light, depriving them of their shadows, before she left the room. Clay was surprised by her departure. Her sudden submission was unusual, suspect, but very welcome.

"Daddy, tell me the story of when you were a little boy and the men came to build the dam," Holly demanded lovingly of him.

"Again? Aren't you tired of that story?"

"No. Please, Daddy."

"All right, Holly. It was the Roosevelt Dam that they came to build. They didn't have the name for it when they first came but that's what it was to be, the Roosevelt Dam. It was in Arizona. I was just twelve years old and I lived out near the dam site with my grandpa and grandma."

"Not your mama and daddy?" she asked, prompting him, knowing the answer before he told her.

"No, they had died when I was very little. I lived with my grandparents. And I loved them very much, but they'd lived their lives and they were old and content to sit and watch things happen . . ."

"But not you?"

"No, not me. I was restless and wild. I wanted to go and see things and do things. It seemed to me that Gran's and Gramp's world was so little, just about the size of their front porch, and there ought to be a whole lot more than that, a whole world more. The men and the dam they were building, they were big and it was big. I started going there to watch. Gran and Gramp just about gave up trying to keep me in school because every chance I'd get I'd sneak off. I'd go out and watch every move those big men were making. It was exciting, Holly, and wonderful, more wonderful and exciting than anything I'd ever seen."

"And there was one special man, wasn't there, Daddy?" she asked.

"You remember this story pretty well, don't you?"

"Yes, Daddy."

"There was a special man, yes. His name was Sam Peters and he was an engineer. He knew everything there was to know about dams. He saw me coming back day after day to watch and finally one day he spoke to me. From that time on Sam Peters was the most important person in my life. I wanted to be just like him when I grew up but since Sam was tall and blond and I was short and dark that wasn't going to happen. I was never going to look like Sam, but I decided I could be like him inside. I could have the things in my head that he had in his. He would tell me what he knew and I would listen and try to remember every word he said."

"Like I do with you, Daddy."

"I think you do better than I ever did, Holly, but I tried my best. I never could make much sense of what I read in books but what Sam told me came alive. I could see and understand the things he told me. Summers when school closed and I didn't even have to pretend that I was going, I was at the dam site from sunup to sundown. I followed Sam around just like a pup. It took six years to build the dam. They had started when I was only a boy and when they were done I was nearly eighteen and thought myself a man. The dam was beautiful. It looked like a castle to me, big stone turrets and all. The sight of it rising up where nothing had been was so beautiful to me, but I hated it, too."

"Hated it?" she asked. He'd never said this before when he'd told the story.

"Yes, I hated it because it was finished and that meant that Sam Peters and all the others would be leaving, leaving me behind."

"But they didn't," she said, sure again of his story.

"No, they didn't. Sam asked me to come along with them. And I went. Ever since then I've never wanted to do anything, never done anything, but what Sam Peters did, build dams."

"What happened to Sam?" she asked.

"He died, died at a dam site in California, the way I'd want to die. I was with him."

Clay didn't speak again immediately. Holly said nothing. They shared their silence, unaware of the family's activity in the kitchen, the front room, and all around them. The others swirled by and time passed. Lily was washing dishes and Rose drying them with clatter and jokes, but Lily wasn't laughing. So Rose laughed alone. Jasmine sat on the floor in front of the unlit adobe fireplace and strung the lavender blossoms she'd collected into a fragile wreath. Not far from her Iris and Poppy dipped wooden spools empty of thread into a plate of soapy dishwater they'd been given and blew bubbles. When Jasmine had finished stringing her garland she walked over to Holly and placed it gently on her head. She left her sister and her father, going out onto the porch, before anyone could speak. Jane watched her family, and waited.

"There was never a dam as beautiful as the old Roosevelt to me, my first. That was the only one I ever stayed to see finished," he told Holly.

"And the day that I was born you went back to see it, didn't you, Daddy?"

"Yes."

"Will you tell me again?"

"It was December 1920, just before Christmas. I hadn't been

home to Arizona in nearly ten years. We were studying a site for a dam clear over on the other side of the state. When your mama had you and I went in and saw you lying in her arms, I just had to go and see old Roosevelt again."

"Why, Daddy?" she asked him.

"I guess because I felt like I was born there, that I'd come to life with the dam, and seeing you having just come to life I wanted to go back and see where it had started for me. I guess that's why, Holly. I drove most of the night and it was dawn when I got there. The sun was coming up and big gray Roosevelt was just starting to feel the touch of it. I stood a way up on top. Oh, Holly, the sweet curve of it, the power and size. Before I knew what was happening to me I was down on my knees thanking God for it and for you, Holly, my beautiful baby girl. You'd been born and the day was being born at this place that had given me my life, the only real life I'd ever known."

"Can we go there someday, Daddy?"

"Yes."

Jane broke in on them.

"It's time for Holly to go to bed."

"Oh, not yet, Mama, please."

"All the girls are getting ready for bed. You're the only one who isn't," she declared. "Your daddy's keeping you up too late again."

Clay looked around the room. His other daughters had all gone.

"I'm sorry, Jane. Go on, Holly, get ready for bed. I'll be in to kiss you goodnight," he said, gently edging her from his lap.

Holly ran lightly away.

"You have five other daughters, Clay," Jane said to him. "Five other little girls that you haven't said a word to all night. Are you going to kiss them goodnight? Or is Holly the only one?" she asked.

"Of course I'll kiss the others goodnight."

"The others! Do you even know their names?"

"Jane, Holly likes to hear me talk. She's more interested than the other girls. They fidget or get bored . . . Poppy falls asleep. Jasmine just stares at me . . ."

"But not your precious Holly?"

"No, not Holly. I'm sorry if it seems I care more for Holly than the others."

"The others again. It doesn't *seem* that you do, Clay. It's obvious."

"Maybe I'm trying to make up for something with Holly," he said.

"What? What are you trying to make up for?"

He was aware of the change in her voice and he answered it. "Her mother," he said coldly. "Her mother who never has a kind word for her. Her mother who gives every indication that she despises her. Don't you think she feels it from you, Jane? You give off your feelings like a noxious fume. It's impossible not to choke. Holly knows and it's a shame that she does."

"What are you saying?"

"That you're jealous of your own little girl."

"She's not mine. She's all yours. Why does she always have to be in your lap? Why do you always take up for her? She's always running to you. You're always telling her your stories. You have to be a hero to someone, don't you, Clay? You have to be idolized, don't you? I remember very well what it's like idolizing you, having you for a hero. I wonder if you'll let Holly fall as hard as you let me. I wonder if you'll let her break into as many pieces."

"Stop it, Jane. My God, can't we ever talk? Do we always have to end screaming at each other?"

Holly was standing in the doorway. "Daddy, I'm ready for bed," she announced. Her parents stared at one another. Again she felt that she was invisible but that she had come between them somehow. "Daddy?"

"Go on, hero. Take her to bed. While you're at it you might say goodnight to your other daughters, too."

"Jane, I . . ."

"Go!"

Holly stood waiting in her long white nightgown, perched on one foot. She fingered the flowers that Jasmine had given her. Jane watched Clay walk toward her.

After he had said his goodnights to the girls he went into his and Jane's room. She was sitting at a mirrored vanity applying thick white night cream to her face. She slathered it heavily and massaged it methodically into her skin. As he watched her now, he thought of the young girl that she had been when he first met her. She'd been so pale and lovely blond, like the children they'd had together, the little girls he'd just left. Only Holly did not look like Jane, like Jane had looked when he'd fallen in love with her so long ago in Kansas. Jane caught sight of him in her mirror.

"I hate this place," she said. "My skin feels like leather. I feel just like a hide that's been put out to be tanned. Look at me," she said, but she was looking at herself. "I look forty years old."

He lay down on the bed. "No, you don't, Jane."

"I do. Don't tell me I don't. I do." She paused, staring over her shoulder at him. "Why don't you, Clay? Why don't you age? Why don't you look a day older than when I met you?"

"I do."

"No, you look the same. I can still see you standing knee-deep in the river. You looked like a little boy playing hookey from school. You still do. You know why, Clay? Because nothing touches you, not really. That's where the lines and wrinkles come from, from life pushing and pulling, bearing down and crushing, but you don't feel any of that. Do you?" she asked bitterly.

She turned back to her mirror. Her viscid face in the glass was repellent to him but magnetic, too. He could not take his eyes from her image.

"Jane, I do feel things. I'm not untouched by life."

"You're such a liar," she said quietly, not in anger or anguish anymore, but quietly, so quietly. She was wiping her hands of the sticky excess. "Lily told me something today about Jasmine."

"Jane, I'm tired. Can we talk about this in the morning?" he asked her.

She approached him slowly, her satiny gown clinging to her thighs and breasts, and spoke. "Tired? You want to sleep?"

"Yes."

She sat down on the edge of the bed and waited. He slipped the straps from her shoulders. The gown slid away from her breasts. . . .

In the darkness he saw her gown shining whitely, lying twisted on the floor by their bed. He lay beside her and tried to think what it meant, how it could be that their bodies could still join when their emotions twanged with hatred and resentment, jealousy and bitterness. His body did not feel the disappointment and rage that his mind and heart did, and neither, it seemed, did hers. They were two people who should never have met, he realized that now, but they had been pulled to physical intimacy when they were little more than children. They had wed, a marriage of bodies, when in spirit they were strangers. He needed to move through life and boldly mark the places he had been. She wanted to remain in one place forever, never go, never travel beyond the safety and security of what she knew and had always known. He wondered what had brought them together. Why had they been fated to meet that day beside that swollen river in Kansas? He knew that Jane's character had been badly scarred by seeing her mother die the way that she had, swept away in flood waters. Ironically, it was the flood that had taken her mother which had brought him to Kansas and to her. It was his first real job with Sam Peters. He had just turned eighteen. And she was a beautiful and lost child, vulnerable, full of sadness. He was drawn to her. That child had grown into a madwoman and still he was drawn. He couldn't help her, and he never had. They hadn't even built the dam that would have been too late, anyway, to save Jane's mother. They'd left without building it, but he'd taken Jane from Kansas with him. He knew this fluctuating life that he thrived upon, Jane detested. He aggravated and aggrieved her, he knew.

Their existence was misery, but being without her was unthinkable. He felt tied to her, guilty and responsible. He hated and blamed her for this. And he couldn't find his way out. He had gone to other women but they had given him only momentary relief, no permanent escape from her. He came back to Jane, always. No one, no other woman, made him want to flood her and drown her the way Jane did. He wanted to kill her with his need of her. He looked at her lying spent on her belly, her face turned from him, covered over with her arms. With his eyes he traced the arch of her back to her waist, the swell of her buttocks, her legs spread in a vee. She lay long and pale in the darkness. He did not know if she slept or not, but he knew that he was stiffening again at the sight of her. He ran his fingers down the dark crevice that split her soft white flesh, halving her. She was wet from him. She moved under his touch. Her body rolled toward his, but still he could not see her face. He didn't want to see it. He let himself slide down into the hot sucking morass of her. She softly surrounded him, held him captive within her.

This was when she knew she had him. At no other time was she sure of him. It dissipated so quickly, the security of having him. When he was gone from her, the safety was gone, and her power, too. She knew his body and its needs because they were hers. Their bodies were in blessed harmony while all the rest of their shared life was angry discord. Tonight she had held him twice, but there had been other nights when she had lain heavily awake next to him, a child between them. And she had waited to loose that child, drop it from herself, so that he might fill her with another. Those were the times when he had gone to whores and she had lost him to them. Now he moved limply away from her and she could not be silent.

"Clay?" she whispered.

He said nothing for a moment. Finally he responded. "Yes, Jane."

"Clay, I wanted to tell you that . . ." She broke off, sensing that he was listening to her with reluctance. "You don't want to hear me."

Once more there was the long pause before he spoke. "Yes. Yes, I do. What is it?" he asked. Exasperation tinged the fatigue in his voice.

"You're tired," she stated and it was a refrain from earlier.

"Yes," he assented.

"You're always too tired for words."

"I'm not."

"You are!"

"Jane, whenever we talk we argue. Why does it always have to be this way?"

"You tell me."

"I don't know," he said wearily. All their pleasure had disappeared. It had floated away like smoke on the wind. He lit a cigarette and watched the pale drift. Yes, just like smoke, he thought. It was gone. And the ugly tension was present again. What was this fire that burned within them and manifested itself in their fierce and fragile lovemaking and then faded? What was it? Desire, he supposed. Fugitive, but endlessly returning, ruling them, binding them with moments of bliss to years of torment.

"I hate you. God, how I hate you," she told him. Now she resorted to her other weapon that held him hostage in their marriage. She grabbed at his cigarette and savagely ground it into the back of his hand.

He leaped away from her. The pain was searing. He stood over the bed. She smiled up at him and put another cigarette to her lips, inhaling deeply.

"I want to hurt you more than you want to hurt me, Clay. Always remember that."

"I don't want to hurt you, Jane."

"Of course you do."

He wanted to deny it, but he couldn't. He wanted to tell her of her madness, but he couldn't speak of that either. He said only, "Jane, maybe you should see a doctor. I don't think you're well."

"I only go to doctors when I have babies."

What she said was true, he knew.

She continued: "There hasn't been a baby in five years. I don't think there will be another."

He heard something in her voice that he did not recognize. He wasn't certain if it was sorrow or sad regret. He knew only bitter pain in her. He came closer, cautiously.

"Are you sorry, Jane?" he asked her.

She began to laugh. Then she was suddenly choking and crying. "I'm glad. I'm glad," she cried. "Sorry. I'm not . . . sorry."

He took the cigarette from her and sat down beside her.

"I wouldn't have burned you again," she said. "Let me see your hand." She bent over the raised and rounded patch of burned skin. "Does it hurt very much?"

"Not now," he answered.

She collapsed back onto the pillows, her eyes slitted.

"That was a pretty little fairy tale you were telling Holly tonight," she said.

"What do you mean?" he asked warily.

"Don't you know?"

"No," he said.

"You even lie about lying, Clay."

"Jane, I think we ought to try and get some sleep." Saying this, he leaned across her and crushed out the cigarette in the ashtray on the bedstand. "Don't you?" he asked.

"Look how puny and paltry you are when you don't want me," she said. "It looks like an old man's. Maybe that will be the only thing that will age, Clay, the thing you care about most."

Once, only once, he wanted to resist her. He wished that she could not bait him to cruelty as harsh as hers. "Like your face,

Jane?" he asked. He hated following this lead, but he wanted to keep her from what she had begun a moment ago, anything to keep her from that.

But she returned to it with the instinct of a hunting dog for a downed bird. "That was a very pretty story you told Holly, but maybe I should tell her how it really was."

"Stop it, Jane," he warned her.

"Maybe I should tell her that your daddy didn't die but just that no one knew who he was, not even your mother. Do you think Holly'd like knowing that you're a bastard?"

"She wouldn't even know what that was."

"But you do. You do, Clay, and that's what matters. Maybe Holly would like to know that your mother ran off and left you. Do you think she'd understand that your mother was a whore? Or maybe she'd like to know what really happened on the day she was born and you went to the Roosevelt Dam. Would she understand, I wonder, that you wanted to die on the day she was born?"

They stared at one another. For all her madness, she told the truth, and he could not say she did not. It was the most frightening thing about her insanity, the veins of hard veracity that ran through it. He'd never known his father. His mother had left him with his grandparents. He had no face or voice to remember of either his mother or his father. It was true and it hurt him still. He watched Jane close her eyes, assured of his pain and her ability to inflict it.

"I hate this place," she said. "Lily told me that she saw Jasmine walking with a man today."

"A man?" Clay asked.

"Yes, a Mexican, a filthy brown Mexican."

"Lily said she saw them walking together?"

"Yes. Out on the desert alone. You know what that means."

"No, I don't, Jane. Maybe Jasmine had gotten lost and he was helping her find her way home. She's only a little girl."

"What difference would that make to a Mexican? She's beautiful and she's white . . ."

"Jane, for God's sake, what are you thinking?"

"I don't want to stay here."

"Have you said anything to Jasmine?" he asked her.

"No."

"Jasmine's not an ordinary child," he said, almost to himself.

"She's normal, perfectly normal. It's this place. I want my babies away from this terrible place."

"All right, Jane. All right."

"Can we go back to Kansas?"

"You could take the girls for a visit," he put to her.

"No. I want us all to live there."

"You know I can't live there, Jane. I can't breathe there," he said. "Besides it looks like Washington is almost a sure thing."

"Almost a sure thing. Is there anything about us that's really sure, Clay?" she asked him.

He did not answer. They lay wordlessly on their bed, two strangers come once more to a hauntingly familiar impasse.

Chapter Three

The first days of May came, and the Calder family had closed in upon itself, the members closely watching and tensely waiting. The month had begun with Poppy's nightmare. She had awakened screaming and in terror, telling of seeing a dark flaming face in the window by her bed.

Jasmine could not get away to meet with Estevanico. She was not forbidden but more insidiously prevented. Someone was always near to keep her near. She was held silently and tightly, kept from leaving the house. If ever she was alone for a moment, still she felt guarded. Now, as she sat on the baked ground in the sun out behind the house, there were eyes on her. There was no one in sight but she sensed that she was trapped within someone's vision, a prisoner of their eyes. Snatches of conversation that she had overheard between her mother and father disturbed her. She was certain that they were planning to move from the desert, and soon. She was oppressed by the quiet and constant attention of her family. Jasmine yearned for solitude and for Estevanico. She heard the door slam and saw Lily and Rose coming from the house. They were arguing. Jasmine was not listening to her sisters but their words came clearly to her and she could not avoid hearing them.

"It's stupid," Lily was saying. "It's a stupid idea."

"It is not," Rose countered.

Lily insisted spitefully, "It is too."

"Nobody asked you to come along. If you think it's such a stupid idea why are you coming with me?" Rose asked her sister.

"I'm not," Lily answered petulantly. "I just happen to be here."

"Why don't you just happen to be somewhere else?"

"You're not really going to, are you, Rose?"

"I really am. Now you know. You don't have to tag along."

"You're going to go out and dig up some nasty old tree and bring it home with you?"

"Yes."

"If you do, Mama won't let you bring it in the house. It's so stupid. Decorating a Christmas tree in May. Christmas is in December."

"So what?" And she turned from Lily.

Now Jasmine was listening carefully to the exchange. She called out to Rose.

"Rose, wait! I'll go with you. I know where we can find a creosote bush that will still be a little green."

She ran over to her sisters.

"Great!" Rose exclaimed excitedly, happy to think that Jasmine liked her idea.

Jasmine was sympathetic to Rose. She trusted her sister's happy instincts and she felt they did need some Christmas now. She was swiftly working out her own plan of escape. She would help Rose find the bush and send her back home with it alone. She would then be free for a few hours.

"Let's go," Jasmine urged, beginning to rush Rose away.

"Mama! Mama!" Lily cried out toward the house.

Jane did not come outside. They could not see her, only hear her voice coming disembodied from the shadowy interior.

"What is it?"

"Mama, Jasmine and Rose are going out on the desert," Lily told her mother.

"No, they're not."

"Mama, please!" Rose pleaded loudly.

Jasmine said nothing.

"I said no."

The tone of the voice made further protest useless.

Rose turned on Lily. "Thanks, Lily. I'll find a tree around here, just you wait and see. Want to help me, Jasmine?"

"No, you go on," Jasmine said.

Rose stumped off.

Jasmine looked at Lily. "Why did you do that?"

"Because I wanted to."

"Because Mama told you to," Jasmine corrected her. "Why doesn't she want me to leave the house?"

"I guess you'd know more about that than I would."

"What do you know about it, Lily?"

"I don't know anything at all."

Jasmine stared at her sister. The pupils of her eyes were dilated and her stare black. Lily looked down, unable to stand the force of it.

"Leave me alone, Jasmine. You leave me alone," Lily said and walked away.

Jasmine went to the shed and got her lizards. She sat down and opened the lid of the box. She took out a desert whiptail. It had a long greenish-gold colored body like a snake and a dark head spotted bronze.

"That's a very pretty one."

Jasmine recognized Holly's voice. She didn't look up at her. Holly was her favorite sister. She moved so quietly and said so little, but she seemed to understand so much.

"Do you want to hold it?"

"Could I?" Holly asked. She sat down beside Jasmine.

"Yes." Jasmine handed her the lizard.

"It's so tame."

"It likes you. You're not afraid of it."

"It's too pretty to be afraid of," Holly said.

"There are some things that are very beautiful that should make you afraid, Holly."

"You mean like rattlesnakes?" Holly asked.

"Yes."

"One time Daddy killed a rattlesnake and even when he cut off its head it still moved. Do you remember?"

"Yes, I remember. Holly, has Daddy said anything to you about leaving here?"

"Yes."

"What did he say?"

Holly hesitated.

"Why won't anybody tell me anything?" Jasmine asked.

"Daddy says that we're leaving very soon."

"Where this time?"

"Washington," Holly told her.

"We've been there before. That's where Poppy was born. You don't remember, do you?"

"No, but Daddy says that maybe we can go to school there, regular school. Mama wouldn't teach us anymore."

"Would you like that, Holly?"

"Yes. Is Washington nice?"

"It rains a lot. I remember walking in a forest. It was so green and the rain was falling but you couldn't hear it because it fell on the moss on the ground. And there was moss hanging from these tall trees. There was no sun. It was wet and green and there were no sounds at all. The rain kept falling and falling but you could never hear it."

"I like rain," Holly said hopefully.

"I like the rain here on the desert, the thunder and the lightning."

"You don't want to go, do you, Jasmine?"

"No," she said. "I can't go."

"But you'll have to . . ."

Jasmine interrupted her. "Look at Rose. She's found her Christmas tree."

"She's so funny," Holly said.

They smiled together at the sight of Rose, her red curls bouncing, tugging and pulling a small scraggly bush along the ground behind her.

"Do you think Mama will let her bring it in the house?" Holly asked.

"Probably not, but if anybody could persuade her, Rose could," Jasmine answered and her smile faded. "Holly, did Mama send you out here?" she asked.

"Yes," Holly answered, making no attempt at evasion.

"Why?"

Holly shook her head. "I only know that you're not supposed to go out on the desert anymore."

"But why? Why stop me now? I've been doing it since we've been here."

"I don't know, but I think Lily does."

"You don't like Lily much, do you, Holly?"

"She's changed. She's not like she used to be."

"She's more like Mama."

"Yes," Holly agreed. She hadn't thought of that, but it was true. "Like Mama, yes."

Without words Jasmine and Holly acknowledged the recent conspiracy of their mother and their sister. Lily had broken the fragile bonds of childhood. She had grown away. They both felt Lily's desertion, and felt, too, her betrayal of them. Holly stroked the lizard and handed it back to Jasmine. Jasmine returned it to the box.

"You've kept these a long time," Holly observed.

"Too long, but I haven't been able to catch any others. It will be hard for me to let them go."

"Why don't you find some new ones today," Holly suggested.

Jasmine glanced toward the house and quickly looked back to her little dark sister.

"Go on," Holly said. "Lily'll be back out here soon."

"Mama will be mad as a hornet at you. At you, Holly, not me," said Jasmine, thinking of her mother's anger aimed always at Holly.

"I'm not afraid."

"You should be," Jasmine warned. "Mama's one of those beautiful things that you should be afraid of."

"Do you suppose if Daddy cut off her head she'd still move?"

"Probably."

"I wish he would," Holly said seriously. "Mama keeps going to the window and looking out at you. You'd better go now while you can. Go on, Jasmine."

"All right," Jasmine said. She hurried away from the house, leaving Holly behind. She was thinking of Estevanico and how soon she would be climbing the rise, then running down to his *morada*. She could see it all so clearly as she fled.

Estevanico could not know that she would be with him soon, but really Jasmine never left him. She was with him when he prayed, when he slept, day and night, always. He felt she was beside him now as he kneeled down beside the still bird. It was a heron and it had flown in during the storm two nights before when the winds were highest. It had been attracted to the *morada* by his torch. When the storm had passed the bird did not leave. Estevanico thought that it was injured, but it was not. It simply sat on the ground and waited, waited for death. It had refused food for nearly forty-eight hours. Estevanico brought a click-beetle and placed it before the bird. The heron ignored the insect. The beetle moved off quickly, its hard bluish shell glinting in the sun. Estevanico watched its flight from the grounded bird. His thoughts were of Jasmine. It had been two weeks since he'd seen her, but nightly he went to the house where she lived with her family and watched the lighted windows go dark. He had been returning from there when the storm had blown up and the heron had been drawn to his torch.

Estevanico knew that it was a good thing that the little girl came to him no more. He was trying to convince himself that his life could return to what it had been before she entered it, but now that she was gone she was with him even more strongly. The bird's bright and unblinking eyes reminded him of Jasmine's.

"Why did you come?" he addressed the bird. "Go from here," he commanded, but it did not move.

He walked back to the *morada* and took up his carving of the Christ figure. It was nearly finished. It was small, easily held in his hand. He intended to put it in the niche by the altar. He cut the Christ with his knife, detailing it minutely and finely. He did not see that the face of the statue was Jasmine's. He was remembering the day that she had first appeared, standing in the doorway, a cool and white intrusion upon his suffering. He looked up from his work and she was there again, so exact a reproduction of his reminiscence that he could not believe her real.

"Jasmine," he whispered.

"They kept me from coming. I couldn't get away until now."

She started further inside but he went to her, stopped her, led her outside with him. She noticed that he had laid aside what he was carving.

"What were you making?" she asked him.

"A figure of Christ."

"Did you make the skeleton in the cart, too?"

"Yes."

"Do you only carve things that have died?" she asked.

He did not want to tell her yes. He gave no answer.

"There is something I want you to see," he said.

They walked to where the heron sat.

Seeing the bird, Jasmine asked, "Is it hurt?"

"No."

"Why doesn't it fly away?"

"I do not know."

She bent and slowly extended a finger, touched the soft feathers. The bird quivered.

"It looks like a lizard, but with feathers," she said.

"The two are much the same."

"How, Estevanico?"

"They both have a backbone. Both have unusual breathing powers. Their young are hatched from eggs. Birds molt their feathers. Lizards shed their skins," he told her. He loved to teach her. It was wonderful to once again be able to give his narrow desert knowledge to her.

"What sin must lizards have committed to be denied the flight of birds?" she wondered.

"This bird denies itself flight," he said.

"Maybe it is punishing itself," she suggested.

"No."

"What then?"

"I think it fears that it has lost its world."

"What do you mean, Estevanico?"

"It came here during the storm. It will not eat. It is killing itself. I have heard of a village far away in a strange land where whole flocks of birds do this. They come only on windy rainy nights and they are brought swooping to the earth by lights. They land and will not move. The villagers kill the birds and eat them."

"But they have really killed themselves."

"Yes."

"Why, Estevanico?"

"I do not know. No one knows. Only the birds know. Could a bird fear that the sky will never again be blue? Could it fear that all the world will forever be nothing but a raging black void? Could a bird have those fears? Could it live with them? Or would it choose to die?"

"Would it?" she asked him.

"No," he answered. "It is only a bird. It does not have human fears. There must be some other reason. Or no reason at all."

"What light brought this bird? No light from the window. There are no windows."

"I had been out walking. I had a torch with me."

She stopped thinking of the bird. "So many nights these last two weeks I've looked out my window and thought that I saw a torch burning in the darkness."

"You did, Jasmine."

"I knew that it was you."

"I fear that I frightened one of your little sisters. I did not want to do that."

"I know."

"I stayed back after that night. I kept at a greater distance, but I could not keep away entirely."

"My family will be leaving soon. I'm not going with them."

"But you must go, Jasmine."

"I won't leave here. I won't leave you."

"This cannot be. All things change. Nothing, no matter how we might love it, remains the same. We were given this time together. Our time has ended. You must go, Jasmine."

"I won't. I won't go. I won't change. I won't grow into my mother or my sister Lily. I want to stay as I am now. Help me, please, Estevanico. Help me."

"I cannot. You said to me once that the dams have come and there is no going back. I cannot stop time, Jasmine, not even for you. And you cannot."

She touched the bird again, and it did not shudder. "It's still," she said. "It has stopped time."

"The bird is dying."

"Yes."

He responded to her thoughts. "No, Jasmine."

"That very first day, Estevanico, you told me that you weren't afraid to die, that you welcomed death. Were you lying to me then?" she asked him.

"I spoke the truth that day. But it is not the same for you, Jasmine, as it is for me."

"Why isn't it?"

"I should never have said the things to you that I did. I should never have spoken to you at all. I should never have looked at you. It was wrong."

"No, it wasn't."

"Yes, very wrong."

They stopped speaking and stood silently over the bird.

"It is so close to death it could be one of your carvings," she said. "When it dies will you carve it in wood?"

"Yes."

"Do you love death, Estevanico?"

"I have lived my life with death in my soul, but you are not me, Jasmine."

"Are you so sure that I'm not?"

"You belong with your family. You must go with your mother and father and sisters," he told her.

"They are not my family," she said and stopped. She searched his face. "You are my family. I belong here with you."

He hated to deny her but denial was his creed. "No. You must go," he said. "I want you to go."

"Don't say that, Estevanico."

"Today we say goodbye."

There was a finality, a rigidity, in his voice that she could not combat, could not bend or alter. She wanted to change him, but she was a victim of change, not a master of it. She knew that she could not wield change.

"Goodbye, Jasmine," he said, and the words came the hardest of any that he had ever spoken. He must make her go, leave him, and live. Her life was precious to him as his own life had never been. He did not know how deeply she had been touched by him and by death. He refused that apprehension.

Jasmine watched his jaw twitch in pain as she had the first day. "Goodbye, Estevanico," she said. She turned and walked away from him, and as she did, she said his name again: "Estevanico."

He heard it and it was like an echo to him, so swiftly had she gone from his sight.

After a while she slowed her pace. It was too hot to travel quickly and she had no desire to hasten home. She felt that she was home here. That place that housed her mother and father and sisters was not her home. She approached the smoke tree. It offered small shade now. Its branches were high and bare. She thought of when she had seen them bent nearly to the ground under the soft weight of thousands of purple blossoms. She gazed out across the flat parched land. There was no wind at all. She was aware of a presence even before it moved into the periphery of her vision. The snake came closer. She was entranced by its soundless and mesmeric motion, the reptilian beauty of it. It was a huge diamond-backed rattler, red and black. It slid along the ground, gliding, gorgeous, and deadly, in a sway. Her skin prickled at the sight of it. It was coming directly toward her. She waited, not alarmed by what it brought. Then it veered and was gone, continuing its capricious winding elsewhere. She followed it only with her eyes and until they failed her.

Jasmine stood and began walking, not in pursuit of the snake. It had made its strike, not killing with its fangs, but with its fatal appearance arousing the idea of death that Estevanico had chastely fathered weeks before. She knew that she could not go and live in a tall green forest, the one from her memory that was covered in moss and misted over with antipathy. Wet Washington. She could see her mother's large white breasts wet from nursing Poppy, and the trees darkly wet, the dripping roofs of the houses, and the slick streets. There was no escape from the pervasive and perpetual rainfall. She could not go there. There she feared that she would be forced to join the conspiracy of women, the sisterhood of moisture, quiet bleeding. Her body was going toward it. She could feel it slipping from her, her own body. When she put her finger up inside herself she could feel the damp and soft convolutions. It was dark within her and she could not see but she could feel the change taking place. She was twelve years old and each day older. It was inevitable and horrible. She wanted to stay as she was now. She did not want to leave the desert and the hard-edged simplicity of childhood. She recalled the plant that Estevanico had pointed out to her once, telling her that it was poisonous. A warning or a prophecy, she wondered. Estevanico was her guide, her prophet, she decided. She must find the plant again. She was sure that she would recognize it. It grew tall with small white blossoms and black berries, but it was the root she wanted. At the base of the pokewood, just beneath the ground, was the venom and the antidote both. She would not have to run after it, but only dig it from the earth and put it to her mouth, swallow it. Then she could stay on the desert forever. Off in the distance she spotted a high flowering spire, its pale sprigs and dark berries mingling. She had found it.

The night was clear and cold, the sky wide and black, the moon fully silver bright, and the stars shone like shards of mica. The perfect stillness flattened the landscape, made it appear to be paint upon canvas.

Jasmine came from out of the house. She had looked upon all the sleeping faces within before she'd gone, a last look. She had hoped to go to the smoke tree but she lay down on the ground in the yard and stared up into the sky. She had secretly eaten the root hours before. She did not know how long it would take. The moon and the stars were far away and then close, within reach of her hand, if only she could lift her hand, but it was so heavy. She felt a weight pressed down upon her chest. She floated out from under it. She was near and far, like the constellations, Ursa Major and the Seven Sisters. The Seven Sisters, she thought, but there are only six. She named each of her sisters, five names, forgetting to name herself. Five sisters on earth and she would float up and join the stellar seven, make them eight, but no, she wanted to stay upon the desert. Not even if she could be a star would she choose to leave here.

The root had tasted bitter. She could taste it still even though she'd swallowed it while the sun was setting and now the moon had risen. She did not believe that it had begun its work yet. Her thoughts came clear as the night and nearly as cold. How long would it take, she wondered. Had she eaten enough of it? She wanted it to be finished by morning. She didn't want to be discovered and saved. This root was rescuing her, taking her to the sanctuary of death, but it was so slow.

It seemed to her that hours had passed since she'd come outside. She began to shake violently. Her stomach cramped. The spasm wrenched her body, brutally bending her in half. It was beginning, she thought. The pain was terrible. She clawed at her skin and writhed on the cold ground. She could no longer see the sky, the stars, or the moon. She thought of the heron. Was its torture like hers, like this? She heard an awful hacking sound, a ragged and raw gagging. It was coming from within her, deep inside her. Her body convulsed viciously. The gagging ceased and she had a moment of calm. She felt the touch of small light hands on her and saw a face over hers. It was Holly.

"Jasmine. Jasmine. What's wrong? What are you doing out here?" Holly asked.

The little thin and frightened voice penetrated, stabbing like needles, and Jasmine closed her eyes. "Go away," she said, managing to speak before another spasm struck.

Holly watched her sister in horror. She could not look away from her suffering. The throe passed and Jasmine opened her eyes. She focused on the figure of the child standing over her.

"Don't tell . . . anyone. I . . . want . . . this," she said.

Holly could not believe what she was hearing or seeing. She thought that she must be dreaming, but she was sure that she had awakened and left her bed. Maybe she had dreamed that, too. If only she would wake now and find herself still in her bed, but she knew that she would not. She was awake. She had gotten up and something had moved her toward the window and she had looked out and had seen the white form lying on the ground. She had run out to it, terrified as she was by Poppy's dream of a black face on fire outside the window, still she had gone outside. Fearful as she was that the face was stalking them and that it was always waiting, she had gone out into the night where the face dwelled and the white shape was lying. She had found Jasmine. It was not a dream. She was too frightened. If she had been sleeping this fear would have awakened her. She was so afraid, more afraid than she had ever been in her life. She wanted her father. He could explain this. He would make it right, make Jasmine come to herself and stop shaking and foaming at the mouth like a mad animal.

"I'm going to get Daddy," she told Jasmine.

"No," Jasmine screamed, but it was a whisper.

Holly stopped. "Why?" she asked.

There was no answer. She saw the white spittle at the corners of Jasmine's mouth turning pink in the moonlight. A great gush of blood flowed from her. Holly ran on collapsing legs into the house, crying for her father.

She woke the entire house with her anguished screams. She was incoherent. Her hysteria was taken for another little girl's nightmare. She struggled to make them understand. Even her father did not comprehend and only tried to soothe her.

"Jasmine. Jasmine," she cried over and over again.

It was Rose who asked suddenly, "Where is Jasmine?"

Holly's tear-streaked face twisted. "Outside!" she screamed. "Jasmine. Jasmine," she resumed sobbing.

Clay started for the door. He called over his shoulder. "Stay in the house, all of you."

Only Holly and her mother disobeyed and followed him outside.

When he reached Jasmine, she was still. She was dead. Jane came flying and fell down beside the white and bloodied body. She gathered Jasmine to her. She began to sway back and forth, her head buried in her dead child's neck, moaning. Holly stood beside her father. She watched with eyes filled with tears and terror. He saw her and took her silently up into his arms, hiding his child as Jane hid within hers. Jane looked up and her eyes met Clay's. Their stricken and ashen faces were etched with moonlight. Jane let Jasmine's body drop from her and she rose up with flailing fists, beating Clay and Holly. She was moaning and screeching now, too. Clay tried to shield Holly. He set her down and attempted to restrain his wife. They battled. Holly watched them. If she did not look at them then she had to look at Jasmine. She chose her father and mother.

"Why didn't you save her! Why didn't you save her!" Jane was screaming.

"Jane. Jane," he said. "I couldn't. There was nothing I could do," he tried to answer her calmly.

"You couldn't. Why couldn't you? Why couldn't you save my baby? My baby!" She paused, moving back to the past with her present hysteria. "Why couldn't you save my mother! Why couldn't you save her? My mother! My baby!" she cried, and she was seeing her mother swept from her in the roiling waters, her mother's face, streaming and horribly resigned, and Jasmine, Jasmine's bloody peaceful face.

"Jane, listen to me," he commanded. "There was nothing I could do. I wasn't there when your mother died, Jane. And Jasmine was dead before I got here," he told her in agony, trying to defend himself, retain his reason, and fight off her insane injustice. "Jane, come away from here."

He reached out for her but she threw off his hand. "Why

couldn't you save me?" she whispered, lost in hushed condemnation.

No one moved. No one spoke. They all, like Jasmine, might have been corpses, but then Jane turned to Holly.

"You did this," she said to the little girl lying on the ground alive. "You."

Holly's raised white face flinched, confusion and innocence upon it. "No, Mama."

Clay took hold of his wife, his hands digging into her shoulders. "Damn you!" he shouted at her.

"You are damned," Jane said.

He dropped his hands from her as if he had been burned. "Holly," he said. He lifted her off the ground gently. "Go in the house, Holly."

Holly moved like a sleepwalker. As she walked, shuffling one foot in front of the other, she listened to her mother's and her father's words, hurling, hurting words.

"She let Jasmine go today, your precious Holly did," Jane was saying.

"Don't. Don't do this," said Clay.

"Holly let her go. She went to him. He gave her something. He killed her. I know he did."

"Jane."

"That filthy man . . . dark creature . . . from Hell," Jane said.

Holly heard her mother and thought of the black flaming face in the window. Jasmine was dead. Her mother believed that she and the man from Hell had killed Jasmine. But she'd done nothing wrong. She loved Jasmine. She wanted to make her happy. That was why she'd told her to go and find more lizards, only to make her happy. She didn't want Jasmine to die. Holly wanted to tell her mother that.

"This is the Devil's work," Jane accused.

Her mother was wailing and Holly knew that she would not be heard by her. She went into the house and closed the door on the awful sounds. She saw her sisters bunched together, their pale arms wrapped around one another, and they were crying. Holly thought of her mother knitting, the needles flashing, and the skein of tangled white yarn in the basket at her feet. Her sisters looked just like that, pale and knotted, their tears meshing. She was crying, too, but she could find no place among them. She sat starkly alone and wept darkly alone.

Jasmine's funeral was on a Thursday morning. Of the sisters, only Lily would attend. She rode importantly between her parents on the front seat of the car. The younger girls stood in the yard and watched them leave for the church. After they had gone, Rose and Iris and Poppy trooped back toward the house, but Holly did not join them.

"Holly, are you coming in?" Rose asked. The sorrow on Rose's comic face was as inconsonant as her pathetic little tree festively decorated with paper streamers standing in the yard where Jasmine had died.

"Yes, in a minute," Holly answered.

Holly was left by herself, but she did not feel alone. She hoped that Jasmine's spirit would come to tell her a last goodbye. She had heard stories of things like that happening. She knew that she wouldn't be afraid of Jasmine's ghost. She wanted it to come and explain to her. She needed to know why her sister had died, and died in such pain. Holly was sadly, strangely angry. No one, not even her father, no one but Jasmine could tell her why and make the anger disappear. Daddy could ease the sadness, but he could do nothing for this terrible anger, could not touch it. She walked slowly over to the side of the house. Then, abruptly, from purposeless wandering her steps took on direction and reason and speed. She ran to the little shed where the box with Jasmine's lizards was kept. In the cramped and dark building by the slatted light of a misfit board in the roof she found the box. She carried it out into the sunlight. Her hands were shaking as she lifted the lid. Jasmine hadn't turned them loose. The six lizards were lying at the bottom of the box. They had yellow numbers painted on their backs. The numbers ran from one to six. Holly confronted this fresh puzzle. Why, she questioned, had Jasmine numbered them? She shook the lizards from the box. They scattered at first but then they found their positions. They lined themselves up according to the numbers on their backs, one to six. Holly stared in amazement and bewilderment at the feat. Jasmine had taught them this. Why, Holly wondered, if her sister could talk to lizards and make them understand, if she could do this wonderful and remarkable thing, why couldn't she talk to her now? Why had she died? Holly needed so many explanations, and more and more. The need grew, the questions, too. How does someone talk to a lizard? And will a lizard talk back? Who is the man with the dark and fiery face? Is he the Devil, as Mama said? How does it feel to die? There were so many questions, so many things that she didn't understand. It made her angry, not knowing.

Holly looked up into the sky, but there was nothing written there, just a brilliant and blank azure slate, an endlessly rising blue desert sky. She shifted her eyes downward, to the ground, the vast scabland, and there were no answers there either. There was only a wildly ugly land that Jasmine had loved, loved so much that she would die rather than leave it. That was the only reason that Holly could give for her sister's death and it was hollow. It was an empty answer and she knew it. She looked down and the lizards were still patiently lined up side by side. Holly did not know what words to say to make them run away, to free them. She did not know what Jasmine had done to them or what must be done to them to release them from her spell. She shouted at them in pitiful despair. She began to kick at them, sending the lizards running in all directions and dust rising up all around. Holly started to cry. The lizards were gone. Jasmine was gone. There would be no returning, no spirit words of explanation.

Through her tears Holly saw a quivering figure standing on a low rise not far away. She dashed the tears from her eyes with the back of her hand, and the figure no longer shimmered but stood solid and dark in the sun. She began to tremble. It was not her sister's spirit she had sensed, but this man. He had been waiting for her, watching for her. She was very afraid. This was the man with the black flaming face from Poppy's nightmare, she was sure. Yet he was real and he was walking toward her. She edged back, away from him. The house wasn't far. She could run to the house and shut the door before he reached her, but she had to run now if she was to have enough time, another moment and he would be too close to escape. His figure grew larger as he came nearer. She must go now. Now! Go! She screamed inside herself, but she could not run. Her legs would not move. This was her mother's Devil and she could not run from him. Her heart was thundering. This was the Devil and maybe he wanted her, too.

Maybe he had come for her and soon she would lie down on the
ground and shake and froth and rage and die as Jasmine had, but
still she could not go. He was very close now. She could see his
face clearly. It was a dark face, but there was no fire in it.
Only his eyes looked burned, red-rimmed, sad, and full of pain.
At the sight of his face Holly's fear left her. This man could not
be the Devil, of that she was sure. She waited to hear the words
that he would speak and began to hope once more that maybe she
could find the answers that she sought. Perhaps this man held
them. He seemed to carry some knowledge heavy as a cross, she
observed. He halted a few yards in front of her. Holly felt that
he was afraid to come closer. He, who had sparked such scorching
fear in her a few moments ago, was frightened of her.

"Jasmine is dead," Estevanico said.

He had not asked it as a question but he appeared to need some
affirmation. "Yes," Holly answered, confirmed. "She died two
nights ago." She paused, waiting for some response from him, but
there was none. She questioned him quietly. "Did you know
Jasmine?"

"Yes, I knew your sister."

"My name is Holly."

"I know. Jasmine spoke of you to me."

"Did she say that I was the dark sister?" Holly asked.

"Yes."

"That's what I'm always called."

"You were her favorite."

"She was mine," Holly told him, tears beginning. "What's your
name?"

"Estevanico."

"Jasmine never said anything about you."

"I asked her not to speak of it. I did not think that anyone else
could understand," he said, desperate now that this child should
understand.

"Did you love her?" Holly asked. This had not occurred to her
until she said it. "You did love her, didn't you?"

"I did," he confessed, but added quickly, "Not in a way that
most could believe or know."

Now his eyes filled with tears. Holly anticipated their spilling
darkly down his face but they stayed instead shining in his black
eyes.

"Why did Jasmine die? Do you know?" she asked him.

He answered simply, "No."

He disappointed her. He was only a poor man who was as lost and confused as a child, as she was. "My mother says . . ." She did not finish.

"What does your mother say?"

"She says that you are the Devil and that you killed Jasmine."

"How does she know of me?"

"I don't know."

Now they were both disappointed, without answers, but without fear of one another. Estevanico could see traces of Jasmine in this little girl's face. He stared, straining to see more. Holly shifted uneasily under his eyes. She expected him to defend himself, to say to her that he was innocent and that he had done nothing to harm Jasmine, but he spoke no words of defense. He only looked at her, guiltily trying to make Jasmine live again in her face. She saw him reach into the pocket of the rough woven woolen shirt that he wore. He brought out some object and held it in his hands but did not offer it to her.

"Did you kill my sister?" she asked, knowing he had not, but needing to hear him say that he had not.

He took a long time answering. "I gave her an image of death that was too beautiful. Do you understand that, Holly?"

"No," she said. He rolled the object between his hands. "What is that?"

"It is for you," he answered and offered it.

Holly took it from him. It was bone-white, smooth and slender, a carved figure with flowing hair and a face that was Jasmine's, unmistakably her sister's.

"It's Jasmine. It's very beautiful," Holly told him.

"I want you to have it, but please, tell no one of it," he asked of her. "Show no one."

"I won't," Holly assured him. "Did you make it?"

"I did."

"Before or after Jasmine died?" she asked.

"Yesterday," he said sadly, thinking of what Jasmine had asked him once, if he only carved things that had died. He saw a hint of her sister's perception in Holly. "After," he said. "Why?"

"You must work very quickly," she said. The look on his face made her wish that she had not said it. She held the little figure and was unsure if she should thank him for it. She didn't want to hurt him any more. He had been hurt enough. "Do you really want to give it away?"

"Yes."

"I guess if you wanted you could make another one," Holly said.

"I could, but I never will," he said. He waited for her to say something that Jasmine might have said, but she did not. Her face was sweet and pitiful. She did not see in him what Jasmine had. There was only the slight physical resemblance that had fooled him, cruelly tricked him, at first, but that was all that there was. This child was pained and saddened by her sister's death, but she did not really know Jasmine or share any of her qualities other than a turn of the head and a way of level gazing that disconcerted and penetrated the object. Whatever Holly saw in him she was unable to communicate or interpret as her sister had. He was amazed that he had even hoped to find another Jasmine. There could be no other.

"I must go," he said.

"Goodbye," Holly said. She opened her palm and looked down at the figure. If he had offered no answer, at least he had given her this. "Thank you."

"Goodbye, Holly."

He turned and left, careful to swing wide around the house and avoid being seen. Holly put the figure in the box now empty of lizards and carried it back to the shed.

The day after Jasmine's funeral Clay told Jane that he was leaving for Washington and that he wanted them to follow in a month's time. Jane accepted this quietly, but his next words infuriated her.

"I'm taking Holly with me now," he said.

"No, you're not."

"Yes, Jane, I am. She can't stay here, not after all that's happened. I want to take her away from here, give her a chance to forget if she possibly can."

"You're afraid to leave her here with me," Jane accused him, her voice rising hideously.

"No more, Jane. No more of that. No more screaming. Believe whatever you like," he said, his voice calm. "I can't stop you and your hateful suspicions. I don't care to try anymore. I can't forget what the doctor said after he examined Jasmine. He said she'd been poisoned. That was a purely medical statement, but it occurred to me that he had spoken a very profound truth. Jasmine was poisoned, yes, and we were the venom, you and I, Jane, our arguments, the atmosphere of hate that we created for our children to try and live in. That's at an end. Jasmine ended it. If we have to live together in complete silence and never again exchange a word, I'm willing, but no more deadly battles. I'm taking Holly with me to Washington. I expect you and the girls to come in a month. That's all I have to say to you, Jane."

Clay and Holly left for Washington the next day. They left feeling as if they had fled some hostile country, but upon arrival Holly was surprised at the similarity of the landscapes. Washington was very like the New Mexican desert, she saw. Their first day they drove out to a place called the Grand Coulee, and she told her father of her surprise as she rode beside him in the big bouncing green truck.

"It looks like the desert, Daddy."

On either side of the narrow road there was sage-covered ground, and the sun baked the long-dry river beds that cut and scarred the earth for miles around.

"It does in a way," he agreed.

"But Jasmine said . . ." She stopped. She had not said her sister's name except to the strange man who had brought the carved likeness since Jasmine's death.

"What did Jasmine say?" he questioned, his voice vibrating with intensity. He carried an enormous responsiblity for his daughter's death. He had to know anything and everything that she had ever said, even now that it was too late for her. He had to know. "What did Jasmine say?"

"She told me that Washington was very green, with tall trees, and it rained all the time. She remembered Washington from when we were here before, but it's not like she said it would be, Daddy."

"You talked together about Washington?"

"Yes. I told her we were coming here," she said, still sensitive to blame. "Shouldn't I have told her? Was it a secret?"

"It was all right to tell, Holly. It was fine."

"But she didn't want to come. She wanted to stay on the desert, but this is like the desert. She would have liked it here, Daddy. Why did Jasmine tell me it was a rainy forest?"

"She was remembering the western part of the state, Holly. That's where we were five years ago. This is eastern Washington. There's a range of mountains called the Cascades that go right down the middle of the state. It's like different worlds on the different sides of the mountains."

"I wish I'd known, Daddy, so that I could have told Jasmine," Holly said.

"I wish that she'd asked me." He shook his head sadly. As if to retrieve his tragic error, make amends for his deadly indifference to one daughter, he said to the other that he still had beside him, "Holly, if there is ever something that you don't understand or that frightens or worries you, whatever it is, I want you to come to me and we'll talk about it. Will you do that, Holly? Will you promise me that you will?"

"Yes, Daddy. Daddy?"

"Yes, Holly?"

"The day of the funeral a man came to the house. He talked to me . . . about Jasmine. He knew her."

"What man?"

Her father's voice was urgent and almost angry. She was sorry that she had started this, but she couldn't stop now. "He told me his name, but I can't remember it. It was a long, funny name. He was a dark man. His skin was very dark. I was afraid of him at first. I thought he was the Devil."

"The Devil?"

"Yes, with the flaming black face from Poppy's dream, but he was very nice, Daddy. He wasn't the Devil. He'd been crying."

"What did he say to you?" he demanded.

She was feeling frightened again. "He . . . he said he didn't think anybody would understand about Jasmine and him. He talked slowly like he wasn't used to talking much. I asked him if he knew why Jasmine had died and he told me that he didn't . . . and then I asked him . . . I asked him . . ."

"What, Holly?" he snapped out the words, pressing and impatient.

"It was something that Mama said that made me ask him and I think it hurt him. I was sorry that I did."

"What did you ask him?"

He was driving her, demanding, almost like Mama. Usually he was so soft-spoken, so ready to explain and to listen to her. She felt pushed to response as she never had before with her father. "I asked if he killed Jasmine," she answered him and said no more.

"What did he say?"

"I didn't understand him, Daddy, what he said, but I know he didn't kill her."

"What exactly did he say, Holly?"

"He said . . . that he'd told her death was beautiful or something like that." It was her final answer. Now she asked, "What did he mean?"

Clay knew that he should be feeling hatred for this dark stranger who had intruded upon their lives and touched his daughters, but he did not. Because of the man he felt less responsible, less culpable for Jasmine's death. It was a relief, this surcease of guilt. Jane had heaped such blame upon him, for Jasmine, for herself, and all their unhappiness. Now this mysterious man that Holly had told him of was lifting the fault from him. How could he hate him? He answered Holly finally. "There are people who believe that death is beautiful. You can't blame them. I don't think you can blame them," he said. He felt it was his turn to relieve the man. "You can't blame anyone."

Holly did not fully understand his words but his tone was returning to normal. She decided not to test his return by telling him about the wood figure. That would remain a secret. She held back, sensing that he had asked everything of her because he knew that she could not give it, no more than he could. She was silently aware of their mutual reticence.

"Daddy, what is the Grand Coulee?" she asked, curious about their destination.

He embarked upon an explanation in his smooth, low, natural voice.

"A long time ago there was an ice age. All the world got very cold and everything froze. The mountains and the rivers, the great beasts called dinosaurs, everything, everywhere, froze. Where we're going, to the Grand Coulee, this happened, too. It was a river but when the ice came it forced the water to go another way. The water cut into the earth and made a new river bed for itself. After thousands of years the ice began to melt and the river must have had some kind of memory because it went back to the old river bed, the one where it had flowed before the ice came and drove it elsewhere. The water left behind a deep gash in the earth. That deep dry gash is the Grand Coulee. We're trying to see if it's possible to put water there again, the water from a dam. It would be something called a reservoir. Does that make any sense to you, Holly?" he asked her.

"Yes, Daddy. When the ice melted did the dinosaurs come to life again?"

"No, they never did. They were gone forever."

Something about the Grand Coulee frightened Holly. She felt uneasy there. She kept looking around as if she expected giant sheets of ice to descend upon them and chase them running down into the ancient river course which looked like a canyon it was so steeply sided. She wanted to leave but her father seemed fascinated by the place. He stepped as close to the edge as he could and she wanted to grab him back. Down in that terrible abyss the huge ghosts of cold dinosaurs waited to swallow her father up, she feared. She could see him falling and falling, endlessly falling. She blinked her eyes and miraculously he was restored to the edge, standing, unharmed and whole, then bending down on one knee and taking a handful of earth and inspecting it carefully. He smiled over at her.

"You can come closer, Holly. I won't let you fall."

She approached hesitantly. It was not for herself that she was afraid, but for him. She did not say what she had just seen in her mind. She did not tell him that she had seen him tumbling downward. Now a new image intruded. He had stopped falling finally. He was lying crumpled and grotesquely twisted at the bottom of the coulee. He was so tangled and still, and over him crouched three enormous dark forms.

"Holly, come closer and look," he urged her.

She went to him. She looked down into the coulee. At the bottom she could discern a jagged rock formation that conformed exactly to what she had seen or imagined moments ago.

"What's the matter, Holly?" he asked her. He put his arm around her. She was trembling. "What is it?"

"It's cold," she said.

"It's almost dark," he noticed. "It is cold. I've kept you out too long. We'll go back right now. Would you like to have dinner in a big hotel dining room tonight, with candles and flowers and waiters in red jackets with silver buttons?"

"Oh, yes, I'd like that," she said, never failing to respond to the magic of his words, eager to forget this Grand Coulee.

In their room a little bed was placed for her beside his large one. That night just after he had turned out the lights she asked him again about Grand Coulee. He explained it all once more.

"Will you have to go back there again?" she asked.

"Yes, of course. That's why I'm here, to find out what can be done with the coulee."

"Daddy, I don't want you to go there. It scares me there."

"Why, Holly?"

"I saw something."

"What did you see?"

"It was a kind of picture inside my head. I saw you fall down into the coulee and in the picture you fell next to some rocks, three big black rocks. When I went over and really looked down there, Daddy, I saw the rocks just like I'd seen them in the picture."

She was sobbing. He could hear her.

"Come here, Holly," he said, throwing back the covers from his bed.

She was beside him. He held her tightly. Maybe it was wrong to have brought her here with him, but he couldn't bear to think of her being mistreated by Jane. He didn't like to have her too far from him and his protection. Jasmine's death had left in its wake these fears and visions of Holly's. It was the naturally awful aftermath of such tragedy, he told himself. Her present distress, fears of losing him, too, were very real to her. He thought only to allay her suffering. Any idea of prescience did not occur to him. Holly was in jeopardy, not he. He rocked his little girl in his arms until she slept. He stroked her hair and her skin, just exactly the color and texture of his own. She was of him, of his body and of his soul, and he loved no one as he loved this child of his. Her warning to him was lost in that love.

The next day as he swayed at rope's end over the Grand Coulee he thought of what Holly had said the night before. He was a rigger-rodman, he told himself. He was a special breed of man, the disciple of Sam Peters. He'd swung down over a hundred

canyon rims. Why should this day, this chasm, be different from
any other, he wondered. And yet he knew that it was. He looked
down. Directly below him were three large and jagged black
rocks. Holly's description came to him. Jolted by the fraying
rope and recognition, he began to fall. He was dying, he thought.
He was leaving Holly just as she had been afraid he would. In the
seconds before he struck the ground, he was thinking of his
daughter. Holly was his last awareness.

He moved in and out of consciousness. Each time that sensi-
bility slipped from him it was a small death, but he knew that he
was alive. He was in a hospital and the men and women in white
who worked over him were doctors and nurses. He knew this,
but he could not speak to them, tell them what he knew. He
battled alone between the worlds of life and death. Jane's face
hovered. He wasn't sure to what side she belonged, the conscious
or the unconscious. Was she really there? Or did he only dream,
dread, that she was? And Holly? Where was she? He thought that
he felt her little dark presence, but he couldn't see her. If he
lapsed into death, he thought, Jane would take Holly. He couldn't
let go of life and Holly. He knew how terribly hurt he was, for
no matter how his mind heaved, his body was like lead. He could
not move. And Jane was there, always there, looking down at
him. His wife stalked the white room like an albino tigress. He
could see her clearly. Then he realized that he would not die, but
that wounded as he was Jane would carry him back to her Kansas
lair and there devour him alive.

PART TWO

❀

LILY

❦

Chapter Four

❦

Kansas, 1932 . . .

The old brick factory dominated the town, both the landscape and its people. It was one of the few factories in the vicinity to keep open its doors in the midst of the Depression. Bad times were rampant and life was especially hard in this rural Kansas community. Poverty had already eaten away the flesh of the people, and now it was gnawing at their pride, their hope, and sucking the marrow of their bones. This factory, they believed, was a bulwark against their fate. Yet it offered possibly a crueler destiny, a prolonging of life, simply a slower death. One entire side of the building was taken up with a sign. In black on a white background were printed the words STRAKER SHIRT CO. SINCE 1882. Fifty long years the sign had stood and it plainly showed its age, proudly, too. The paint was peeling like burned skin. The stubbornly red bricks of the building absorbed the sun, held the heat in a way that a woman with a cooling lover would envy.

Within the building there were three levels of activity. On the top floor the shirts were made. From the high transomed windows came the incessant drone of sewing machines. It was darker and quieter on the ground floor where the shirts were pressed and boxed. In both of these areas the workers were female. Girls and women in white smocks and brightly colored bandannas sewed and steam-ironed and packed the men's shirts, a kind of institutionalized housewifery. For many of them it was this job alone that stood between their families and starvation. Down below, in the basement, was the shipping department, a strictly male domain.

It was nearly time for the half-hour lunch break. Things were beginning to slow slightly in anticipation of stopping, but Lily continued to pack the shirts as they came to her and at her usual speed. She was not a particularly fast worker, but diligent and painstakingly neat. Occasionally Lily would glance searchingly around the dim airless room. She was looking for someone. She had been looking for him all this morning, and the day before, and the day before that, watching and waiting for him to appear. For five days she had kept her furtive and futile vigil here in the factory, but it had really begun last Sunday outside these walls.

Lily deftly folded the shirts, white and blue, yellow, striped and checkered, each into its box. Her movements were a constant flow, so unthinking and menial a task, and repeated so often, that it had become involuntary, like breathing. She had been working on the packing line since just before her sixteenth birthday. Soon Lily would be seventeen. Close to a full year of her young girlhood had been spent at this labor. The shirts came at her unceasingly. Whether it was summer or winter outside, whether her heart ached within her or her eyes misted and stung from the tears of watching and waiting for someone who did not appear, still they came, the shirts, white and blue, yellow, striped and checkered. The season or her sorrow made no difference to them.

It was too far for Lily to travel the twelve miles in from the family farm every day and so she lived in the factory dormitory, a large frame house next to the factory itself. Her wage was ten dollars a week, most of which she gave to her mother. Nine hours a day she worked, Monday through Saturday. Sunday the factory was closed, God's and Mr. Straker's day of rest. On Sundays Lily went out to visit her family on the farm. She always had until Earl had entered her life and became her life, all her life. Then she began to make excuses to stay in town on Sunday. She gave her mother every reason but the real one. Earl. Four months of Sundays they had had together, she and Earl, and then last

Sunday she was suddenly alone. Lily had waited, but he had not come to her.

It was Friday now. She looked for him still. All week he had not shown up to work in the shipping department. Lily had risked being late in the morning, had stood at the door expecting his arrival, and finally had to turn and go inside alone. She couldn't bring herself to ask anyone where he was, anymore than she could go and knock on the door of his room. Earl had been so adamant that they not be linked in any way. And she had thought she understood why. Factory gossip was fierce. To think of anyone else roughly handling or coarsely using what she and Earl shared was terrible. She was sure he felt as she did and that was why they concealed their love. Earl was hers. And she was his. How many times he had pleaded with her to prove this, and she had, she had, but now she was afraid.

Her hands and arms working like steady machinery, Lily's thoughts were quaveringly human, swinging from the poetic to the mundane. She was remembering their Sundays. The first had been in December. Earl had asked her often to meet with him, but she had said no time after time. Then one day, unaware of any change or difference in the day or in herself, she found that she couldn't say no. So she said yes. They met and walked in the snow together. He had held her hand and tried to kiss her. She wouldn't let him until hours had passed, miles had been walked, and then they had kissed and kissed. Their mouths touched and lingered, and where they were joined was the only spot of soft warmth that frozen Sunday.

Every Sunday Earl had begged for more of her. Once in the late-afternoon darkness in the grove of bare-limbed trees out behind the town's main street he had opened her coat and un-buttoned her sweater. She had watched him, unable to stop him. He had put his hands to her breasts, reached inside the tightly overflowing white cups of her brassiere. When he bent to kiss her nipples, reddened and taut from the cold and his touch, she had pulled away from him and hurriedly covered herself. She refused him for a while, but Lily could only say no to him for a while. Ultimately she acquiesced, inevitably acquiesced. The day had come when Earl had sneaked her up to his room over the grocery store, but she wouldn't go inside. The next Sunday she had gone home to the farm without telling him. She had wanted to run from Earl and his too insistent demands and desires, but she had discounted her own. She had missed him, his touch, and what she believed to be his love. After that Sunday spent apart she had gone up the stairs and into his room with him. She refused him no more and nothing. No longer did they kiss in the falling snow. The snow had begun to thaw and Lily climbed the stairs to his room where the kisses were passionate but strangely perfunctory, too, no longer sweetly complete in themselves but always leading to other things.

Now Earl was gone and she did not know where. He had left her, run from her as she had run from him once, but she feared that he would not be returning to her as she had returned to him. There was nothing undone between them now as there had been when she had fled to the farm. She was afraid that Earl had had his fill of her. He was satiated. Yet she stirred still. She could almost feel his hands unbuttoning her sweater that first time, slowly unbuttoning . . . she buttoned the shirt, folded back its sleeves, and enclosed it in its box. Lily sensed the closing, felt the finish of it, even while she looked up once more seeking the sight of him.

The bell rang for lunch. Everyone stopped work and rushed away. Lily slowly walked over to the Coke machine. She stood beside Ruthie Ette. Ruthie slept in the bed next to hers in the dormitory. Lily had no real friends among the factory women. Ruthie, by her proximity, was as close to one as she had. Lily opened her bottle of Coke and took a drink from it. The sweet burning liquid bubbled down her dry throat. Ruthie was staring at her. Lily had the most lovely and unlikely mouth.

"Hello," she said to Ruthie.

"Hi," Ruthie responded.

"Ruthie, will you sit with me at lunch?" Lily asked. She couldn't be alone with her thoughts of Earl. There had been a time when that was all she wanted, to sit and remember, every detail, every Sunday moment, but she couldn't stand that now, not now. The tingling of the Coca-Cola in her stomach was making her feel qualmish, strangely sick. She swayed slightly. "Can we go sit somewhere?" she asked Ruthie.

"Okay, Lily. How's about outside?" Ruthie was agreeable, easily available.

They went out into the yard that fronted the factory. There

was a high fence all around and a few benches scattered here and there, but mostly everyone sat on the ground. Ruthie and Lily were among the last to leave the factory and tight knots of already seated women stopped their conversations and turned to look after them as they walked past. They all liked Ruthie or knew her anyway, but after a year Lily was still a stranger among them. She kept to herself and was disliked for her reserve, her unwillingness to reveal herself to them. It was common knowledge that something was going on between Lily and Earl Mahoney. They had been seen together on several Sundays. Those who hadn't seen for themselves had been told. So everyone knew. The reticence that had earned Lily the women's enmity was a childhood defense, a protective pose, and now ingrained. It was not snobbery or prudishness that held Lily back from them as they thought. Fears and pain from long ago, layer upon layer of them, had shelled Lily over. It was sadly ironic that the only secret that she had consciously tried to keep was Earl, and Earl was the only thing that they all knew of her.

"Why don't you take your smock off, Lily? It's hot," Ruthie said.

"No. I'll keep it on." As she spoke Lily fingered the buttons of her smock.

"Suit yourself. I wish I could take all my clothes off. I just hate clothes. They bind me something awful. Someday I'm gonna live in a big house where I can walk around nekked as a jaybird with all the blinds open, wide open. And if anybody looks in at me I'm gonna laugh in their faces. 'Cause if you've got a big enough house you can laugh at them all and go nekked, too," she declared. Ruthie was a product of her times. The Depression had imprinted on her young mind that financial security meant everything, to have money was to have beauty, courage, morality, everything. She was struggling out of her smock and unbuttoned her blouse, too.

"Ruthie, you can see your bra," Lily advised

"What do I care? It's just us girls," she answered.

Lily looked around the yard. "There are some shipping men over there," she said and couldn't help searching for Earl among them.

"I guess you'd know if there were any, Lily," she said archly.

"What do you mean?"

"You know what I mean." Ruthie winked at her.

"No, I don't."

"Well, what I mean is that men just seem to find you or you find them, I don't know which. Some of the girls and me were talking about you the other day . . ."

"Talking about me?" asked Lily.

"Yes, about you, and we were saying that there's lots of girls around prettier than you, but you sure do seem to attract the men to you. I was looking at you today and I think it's your mouth. If I were a man I'd want to kiss you, Lily." Ruthie stopped talking. She was hungry and digging into her lunch sack.

Lily felt a wave of dizziness, a hot rushing of blood to her face. "You think, and the others, too, that I attract men?" Lily asked her.

Ruthie was tearing away the paper from her sandwich. "Oh, don't play so dumb. What about Earl Mahoney?"

"What about Earl?" Her heart was pounding. To speak his name aloud was torture. She hoped that Ruthie hadn't heard her voice crack.

Ruthie hadn't heard. She was completely occupied with eating. She took an enormous bite and while chewing said, "You two are pretty good friends, I hear." She swallowed noisily. Ruthie was not a malicious or mean girl, only shallow and crassly simple. She said whatever occurred to her. She had little sensitivity and less perception. Nothing penetrated too deeply or meant very much to Ruthie.

"What have you heard?" Lily asked.

"Just what everybody else has. It's all over the factory. Betty Turnel saw you and Earl going up to that room of his over the grocery."

"She saw . . . but how did Betty know it was Earl's room?"

" 'Cause she's been there, I guess. Lots of the girls have. That Earl, he was a real sly one," she said and smiled at Lily while taking another bite of greasy bread and reddish-brown meat. "I wish he'd asked me up there. What was it like?"

Lily said nothing. She put her hand to the back of her neck and her skin felt on fire. From all over the yard eyes bored burning into her, she could feel them. Ruthie's voice was like the sound of a tiny stinging insect dimly buzzing and faraway, then flying close, deafening, blaring inside her ear. The words flew around within her. They all knew about her and Earl. Earl. Earl had had other girls. They all knew Earl. Earl.

"I sure wish he's given me a tumble before he left," Ruthie was saying.

Everything went very still. That one word stopped the beating wings of the others in her brain. "Left?" she asked.

"Sure, left. Gone. You knew Earl was gone, didn't you? He hasn't been to work all week. He told you he was going, didn't he?"

"No."

"Well, maybe he thought it would be easier this way. They come and go down there in shipping, come and go all the time."

"Where did Earl go? Do you know?"

"Come on, he told you, didn't he, really?"

Lily reached out and took hold of Ruthie's wrist. She did not want the sandwich going into the greased and shining mouth and stopping her answer for even a second. "Ruthie. I don't know. He didn't tell me anything. Where has he gone? Tell me," she said hoarsely, rapidly.

Ruthie stared blankly at her. "He went home to his family in Missouri, I guess."

"His family? His mother and father?"

"Mother and father, that's a good one!" Ruthie laughed loudly. "Earl Mahoney went home to his wife and three kids."

Lily dropped her hand from Ruthie's wrist. "How do you know?" Lily demanded.

"Know what?"

"That he's married, that he has children," she said. The words "married" and "children" that roared inside of her brain came very calmly from her mouth.

"He didn't tell you that either? Everybody knew. Anyone of us girls could have told you about Earl, Lily. You never asked. Kitty Vander told me that he . . ." she trailed off. Lily's face was too clearly stricken for even Ruthie not to see. "You look a little sick, Lily."

Lily was already drawing back. She knew instinctively that she had come out too far toward Ruthie, made herself vulnerable. "No, I'm all right."

"You sure? You're awful white. Maybe you should eat something. All you had was that Coke. Want a bite of my sandwich?"

she offered. She held out the remains of it to Lily. A smear of red lipstick and her teeth marks were left on the small piece of meat-stained bread.

"No, thank you," Lily declined. She turned her face away.

"Suit yourself," Ruthie said. She shoved it into her mouth and started licking her fingers, sucking greedily. "It's too bad Earl didn't even say goodbye, but he was a real bastard. Good riddance to bad rubbish."

Lily stood.

"Hey, we've got ten more minutes. You're not going in now, are you?" Ruthie looked up at her in amazement. "Ten more minutes," she repeated.

"I want to comb my hair," Lily said.

"Well, see you later."

"See you later, Ruthie."

Lily walked quickly through the women in the yard, but she couldn't escape their faces and their voices. She thought she heard her name and Earl's and then laughter. She hurried on. Inside it was cooler, darkly quiet. She had a sudden urge to lock all the doors behind her, to keep them all out and away from her. She sat down at her place and laid her head on her arms, hiding her face. A stack of shirts was piled and waiting for her. She couldn't lock the women out. This was their place. Their place, and she couldn't stay in their place. They all knew. Earl was gone. Earl was married. And they all knew. Only she hadn't known. He'd never loved her. He had only wanted to take her up to his room. There had been others, so many others there before her, and after her, too. They all knew. This was their place. She couldn't stay here. Only she hadn't known about Earl. Now she was going to have Earl's baby and only she knew that.

They began to come in from lunch. Lily lifted her head. They must never know what she knew. None of them must ever find out what she carried inside of her. She would stay on in this place of theirs for four hours or forever if she had to, but they mustn't know. She began packing shirts slowly steadily but she wanted to run screaming away.

Lily did not stop until the final bell at five o'clock. Then she quietly approached the floor lady and told her that she was feeling sick. She whispered that she had bad cramps and was flowing heavily, women's lies. She said she wanted tomorrow off, that she'd be going home for a couple of days. The floor lady accepted her lies, women's belief, and Lily left the factory.

She packed only a few things, leaving the rest for her return, but she knew she would not be coming back here. No one else must know, so she left a few smocks and a blouse as security. She gazed down the long row of narrow iron beds. She could smell the heavy sweet odor of women. She often had lain awake at night, heard their breathing, breathed their smell. She had lain and longed for Earl, wanting the strong acid smell of him, contributing with her desire to the heavy sweet woman smell in the room with many beds and many women. She would send for the other things later when it no longer mattered what they thought or thought they knew.

One of the girls and her boyfriend gave Lily a ride six miles up the road. Then they turned off and Lily walked the rest of the way. She arrived at the farm in the early evening. Her father was behind the closed door of his room. Her mother and sisters were surprised to see her on a Friday. She said that she was not feeling well. She went in and sprawled across her old bed in the room she shared with Rose. Rose joined her and chattered on for a long time. Lily pretended to fall asleep. Rose undressed for bed, turned out the light, and said goodnight, but Lily did not respond. Lily listened to Rose's even breathing near her. She touched her breasts and tears squeezed from her eyes. Her hands were her own, not Earl's, and she wanted Earl's hands. She couldn't make herself feel the way that he had made her feel, the way she craved to feel. She moved her hands down to her stomach. It was swelling with Earl's child, but Earl had three other children. He was with them now and this one he would never see. Still she loved him. The tears streamed down her wan, spare face. She took the pillow from under her head and laid it on top of her. She pressed it hard against her, but it was so light. She'd grown used to the weight, Earl's weight. At first she had felt that he was crushing her, but she had come to love the feel of his body upon hers. She would beg him not to leave her, to stay within her, heavy upon her, and now he was gone. He was with his wife in Missouri. Was he doing to his wife the things that he had done to her in his room on Sundays? Lily wrapped her legs around the pillow. Was Earl's wife wrapping her legs around him? Was he deep inside his wife, hard and driving, then releasing, going soft and slipping away from her? And was she, his wife, sighing for him to stay, to stay within her, to stay with her? Was he staying? Would he always? Earl. Earl. Lily went to sleep saying his name.

Throughout the morning Lily waited for a chance to be alone with her mother. Since it was Saturday and the girls were not in school the house was crowded. Lily had not yet seen her father. He had been for hours in the fields before she was even up, but she had heard him from her bed, heard his limping through the house in the predawn darkness. Rose had gone into the parlor and the three younger girls had run outside, leaving Lily and her mother in the kitchen. They sat at the table alone together. The moment Lily had waited for and dreaded had arrived.

"Mama, I have something to tell you," Lily began. "Something has happened."

"Happened? What's happened, Lily?" she asked. Jane Calder drank her coffee and looked inquiringly at her daughter. She was well enough pleased with this child, her first. Jane had grown calmer since they had come to the farm. She and Clay did not argue any more. They barely spoke to one another. She controlled all their lives and that control was like a drug to her. She seemed saner than she had during their deracinated traveling days, but the treacherous potential for utter madness was still within her. The only one who could now bring on her old rages was Holly and Holly shied away from her mother. The rages were rare. Jane steadily lowered her cup, convinced that whatever had happened to Lily was within her power to correct or change at her will. "Is there anything wrong at the factory? You haven't lost your job, have you?"

"No, Mama."

"What then?" she asked and raised her cup to her lips confidently.

"Mama, I met a man."

Jane's coffee cup trembled slightly. She had not expected this. It seemed so soon, too soon. "You're too young, Lily."

"I'll be seventeen years old next month," she said.

"No, you won't."

"Mama . . ."

"Not seventeen. Not next month. Not yet. It can't be."

Lily looked at her mother fearfully. "I'll be seventeen April the twelfth, Mama."

"I know the date. I remember very well. Seventeen is too young."

"You were younger when you married Daddy."

"I was very young and very wrong. So you want to get married, is that it? Is that what you wanted to tell me?"

"No."

"Engaged?" she asked. "That's better. That might be all right. Of course I'd have to meet the boy." She was relenting somewhat.

"He's not a boy," Lily said. She strained to keep her voice even. "And he's already married."

Jane's voice rose. "I won't have it. I won't have you seeing a man who is divorced."

Lily took a deep breath and plunged. "He's not divorced. Mama, I didn't know . . . I had no idea he was married when I met him."

"Just what are you saying?"

Lily had always been obedient to her mother in all things. She had tried never to displease her and these words came hard, words of disobedience and disgrace. "I fell in love with him before I knew."

"But now that you know you've stopped seeing him?" Jane questioned hopefully.

Lily wanted one more moment of her mother's love and approval and so she answered, "I haven't seen him for a while."

"And you won't see him ever again," she announced.

"I don't think I will, Mama," Lily said quietly.

Jane eyed her sharply. "Lily, I hope that you've learned something from this. Men are . . . can be . . . dangerous. They see a young girl and she's fresh and pretty, and they want her and they lie to have her. You mustn't believe their lies, Lily. You're hurt, I know, but you didn't really love this man. You don't know what love is. You'll get over him. You'll forget, sooner than you think possible. In time you won't even be able to remember his face or his name."

"I'll always remember him, Mama," she said. She knew that she could wait no longer. "Mama, I'm pregnant."

Jane stared down into her coffee cup. She was silent and motionless for a long, long moment. When she finally looked up at Lily, her eyes were hard and glittering. "You let him. Like a whore, you let him. Whore. You're your father's child."

"Mama, please . . ."

Now Jane was screaming. "Holly! Holly!" She wanted the miniature of her husband, Holly, the easy object of her anger. "Holly!"

Holly ran into the kitchen from the yard. The screen door banged behind her. She looked from her mother to her sister and said nothing. Rose had come from the parlor and was standing in the doorway. She, too, silently watched. Jane was working her hands together. Lily, head bent, tears falling, stared down into her lap.

"Holly, go get your Daddy," Jane commanded.

"Mama, I'll go," Rose volunteered.

"No." Jane did not even turn toward Rose. Her eyes were fastened on the little dark girl who stood with her back to the door. Dementedly, she demanded, "Holly. I said for Holly to go."

Holly didn't move.

"Go. Go get your Daddy. Bring him here. Tell him that his whore-daughter Lily has something to say to him."

"Mama, please, I'll go," Rose said again.

"No!" Jane screamed. "You, Holly, go!"

Still Holly stood as if paralyzed, stood like some feral creature stunned by a sudden hypnotic beam of light shined through the darkness, but not seeing the immediate danger, looking beyond to a more insidious threat. Holly wasn't seeing her mother's white enraged face, but something else, something worse, beyond it.

"Go!" she screamed. She hurled her cup at Holly. The child ducked and the cup shattered against the wall. Hot coffee splashed onto Holly's arm. It burned, but she did not wipe it away. Her first protective reflex was to turn and run.

Jane screeched after her, "You bring your Daddy! You bring your Daddy here!"

Rose left the kitchen and went back into the parlor. She looked out the window. In the yard Poppy and Iris were laughing and playing in a shallow puddle of water. Beyond, Rose could see the lone running figure of Holly. As she watched her cut across the field, Rose could almost feel her own skin scalded from the coffee burning further in the sunlight, her own breath coming fast, the tall grass wetly slicing into her own legs. She should see and feel it all too vividly. Rose shortened her focus to the two blond and oblivious children squealing in the mud. Her little dark sister, Rose blurred.

Holly was tall for eleven, and thin, painfully thin. The muscles in her legs and arms were long and hard from constant use. Her dark hair was cut short for convenience. She looked like a boy, strongly resembled old photos of her father at her age. Her mother was always saying it, that she looked like her father, that she should have been his son. It was said spitefully, but Holly was proud. She was so estranged from her mother now that she did not even hate her. She avoided her. She dreaded her outbursts, knew that she somehow provoked them, and tried to stay clear. When she was forced near her mother she looked through her, past her, to a memory of her that she hated, but there was no current hatred, only a kind of emotional deflection, a studied shunning.

Her heart was pumping hard, slamming against her chest, not from exertion but from the strain of her thoughts. Holly was afraid for her father, of what he would have to face when she brought him back to the house. Her mother could hurt her in no way but through her father. His pain traveled through Holly and she was frightened. She tried to think what Lily could possibly have done or said to her mother. Ordinarily she, Holly, was the only one of all the girls who could bring on her mother's anger. It had always been that way. Always she had raised this horrible and special response in her mother. She could remember it even when she had been very small, especially then, looking up into her mother's face.

Holly thought of the time when Jasmine had died and her father had had his accident. In her mind these two events seemed to have happened within moments of one another. She knew that it had been days, but in her memory it would always be the same day. Jasmine's death was vivid. It had happened on a cold and dark night, outside. Then everything turned white. It was a hospital room and her father lay in a bed way up high. She had tried to talk to him but he wouldn't answer. She remembered thinking that he didn't answer because the bed was so high and he was so far from her that he couldn't hear her. She had wanted to tell him something. Had she said it and he had not heard, or had she not said it at all? She couldn't remember what it was, only that it had remained unspoken or unheard between her father and herself. Then her mother was there. She hadn't been, but suddenly she was. Holly had looked up, way up, and saw her mother bent over the tall white hospital bed. And from her low, distorted, childish view Holly saw her mother's face. There had been no sorrow in it but only an ugly satisfaction, a pleasure for his pain, a quick sharp smile at his senseless and helpless state. Holly had seen it, plainly, and that was what she would forever after see when she looked at her mother. Now when she was near her and it appeared that she was looking beyond her, it was that face leaning down over the tall white bed of her father that Holly saw.

Holly was not very curious or concerned about Lily. She sensed that her sister had done something wrong, something bad that men did not do but only women did. There were so many things that only women did, Holly thought, and not good things. She knew that she must grow into a woman, but she wasn't at all sure that she wanted to do that. She didn't think that she would ever want to go to that big blue box in the hall cupboard and take a white pad from it and carry it into the bathroom the way that her mother and Lily and Rose did. She couldn't imagine her sister Jasmine taking part in such a ritual. She had no memory of her doing such a thing. And Holly remembered so many other things about her sister who had died, her death most graphically, but not this ceremony of the white pad and the blue box. Somehow Holly felt it all related to Lily's tears in the kitchen and her mother's anger, but her concern did not touch the immediate players in the scene. She was thinking of her father, how it might hurt him, ensnare him once again in the madness of her mother. Holly could see the look that would come into his eyes at her appearance, the joy, and then the pain at the words that she had come to say. The pain would surface, a real true pain, palpable, like the throbbing in his injured leg when it was cold and damp. And it was cold and damp so often here in Kansas. She recalled the hot dry days on the desert and wished for them back for him. She wanted to ease his pain, not bring him more. Holly knew why her mother had chosen her to come and tell him and bring him to the house. She knew that her mother wanted her to witness her father's pain, knowing that she had brought it to him. Her mother wanted her to be helpless before his hurt as he would be helpless with it. Holly slowed her pace, but then quickened. Better it was her, she thought. She was suddenly glad that her mother had sent her because at least her father would have the happiness of seeing her running toward him before she had to shatter that sight with her words of trouble from home. In the distance she saw him behind the plow, the old gray horse plodding ahead, and he guiding so surely. She saw the straight furrows wending steadily and she shuddered at how people marveled that a cripple could plow the earth so strongly, so rightly. Those people thought that because he was bent that everything he touched must twist and deviate, and Holly shook with hatred of them and their warped ideas.

Not yet, Holly thought, not until he looks up, no words until he sees. He saw her. He stopped and took off his hat and waved it widely to her. Already she could see his smile, spreading bright and big across his face. For her. It was all for her, for the sight of her, Holly knew. And she knew how his heart must be swelling just as hers was.

"Daddy! Daddy!" she called out to him and sprinted the space between them.

He watched her run, the smooth long strides of her slender legs, the clear outline of them beneath her red skirt that the wind drew tightly back from her supple body. Soon he would feel her arms around his neck, her hard warm brown arms softly entwining. He was torn between wanting her to come faster and to slow. He wanted to watch her and to feel her, too. Holly was the one thing, the only thing, that he loved completely and still in life. She was his last chance to love himself again, to escape the self-loathing and pity that had overcome him since his accident. She was there. Her arms were around him as he knew they would be, as he had felt them long before she was actually within his grasp. He could feel her whole and perfect body pressed to his as he had felt it while he watched her run, as he had felt it all the morning while he ployed his straight furrows. Holly was his straight furrow, his own clear sweet straight mark upon the earth.

"Daddy."

"Holly."

Then they stood away from each other.

He looked into her face. "What's happened?" he asked her. He did not know what had happened but only that something had. "What is it?"

So soon, she thought, how quickly he can read a face without a word spoken. "Mama sent me," she answered. Her reply said far more than the few words she spoke. If Mama had sent her, the implications and ramifications were many and perilous. They both knew that well.

"What does she want?" he asked. His voice had gone weary.

"She wants you to come home. It's something about Lily. Daddy, she called Lily a whore."

"Let's go," he said in the same thin and frayed tone. He returned his hat, so joyously waved only a moment ago, sadly to his head.

Now his face was hidden from her. She couldn't see his eyes, and that was easier for him and for her. They walked. His was a difficult gait to follow. She began to limp as she moved along beside him. It was an unconscious and totally loving gesture and imitation. There was no hint of mockery. She was not even aware that she was doing it, but he knew.

"Why would she call Lily that? Lily was crying," Holly said.

"I'm sorry that I don't know why, Holly," he said. Seeing a ragged circle of small raised blisters on her skin, he asked. "What happened to your arm?"

"It was Mama," she answered. Her voice showed no emotion. "She threw her coffee cup at me."

"God help me, Holly, I wish I could make her stop, but I don't even know why she does what she does. I used to think there were reasons, but I don't know anymore. I only wish I could stop her from hurting you."

"There's no stopping her, Daddy. There's no knowing when she'll start or why," she said. Her mother was a volatile and violent woman. These were two terrible truths that Holly had come to live with. "It doesn't hurt," she told him, trying to soothe him. "She doesn't hurt me anymore."

"I was afraid of that," he said, and he seemed sadder still.

They walked unevenly, haltingly, toward home.

"What is a whore, Daddy?" she asked him. She kept her eyes straight ahead, not even attempting to see his face under the shadow of his hat brim. "I've heard that word before. It's Mama who is always saying it. What does it mean?"

"I don't know if there's any such thing really."

"Did Mama make the word up?"

"No. It's a very old word, and like a lot of words, an empty one. Sometimes people like to put a word or a name to a thing that they fear or don't understand. It makes them less afraid, but a lot less able to understand. It's much easier to have a name that you can call something and then it becomes that name, only a word, and you don't need to think about it anymore."

"Like ghosts? People are afraid of them. They don't understand. Are whores like ghosts, Daddy?" she asked.

"Kind of like that, yes," he answered her.

"What's going to happen to Lily?"

"I don't know what has happened to her, and I don't know what will, but I have a feeling that Lily will be all right. I'm sure of that."

"Lily reminds me of Mama sometimes," Holly said.

"Does she?" he asked. "How?"

"This morning when Mama called for me and I came into the kitchen, they were facing each other, Mama and Lily were, across the table and they looked just alike to me."

"Lily is like your mother."

"They all are, but me. I'm like you. I'm yours, aren't I, Daddy?"

He removed his hat and squinted at her in the high bright sunlight. He put his arm around her shoulders. He held his hat in that hand and the straw of it scratched her bare skin, tickling her. She smiled up at him. "Yes," he answered.

"It takes two people, a man and a woman, to have a baby, doesn't it?" she asked suddenly.

He replaced his hat. "Yes, it does. The man plants the seed and it grows inside the woman, grows into a baby in her body, and then the baby is born."

"And I grew inside Mama?"

"You did."

"You're sure? You're sure I didn't grow inside of you, Daddy?" she questioned doubtfully.

He smiled slightly. "It doesn't work that way. The woman carries the baby, always."

Again, she thought. Another thing that only women do. "It just doesn't seem right to me that I grew inside Mama. Maybe it was another woman who carried me and then gave me to Mama."

"No, she is your mother, Holly."

"But how can that be, Daddy? I'm not her child," Holly said.

He had no solution to offer her. He gave assurance instead. "You're mine."

They came in sight of the house. Iris and Poppy still played in the yard.

"Stay outside, Holly," he told her, hoping to keep her from what he imagined must be waiting within the house. He looked down at the burn on her arm and knew that he was too late to protect her from that. It was with self-loathing that he faced his imperfect defense of Holly and his impotence with Jane. "Don't come in," he said.

"All right, Daddy," she said and went to join her small blond sisters.

Clay walked to the back door, hesitated for a moment, and then pushed open the screen. He saw Jane sitting alone at the table. She stared down at the empty saucer before her and did not look up at his entrance. He stepped toward her and one of the pieces of her coffee cup was crushed beneath his foot.

Jane heard the breaking sound. Clay was near her. She was working out a plan, desperately fighting to regain control. She had decided that a marriage must be arranged between Lily and a nearby neighbor named Workman Banner. Jane needed her husband now only to blame. She spoke to him.

"Lily is pregnant."

Clay had almost expected this. "Who is the father?" he asked. He walked carefully, avoiding the shattered porcelain fragments of her anger, came and sat down opposite her. "Who is it?" he asked again. He wanted to care, wanted to feel rage at the man or disappointment in his daughter, but he didn't.

And Jane knew that he didn't. "Why ask? Why pretend, Clay? You don't care about Lily even though she is your daughter, your whore daughter."

"Don't say that, Jane."

"I didn't raise her to be a whore. You gave her that, passed it down from your mother."

"Jane . . ." he began and stopped. "Is that what you wanted to say to me? Is that why you sent Holly for me?"

"Holly," she said. "Where is she?"

"She's outside. I told her to stay there."

"Away from me," she said.

"Yes, away from you. Why did you have to hurt Holly? Couldn't you have waited, saved it for me?"

"No, she deserved some pain," Jane answered.

Clay couldn't address this insanity. He said nothing. Jane continued.

"It's always Holly for you. She's all you care about. What about Lily?"

"I don't know," he said. "What about her? What are we going to do about Lily?"

"I'll take care of it," she told him.

"What are you going to do?"

"I'll take care of it," she repeated.

He knew he would let her. She knew it, too. He watched her stand and gather her white merino shawl closer to her. She walked out the door and he didn't ask where she was going.

It was three miles to Workman Banner's place. Along the way she rehearsed what she would say to him. Head down, the fringe of her wrap softly dancing, her lips moving silently, she was a pale and mad figure set against the hale Kansas land. When she arrived at the farm she had a touching and lucid story to tell Workman, a recent widower. He listened to Jane with interest. He was obliging. His wife Matty had died in childbirth six months ago. Now a woman came in to clean the house, fix meals, and care for his infant son while he worked the farm. He missed Matty terribly. He knew that he could never replace her. She had been his one love, but he was lonely and the housekeeper could not fill all his needs. He didn't want to disappoint a young girl who might marry him looking for love that he could not give. Still he wanted the things done for him that a wife did. Workman Banner wanted a wife, a functionary. He listened to Jane Calder and thought that her daughter Lily, damaged though she might be to other eyes, would suit his purposes perfectly. All that he could remember of Lily was a young girl of fourteen when the Calders had first come to Kansas. She'd been fair, blond-haired then, but oftentimes children grew darker as they grew older. He liked to think that she had kept her blondness. Matty had been blond. Still he didn't want to hope too much, expect too much. He told Jane Calder that he would come by that evening.

It was a beautiful spring twilight. Jane arranged for Workman and Lily to be left alone on the porch. All the family was herded carefully into the house. The sound of high girlish giggling faded. The swing creaked from Lily's nervous swaying. Workman stared down at his hands. There was a long silence. They knew so little of each other and yet they knew, too, that they were here to consider binding their lives together. There was no love or liking but a mutual need. Lily needed his name to expunge, or at least to hide, her sin and shame, to satisfy her mother. Workman needed her young and fertile body, a woman who was not hired to stay between the hours of seven and five but who would remain with him through the nights, which were the hardest for him. Workman needed a warm and breathing girl beside him to drive away his dreams of his dead wife. He often dreamed of Matty lying in her coffin like a cold waxen doll. Workman would have given his arm to have her alive again if only in his dreams, but his wife was thoroughly dead for him. He needed someone to dispel death, someone who lived, and lived with him, even if not for him. The dusk had turned to shadowy darkness before he finally spoke.

"Jonathan, my son, is a good baby," he said. He was unaware that his words were following the pattern of his thoughts. He did not think that they might seem strange or abrupt to her, she not knowing what he thought. "Mrs. Brown says that he's never any trouble at all."

"I like babies," Lily said, moving from the personal to the general. She saw him look to her waist. She placed her hand on her stomach. She felt forced back to the personal. "This one, too," she said.

Someone turned on a light in the parlor and the glow of it touched Lily's hair. She looked very blond in the night. Slowly he reached out his large hand and covered hers with it. "I like babies," he repeated after her. "This one, too," he promised her. Workman Banner was an honest man and not unkind. He smiled for the first time when Lily smiled at him. "It's a good thing, Lily."

"Yes," she agreed.

Though they were utter strangers, their needs were meshed. What had begun as a desperate idea of Jane Calder's only a few hours before was now inevitable.

The wedding ceremony was a small one. In the Calder parlor, Lily, dressed in her grandmother's wedding gown, and Workman, wearing a blue suit slightly small for him, stood together before the preacher and became man and wife. Workman had no people other than his baby boy who was home in the care of Mrs. Brown. The only witnesses were Clay and Jane Calder and Lily's sisters. There was a quiet dignity, a solemnity, to the moment of union, but beneath that a certain sadness, an aura of lives being settled, of people surrendering and resigning themselves to life as it was and not how they had wanted it to be. The occasion had a funereal feeling, the death of dreams.

The groom kissed the bride. It was the first time that Workman and Lily had kissed. The pregnant girl and the grieving man shared their first chaste and tender embrace, prompted by ceremony and in the sight of others. It all appeared as it should be. Everyone went easily through the motions, easily through the emotions, empty in themselves.

A party had been planned for after the ceremony, a party to prove that there was reason for celebration. This was a happy occasion and it had to be loudly declared as such. The Calders could not afford the expense, but Jane had insisted on the show, and somehow it was managed. Tables, laden with food, were set outside. Rose had strung paper lanterns in the five budding elms. There was a three-tiered, pink-tinged wedding cake, another of Rose's creations. With the arrival of the guests hungry for pleasure, and the flashing fireflies, and the stirring mild-aired breeze, it all began to grow more and more beautiful. There was dancing and laughter. Neighbors and townspeople and even some from the factory came and celebrated the marriage of Lily and Workman. Soon the reason for the celebration was obscured by the pure joy of a party. Lily had especially wanted her co-workers to attend. It was imperative to her that they see her happiness with Workman. She was trying very hard to be happy for them. Lily had given up being happy for herself.

Jane and Clay sat silently side by side. There were no words between them and yet their minds were aligned, their thoughts the same. Twenty years of time, a shared life, was powerfully with them. Across the regret and torment of their marriage they remembered their beginning. They had been happy. They had been in love. There had been nothing that they had wanted more than to have each other. It should have lasted forever, both believed. They had been fools. That was clear. The deep disappointment and humiliation was shared by them, too, silently. Jane and Clay watched Lily and Workman. This bride and groom were very different from the bride and groom that they had been. Wordlessly, they prayed together that this marriage would be different from theirs, too.

Rose was jubilant. This party was hers, she felt. For the very first time in her life her vision had been turned to reality. She had worked so hard to bring her conception to beautiful life. The lanterns and the cake, the paper-lace decorations, the flowers, were all hers. Never had she felt such happiness and excitement. She wasn't thinking of her sister Lily. Rose thought of herself. She loved all the people and the lights and the laughter. She loved the music. This was the way life was meant to be. She wanted to dance, and like magic her wish was granted. A boy appeared and asked her to dance. Her partner's name was Clyde. Clyde had blue eyes and hair redder than hers. He talked steadily while they danced. She learned that he was a mechanic at the shirt factory and that seemed to her a wonderful thing to be. He wanted especially that she should know he wasn't one of those bums in shipping, he told her. The intricacies of the industrial hierarchy at the Straker Shirt Company were lost on Rose, but she loved listening to Clyde talk in her ear, loved the feel of his warmth and earnest breath on her skin. She loved dancing with him. Tonight Rose loved everything and everyone. She was sorry to have to leave Clyde, but she explained to him that she had to get her little sisters ready for a song they were to perform. He made her promise that they would dance again later. She turned to go into the house but looked back over her shoulder to Clyde. And he was watching her walk away.

Once inside the stuffy house Rose began to feel stifled. She was eager to be back out in the night at the party. She quickly fixed the costumes she had made on Iris and Poppy. They were going to sing a duet as little Chinese girls. Poppy was heavy-eyed with sleep, but Iris was awake and vibrant. At last the pair stood before Rose, perfect in their pink and yellow cheesecloth dresses, wide sashes, fans, and flowers. Rose was rushing too fast to notice the disparity between the sisters. She saw only that they were ready. Poppy took hold of her hand and they walked from the room, but Rose had to go back for Iris. She found her standing in front of the long mirror. Her face, whitened with powder, stared from the glass at Rose. Iris touched her own face and smiled. She was as beautiful as she thought she was.

"Come on, Iris," Rose said impatiently. "Everyone's waiting. Come on," she urged. She hustled Iris from her image.

Iris positioned herself under the lanterns. Poppy stood just a little behind in the shadow. Everyone gathered around them. Poppy nervously watched Iris for the signal to begin. Iris started to sing. So did Poppy, but no one heard her. No one saw her. They heard only Iris and saw only Iris. She deafened and blinded them to anything but her own shining self. All eyes were riveted upon her, admiring her, and loving her. She could feel them, the caressing waves of adulation that flowed from them and flooded over her. To stand singing with the light shining through her dress, to stir, to arouse them, this was bliss for Iris. At the finish of the song there was quiet and then the applause burst out. Iris and Poppy curtsied as they had rehearsed. Poppy had forgotten the words to the other song that they had practiced and so Iris was forced to sing their encore alone.

Holly stood apart and observed. She had taken nothing from the tables. Her stomach felt queasy. That afternoon she had begun bleeding. She had gone to Rose and Rose had taken her to the blue box in the closet, given her a white pad, and sent her into the bathroom. Holly had stood in there and watched the slender thread of blood run down her leg. She had thought of her father's accident. She had felt that something inside of her had died or was dying and was pouring out blood from its wound. She hadn't told her father. Holly felt, without knowing why, that a barrier had risen up between them, that she was different now and that she must move away from him. Without him, Holly was all alone. The stunning and pale vision of Iris, her lovely white face, made Holly think of ghosts and whores. She watched her father beside her mother and struggled to understand what had happened to her today.

A circle was formed and in the center Lily danced with her new husband. Workman was awkward and shy. Lily did not like

having an audience. She feared being seen. Yet they danced and
smiled as best they could. It was Sunday. Lily's thoughts were of
other Sundays. She remembered her days with Earl, days that had
led to this one, her wedding day. She had just pledged to spend
a lifetime of Sundays with this man who was turning her in
clumsy circles.

"I'm faint," she whispered to Workman.

He led her away from the crowd.

Chapter Five

The summer of 1938 was ending when Lily had her fourth baby. Her labor lasted thirteen hours, through the night and into the morning. It was noon when the little boy was finally born. During the six years of their marriage Lily had given Workman Banner three sons. She had suffered greatly giving birth to them, each one having to be torn from her. Her first baby, her lover Earl's child, was a daughter, and she had come easily. She was named Hope. She had been born too soon, a bare six months after the wedding ceremony. It had been announced that the baby was premature, but it was whispered otherwise. Hope was now five years old, blond like her mother, and the whispers about her had quieted. Too many babies had been born since for any gossips to still be troubling themselves about a little girl who had come three months early to this earth, but the ease of her arrival continued to disturb Lily. Hope, the child of sin, should have caused her more pain, she believed.

Hope did not know that she shared only a mother with her younger brothers, that their father was not the same. That was a secret that few knew. Hope was aware that her mother was not her older brother Jonathan's. His mother had died a long time ago. Jonathan had told Hope and he had cried when he did. They did not speak of it again, but sometimes their father mentioned Jonathan's dead mother. Usually it was after he had been to her grave to take flowers on her birthday in April that he talked of her, but the two children tried not to hear him. Hope hated the look that came into Jonathan's eyes and into her mother's, too, at the sad reminiscence of her father, but it happened only rarely, in the spring, in the month that the dead woman had been born.

Hope and Jonathan were very close, in age, and size, and appearance, tangibly tow-headed, snub-nosed, and overalled, but the bond between them went deeper than what could be seen. There was no blood binding them, no corporeal chain. They were connected by a thin but unbreakable silver cord of spirit.

Today these two had escaped to the barn, running from the sound of Lily's cries. Both of them had heard this sound before. Among their earliest memories were her cries, rising, and then capped by a new and separate cry, a baby's wail. Hope and Jonathan huddled together far into the darkness of the barn. From the wide opening door a large square of light fell and they drew back away from it, but came forward when they heard their Aunt Rose's voice.

"Hope! Jonathan! Are you hiding in here?" she called, her tone good-naturedly seeking and not angrily probing. "Where are you?"

Jonathan's voice piped, "Here we are, Auntie Rose!"

She approached their shadowy corner. "So there you two are," she said, and smiled at them. They were such a pretty pair of children. Rose's throat constricted and her heart tightened at the sight of them. "Your mama has a wonderful surprise for you," she told them.

Hope's eyes gleamed up at her from under flaxen brows, shining in the darkness like a barn owl's.

"You mean a baby?" she asked her aunt.

"Yes, a brand-new beautiful baby brother."

"We knew it was a baby, Auntie Rose," Hope said.

"You did?" Rose laughed. "Now how could you have known? Why, the stork just flew in this very minute and dropped the baby off."

Hope listened silently in innocent but instinctive disbelief. Jonathan questioned seriously.

"Truly, Auntie Rose? Did the stork truly come? Is that where babies come from?"

The little boy's question and the little girl's quiet prevented Rose from perpetuating the silly fable. She said nothing. Hope spoke.

"Another boy, Auntie Rose?"

Grateful for an easy answer, Rose said, "Yes."

"I wanted a sister," Hope said, clearly exasperated at this male pattern.

"How about you, Jonathan?" Rose asked. "Did you want a sister, too?"

Jonathan turned to Hope. "I have a sister," he answered simply and it was evident that Hope was all that he wanted.

Hope was looking at her aunt with her owl eyes. "Why don't you take this baby, Auntie Rose?"

"I couldn't do that."

"Why not?" Hope asked.

"It's your mama's baby, not mine."

"But Mama has so many . . ." Jonathan began.

"And we heard Grandma say that you lost your baby," Hope finished.

Rose's smile faded. It had been six months and still the old pain waited to spring up raw and new. She thought of her stillborn baby and there was an ache, an empty place within her that could never be filled. At first Clyde had cried with her, but no more. He had recovered and his grief had gone, but hers remained. Rose knew that she would never again be the girl she was before her baby had been born dead. She wanted to go back to what she had been before she saw her lifeless child in the hands of the doctor. She wanted to go back. She did not think of going forward.

"How did you lose your baby, Auntie Rose?" Jonathan asked. "Did you put it someplace and forget where? Hope did that with her dolly. We looked and looked but we couldn't find it. She can't remember. Is that what happened to you?"

Rose fought backward to forget, back to a time when there was no need for forgetting, but she kept losing the fight, losing the child, losing, and losing. She looked at Jonathan, his waiting face. "No, that's not what happened, Jonathan," she said.

"Auntie Rose's baby never cried like Mama's," Hope said. At the age of five Hope faced her small world squarely. Hers was still a simple existence. She did not know yet that life would not remain so straightforward, that the rules she now believed so inflexible would one day be flouted or forgotten. She lived in a child's world and she was a sharp and childish realist. Her truth was brutally solid. She had not yet discovered that human beings were infinitely susceptible, fragile, fallible, and that she had come to life a crying offspring of these gray creatures. "Isn't that right? Your baby never cried, Auntie Rose?"

"My baby never cried," she answered. "My baby was born dead."

There was silence.

"There's ice cream to celebrate your new baby brother," Rose said finally.

"Did you make it?" Hope asked.

"Yes."

"You make the best, Auntie Rose," Jonathan told her.

"Let's go get some," Rose almost shouted.

They left the barn eagerly for the light of the day and the sun-softened ice cream that waited.

Later, after she had gone, Rose thought of Hope, her niece's sweet and melting ice-cream face. She wondered if there was something more she could have said, but she couldn't think what it would have been. Rose still had difficulty believing what Hope believed so effortlessly. Her baby had never cried. She passed restlessly through the rooms of the apartment that was hers and Clyde's. They'd come here as newlyweds three years ago in 1935, only three years after their first dance. The apartment building was within walking distance of the shirt factory where Clyde worked. Rose went to the kitchen window to see if he was coming up the street, home to her, but there was no one, only a tired-looking yellow dog with its bony hind leg lifted and its tired-looking yellow stream wetting the street.

Rose began unconsciously cataloguing, contrasting and comparing her life to the lives of her sisters. Rose wanted a child badly. Lily had a house filled with children, but there was something wrong in Lily's house. Workman was a fine man, a hard worker and good provider, but he showed affection only to the children and never to Lily. Rose wondered if Workman and Lily

loved each other. It had been a marriage of necessity, she recalled.
Rose knew that she loved her own husband, had loved him from
the first time she saw him at Lily's wedding. Clyde loved her, too,
but they were so young when it began and they had loved each
other so long. Instead of being confident, Rose worried sometimes
that it might wear out, their love. Clyde had fallen in love with
a fourteen-year-old girl and he'd married her when she was
hardly eighteen. Now she was twenty-one. What if she was
growing too old for Clyde? Rose closed the kitchen curtains.
Maybe she should make new ones, she thought. These were only
a few months old, but she was tired of them already. Suppose
Clyde was, too? The pattern of the cloth made her dizzy. She
thought of how dizzy she'd been when she was pregnant, so light-
headed and happy to be. If only she had her baby now. If only
she could go and find it lying in the crib that stood empty in the
bedroom. She refused to remove the crib, left it waiting. There
would be another baby. There had to be, she believed. There
would be a baby for her to hold while she waited for Clyde, a
baby to bring fresh life here and make her feel young and sure
of love again. No, she did not envy Lily her life, but she did
envy her her babies. Rose's thoughts returned to Hope. Hope
reminded her of Jasmine. Sometimes at night, just before she fell
asleep, Rose would feel a strange loneliness. It was then that she
remembered Jasmine, her silver-white sister who had died. When
this happened she would move closer to Clyde. Whether he was
asleep or awake he comforted Rose with his firm presence, his
bare chest covered with coarse coppery hair, his muscular arms,
and the freckles on his back that massed along the top of his
shoulders. Jasmine and the shadowy sensations that her memory
evoked would disappear, vanish before Clyde and the strong
reality of his strong body. It was good to be alive and beside her
husband, not dead so young like Jasmine.

Rose opened the curtains again and looked down the street.
Clyde might have stopped to talk with Holly as he sometimes
did. But that couldn't be, Rose remembered. Holly wasn't working at the factory anymore. Her summer job there was finished.
Rose realized how different she and Holly were, but there was no
jealousy between them. There was an understanding and an
acceptance of one another, something that Rose felt with none of
her other sisters. Whenever she saw Holly's serious face she was

glad, happy for her own ability to laugh and make others laugh with her. Rose prized her humor highly. She placed it equally alongside Holly's intelligence. Holly was smart, no doubt about it, and she would surely make something of herself one day, but Rose had no desire to be Holly. Holly was a target, their mother's mark. Rose had seen it all her life. She could never really comprehend the cruelty and it was terrible to watch. That was one of the reasons she had been so eager to marry Clyde. Rose had come to this little apartment, thinking of it as a haven where people who lived together loved each other and hatred was absent. Hatred had been so much a part of her childhood home. Mama's hatred had spilled over like a kettle of boiling water filled too full, splashing, burning, uncontrolled. Poppy was the only one who their mother completely loved. Rose begrudged her baby sister Mama and the only thing that she begrudged Holly was Daddy.

Rose paced the living room and returned to the kitchen. She closed the curtains. Where was Clyde? He was later than he'd ever been before. She opened the curtains. If it wasn't Holly he had stopped to talk with, who was it then? There was only one person she would have minded her husband talking with, and that was Iris. What if Iris was in town? She was always coming in to do something. Rose knew how she hated it out on the farm. Don't let it be Iris that Clyde is with, Rose begged inside herself. She couldn't stand it when Clyde was near Iris, the way his eyes traveled up and down her. Rose feared, and hated fearing, that Clyde might be wishing it was his hands and not his eyes that moved along Iris's body. Iris was too beautiful. If Rose hated any one of her sisters, it was Iris, and yet she let herself be used by her. Iris and her golden hair and green eyes and that long-striding walk of hers. Holly described her once as lissome, a word Rose knew she must have read somewhere. No one ever used those kinds of words; only Holly would because she'd read them somewhere. The word fitted Iris, the sound of it suited her. Rose lifted a corner of the closed curtain. He was nowhere to be seen. She tried to think of how she could make Clyde laugh when he came in the door, how she could laugh, and make it all right. She opened the curtain fully and leaned out the window, stretching and straining for the sight of Clyde. She saw him. She wanted to scream out to him that he was late and demand to know where he had been all this time, but that was what her mother would have done. She drew back quickly as if scalded. Rose searched for a joke to make, but she didn't feel like joking. If only she hadn't spent the morning at Lily's, she could have made a cake and had it waiting for him. Clyde loved her chocolate cake. Why was there no cake and no joke, but only herself to present him with?

She ran smilingly to open the door. As she stood there she thought again of new curtains. New curtains would make the place look so much cheerier. Why had she ever picked that dark heavy cloth and the dizzying pattern? Clyde came home later every day. Maybe if things were brighter-looking he would begin to come home earlier again. She waited in the open door for him. Why did he walk so slowly? Why did he drag his feet? Her face felt ready to crack from the forced smile, but she held it until he saw her. Why didn't Clyde smile back at her? He was probably too tired, she excused him, too tired to smile and run into her arms the way he used to. Was three years the limit, the end of love and longing? She smiled wider, swung the door open wider, and the emptiness widened inside her.

Jane Calder was thinking of Lily and of the baby boy born to her daughter that day. The infant was hours old now. It was early evening. Jane was fixing supper. She didn't hear Holly come into the kitchen. Holly stood watching her mother. The long pale hands working in the white dough held a fearful fascination for her. She forced herself to look away and spoke to her mother.

"Mama, I need some black thread," she said.

Jane turned toward her. "In my sewing basket on the credenza," she told her. "Are you all packed?"

"Yes, nearly. I just noticed that the hem is coming out of my black skirt. I have to stitch it."

"I guess you would have liked some new things for school."

"No, Mama, what I have is fine."

"The other girls will probably have nicer things, fancier, the kind of things that girls who go to fancy schools have," Jane said.

"It's not a fancy school. It's a teacher's college."

"In California," Jane added.

"Yes, in California, Mama."

"I guess the schools in Kansas weren't good enough for you."

"No school in Kansas offered me a scholarship."

"You wanted to leave home, leave Kansas. You know it's true," Jane accused her. She thought that Holly grew more like Clay daily. She was about to say more, charge her further, when she heard a car drive up. Iris's laughter reached the silent kitchen. Swiftly the car pulled away and Iris was entering through the back door. Jane's attention was diverted from Holly. "Why are you so late? Whose car was that? Whose car were you riding in?" she asked Iris.

"It was Bobby Jackson's daddy's old Model T."

"What were you doing with Bobby Jackson out at night in a car?" Jane asked.

Holly took this opportunity to escape the kitchen and her mother. "I've got to sew my skirt," she said quietly.

Neither Jane nor Iris heard her, but as she was leaving Holly heard Iris.

"It's only five o'clock, Mama. You talk like it was midnight. Bobby saw me walking home from town and he gave me a lift, that's all. . . ."

Holly heard no more. She went and found the black thread in her mother's basket and returned to her room. The old brown valise that had been her father's sat open on her bed. He had given the suitcase to her, not saying that his need of it was gone and not needing to say it. Her few items of clothing barely filled it. Holly did not have many things but she had a knack of putting together what she had cleverly. She carried in her mind the way that she wanted to look and she was excellent at reproducing mental images. Holly was obsessively neat. Her clothes were always pressed to perfection, matched beautifully, and well-fitted to her long slender body. Her appearance heightened the impression of untouchability, the aura of unbending and scrupulous order that surrounded her. She lived within herself, behind well-tended walls.

After she had finished repairing the hem, she carefully folded the black wool skirt and placed it on top of a white sweater in the valise. Holly rarely wore bright shades and never red, the detested color of her childhood. Since the age of thirteen she had silently gone her own way. She did not openly defy her mother, but subtly circumvented her. Her application for a scholarship at a school in California was a perfect example. Holly was eager to leave Kansas and have a life completely her own in another place far from here. Her mother knew this, but she couldn't prevent her going. Even Jane could not find a reason to deprive Holly of a free education, though she had tried and finally given up, settling into general disapproval.

Holly was glad to be going, but she would miss her father. He would miss her even more and that hurt her more. Their relationship had been tempered by the years. She was no longer a little girl who could take refuge from the world in his lap. She couldn't kiss his face and hands as she had when she was a child. Convention had forced them apart. Even if they were father and daughter, they were man and woman now, too. The distance between them did not lessen their love or need for one another. Only now it went unexpressed, except when an occasion justified a touch. They were allowed rare caresses on a birthday or Christmas. Once the love between the father and his little girl flowed freely from the emotional to the physical, but now because she had grown they would be damned for any unexcused display.

Holly looked up at the entrance of Iris. She hadn't knocked. She never did. Iris came and stood before the small mirror on the wall for a few minutes before speaking.

"You packed your perfume yet?" she finally asked. "You know, that stuff Daddy gave you?"

"Yes, but you can have some if you want it. I haven't closed the suitcase yet."

Iris walked over.

"You have such pretty things, Holly. You keep them so nice."

"You have pretty things, too, Iris," Holly said, but she couldn't help noticing a tiny grease spot on the bodice of Iris's green dress. "Here." She handed her the dark blue bottle of perfume.

Iris dabbed and dabbed, putting on far too much, until she reeked. The scent on her throat and between her breasts was blatantly inviting. She gave the bottle back to Holly. Holly took a tissue and wiped the perfume that Iris had spilled down the label on the bottle. She returned it, after carefully capping it, to the little silk side pocket in the suitcase.

"Do you have any rouge?" Iris asked.

"Does Mama let you wear rouge?" Holly asked her.

"Do you have any?"

"Does she, Iris?" Holly persisted.

"I wear it and she doesn't say anything."

Holly thought that even if anything had been said to Iris she probably hadn't heard. She rarely listened to anyone. Holly had noticed that she did pretend beautifully to listen to men. "I don't have any rouge," she told Iris.

"How about powder?"

"Sorry, no."

"You're almost eighteen, Hol, and you don't wear rouge or powder. Boy, if I were eighteen . . ."

"What would you do?"

"Get out of here. I wish I was eighteen right now," Iris said. She was pinching her cheeks to redden them.

"Are you going out tonight?"

"Yeah, there's this dance."

"A dance, that's nice," Holly said.

"It'll be real hoky. They always are, but it's better than staying home."

"I guess so."

"You don't like dances, do you, Hol?"

Holly was surprised at the question. Ordinarily Iris never asked about anything that did not pertain directly to her or something she wanted.

"You never go to dances," Iris continued. "I guess you don't like them, huh?"

"No, not very much," Holly answered.

"I guess you wouldn't want to go with me, huh?"

Now Holly was more than surprised. She was shocked. Then she realized that it couldn't be a simple invitation, that there had to be some other reason, probably a selfish one.

"Why are you asking me, Iris?"

Iris was an expert manipulator. She weighed whether to tell her sister the truth or flatter her. With her mother or her other sisters she would have applied flattery, but with Holly, she decided, honesty was better, more apt to get results.

"Mama says I have to be home by ten, but if you're along maybe she'll make it eleven."

"I'd like to help you out, but I still have some things to do."

"You're all packed," Iris observed.

"My train leaves at eight o'clock in the morning, Iris."

"That's a good reason to celebrate, isn't it? Please, Hol," Iris cajoled.

"All right, all right, but we can't stay past eleven."

"I'll go tell Mama!" Iris said gleefully. As she was leaving she caught a glimpse of herself in the mirror. It stopped her. She preened and danced before the glass. "Am I beautiful?" she asked her sister.

"You know you are," Holly answered.

"But I want to hear it."

"You'll hear it often enough tonight. You don't need me to tell you that you're beautiful, Iris."

"But I am, aren't I?"

Holly looked at her. Iris's eyes were the color of the dress Rose had made for her, deep and shining green, straining with a pleading hunger. She was gorgeous in the stained dress. Iris managed to look wonderful despite shoes with broken straps and safety-pinned slips that showed. "Yes, you are beautiful," Holly said. It was undeniably true.

They hadn't been at the dance long. It was a clumsy, crepe-papered gathering of farmers. Holly was standing by an open window recovering from a rollicking square dance when Iris approached excitedly.

"I've met two fellas, Hol," she said rapidly.

"That's nice," Holly commented unenthusiastically. She was wishing she'd stayed home. She searched Iris's face, trying to find what it was about her that made her so irresistible. "So you met two boys."

"Not boys. And not from around here. They're salesmen, traveling salesmen, and they're real good-looking, both of them. They're over there," Iris told her. She gestured across the room.

Holly picked them out immediately. They were large men dressed in blue suits and loud striped ties. One was red-faced with short-cropped sandy hair. The other was dark with slicked-back hair, and had a blue-black shadow of heavy beard. They smiled. Iris waved. Holly made no move.

"The dark one kisses real good," Iris whispered. "His beard scratches, but I kind of like it."

Holly had noticed Iris's disappearance earlier but she hadn't given it much thought at the time. Now she linked it with what Iris had just told her. "You went . . . where did you go with him?" she asked.

The self-satisfied smile did not leave Iris's face. "After we danced he took me out to his car. He has a car, Hol, a big new black one. And we had a drink from his flask. The flash is silver, real silver."

"Iris, does he know you're only sixteen?"

"I told him I was eighteen."

"Maybe I should go over there and tell him the truth."

"Won't matter much now." Still she smiled.

"What is that supposed to mean?"

"He wants me too much to care how old I am. He kisses with his tongue. I'll bet you've never kissed that way. None of the boys around here do. They don't know how to do anything around here but grow corn. They're just a bunch of dumb farmers, but these fellas are different." She waved again to them. "I'm going to the Bluebird Café with them."

"Not alone, you're not."

"Then c'mon along," Iris challenged. "You can have the blond one. His name's Bill," she tossed over her shoulder as she headed across the dance floor toward the salesmen.

Following her, Holly asked, "What's the dark one's name?"

Iris stopped and turned. "Al," she answered. "Do you like him better?"

"I don't like either one of them. I don't even know them."

"Well, if you want Al, just say so."

Iris walked on. They reached the waiting men. After introductions and grinning compliments, they left. Al smoothly maneuvered Iris into the back with him. Bill slid behind the steering wheel and Holly hugged the door on her side. Holly learned from Bill that he had been selling sewing machines for six years and that his territory was west of the Mississippi. There was no conversation coming from the back. Holly glanced behind her and saw Iris's dress gaping open. She looked away quickly and stared out the windshield. When they finally pulled up to the Bluebird Café, she nearly leaped from the car.

The Bluebird Café had been painted blue once long ago. There was a string of tin-coned lights hooked haphazardly to the eaves of the roof. It was a ramshackle old barn with a bad reputation.

To Holly, after the long dark ride with the two strangers and her wayward sister, the dilapidated roadhouse looked heavenly.

Just within the entrance stood an enormous, peacock-blue, chipped ceramic bird, the café's mascot. Beyond, there was a bar and a few tables. A juke box played Benny Goodman. The bird watched over all impassively and blindly with a flat-eyed enamel stare. Bill ordered four Cokes. After the waitress brought them, Holly saw Al produce his flask. She didn't know what kind of alcohol it was, only that it was amber-brown and smelled strong. No one asked her if she wanted any or not, it was quickly poured into her glass. She left it untouched.

Iris was laughing, a lovely tingling laugh. She was performing. Holly was reminded of her sister's performance at Lily's wedding. Iris had worn powder that night, but tonight she was doing without. Iris was beginning to tell of a time when she was eleven years old and it was summer. The image of the softly powdered singing child-Iris faded, and the loose, laughing words called up a hard memory in Holly.

'I thought I'd die that summer," Iris was slurring. "It was so quiet and hot. I wanted something to happen. I wanted that real bad and nothing did. Everybody moving so slow, sticking to themselves. My mama would be out on the porch nights, fanning herself. She moved that fan so slow. That slow swishing sound was worse than the quiet. I just knew that nothing was ever going to happen unless I made it happen and so I did. I started setting fires. . . ."

Holly was listening intently. She remembered the summer of the fires, the heat and heavy apprehension. She didn't want to believe that Iris was responsible. Still, here her sister sat in the Bluebird Café, loudly and laughingly taking the blame and the bows.

". . . just little ones at first," Iris went on. "In the evening around suppertime. The smoke would come rising up in the sky and everybody'd come running. The fires made the sunsets redder, made everybody's faces red, too. The men would work to put out the flames. They'd take off their shirts, and their bare chests were shiny and red and big. I did it all summer long. Nobody knew where there'd be a fire next. It was exciting, real fun, about the best summer I've ever had, I guess . . ."

Holly tried not to hear any more, but Iris could not be resisted.

"The little fires got to be no fun after a while, though, just a patch of ground lit up somewhere off and away from everything. Not so many people were coming running as at first. I knew what I'd do. I'd give them a fire that they'd never forget, that they'd talk about for years, tell their kids about. There was this orchard gone real dry. The fruit had just shriveled up before it even got ripe and the branches of the trees would snap in two if you just touched them. I knew it would burn fast and glow in the night for hours," Iris said. "And it did. They tried to put it out, but they couldn't. We all stood watching. It was like the end of the world. My sister Lily kept saying things from the Bible. The wind came up and the fire jumped and spread. Everybody scattered, running for their lives, screaming and yelling."

Iris's green eyes blazed with her story. Holly and the men stared at her, enthralled, trapped by her and her beauty and her hideous story. Looking at Iris was like looking into the fire itself.

"I guess that was the most exciting summer ever. Wasn't it, Hol? Do you remember?" Iris inquired lightly.

Holly stared at her sister. "Yes, I remember," she answered. She was remembering, too, the twisted, charred, and smoking-black grove. She looked at Iris and wondered if she remembered any of the aftermath, but she knew that she did not. Iris's love was excitement. She was beyond guilt and oblivious to consequences. Holly believed her sister's story and she asked, "Do you remember after the fire, Iris?"

"No, what happened then?" Iris tilted her head and smiled. The question was almost innocent, certainly ignorant.

The men were turned to her. Iris still smiled. They were all waiting for her to answer, to speak. "Nothing," Holly said.

With three glasses of spiked Coke lined up before her, Holly finally asked the time. Bill took a heavy gold watch from his pocket.

"It's quarter to eleven," he said.

"We have to go." Holly directed her words to Iris.

"Can I hold your watch, Billy?" Iris asked, attracted by the dull gold shine of it.

"You can hold mine, honey," Al said. He winked at her. "It's bigger."

Holly said again, "Iris, we have to go."

"Let's go," Iris said. "I promised my mama I'd be home by

eleven. You wouldn't want me to break a promise to my mama, would you?"

Iris's laughter filled the café, and the bluebird blankly stared on.

Holly interrupted Bill's stories only to give him directions. She guided him carefully along the winding back roads to the farm. She avoided looking behind her to the back seat where Iris and Al were. She was grateful to Bill and his twanging voice for drowning out the sounds that the other two made. When they arrived at the farm, Bill made a feeble attempt to persuade her to sit for a while. She declined and he accepted her rejection affably. He seemed willing to let her go, eager even.

"So you're going off to school tomorrow?" he asked, knowing that she was.

"Yes."

"Well, good luck to you."

"Thank you, Bill."

"You'll make a good teacher. You put me in mind of an English teacher I had once. You'll be good at it."

"I hope so. Goodnight, Bill."

He shifted, hitching one shoulder, made awkard by this dark slender girl with her appraising stare. He felt she was grading him just like his prim old English teacher who, with her fine hand, had marked his mistakes but left them for him to correct. "Should I walk you to the door?" he volunteered.

She realized how silly she'd been to feel any threat from this man. He was afraid of her. She smiled. "No, thank you, Bill," she said. She didn't look back, but with her hand on the door handle, spoke. "Good night, Al. Iris, are you coming?"

Iris's voice came muffled, pleasantly heavy. "You go on in, Hol. I'm going to sit out here with the fellas for a minute."

"Don't be long."

She stepped from the car. Before she closed the door, Al called out.

"Bye, Sis."

"Goodbye."

She closed the car door quietly and walked toward the house. Inside, she tiptoed, mindful of her sleeping family. She went to her room and began to undress. She hung her dress, smoothed it with her hands. Tomorrow she would wear it to the train. She heard the car drive away. She waited for the sounds of Iris's loud entry, but there was only silence. All night Holly listened for her sister's return, but Iris did not come home.

In the morning Holly accepted what she had tried in the darkness not to know. Iris had run off with the two salesmen. Holly had hoped that something, anything, would bring her back, but now she realized that nothing would, that Iris had run. She heard her mother in the kitchen and she reluctantly pulled on her robe and left her room.

"Good morning, Mama."

"You're up early," Jane commented.

Holly fixed herself a cup of coffee and sat down opposite her mother at the table. Her mother's blond hair was beginning to whiten. She was not softened by age, but made colder, as if a hard frost had collected along with the years. "I couldn't sleep," Holly said.

Jane eyed her, scanning her face. "You don't look like you did."

"I was concerned about Iris."

"Iris? Why?"

"She didn't come home last night."

"What are you talking about? I heard you come in at eleven."

"You heard me, Mama," Holly started to explain. "We got a ride from the dance." Under her mother's icy blue eyes she amended the stop at the road house. "Iris stayed out in the car. I came in, but she didn't."

"You just didn't hear her."

"Her bed hasn't been slept in. Iris is gone."

"Who gave you a ride home?"

This was the question Holly had been dreading. "Two men, strangers," she answered baldly. She tensed, alert for any movement by her mother in her direction, but Jane ran from the kitchen.

When she returned her face was white, whiter than usual. She sank down into a chair. Holly waited.

"You're to blame for this," her mother said.

It was what Holly had expected. She was ready. "Mama, I thought she was coming right behind me. How could I know that she'd do something like this?"

"She did nothing. Those men forced her. Iris is so pretty."

Holly knew that her mother thought she was ugly. She heard it without the words being said, that she was dark and unwanted and home safely.

"They took my beautiful baby. You should never have left her alone with them. You should never have gone with them, never have gotten in their car with them."

Holly spoke before she thought. It was the truth but unthinking truth. "No one forced Iris. She went with them because she wanted to go. She hated it here."

"Liar!" Jane shouted.

Holly was poised to deflect a blow or evade a lunge from her mother. Her stance was practiced and pitiful. She heard her father's steps. He was in the kitchen.

"Daddy," she said.

"Always Daddy," Jane breathed harshly.

"Daddy, Iris has run away," Holly told him quickly.

"Iris has been taken away. It's all her fault," Jane said, glaring at Holly.

"Mama, I tried to tell you . . ." she faltered.

"Tell me what happened, Holly," Clay said softly.

She told her parents about the night's events, omitting nothing, not taking her eyes from her father. Holly knew that whatever she said would make little difference to her audience. The words meant nothing. Her father's faith and love were with her, had been long before this morning's words, and would be long after. And her mother, she'd never had her mother's faith or love, never would. So the words were really nothing at all. When she finished, her mother's blame continued and her father's silence stretched.

Holly dressed. The faint smell of the traveling salesmen's cigar smoke remained in the cloth. She closed her suitcase and carried it from her room. It was time to leave. Her father waited outside in the car. Holly said a quick goodbye to her sleepy little sister Poppy. She walked to the kitchen. Standing in the doorway, Holly heard her mother's last words. Jane spoke into the telephone. She was reporting Iris's kidnaping to the sheriff. Holly knew that her mother was aware of her presence but was not acknowledging it. She stood a moment longer. Her mother would not turn and look at her. Holly left.

They were in town, only a block from the train depot, when Holly spoke, ending the silence of the ride.

"Daddy, take me to Rose's. She'll see me off."

"Why?" he asked.

"Because I can't say goodbye to you, Daddy, not to you. Please take me to Rose's."

He understood. "All right, Holly."

He stopped the car in front of Rose's building. Holly leaned over and pressed her face to his chest. He stroked her hair.

"Holly. Holly. Don't come back," he said.

"I have to come back. For you, Daddy."

"Don't come back. For me, Holly."

And as always, he gently, so gently, forced her from him.

At the station Rose laughed and made jokes, but Holly was already gone, distant and unresponsive. She was far ahead of her train. She kissed Rose goodbye and boarded. Rose waved and waved. The train left. Holly was gone. It seemed that Iris was, too. And Rose, without realizing, began to want to go, to want to watch a red-haired, waving, smiling girl recede to nothingness.

Chapter Six

In her first year at school Holly wrote home regularly, but her letters to the farm were strangely perfunctory and always addressed to the Calder family. Not knowing why, she seemed unable to write to her father warmly or separately. She only hoped that he could understand what she didn't herself. It was in writing to Rose that Holly was capable of conveying the feelings and changes she was experiencing at college in California. She felt that her sister appreciated and was not hurt by her new life.

Rose, slowly recovering from a miscarriage, anticipated Holly's letters eagerly and answered them swiftly. After the stillbirth the year before, all that Rose had wanted was to try and have another baby. She had tried again, but in the effort she had lost the five-month-old male fetus and more than that. In the Wichita hospital they had cut away Rose's ovaries, removed the incompetent pieces of her. When she returned to the apartment she allowed the crib to be taken from her, too. Now she spent her days waiting for Clyde to come home, which often he did not, and waiting for the letters to come into the post office from California. They played a sadly large part in Rose's stripped life.

Lily was pregnant again and had been confined to bed, which was why fifteen-year-old Poppy was walking across the countryside this morning. She was on her way to her sister's to help with the children while Lily rested and tried to hold on to the new child within her.

Poppy was small for her age, looking no more than eleven or twelve. She was a timid girl, her eyes lit with a bright scared light. She had a pale and soft rabbitlike quality. Her mother believed her to be a frail and delicate child. Poppy was weak and completely under the power of her loving mother. Only once in a great while a surge of anger would break from her. She suffered rare but fierce and racking seizures that she could not control any better than the horrified observers of them could. She would go rigid at first, then rabid, biting and tearing at any hands that touched her. Finally falling limp, totally drained, she would sleep as if dead. She had never experienced one of these convulsions without her mother present. Even Jane could not subdue Poppy but she was somehow essential to the attacks her child sustained.

Jane Calder said that her youngest, her best-loved child, had temper tantrums, that was how she explained them away to others and to herself, but Poppy's fits were terrifyingly arbitrary. No external force incited or stopped them. They came and went, the first when Poppy was only five years old, without warning. These few violent episodes had so scarred her family's perception of her that Poppy could go for years without having a seizure and still those near her could only watch and wait for the next to come. Poppy didn't know what happened to her. There were gaping holes in her memory that frightened her. The fabric of her life was torn away in places, the threads ripped, dangling uneven and ragged. Her mother said that she would outgrow them, and Poppy believed completely in her mother, but she did not know what it was that she would outgrow. She could only guess that someday she would remember all her days and that there would be no more dark spaces.

Poppy picked her way along the road. It was rutted and muddy from the rains, but the sky was clear today. For the first time in nearly two weeks the weather was mild, sunny, and blue. She loved feeling the sun on her face and looking up into the sky, but she had to watch where she stepped. She tried to keep her eyes down and avoid the deepest green-brown puddles, but the sky was so pretty to see.

Lily listened for her sister. She had the baby Jeremiah on the

bed beside her. Three-year-old Franklin and five-year-old Luke
were playing outside. Hope and Jonathan sat on the porch steps
and watched their little brothers. They saw, both at the same time,
Aunt Poppy coming up the road, a small pinkish figure. She
waved to them and they ran to her. Her pink dress was splashed
with mud.

"What happened to your pretty dress, Aunt Poppy?" Hope
asked.

Poppy looked at her dress. "I guess I fell down," she answered
quietly.

Hope took her one hand and Jonathan the other. She seemed
more a child than they. Hope guided her gently toward the house.

"Come inside," Hope said. "We can clean your dress."

They entered the house.

"Mama," Hope called. "Aunt Poppy's come." Hope looked at
her aunt. "Maybe you should clean off the mud before Mama
sees."

"Yes," Poppy absently agreed.

Hope walked into her mother's room. She liked the pictures on
the wall there. She always stopped and looked at them for a
moment. The faces of the young, pale, long-haired man and the
older, heavy-eyed one belonged together, side by side, as they
were. Hope knew that the one was Christ, the son of God, and
she believed the other was God Himself. It was years before she
discovered that the second picture was of President Franklin
Delano Roosevelt.

"Mama, Aunt Poppy's here."

"Where is she?" Lily asked.

"Oh, she's coming," Hope answered vaguely, stalling.

Lily looked at her only little girl. Sometimes she could see
glimpses of Earl in her. It bothered Lily. Hope was a good child,
but she reminded Lily of things she would rather have forgotten.
It surprised Lily that Workman was especially fond of Hope. He
blamed neither the mother nor the child for a past of which he
was no part, but he found more to love in Hope than he did in
Lily. Lily patted Jeremiah. She wanted not to resent Jonathan,
her husband's son by another woman, but she could not be as
magnanimous and misremember the way that Workman did. She
hoped this coming baby would be a girl. She wanted to give
Workman a daughter that was truly his. When she had hinted

this to him, he had told her that he had forgotten that Hope
wasn't his, and Lily was sorry she had reminded him. She was
beginning to speak to Hope when Poppy came in from the hall.
Lily noticed the wet spots on her sister's dress. Poppy stood shyly
in the doorway. Lily thought how much younger than Hope she
looked and how little help she would be. Mama had kept Poppy
a child too long, Lily judged. She glanced at her own daughter
and prided herself on the difference. Hope was not half Poppy's
age but she appeared older and more assured. Lily almost had
to laugh every time Hope said "Aunt Poppy." It was funny to
her, hearing a child call a child that, and few things amused Lily.
Her laughter was a thin and scarce thing. She could not have said
if she was happy or sad, having no inclination to ask and no
insight to answer. Her family was her life. Her religion was her
strength, she believed. Her church-going and Bible-reading were
thoroughly approved activities. Lily's ardent religiosity was clear
and moral and clean. No one could possibly fault her on her
fervor. She was safe and blameless at last, loving her Lord and
lavishly displaying that love. The loving of men, even her baby
boys, tended to get tangled and muddied and troublesome. Her
sons would grow and leave her, but the church would abide. Lily
had left the family into which she was born and the family that
she had borne would splinter likewise. Hope was already inde-
pendent of her. She was like her father, Lily thought, like Earl
who had only needed her, desired her briefly, and had gone. Earl
was the first and last human being that Lily had loved without
reservation. He had betrayed her and his was a double betrayal.
Not only had he deserted her, but he had driven a wedge between her and her mother. And Lily had revered her mother.
After Earl that reverence was ruined. But now Lily had her faith
and that would remain with her always.

"Don't just stand there, Poppy," Lily said, thinking that she
hadn't been much older than Poppy when she had gone to work
in the shirt factory. Not knowing why, her voice grew impatient,
almost angry. She picked on the water-spotted dress. "What happened to your dress?" she asked, and couldn't understand why
Poppy looked afraid.

"Nothing," Poppy answered. She took a tentative step into the
room. "I fell in the mud, but it's nothing. Really, nothing, Lily,"
Poppy pleaded for belief.

"You're always stumbling around," Lily said in disgust.

Poppy cringed and wiped at the wet spots.

Hope looked from her mother to her aunt. The shape of their faces was faintly the same, but that was all. Hope knew, though she certainly hadn't been told, that her mother was going to have another baby. If this time it was a girl, Hope wondered, would her sister be like her or would they be as far from one another as her little Aunt Poppy was from Mama, who seemed enormous to Hope. It would probably be a little boy again, she decided.

Poppy had been at Lily's for two days when the rain began again. Late in the afternoon the sky blackened and what should have been only a cloudburst continued for hours until the sun had set darkly down among the thick and thunderous clouds on the western horizon. The storm ceased for a short time and then broke again with greater force and fury. Gathered around the supper table that evening, the Banner children were quiet. Poppy and Workman did not speak. The poorly cooked food that Poppy had prepared passed silently into mouths and the rain pounded steadily on the roof.

Poppy put the children to bed. When she returned to the kitchen, Workman was sitting at the table and Lily had gotten up from bed. She was reading aloud from the Bible. Poppy sat down and listened. Lily's voice was high and grating. The biblical phrasing was arcane, and the story cruel and incomprehensible to Poppy. The reading went on and on. The rain continued. Finally Lily closed the huge book and carried it back to her room. She did not say goodnight. She had never spoken at all, only read from the Bible. Workman soon silently followed his wife. Poppy scraped the dishes and collected them in piles. She filled the dishpan and began to wash the plates and bowls and silverware.

After cleaning the kitchen she still was not tired. She wandered through the unlit rooms to Lily's. She stood there and listened. She could hear Workman's heavy breathing. Poppy did not know what she had expected to hear but she felt disappointed. She looked in on the children. The four oldest slept in the same room. The baby Jeremiah had his crib in Lily's room. When the new baby came he would be put into the room with the others, expelled from his crib and babyhood. Poppy was glad that she was youngest, lucky never to have been shunted aside by another new baby. She would always be Mama's baby.

She did not undress. She wrapped herself in a blanket and stood by a window watching the rain. It beat harder and harder. Poppy closed her eyes and tried to hear her own heart, but she could not. She clutched the blanket in one hand and with the other she touched the vein that always pulsed so strongly, so close to the surface, in her throat. She could barely feel its throbbing. She opened her eyes. The constant pelting without had usurped the rhythm within her. It was robbing her, taking something from her, Poppy feared. She wanted the rain to stop. She wanted Mama. She started for the door, but she thought of her sister. She went and knocked softly on Lily's door.

"What is it?" Lily asked.

To Poppy the voice did not sound sleepy. She pictured Lily lying in bed awake, staring up at the ceiling, hearing her husband snore and the rain fall. She spoke through the door. "Lily, I want to go home," she said.

Poppy listened. Lily's bare feet hardly made a sound. The door opened.

Lily saw Poppy standing fully dressed. "What are you doing up? Go to sleep," she commanded.

"I can't sleep. I want to go home," Poppy said.

"You're a big girl, Poppy, much too old for this. Stop acting like a child. Go to sleep."

"I can't," she said, tears sounding in her words. "I can't," she repeated, more loudly.

Workman's snoring stopped. They heard him stir.

"Lily?" he questioned. His voice full of unhappy and aroused sleep. "What's the matter?"

"It's nothing," Lily told him. She stepped out toward Poppy and closed the door behind her. "See what you've done?"

Poppy backed away from her sister. Lily's shadowy face was frightening. "I want to go home." It was a wail.

"In the morning," Lily said.

"No, now. I want to go home now."

Lily put her hands on Poppy's narrow shoulders. "You can't leave now." She spoke slowly and sternly, her hands tightening their grip, controlling. "In the morning. Now go to sleep."

The words and the hold of her sister made Poppy's heart begin to pound. She could feel it now, wilder, harder than the rain. The back of her neck was cold but her hands were hot. Her whole body was patched with panic, fire and ice. Poppy wrenched away from Lily, but once free of her, she could not move. She stood staring, her scared rabbit eyes bright and rapidly blinking.

"What ails you?" Lily demanded.

"I want to go home."

"Stop saying that. You're not five years old, Poppy. You're a big grown-up girl. You can't go home tonight. In the morning, I said."

"No." It was a blank refusal.

"Poppy." Lily said her name warningly. There was fear in her voice. She had seen Poppy's fits and she was afraid of them. "Poppy, don't do this."

Poppy knew that her sister was remembering what she could not, knew that Lily was thinking of the times that were only dark spaces in her own memory. She knew, too, that Lily was about to reach out for her and try to stop her. Poppy ran down the hallway.

Out from under Lily's roof she felt frightened but free. The rain was cold, cutting like glass as she fled into it. She had run in the wrong direction, but circled back and found the right way. It wasn't far to the bridge. Poppy feared crossing it at any time, hating the sickening sway of it, but now it was more terrifying than ever before.

The night was so black and wet that she did not see the bridge until it was only a few yards away. The water of the river had risen swiftly. It nearly overflowed the banks, rushed white and black just beneath the gaping boards of the bridge. Poppy stepped out onto it, grasping the soaking ropes, inching along, not looking to the river raging below, but hearing it, feeling it. She tried to move faster, but slipped. The bridge was swinging furiously and the water touched her face. Unable to stand, she began to crawl along the slippery slatted planks. She had to get home before it overtook her. For the first time feeling the descent into darkness beginning, she fought back, gripped the bridge and consciousness. She must get to Mama before letting go, Poppy knew.

The swinging sensation had stilled. Poppy had held on and reached the far bank, the home side of the river. Standing on the sodden but solid earth she saw the bridge collapse, watched the pieces of it, like so many matchsticks, swept downstream. She staggered homeward.

There was one light in one window of the farmhouse, a burning beacon. Poppy saw the door opening, and her mother was there, arms outstretched. Once in that embrace she felt her body stiffening. Everything was swirling blackness like the river. For one moment she feared this homecoming was a dream and that she had really fallen with the bridge. Poppy pressed her lips to the dear dreamed hand and then sank her teeth to test, to taste, the reality of the flesh. She did not hear her mother's cry. There was only sweeping senselessness.

Jane Calder knew better than anyone how to care for her seized child. She drew back her marked hand and stood watch over the violent writhing. When it passed she carried Poppy to bed. She undressed and dried her. Jane hurried away to get one of her own long white dressing gowns. Clay was asleep in the room. He had not awakened, not at the sound of the telephone ringing when Lily called, and not at the frenzied arrival of Poppy. She was glad that he slept. Poppy had come home to her alone. Clay Calder had nothing to do with this, no share in her child, Jane thought as she stood holding the nightdress. Leaving him asleep, she returned to watch and ward.

Poppy would lie inert for hours. With a gentleness that this child alone knew from her, Jane brushed back the damp pale hair and fastened the tiny pearl buttons. She loved Poppy best. Lily was a disappointment. From Rose she had expected little. And Iris, beautiful, but gone. Jasmine, her dead baby. Holly, Clay's child. Like runners, her children raced through Jane Calder's mind as she sat with the victor, her last child made first. Poppy slept on. She had a high fever. Jane gauged the heat with her cool pale hands, her touch so tender and Poppy so unconsciously accepting of it. The hours went by. Poppy turned and tossed, a difference from the usual trancelike state into which she fell. She spoke incoherent words that Jane strung together in a pattern of reason.

"The bridge . . . falling . . . all fall down . . ." whispered Poppy. "The bridge . . . London Bridge . . . all fall down . . . falling . . . falling . . ." Her singsong voice mingled nursery rhymes and reality. "I want to go home, Lily. I want to go home. The river runs so fast . . . I want to run that fast . . . as fast as the river . . . run home . . . run home. The bridge is falling . . . I'm falling . . .

Mama, don't let me go. Don't let me fall, Mama!" The whisper rose to a bleating plea. "Mama!"

Jane held her and rocked her. "I'm with you. You're safe. I won't let you fall. I won't let the river take you, Poppy. It can't have you. You're mine. Home. You're safe . . . home . . . mine : . . safe . . ."

Jane's words were becoming as disjointed as Poppy's but Poppy responded to them. They moved together and the murmured expressions soothed. Jane had no way of knowing if the bridge had actually fallen but the threat of it shook her. She knew too well what the flooding river could do. Its waters had taken her own mother, but Poppy was saved, Jane knew. Poppy was saved.

In the morning Jane slept with Poppy curled against her. Clay found them this way. He had seen the sight before. He did not wake them, but wordlessly left for the fields. The storm had spent itself. He limped out into the sunlight. He thought of Holly, so far away, and how she had once slept beside him. There was a pale rainbow arching across the sky. He looked for a long time until its tremulous light faded and disappeared.

There was no rainbow to be seen in town, only clearing skies over the still wet street. Rose's shoes were thick with mud by the time she had walked the block from her apartment to the post office. It was Thursday. Today a letter from Holly would be waiting for her. Without fail, every Thursday, there was one. Holly could not have known how much the letters meant to her sister, but she kept them coming like promises, unbroken, a steady stream of them. They were more than important to Rose. Their arrival, her name written on the envelopes, gave her a sense of identity. Holly had left Kansas and found another world, maybe she could, too. The letters said to Rose that her life was not over, that somewhere there might be something else for her. There was for Holly. There must be for her. Whenever she lifted the kitchen curtain she saw the same main street of the tiny Kansas factory town, Marysville, named for Mr. Straker's invalid daughter who had died when she was only a girl. How many girls had died in a small way, a part of them dying, their dreams

expiring, while they worked in Mr. Straker's factory in Mr.
Straker's town, Rose wondered as she walked. And this street,
the reluctant route home of her husband, there had to be more
than that. When Rose read Holly's letters she could see beyond
Marysville. She had lost Clyde, Rose knew, as surely as she had
lost their babies. The miscarriage had ended her hope. She would
never be a mother. She felt to blame. It was her fault. She had let
Clyde down. And her sorrow was defined by his disappointment,
the edges sharpened by it and by her guilt.

She waited nervously at the counter while the clerk went to
look for her letter. When he came toward her with it in his hand,
she breathed again. She placed it in the pocket of her coat and
hurried home. Back at the apartment, the site of her failure as a
wife and a mother, she opened the letter and escaped into it. The
single page was closely covered with Holly's long precise black
pen strokes.

Dear Rose,
    This is going to be a short one. Midterms are upon me and
I am studying night and day. I can't help but think that
there is something wrong with a system of education that
asks students to stuff themselves with facts like a Thanksgiving turkey is stuffed. The facts are eaten, devoured by
a test, a midterm, a final, and the students are left with no
knowledge at all. There's not even a bulging stomach. It is
simply let go, of no further use after it has been tested. I
hate cramming, but everyone does it. I guess all this must be
pretty boring for you. I won't go on with it.
    California is such a beautiful place, so different from
Kansas. It grows more beautiful to me every day. Doesn't
it seem right that Iris was born here, beauty to beauty? I
think of Iris often, try to imagine where she is and how she
is. I feel that she is all right. It was a good thing that she
got out of Kansas, but the way she did it was all wrong.
Still, it was pure Iris to run off like that without a backward
glance, a goodbye, or a thought of who she might have hurt.
You'll probably think that this is strange, but I have the
feeling that Iris is near here, close by, in California somewhere. Maybe that sounds crazy but I can't shake the
feeling.

I've told you that the school is only blocks from the ocean. I walk there often. Do you remember the ocean? I didn't. I don't know how I could have forgotten it, but I guess I was so young. Now, though, I'll never forget. It's so big. That's not a very original observation, I know, but it's the first trite thing that strikes me about it, its vastness. I'm very glad that I came here. I have learned a lot, not necessarily all from my classes. I don't know that any of us realized how isolated we were within the family. It is good to come in contact with other people, but I'm shy still. I don't mix much, but I keep my eyes open. I'm not completely happy with school. I'm probably suffering from the midterm blues. I've always hated being in the middle. It's funny that I'm right in the middle of the family. Maybe that's where my dislike comes from. But don't worry about me. I'm all right. I'm fine.

How are you, Rose? Your last letter made me want to take a train to Kansas, come knocking on your door, and sit and drink coffee and talk with you for hours. I want so much to talk with you. Letters are fine, but I want to see your face. Your letter made me sad and also made me feel the distance between us. Maybe you could come to California for a visit? This summer? I won't be going back to the farm this summer. Did I sneak that in fast enough? I want so badly to see you and Daddy, but I have a chance at a summer job here. Summer jobs are few and far between. It's not for sure, but it looks very promising. So I probably won't be seeing Kansas again for a while anyway. But couldn't you come here for a week or two? Would Clyde mind? It would be so wonderful. Think about it, Rose. Really there aren't many things that I miss, but you are one of them.

Love,
Holly

Rose set the letter aside. Holly never referred to coming back to Kansas as coming home. She might head east or visit the farm, but a homecoming wasn't mentioned. Rose guessed that this was no longer Holly's home. She thought of her sister's desire to see

her and their father, but Holly said nothing about the rest of
the family. Rose suspected that Holly honestly didn't miss Lily
or Poppy or their mother and refused to pretend that she did.
That was like Holly, telling the truth no matter how much it
hurt. It was an admirable trait but difficult, too. Rose realized
that she did not have that kind of hard honesty. She looked
around the apartment. She would love to leave here and make a
trip to California. She had to smile over Holly's fear that Clyde
might mind. He would like to have her go. She wouldn't be
around to remind him, to interfere with his plans, to hinder his
pleasure with her presence. Now that the letter was read and
would soon be answered, the rest of Thursday and the week
spread empty before her. That was the worst thing about Holly's
letters. They were like Christmas, anticipated, and planned for,
and then past, too soon. Rose faced her life beyond writing a
response to Holly and she saw nothing.

Clyde came home early. She had fixed dinner, expecting to eat
it alone and wrap up the remains for Clyde to swallow coldly
at the sink sometime in the night when he finally returned, but
tonight they shared the meal. Since her time in the hospital there
had been too many missed suppers between them, too much anger
and pain, to ever have again what they had once had when she
was whole, Rose thought. The memories of their good times together only made this evening more glaringly unhappy in
contrast.

"How's the beef?" Rose asked.

"Good," Clyde answered.

"Is it tender?"

Clyde looked up from his plate. "You're eating it too, Rose.
Yes, it's tender. You know it is," he said.

But she hadn't known. She hadn't even tasted the meat. She
had relied on him for reasons and responses, reacted to him for so
long. Rose had experienced everything through Clyde since she
had become his wife. If Clyde was happy, then she was. If Clyde
was sad, she was, too. And if Clyde was angry, she did not feel
his anger as her own but cowered before it. She took a mouthful
of beef, held it on her tongue, and tried to taste it. It was good
and it was tender. She swallowed, feeling as if she hadn't eaten
in all the years of her marriage. She had been sucking all

sustenance from Clyde. She took another bite and it tasted even better.

"I got a letter from Holly today," she said.

"It's Thursday, isn't it?" asked Clyde. He was tired of her, weary of her mournful laughing eyes, used to her routines, bored by knowing everything that she would say before she said it, but he didn't want to hurt her. "How's Holly?" he asked. He only wanted to be rid of her.

"She's fine, studying hard. She's staying in California this summer."

Clyde helped himself to more corn and said nothing.

"She wants me to come and see her," Rose added.

"In California?" he asked, trying to hide the hope in his voice.

"Yes."

"That'd be nice for you, Rose," he said and continued with his corn.

She didn't know what she wanted from Clyde anymore. She knew she still wanted, was still asking, something. He was giving her nothing.

"Could we afford it, Clyde?"

"I think so."

"I wouldn't stay more than a week or so."

"That's not very long," he said.

There was a time, Rose remembered, when a day apart would have been forever to them, but now two weeks wasn't very long to him. And it wasn't very long to her either, not long enough. Rose wanted to leave, but it was Clyde who made the move, an abrupt pushing back of his chair.

"I have to go out," he said.

She started to ask where he was going, when he'd be home. The questions wouldn't come. They lay heavily inside her but she couldn't speak. She sat silently at the table listening to the door open and close. She had certainly lost Clyde. Yet she felt lost. She wished that Holly's letter hadn't come today. If only it was due to arrive tomorrow and she still had something to look forward to, but she didn't. She decided she would telephone the farm and see how the folks were. She hadn't heard from them in days and she was hungry for the sound of a human voice other than her loath husband's.

Clay answered Rose's call. From her father's tone when he spoke of Poppy's illness and Jane's nursing of her, Rose knew that he was lonely. She invited him to dinner the next night and he accepted.

He arrived at the apartment at just the time he had said he would. They were sitting down to dinner, neither having mentioned Clyde's absence, when Clyde entered. Rose set him a plate. He began to eat quickly. After a while, feeling the quiet, he spoke.

"Did Rose tell you that she's planning to go to California this summer?" he asked her father.

"No," Clay answered.

"I was just going to tell him about it," Rose said.

"I think it would be a real fine thing," Clyde said. "Rosie's had it pretty tough these past months. She needs a vacation."

"I agree," Clay said softly.

Clyde felt uncomfortable. He said hurriedly, "I'd miss her like crazy, but it would be good for her."

Rose said nothing. The silence lengthened.

Clyde got up from his chair. He did not notice that he was taking the tablecloth with him. Rose reached for the bunched cloth to save the dishes from being pulled to the floor. Clyde, still unaware, extended a hand to his father-in-law.

"Sorry I can't stay."

Clay shook his hand. He looked at his daughter's husband and knew what it was not to want to come home nights. He easily recognized the guilty and reluctant defiance in Clyde. He sympathized. And he was sorry for his daughter. Clay was torn, seeing both sides, and feeling almost anxious to be back at the dark house where the only light burned in a room with a delirious child and a pale vigilant woman. There, at least, everything was clear, decided long ago.

"I have to be going myself," Clay told his seated daughter and her standing husband.

Rose walked him to the door. She watched until he was in his car. She turned back to the dining room and Clyde. Clyde stood and ate the remains on his plate. She went into the bedroom, thinking that she would wash the dishes in the morning. Clyde did not come into the room until long after Rose's feigned sleep had become real.

Clay had just returned from Rose's. He was sitting in the dark parlor when the telephone rang. He knew Jane wouldn't answer. She was with Poppy. He got up and walked to the kitchen. It flashed through his mind that it might be Holly calling. He quickly picked up the receiver. It was Lily. She immediately asked for her mother. Clay went to the closed door of Poppy's room and knocked softly.

"Jane," he said. "Lily is on the telephone."

"Tell her I'll call her later."

"You always say that and you never do, Jane."

"Just tell her," the muffled voice came angrily.

He walked back to the telephone and told Lily. There was a pause and Lily said goodbye. He told her goodbye. There was another pause. Then Lily broke their connected silence. Clay left the kitchen, going slowly into the darkness of the parlor again.

Lily stood staring at her telephone, hoping it would ring and that it would be her mother calling her back, but she had waited for this too many times and heard nothing. She bit back her lip and walked away. She went silently past Workman, who was dozing over a seed catalogue, and in her bedroom found Hope diapering Jeremiah.

"Give him to me," Lily told her. "Go and check on the others, Hope."

Hope watched her mother lie down on the bed with the baby. She left them. Hope was rapidly becoming a mother herself, the child in her being buried under the load of duties and responsibilities that she bore, that Lily heaped upon her. Hope gathered her brothers together and organized a game of hide-and-seek, but it did not go smoothly. She had to convince a tearful Franklin that when he closed his eyes and couldn't see, it didn't mean that no one could see him. Finally the game was gotten under way. Hope was searching for Franklin. She passed her mother's room.

The door was slightly ajar as she had left it. Through the crack she saw her mother holding Jeremiah and reading from the Bible. She listened to Lily's thin sharp voice.

"Death consumes sinners as drought and heat consume snow. Even the sinner's own mother shall forget him . . ."

From the cries at the other end of the house, Hope knew that Franklin had been found. It was her turn to hide, but she couldn't think of any place to be safe. She hoped that Jonathan would find her first, squeeze next to her in the darkness she would find, and they could hide together from the others. The words her mother had been reading came to her and she tried to make some sense of them. She knew that there was no snow in the summer, but Hope wondered what it was to be a sinner.

PART THREE

IRIS

Chapter Seven

The Imperial Valley, California, 1940 . . .

They stared from the dusty windows of the stores and cafés. They stepped back off the streets when she came by. She walked, undulating, ungrounded, openly inviting. Medusa-like, her appearance stunned them, stopped them all, men, women, and children. Iris had been a pretty and careless girl when she ran away from Kansas. Two years of sordid road experience had given her a strong corrosive beauty. She was a corrupter of saints, a consort of sinners.

The two salesmen had brought her as far as California. They were willing to keep her with them forever, but one night she had softly crawled from in between them on a motel bed in Stockton. She had gone, but not before taking their heavy gold watches from their trousers hastily dumped on the floor. In the beginning she'd been Al's girl, but in a Colorado roadhouse she had danced with Bill and had known that he wanted her, too. He had pressed her against him and she had felt him hardening and softening. She had kept the men separate for a while until the idea of a *ménage à trois* became irresistible and she had drawn them both into bed. It was fun, not knowing if it was Al or Bill inside her, not quite sure whose mouth was kissing hers or whose hands were rubbing and stroking her. When it ceased to be fun she left them in bed together without watches in their pockets.

It had been that gray and misty dawn of her escape in Stockton that a Filipino boy named Rafael first saw her. The streets had been deserted and he had felt safe in sitting beside her on the park bench. He could not believe his good fortune. He'd won that night at cards, too. She was the most beautiful girl that he had ever seen. Rafael was beautiful to Iris, too. He was so darkly fine and lean, very different from the salesmen. Iris loved the look of him. For the first time in her life she had forgotten her own beauty for a moment. They had spent the day spending his poker winnings and were together from that time on. They were both aware that their liaison was dangerous. Rafael believed that he alone possessed Iris, but she had other men. Still she cared enough to keep them secret, to deceive him. He couldn't stand it when other men even looked at her. He was helplessly, constantly angry, tortured, wanting to fight them, but knowing that he could not. Rafael was a stranger, a foreigner, and to fight would mean almost surely to die. He had lived in America for ten years, but he was not a citizen. He was the eternal outsider, but in love with a beautiful blond American girl. He could not defend her, or protect her, or proclaim his possession of her. Rafael believed that Iris hated this as much as he did. He didn't know that she liked things as they were, that Iris welcomed the situation because it gave her him and the freedom to take others, too. His love was not enough for Iris. Her need was insatiable, but he did not know. Rafael had faith in her and he was sure that she was as shamed as he when he was made to stand impotently and allow other men to look at her and speak to her.

They had traveled up the California coast from Stockton and then down the length of the state, following the crops. For more than a year they had been together, he in the migrant camps, sleeping in boxcars and tin bunkhouses, and she in the closest motel. She was on her way back to her room now while the town watched her passage.

She turned the corner to the motel. It was a dirty place, but Iris rarely ever noticed her surroundings. It did bother Rafael to think of her there in a foul fifty-cent room. He could almost ignore the motel's sign, having grown used to the prejudice but not to the filth of the country. Iris did not even give a glance at the fly-specked placard posted beside the door: POSITIVELY NO FILIPINOS ALLOWED. She entered and crossed the grimly tiled foyer. That the money with which she paid her rent here was provided by the stoop labor of a Filipino, her lover Rafael, did not seem ironic to her. She no more saw the irony than she did the sign. She knew only that no man had ever worshiped her as Rafael did, and that he was forbidden to her, therefore she must have him. He would slip up to her room tonight as he did every night. Later they would go out to his camp. It was exciting to Iris, the way the atmosphere thickened with tension and desire when she appeared there.

Once in her room she immediately put a Glenn Miller record on the phonograph that Rafael had bought for her. Moving around in time to the music, she began to undress, slowly shedding her clothes, dancing out of them, and throwing them to the floor. When the record ended she tied a robe loosely around her and walked, a bottle in each hand, down the hallway to the bath. From one bottle she poured pink bubble bath under the streaming faucet. With the tub billowing suds, she immersed herself. Now she tilted back the other bottle and took a long pull of tepid red wine. The room was ugly, old rusted pipes bleeding into the grouting and yellowed porcelain stained with use, but Iris was oblivious. What occupied her totally was her own steaming and slippery body, the way that it glowed up incandescent through the water. She swallowed more wine. The warmth seeped inside her. Someone came banging on the door but Iris didn't hear. She touched her soap-surfeited legs and arms and breasts. She lay in the tub for hours until the water was cold and murky around her, her skin sodden and crepey. She dried herself, drained the bottle of wine, but did not bother with the tub, and left the squalid room. Back in her room, before the mirror, she began to apply her makeup. Iris knew every trick to enhance her face, heightening the color, smoothing the shape. No one knew her beauty as well as she did, or loved it as well.

She was wearing a white lace slip when Rafael quietly knocked. He had waited until the desk downstairs was unoccupied, the clerk gone to eat his supper, before coming up. Iris was satisfied, intoxicated from her afternoon of narcissistic grooming, wine, and self-adulation. She opened the door. She made Rafael pick the

dress that she would wear that night. While he watched she put
on his choice and then removed it, and her slip, her stockings, her
panties. He did not go to her, knowing that she would tell him
when she wanted him. He stood in the center of the room and she
went to the bed. He was tired from the fields, his back ached,
but he could hardly restrain himself. He wanted to cover her
naked body with his own. She displayed herself to him in perfect
dispassion. She smiled and stretched out her hand. He stumbled
to the bedside, kneeled down and kissed her. She smelled sweet.
Her skin, soft and smooth and white, tasted of vanilla. He ran
his hand down her body until his fingers felt the eruption of
floss, silken like the golden strands on corn. He had had other
women, ones that he had bought, and he knew the coarse mass
that hid them. Iris was not like them. He stood to remove his
clothes. She was spread out before him. He started down to her.
Her face was painted and her hair curled. He knew not to touch.
He believed that he had learned what of her was his, but he had
not. Iris belonged completely and only to herself.

Iris left the room first. She diverted the attention of the desk
clerk. The huge man, pleasantly full from his supper, and smitten
with Iris, did not see Rafael come down the stairs and duck out
the door. This maneuvering was fun to Iris, part of the danger
and excitement in knowing Rafael. She didn't care that he was
hurt and enraged by the evasions, the cat-and-mouse game that
fat bigots forced them to play.

He followed behind her. They could not walk together. They
were headed for the camp. Even there, among his own people,
there was resentment of them. He had been warned by several
of the men about the risks he took loving Iris. They claimed that
they were concerned for his welfare. They told him that they
did not want to see him beaten or shot because of this white
woman. She was very beautiful, but was she worth his life, they
asked Rafael. He listened to the men's questions, questions cal-
loused and worn down like their hands, and he heard envy, not
solicitude. He thought that Iris was worth his life, worth anything.
Besides, he told his friends, they were careful. The camp was the
only place other than a motel room where they could sit together
and he could hold her hand, kiss her, openly adore her, but when

they appeared the Pinoy smoldered. They wished that they were Rafael, wished for one night between her legs, and they hoped that she would not bring trouble. Life was hard enough. She brought beauty to the camp. She was wonderful to look upon, but they rubbed their hands together and wondered, might not she bring death, too?

As they neared the camp Rafael came closer to her. They could hear a guitar. He put his arm around her. The tin boxes where the men slept came into sight. The sky was darkening. The long furrows in the fields were beginning to disappear, eased by the night. The men were gathering out in front of the metal shacks to witness a cockfight. Iris and Rafael joined them.

Rafael knew what was about to happen. "I don't think that you will want to see this," he said to her. His English was clear, with only a trace of accent. He had learned the language when he was a child at home, learned it easily and well. It was as if he knew even then that someday he would come to America. Rafael had prepared himself as best he could but he could not know what he truly faced. America, the dream, was more than a disappointment.

"This you will not want to see, Iris," Rafael said. He watched the cages being brought and the birds that waited within. He did not love cockfighting as his friends did. It had no thrill for him. He was sickened by the combat. Still, he sometimes had bet on a bird. Only to feel a part of the crowd that howled, he had howled. Only to feel one with the other gamblers, he had gambled. He needed to feel companionship, to belong to something. Then he had found Iris. He didn't want her to be a witness to the brutality that he had once wagered upon, crouched down in the earth and screamed for.

"Let's go before it begins," he said.

"What is it?" Iris asked. She sensed the excitement and it was like alcohol to her. She drank it in from the air around her, was stimulated by it, vibrated in tune to the stirrings. "What's everybody waiting for? Are those chickens? What's going to happen?"

"It's a cockfight," he told her.

The men were taking the birds from the cages now. They held them in a special way, carried them to the ring of dirt that had opened in the circle of dark men. Their eyes shone like the tin houses in which they slept. The men clutched money in their hands and the handlers clutched the birds. One was set down first.

Rafael spoke to Iris in a whisper. "You will not like this," he said. He was so sure of the sweetness of her, the softness. He didn't want to see her cry. He didn't want her hurt by the sight that she would see if she remained. "Let's go and listen to Fidel," he suggested to her. The guitar music struggled plaintively to them over the shouts of the men. "Let's go to Fidel."

"I want to watch the fight. I've never seen one before. I want to stay, Raf," she said to him. She was aware of the men's fierce and slanted faces. The bird that waited was a scrawny-looking thing, she thought. Its neck feathers and its long tail plume were ragged, but the sharp pointed beak and the clawed muffs were impressive. More than the fight she liked the feeling that the fighting created. "What happens now?" she asked.

He knew that she would not leave. He answered, "The other bird will be pitted and then comes the first strike." His voice was muted.

She looked at him and saw that his eyes were not like the other men's. Her attention shifted from him to the birds. The second cock was set down. Immediately they were engaged in midair battle. The roar from the men was loud, beginning as a growl and escalating. Rafael watched Iris. He hoped that she did not know this was a fight to the death. If she did know, how could she smile as she was smiling, her breath coming as it did when he made love to her, her eyes gleaming? Her green eyes mirrored the dark ones all around her, the eyes of men dehumanized, demeaned, and exploited, men who craved some cruelty inflicted on any object other than themselves. He wondered how she could so sweetly resemble them. She could not know what was coming. She must think that it was some innocent game, harmlessly resolved, that neither bird would be killed by the men's sport, that they would simply fight and then be separated and returned to their cages until they played the game again. Iris couldn't know that death was near, he told himself as he gazed at her, but something in her that he saw, was seeing, for the first time, told him that she did know and was eagerly anticipating the final moment.

The smaller bird, stunned by a collision, was down, and in an instant the bigger one hit hard with both his clawed muffs. It was over. One was alive and the other dead. Rafael waited, hoped, for Iris's tears. They did not come. She turned to him.

"Why didn't you bet?" she asked. "I knew the big one would win. Next time can we bet?" she asked, watching the money being gathered. She did not even look to see the one cock being taken to its cage and the other to be buried. "Can we?"

"Yes, if you want," he said.

It had grown very dark and the excitement had gone. The tin bunkhouses looked leaden and the men's faces bitter, sullen, and weary. Paco lingered near Rafael. He lit a cigarette, the match flaring in his face.

"Benigno, he come tomorrow?" he asked Rafael.

Rafael nodded. "Tomorrow."

Paco stared at Iris for a moment. "One more Pinoy to shit on," he said and walked away.

"Who's Benigno?" Iris asked.

"I have been meaning to tell you. Benigno is my little brother. He has come to America. I am to pick him up at the bus tomorrow."

"Oh, that's nice, huh? You'll be glad to see him."

"Glad, and sorry, too. It is like Paco says, I'm afraid."

"It can't be all that bad," she said, eager to get off the subject. "Raf, let's go dancing."

"You know that I can't take you dancing."

"But I want to go."

Fidel's guitar could be heard clearly again.

"We can dance right here," he said.

He took her in his arms. They danced across the ground to the fragile chords, but Iris stopped.

"I don't want to dance here. There's a place in town that I've heard about. I want to go there.

"I can't."

"Are you afraid to take me?" she taunted him.

He was afraid. Once in Salinas he had seen two Pinoy boys stripped naked by a mob of young white men and beaten by them and thrown into an irrigation ditch. He was left to guess what their crime had been. He was afraid. And yet he couldn't let Iris know that he was. "Where is this place?"

"On Main Street."

"I'll take you there," he said. "Iris." He stopped her.

She was impatient at the delay. "What?"

"Iris, you are so beautiful."

He barely brushed her face with his hand.

"Don't," she told him. She took her compact from her purse and strained to see her face in the dark, seeking herself in the mirror, refusing him and his touch.

"I'm sorry," he said.

"C'mon, let's get going."

"Wait, there's something that I want to say to you."

"What? About your brother coming?"

"No. Iris, I want us to be married."

"Married," she said. "Isn't there a law against it or something?"

"In California, yes, but I have asked, and we could go to New Mexico. Others have."

"I lived in New Mexico when I was a kid. I didn't like it there much."

"We would stay only long enough to be married. Will you marry me, Iris?" he asked.

"Sure, Raf. We'll get married, but not right now," she smiled at him, placating him, eager for the lights of town. "Are you going to take me into town?"

"Yes. You know they won't let me inside the dance hall. I'll wait for you."

"Okay."

He stayed well behind her. He could see the laughing groups of men and women, white men and white women. They gathered by their automobiles outside the hall. Iris was far ahead of him. She glided through the crowd. She belonged among them. He did not. He could not enter the building. He did not know what would happen to him if he tried, only that his punishment would be swift and terrible and dealt from the hands of the big pale men who stood so calmly with their arms around their women. They were the proprietors of this place. The women were theirs. The cars. The land. The country. They owned the air that he breathed and they did not like sharing it with the likes of him. He was good for labor, for taking the food from the ground for them, but for nothing more. Rafael knew that he shouldn't wait, that he should return to camp quickly. He thought of Iris dancing, smiling, being held and touched. He could not leave and leave her to them. He walked around to the back of the hall. No one was there. He sat and started to wait. He listened to the band playing, waited for it to stop, waited, as he had promised, for Iris. He closed his eyes, feeling suddenly how tired he was. He fell into a kind of sleep, half dreaming and half remembering home, the islands where he would return one day and find peace. As soon as he had collected enough coins he would go, but he couldn't save. He spent all his money on Iris. He squandered all his love on her, too.

The band was better than most she had danced to in the small towns where she'd been. Someday, she decided, she was going to a big city, Los Angeles or San Francisco, and hear Glenn Miller or Benny Goodman. She'd worn their records thin on her phonograph. Iris loved music. It was the only thing that she could lose herself in for any length of time. In the beginning Rafael had made her forget herself. She had been intrigued by him, his carved body the color of deeply stained wood, but no more. She was tired of him. He followed her too closely lately. A man with white-blond hair approached her and asked her to dance. She accepted. He wasn't much of a dancer and his arms were not so strong and hard as Rafael's, but this soft, light difference was welcome to her. She danced with him and again and again. When she looked at him she recognized the desire that she had seen, had sparked, in a hundred other men. They walked over to some chairs and sat down. He edged his chair closer to hers.

"I think you're about the prettiest thing I've seen around here."

"Have you been around here long?" she asked him.

"Just all my life," he laughed.

Iris laughed with him, but behind her laughter she was thinking that it was no joke to be stuck in this dirty little hole of a town. She couldn't wait to leave. It reminded her of Kansas. She'd be gone soon and she wouldn't be going with Rafael.

"How'd you happen along here?" he asked her, still chuckling.

"I'm visiting my aunt," she told him.

"I hope you're planning a nice long visit."

"Maybe. Maybe not," she answered vaguely.

"You want to dance some more?"

"Yeah, I like dancing with you," she said, lying easily again.

"Let's go," he said eagerly.

As the night progressed he became more and more possessive of her. If she danced with someone else she would see him glowering on the edge of the floor. He acted as if he had brought her, bought her, even. There was no escaping the greed and jealousy of men. Really, Iris didn't want to escape. She liked exciting these emotions, but sometimes it was just too easy. This one was too easy. He wasn't even fun. She'd spent an hour or so with him, danced with him a few times, and he was acting like a husband. He caught her roughly by the arm as she passed him.

"Say, I thought you liked dancing with me." He was slurring his words.

Iris twisted from under his grip. She guessed he'd had a lot to drink.

"I just love dancing with you," she said and smiled for emphasis.

"Well then, how come you've been dancing with all those other guys?" he demanded.

"I was only trying to make you jealous," she coyly confessed to him.

That was what he wanted to hear from her. "Well, okay. I'm jealous. Come on and dance with me now. Only me from now on. You're my pretty baby. I saw you first," he said. He was moving her back out onto the dance floor.

She leaned close to him. "I have to go to the little girl's room. I want to powder my nose. And I have to tinkle," she whispered to him.

She felt him watching her so she went to the ladies room. There were several women chatting at mirrors, putting on lipstick, studying their faces, and considering their chances. Iris patted her hair into place.

"That's a real nice dress," a thin brunette seated on the sink's edge told her.

"My boyfriend gave it to me," Iris said.

"Is your boyfriend here tonight?" the girl asked.

"No."

"I didn't think so. Otherwise you wouldn't have danced so much with Fred."

"Is that his name? Fred?"

"Yeah, the big blond."

The entire room had quieted and everyone was listening to the exchange.

"Do you think your boyfriend would mind about Fred?"

"If he knew he would," Iris answered.

"He might not buy you any more pretty dresses," a blond in a tight black dress threw in.

"Maybe Fred would," Iris said to the group.

"You'd better be careful with Fred," the brunette warned her. "I hear he can get real mean."

"He doesn't scare me," Iris boasted.

"Fred carries a gun in his truck. He's a mean one. That's no lie. You watch yourself."

"Thanks, I will."

Iris left the bathroom. She wondered if she'd misjudged this Fred, but then again maybe those girls were just having fun with her, trying to frighten her. Girls were like that, Iris knew. She didn't know a lot about women, but that much she did. She preferred men and men preferred her, which was probably why girls said the things they did to her. Still, she left the dance cautiously, making certain that Fred didn't see her departure.

Rafael saw her walking down the street from the dance hall. He ran toward her. He had missed her too much to be circumspect. He put his arm around her waist. They stood together in the circle of light from the lamp post and kissed. They were plainly visible from the open door of the dance hall.

The next day Rafael walked to the bus station. He hadn't seen his brother Benigno in ten years. Benigno had been only eight years old, a small child with enormous black eyes, when Rafael had left the Philippines. Now that little boy was grown and had come to America. Rafael was frightened for his brother. He hated to see his dream die as his own had. To witness the killing of his brother's dream was too much. He walked quickly. He didn't want to be late and have Benigno left waiting alone in this strange and hostile place that he could not yet understand. Rafael hoped to teach his brother the lessons he had learned, to help him as no one had helped when he first came to America.

Rafael was only a block from the station when the single shot fired from a truck passed into his brain. He was dead instantly, the victim of an arbitrary violent act, the town's sheriff decided. The sheriff treated the case with nonchalance, as if a deer had been shot out of season. Benigno sat patiently on a bench at the station, looking up at every sound, hoping to see his brother's face, afraid to speak to anyone, not knowing if he could make himself understood.

In a restaurant near the motel where Iris was eating lunch she heard the waitress and some men talking about a shooting. There was no sadness, only mild interest, for the loss of a life on the street near the bus station that morning. Iris listened to them and the pieces of information began to fit too well. To the waitress in her orange uniform and the men drinking thick coffee from thin white mugs at the counter, the death was nothing but gossip, a slight respite from the boredom. To Iris it was something else. She knew that today Rafael was supposed to meet his brother, but it couldn't be Rafael, she told herself. Then she heard the one man say that the dead man was a Filipino. In the same breath he asked for a piece of apple pie. The waitress lifted the big glass dome from the pie and cut a slice. The man attacked it with his fork, eating it all in three bites. Iris went up to the counter to pay her bill. She glanced at one of the men and was about to ask if he knew the name of the man who had been shot. He winked at her. She smiled and said nothing.

She stayed in her room until late that night. She went out to the camp finally. She found it quiet and the yard empty. There were no tired singing men sitting around fires. There was no cock-fight. There was nothing, no life. Something had happened. Surely something terrible had happened. She went to Rafael's bunkhouse and knocked on the door. An older man whose name Iris could not remember opened it a crack. When he saw her, his face flinched, contracted as if in pain.

"Where is Raf?" she asked.

The man shook his head.

"Where is he?"

Another man came to the door. This was Paco.

"You don't know?" he asked her. His eyes raked her.

"I heard something . . . Rafael didn't come tonight . . . to see me. I wanted to know where he was," she said. She couldn't say what she suspected. She listened for one of the small dark men to say it.

"Rafael is dead," Paco said coldly. "Shot this morning."

Now she knew. It was certainty, not suspicion, but certain death.

"Who did it? Why?" she asked.

"Nobody know. Nobody care. So . . ." He spread his hands in awful resignation.

"Where is he?"

"In the ground. He buried this afternoon."

It was hard for her to believe that she would never see Rafael again. Only the night before she had decided to leave him and now he was dead. Dead. And gone. She should go but something kept her standing there.

"His brother," she said. "His little brother was coming today."

"He come. Helped to carry his brother's box."

"I want to see him," she said.

The old man, who had been listening to their words and saying nothing, shook his head violently. "No. No," he said.

Iris looked to Paco. "Please, Paco. I want to see him."

He couldn't refuse her. He felt hatred for her. He blamed her for Rafael's death. She was responsible somehow for the murder. If Rafael had not loved her he would be alive, Paco believed, but he could not say no to her.

"Benigno!" he called inside.

The old man pushed past Iris, went out into the yard, and spat. He returned to the bunkhouse and lay down on a bare striped tick. The boy came to the door.

"This Benigno," Paco said, and he walked away, crossed to the old man, and sat down beside him on the frayed mattress.

Benigno stood before her, his hands clasped together. He looked like Rafael.

"My name is Iris. I was a friend of your brother's."

"Yes, I know."

The voice was the same, in timbre so like Rafael's. Benigno had been taught in the same school as his brother. He had dreamed the same dream. He had come to America and his brother had been killed. Benigno mourned him, but he felt that he was only just beginning. It was sad that Rafael's life had ended, but he wanted to begin. He wanted to realize the dream. Rafael had not had time enough to warn his brother and perhaps Benigno could not have been warned. Benigno couldn't stop staring at Iris. The others had told him about his brother's beautiful blond girl and here she was. She reached out and brought him closer, closed the

door behind them. It made him feel better, less lonely and frightened, being near her. She had been his brother's. His brother was
dead. This girl was white and gold. She swayed against him.

"Let's go for a walk," she said.

They started out into the darkness.

Holly was surprised when they told her that her sister was
waiting for her in the lounge of her dormitory. She expected to
find Rose, thinking that she had finally come for the visit they
had written about and planned for so long. She hurried into the
room. There, seated on one of the worn sofas, was Iris. Poor
Rose, thought Holly, trapped in Kansas, as she saw Iris for the
first time in two years, Iris who had gotten out ahead of them all.
Holly walked over to her. Iris rose. They faced each other awkwardly and appraisingly.

"How did you know to come here?" Holly asked.

"I remembered you were going to school in Los Angeles. I
took a chance you'd still be here. God, how long will you be
here?" she asked.

"Two more years. I'm halfway through."

"I'm on my way up to Washington. I dropped my bag in a
locker at the bus station. Thought I'd stop and say hello. It's been
a while," Iris said smoothly.

The same Iris, Holly thought, casually throwing bombs, heedless of outcome. "It's good to see you," she said, meaning it, but
feeling that she should take cover.

"Yeah," Iris said.

"What have you been doing? Where have you been living?"

"Oh, Hol, that's too many questions. I don't know, I've been
around, California mostly. Is there some place we could go? That
old lady at the desk, the way she keeps looking at me, kind of
gives me the creeps."

"Mrs. Thompson," Holly identified her. "We don't see too
many girls like you here," Holly said. Iris was dressed in a white
suit with a bright yellow blouse. The suit fit her like skin. Her
hair was long, swept high off her forehead, but falling to her
shoulders. Holly noticed that her sister's white shoes were scuffed.
The same Iris, she thought again.

"There's a coffee shop," Holly said.

"Coffee, huh? Is there any place I could get a drink?" Iris asked, lighting a cigarette. "Oh, coffee'll be okay, I guess. Let's just get out of here."

At the coffee shop Iris began to tell Holly about the last two years. Holly listened, fascinated by a life so different from her own. Iris said more than she intended. After all the strangers, the passionate strangers, and the changing scenery, Iris had not anticipated the pleasure of having Holly, a sister, beside her.

"How do I look, Hol?" she asked.

"You're not a little girl anymore. You're more beautiful, if that's possible, Iris," Holly answered truthfully.

"Yeah?"

"Yes."

"Wait till I've been on that bus for a few days."

"Did you say you were going to Washington?" Holly asked her.

"Yeah, Seattle. Why don't you come with me?" Iris asked suddenly, surprising them both. "There's a lot of Navy up there. It'd be fun."

"I couldn't."

"No, I guess not." Iris stubbed out her cigarette and took another from her purse. A man from the booth across from them leaped up and held out a gold lighter. Iris's eyes flicked across the man and the metal. "Thanks," she said. He returned to his seat but continued to stare at Iris. "I don't know. This place isn't so bad. Maybe I should stay here instead of going to Seattle."

"I like it," Holly said simply.

"Yeah. You seeing any guys? You probably have a steady guy, huh?"

"No. No guys, steady or otherwise."

"Why don't you come along with me? You don't really want to be a teacher, do you? Try to teach a bunch of kids who'll hate your guts. I hated school and every teacher in it. Why do it, Hol? You've gotten real good-looking. You have, I swear. Why don't you come with me? We'd be a great team. We'd have a ball up there."

"I couldn't quit now. I'm only two years away from my degree. As far as teaching goes, I have to admit I have some doubts about it."

"I'm telling you it'll turn you into a shriveled-up old lady before your time. Like that Thompson dame behind that desk. Well, listen, I've got to get going."

"But you just got here."

"There's a bus to Seattle tonight and I'm going to be on it."

"What will you do in Washington? Do you know anyone?"

Iris inhaled deeply. "I make friends easy." She stared through her exhaled smoke at her sister. "I thought I might do some singing up there."

"Singing?"

"Yeah, with a band, you know." She liked the way it sounded. "I'm a pretty good singer. You don't have to be too good if you have other things going for you, you know."

"I think it's a wonderful idea. You have such courage to try it. I'm sure you'll succeed."

Iris felt something fleetingly like shame. "Yeah, well, it was good seeing you, Hol. It really was," she said and stood.

"I'll walk with you."

"No. Finish your coffee. It's not far to the bus. I'll manage."

Holly followed her look to the man in the booth. "Goodbye, Iris. Will you keep in touch? Call me from Washington and give me your address as soon as you get settled."

"Sure I will. Bye, Hol." She leaned over and gave her a quick kiss on the cheek.

Holly watched her go. She saw the man leave his booth and follow Iris out. The same Iris, but more destructively lovely than ever. She drank the rest of her coffee and contemplated facing Mrs. Thompson back at the dormitory. She paid the bill and walked for a long time before returning to school. She wished that she never had to go back.

Chapter Eight

It was an evacuation sale. As Holly walked by the immaculate yellow house that she passed every day, she felt a difference before seeing the notice and realizing what it meant to the residents of this house. She had often seen the androgynous, twinlike couple and their children. These people were being removed from California, taken from the coast. They faced a shadowy fate somewhere in the interior of the country where they would not be a threat to security. But what possible threat could they pose, Holly wondered. She stood for a moment before their house and confronted their fate. It was a part of war, she had been told, but it disturbed her. She thought of the scavengers who would come here, attracted by the sign of displacement, like vultures to a death, jackals who would buy pots and pans, rugs, chairs, snatch up the possessions of this family at bargain prices. The family was Japanese and because their countrymen across an ocean had become aggressors, they, by association of race, had become prey.

She hurried on. She was not responsible. She was not to blame, but still she felt guilty, one of the acquisitive and avenging pack. She would not go into the house and browse and buy, but neither would she stop and say anything to those who did. She would merely recognize the greed and injustice and feel sorry and disgusted. The studio with its tall gates was just ahead. The buildings were drab-looking, a disappointment to anyone who expected glamor from a movie lot. Henry, the guard at the gate, waved at her as she entered.

Holly had not become a teacher. After Iris's visit she had remained in school for several more months. Then one day she had simply walked into the dean's office and announced that she was leaving. The dean was shocked. Great ordinary things had been expected of Holly Calder. She had been a scrupulous student and she would surely have made that sort of teacher. The dean had told her this and Holly had answered by saying that she didn't want to teach, that it seemed pointless and futile to her, that she guessed she had never really wanted it. Holly had taken away with her the dean's promise that she could return at any time and finish her work toward her degree. It was a promise that Holly had not solicited and that she knew she would never redeem. She had left.

During two summer vacations she had worked as a typist at Warner Brothers. The same day that she quit school she went to Burbank and applied for a full-time position at the studio. She was accepted. For a year she had been typing, a tedious occupation, but never once had she regretted leaving school. She did miss the nearness of the ocean. It was a long trip on the Red Car to the beach from her apartment in Burbank, but most weekends she made it. She would go to the Santa Monica pier, take a walk on the sand, eat dinner in a restaurant with an ocean view. The pier was always packed with servicemen and their girls, but Holly was always alone.

She returned the guard Henry's wave and tried to forget the Japanese family's plight. There was nothing she could do for them. Her thoughts went nervously to herself. Today she was starting a new job at Warner's. From now on she was Arnie Ross's secretary. She wasn't sure why she had been chosen for this promotion. Ross would gladly have told her but she would never have asked. He had picked her from the typing pool because he liked the way she looked. He didn't want to sleep with her. The studio gossip grapevine speculated that he already had. Ross could sleep with almost any girl. He knew that well, but it was just the opposite with Holly Calder. He guessed that he probably couldn't take her to bed even if he'd wanted to. And he didn't. He admired her cool, pristine appearance, the way she called him Mr. Ross, that aloof stance of hers, the distance that she kept between herself and everyone else. She didn't physically stimulate him, but she would give an attitude to the office that he himself, unkempt and loud-mouthed, knew he never could. Arnie Ross was smart and he had taste. He could spot class without possessing it. His only worry was that some slick vice-president would steal Holly away from him.

Holly entered the office. There was only a desk, a filing cabinet, and one chair in the small room, but it was a space all her own, a real luxury after the typing pool. She opened the door to the inner office, knowing that Mr. Ross hadn't arrived yet. It was a shambles. She backed out and bumped into her new boss.

"Scare you in there?" he asked, grinning at her.

"No, sir . . . well, yes, a little," she answered uncertainly.

He looked past her. "It's a mess."

"Shall I open the blinds, Mr. Ross?"

"Sure, go ahead. Do anything you like to neaten it up. The only thing I ask is that you leave my desk alone. I have a system that's all my own. It may not look organized, but it makes sense to me."

"Yes, of course. Would you like some coffee?"

"Yeah, that'd be great."

She started to move around him. He went to get out of her way. They danced back and forth into each other's path for a few moments. Finally he reached out and took her by the shoulders, stepped around her. She left the office to get his coffee. As she poured a cup she realized that she didn't know how he took it. She went back down the hall. His door was open. She stuck her head inside.

"Mr. Ross, cream or sugar?" she asked.

"Both, lots of cream and two sugars."

"Yes, sir."

She turned to go.

"Holly?"

She came back into the doorway.

"Yes?"

"How do you take your coffee?"

"I? I take it black."

"Figures."

Later in the morning he called her into his office. She came in with her dictation pad and a sharpened pencil. He noticed.

"I don't do much dictation, Holly."

"Yes, sir." She dropped the tablet to her side as if to hide it.

"I'd like you to read this script. Tell me what you think of it."

She took the gold-bradded script that he held out to her.

"Why would you want me to read it?" she asked.

"Have you ever read a script before?"

"I've only typed them."

"That's what I want. A fresh viewpoint," he said. He noticed the way she gripped the script to her chest, like a little girl carrying school books. "I think it's shit. I'd like to know what you think."

"Yes, sir."

He followed her out of his office.

"I'm going to lunch now," he told her. "Yeah, I know it's only eleven-thirty, but I'm hungry," he said, feeling that he had to explain himself to her and not knowing why. "I didn't have any breakfast."

After he had gone Holly began reading the script. It wasn't a very good story, but the form fascinated her. It was past two o'clock and she was just finishing when Arnie Ross returned. He didn't speak, but went directly to his office and closed the door. He had been in bed for the last two hours with a young, red-haired actress. Her name was June. She'd been eager and cloying, avidly bursting from her clothes, but he'd left feeling cheated. She'd tasted stale to him.

Holly went to get herself some coffee. She'd been so involved in reading that she'd forgotten to eat lunch. When she returned to her desk his door was open.

"Holly!" he called to her.

She put her coffee down and went in to him.

"Go get your coffee," he told her.

She did as she was told.

"Sit down," he said. "Have you started on that script yet?" he asked her.

"I read it."

"The whole thing? You read it all?"

"Yes."

"So what'd you think?" he asked incredulously.

"The story's not very original. The end is stronger than the beginning. The best character is the old man. If it was more his story . . . if the focus could be put on him, you'd have something. The other characters are just stick figures. They don't make you feel anything for them. You don't care what happens to them. And really nothing much does . . . happen, I mean," she stopped. He was looking at her very strangely. "Mr. Ross, I don't know anything about scripts."

"You know plenty," he said. "You're sure this is the first script you've ever read?"

"Yes, sir."

"We share the same opinion on this one. You put it a little more politely than I did. God, you're a polite girl," he mused. "I want you to read another script and this time I want you to write down what you think of it." As he spoke he was digging through piles on his desk. "Here it is. This is the one."

"May I take it home with me?"

"Yeah, sure."

She took the script with her to the outer office. He dialed the redhead's number, deciding to give her another chance.

Holly returned home after her first day as Arnie Ross's secretary carrying the script he had asked her to read. Home was a one-bedroom apartment half a mile from the studio in a court of flat and square pink stucco boxes with red tile roofs that the landlady liked to describe as old Spanish. The grounds were not well tended. The patch of lawn in back struggled along on its own except when the landlady's son gave it a desultory monthly mowing. He always cut it too close and it turned brown. Slowly it would fight its way back to overgrown green only to be lazily chopped again. There were camellia bushes that never bloomed and beside them oleanders that were in constant poisonous flower.

Holly was lucky. Housing was scarce now. It was almost impossible to find an apartment. She had happened on this one more than a year ago and had settled on it thinking that she would find a better place in no time, but the war had come and she had found herself in sudden possession of a gem. Several of the girls from the studio had offered to move in with her, sympathizing pro-

fusely with her single state, but she had refused. The idea of
sharing her apartment and her life with one of them was repugnant to Holly. She had come to the conclusion that she was a
solitary animal. When girls spoke of hating to eat alone or going
to a movie unescorted, she didn't undertsand. A girl, if she couldn't
find a man, which was the number-one priority, was supposed to
gather into a covey of other girls, Holly had observed. She sometimes felt very odd not being in the market for a husband or a
roommate but liking her life alone. Guilt made her wonder if she
liked it or was resigned to it. She put her key in the lock and was
happy to open the door to silent emptiness, happy at that moment
anyway.

She laid her purse and the script down and went to raise the
windows. It was warm for March, a soft evening that held the
promise of rain sometime in the night. Holly heard heels clicking
quickly on the walk outside. Her neighbor was coming home.
She too lived alone but rarely was. Although Holly had never
spoken to her, she knew the woman's name. On her mailbox it said
L. Sparks. The L. stood for Laurette, Holly had learned one night
when a man stood in the courtyard and called it out over and over
again. The radio came on next door, first blaring and then lowered
to a roar. Holly listened to the plaster-distorted din, thought of
knocking on the wall, and decided to try and ignore the sound.

Holly's apartment was very bare. She had decorated it the way
that she dressed, colors neutral, little ornamentation, simple and
straight utilitarian lines, clean, and uncluttered. She did not have
guests. This place was solely hers, the realm of her inner life. On
a small table near the door there were two framed photographs,
the only pictures in any of the rooms. One was an oval, soft,
sepia-toned portrait of a young boy sitting cross-legged in a chair,
a boneless blond pug dog slumped in his arms. The boy's face
was alert, fine-boned, and dark. The high-backed wicker chair
and the stiff satin tie at the neck of his shirt contrasted sharply to
the eager face. The elegant, old, somnolent dog seemed more a
prop than a pet. The other photograph was square and larger,
more harshly black and white. It held seven people in a moment long ago, escaped to wherever moments go. There was
a quite beautiful woman in the center, surrounded by six little
girls in white. They stood outside, the morning sun bright on the
white dresses. The woman wore a dark thin dress that fluttered

slightly in the stillness of the framed paper plane. Her hair was so fair that it caught the light in exactly the way that the pale dresses did. No one smiled; one puckish child's face appeared to, but it was the effect of the facial structure and not a smile.

Holly kept these pictures of her father as a boy and of her mother and sisters dusted and polished but she did not look at them. She was well aware of her choice, the significance of these particular photographs. The only adult pictured in them was her mother. Now all the family was grown or dead, but in Holly's stark apartment they were as they once had been and would never be again.

The radio went off. She heard Laurette click past. It seemed that she was forever listening behind her door to the comings and goings of others. She wondered where Laurette, girls like Laurette, went nights. Holly realized that she lived her life very differently than others, but that difference, her apartness, had been with her for so long that it had hardened into instinct, become character. She tried to think back, remember when it was that she had taken the first step toward becoming what she was now. She guessed that she had always been this way.

Holly sat down with the script, began to read, never slumping in her chair, steadily turning the pages. It went quickly. It was a wonderful story, she thought. She considered what she should write for her boss. She had been amply prepared for Arnie Ross, warned about his blatant use of women, his conquest of them, their bodies. With her, Holly decided, he had set about using her mind. She didn't think that she was beautiful enough to attract him, but being what he was, he would have in some way to consume her. Arnie Ross was an obese jackal, a creature dropped fortuitously into a place and time where carrion was plentiful. He was in the perfect business to indulge his appetites. Holly was certain that he would have bought something from the house of the Japanese family about to be interned. She saw quite clearly what he was. She carefully phrased her opinion of the script in a single page for him. It took her several hours to get it in exactly the form that she wanted. At midnight she left it on the table and went to bed.

Sometime in the early morning a door slammed, Laurette's door, and jarred Holly awake. She lay in the darkness and listened. Laughter came through the walls, high shrieking giggles interspersed with a lower masculine rumbling. It sounded as if Laurette was having a very good time, but Holly anticipated, waited for, something else. There was a long silence. The clock ticked metallically, mechanically, inches from her. Glass shattered, broken against something in Laurette's apartment. Holly sat up. She heard shouting and a slap, angry words and blows. Laurette's cries sounded like her laughter. Then there was quiet. Holly remembered her parents' closed doors and the sounds and the silences that came through them. She realized now what those silences must have been and that realization was like a stone within her, a rock of resentment veined with jealousy. Possibly she should call the police, but the battle next door seemed to have ended. It was over now. The argument and dissension had died away. Now they were in bed together, the man and Laurette were, just as her mother and father had been.

In the morning Holly woke before her alarm went off. Outside, high heels sounded sharply. She got up and went to the window, caught a glimpse of platinum-blond pompadour and swinging short red skirt. Laurette again going, and here she was still watching, Holly thought. She didn't believe that she wanted a life like Laurette's or her sister Iris's, but she questioned whether her own was a life at all. This morning she felt caught, trapped, in frightened and rigid reflex. She doubted this tangle of solitary and exact routines that was supposed to be her life. Walking into the living room, she saw the page she had written the night before. She read over her words. They sounded stiff to her, stilted, conveying none of the feeling that she had for the script. She crumpled the page angrily. She'd go into the office early and type another, but she'd have to hurry. She picked up the wadded paper from the floor and took it to the trash. She was willing to scrap what was hopelessly ruined, broken, or incurably stunted. She had discarded teaching. She had left her family and Kansas. She wondered now if this bystanding, onlooking life of hers should end, and if she was capable of ending it.

It was late in the morning when Arnie Ross arrived at the office. He looked as if he hadn't slept all night. He said only one word as he passed Holly's desk.

"Coffee."

She brought him a cup and was turning to leave.

"Did you read that script?" he asked her.

"Yes."

"And did you write that page for me?"

"Yes."

"I want to read it."

"Now?" she asked.

"Yeah."

She went and got it. He took the single sheet of paper. Again she started out of his office.

"Stay here," he said. "Sit down."

She watched him while he read. After a few minutes he looked up at her with bloodshot eyes.

"Not bad. I want you to do some more for me."

"Yes, Mr. Ross."

"There's one you've got to read right away," he said and began shuffling through papers. "Shit, it's Friday. I forgot. You don't want to spend your weekend reading a script."

"I don't mind."

"Won't they miss you at the Coconut Grove?"

"No."

"C'mon, you've got to have better things to do with your weekend," he said.

Holly said nothing and extended her hand for the script. A man like Arnie Ross would never understand the way she spent her days and she had no intention of trying to explain it to him. He gave her the script and she left his office.

On Saturday Holly went to the beach. Her old school stood beside the Pacific Electric track and she looked out the window of the red car for the sight of the big stone building. It came into view. She missed none of the people, not the ones who had tried to teach her, and not the ones who had tried to learn there. She was glad that she had left and grateful that the train traveled rapidly past. She wore a large straw hat, hiding under the wide brim. She averted her eyes from her fellow passengers and wished that they would do the same. She felt that they were staring at her, especially the older woman on the seat beside her. Her father had taught her to drive years ago. She was saving her money to buy an automobile. It would give her such freedom and in so many ways. More than anything she wanted to be alone, not under the scrutiny of strangers. Instead of feeling any kinship with the people around her, she was revulsed by them. She hated being near them. She was happy when she could smell the ocean and leave the car.

On the pier there was a carousel. Its music was loud, sweetly brash and blaringly sad. There were sailors everywhere. Some with girls and some without. Those who were alone looked at her, craning their necks to see under her hat. One of them whistled softly. And another said hello. Holly did not acknowledge them. She concentrated on the ocean, her mouth full of sugar from the melting praline bought at a candy stand painted like a striped peppermint. The wind was blowing colder off the waves and she took a sweater from her neatly packed satchel.

She stood back and watched at a shooting gallery. Men would take the rifle and try to shoot the targets, winning for their girls one of the stuffed animals that hung from a line festooning the booth. A man won and his tittering girl picked a bear as pink as her rouged cheeks. The man who ran the game shouted loudly to draw attention to the winner. Everyone wanted to be a winner, Holly thought, watching the crowd. She walked on. There were myriad games and players, but so few winners and so many losers. Holly sat on a bench by the stone steps leading down to the sand. She removed her shoes and socks, rolled the socks into the shoes, and put them in her satchel. She started down the steps, carefully sidestepping gum and glass. She reached the sand and it was warm from the day's accumulation of sun. The sand felt good to her bare feet. She headed for the hard-packed, damp ground nearer the water. Someone was behind her, following her. She looked around and saw many people still on the beach, lots of squealing children and striped umbrellas. She was not frightened by the trailing presence, only sorry that someone was so lonely. She hoped that he would be satisfied to follow, but that he would not speak to her. As she wished for this, he spoke.

"Hello," he called to her.

She kept walking.

"Hello," he repeated his call.

She looked back at him over her shoulder.

"Hello," she said.

"Nice day," the sailor said, coming alongside.

"Yes, it is." She edged away from him. He looked young and

scared. He did not have the bearing of a winning rifle shot. He would never provide any girl with pink stuffed bears no matter how hard he might try. He was very skinny. His walk was a sad and cocky shambling. The bell bottoms of his trousers looked enormous compared to his concave, jumper-clad chest. His skin was pimply, still adolescent. The stripes on his sleeve spoke a language that she couldn't comprehend. Holly watched him while he struggled to think of something to say to hold her. She wanted away from him as fast as possible.

"My name is Roy Kincaid," he told her.

She knew that she was now supposed to volunteer her name. That was the way the exchange worked, but Holly found it difficult to speak. This boy was most likely doomed to some Pacific atoll that no one had ever heard of and even when they read it in the papers they wouldn't correctly pronounce the name of the newest bloody battlefield. There was a good chance that he would die and she was standing hesitating about offering her name to him.

"I'm Holly Calder," she said, giving in to her guilt.

"Do you mind if I walk with you?" he asked.

Yes, she wanted to say. "No," she said.

"I'm from Iowa," Roy said. "Isn't this ocean something?"

"Yes," Holly quietly agreed, staring out at the huge Pacific. Roy Kincaid was using it as a conversational gambit at the moment. Soon he might be sailing across it to fight and die. He could ride the sea until it swallowed him, Holly allowed. "It's very beautiful, especially at sunset."

"Where're you from, Holly?" he asked.

She cringed at his questions, his pathetic probings. "Kansas."

"Say, we're almost neighbors."

"Almost," Holly said.

"I sure would like to take you out tonight."

She looked at him. "I'm sorry." She looked away. "I can't."

"Already got a date, I'll bet."

She lied. "Yes."

"I should have known. The pretty girls are always taken."

She smiled. A question escaped her. "Do you think I'm pretty?"

"I sure do."

"Thank you, Roy."

"I think you're about the prettiest girl I've ever seen."

He was anxious, hoping she'd break her date. The date was a lie and so was the compliment, Holly thought. It was funny. And sad. She wished that he had stopped at simply saying she was pretty. She was angry with herself for asking his approval, for forcing the exaggeration. She wasn't angry with him. "I have to be going," she said.

"Are you sure?"

"Yes."

They were back at the steps. The light was fading. It was an unseasonable hot spell but the days still ended early. She climbed the stairs. He was behind her. Her feet were cold now. She sat on the bench and brushed the sand from her soles. She put on her socks and shoes. Before she could stop him, Roy Kincaid had kneeled at her feet and tied her shoes for her. It was a gentle gesture. She was touched by it. He stood and so did she. She looked at the white hat set jauntily back on his head, the bad skin, and soft brown eyes. There was sand on the knees of his trousers where he had bent to the ground. Why not have dinner with him, she asked herself, or maybe go dancing or to a show? She imagined his thin arms around her, fending off his kisses and his hands, the closeness on the dance floor or in the balcony of a dark movie house. She was repelled by her thoughts.

"Goodbye, Roy," she said and walked away.

"Goodbye," he called to her as he had called hello.

The ride home was long. That night she heard Laurette Sparks come clicking home late. Holly had not been asleep. She looked out her living room window and saw Laurette fumbling with her keys while a sailor rubbed his hands across her shoulders and down her back, lifted her hair and kissed her neck. Holly couldn't make out the sailor's face. Maybe it was Roy Kincaid, she thought. Of the thousands of sailors in the city, she hoped that it was Roy. She hoped that the gentle losing boy had found some warm and easy body somewhere that night and that, just once, he'd won.

Chapter Nine

The air was heavy and still, weighted with anticipation. The sky and the land were coated in a coppery film, the color of the coils through which electric current passes. Poppy had gone into town. Jane was seated in the kitchen, alone in the farmhouse. Her hair was totally white now. She looked far older than her forty-five years. War slaughtered men, aged women, and America was in its second year of war, but Jane Calder had no sons and the army had no use for her crippled husband. Other things had aged her. She felt that she was ancient, that she'd lived a century at least, and that feeling was stamped upon her face. Clay was out in the fields. He worked longer and longer hours to be out from under her roof. The house was deadly quiet, cold at its core. Only Jane could stand to stay within it. It was hers, her creation and her destruction, too. She'd brought them, all the family, here after Clay's accident when he could no longer work the dams, but now nearly all had escaped. Poppy was with her still. Poppy loved her, but where was she now? Why didn't she come home? Jane got up from the table and went to the window. The sky had darkened and the wind had risen. Jane crossed her arms in front of her and rocked against the glass aperture, unseeing, softly banging her forehead to the pane. She could not see beyond herself. Her eyes were turned inward, not looking for the return of her adored daughter or registering the twisting spiral in the distance, off on the horizon. Her horizon was her pale-lashed eyelids. She did not see her husband come running, taking jagged strides, from the fields.

Clay burst into the kitchen. She did not turn.

"Do you see it?" he asked her.

She did not respond with words, but her back stiffened at the sound of his voice.

"Jane?" he asked. His hand lightly brushed her. She turned now, more to evade than to acknowledge him. She looked at him with blank, slatelike anger.

"Jane, did you see the cloud?"

"What cloud?" she asked.

"Look out there," he said. He looked out the window when she did not. The cloud was nearing. "A funnel cloud."

"Where?" she asked, not caring.

"There. It's a tornado, Jane. It's coming right for us. We've got to get out of here."

"Why?"

"It's a tornado," he repeated.

"I'm not going anywhere."

"Jane, please," he said. He touched her, hoping to pierce her insane apathy.

She pulled away from him. "Don't."

"All right. All right, Jane, I'm sorry, but you have to listen to me. . . ." He didn't know what to say. He didn't know what words would reach her. "Listen to me . . ." he began again, and broke off in frustration.

She was staring at him. "Is it lunch time?" she asked, as if she had become aware of his presence in the kitchen for the first time. "Why have you come in so early? I haven't fixed your lunch yet. It's not time. Don't try to tell me that it is."

"I didn't come for my lunch, Jane," he said, making an effort to speak quietly and slowly. "We have to get away from here."

"You never wanted to be here. You always wanted to run away," she accused him.

"For Christ's sake, Jane, don't start this now. There a tornado coming. We don't have time." He was beginning to shout.

"Shhh . . . shhh," she hushed him absently.

He held back from shaking her into focus, sensing that force would only drive her further from him. Her eyes were on him, but she wasn't seeing him, he knew. "Jane," he said, thinking her name might bring her around. How long, he wondered, had she been like this and he so unaware? Months? Years? Had he become as blind and blank as she not to have seen this mad blind blankness of hers?"

"I'm not going anywhere," she told him.

He checked out the window. The cloud was huge now. He reached for her. She lunged away from him. She shrank back into the corner, her eyes glassy and wild.

"You can't make me go. This is my home. I won't go with you anymore, Clay. You took me away, so far away, so many times, but no more. Never again. You can't make me go."

"I'm going, Jane."

"Yes, I know. I knew you would. You always run. You always have. You always will. But you'll come back."

"There may not be anything to come back to. Jane, come with me."

"I went with you, too many times. I never will again."

"Do you want to die here?" he asked her.

"Yes," she answered. "I do."

"I don't."

"Then go. Save yourself."

"I want to save you too, Jane," he said, and he did still.

"Too late. Too late for that."

"No."

"Yes, Clay."

"Come with me," he said.

"Stay with me," she said.

They stood facing one another. All their life was distilled in those two sentences, condensed into a single confrontation. He went and took the key to the car from the hook on the wall. He said nothing else to her. She said nothing else to him. There was nothing else for them to say.

He ran against the wind across the yard to the car. The cloud was almost directly overhead now. He started the engine and drove off. He went in no particular direction, only away.

Jane returned to the table. She sipped the dregs of her coffee, taking in the cold and bitter liquid. She was on her way to the kettle on the stove when the house collapsed upon her.

Holly received the telegram at work. It was from Rose. The words were few but potent. She placed the yellow square of paper in the center of her desk and walked through the open door to Arnie Ross's office. He did not look up at her entrance.

"Mr. Ross," she said and her voice was steady and firm. She was amazed at herself.

He stopped writing. "What is it, Holly?" he asked before he saw her. Seeing her, he demanded, "What's wrong?"

"I've just had a telegram," she told him.

In 1943 a telegram meant a death, a war death. Ross was puzzled. Clearly, this ashen girl had had news of a death. The loss was plain to see, but he hadn't guessed that Holly had a boyfriend in the service. Maybe her brother had been killed.

"I'll have to go home," she said steadily.

Her control was admirable, but her voice sounded hollow to him.

"Yeah, take the day off," he said.

She shook her head. He was being kind and generous but he had misunderstood her. "I mean I'll have to go back to Kansas."

"Kansas?" he asked, confused.

"For the funeral," she explained. She didn't know why she had made it singular. There would be two, together. They were dead, together. Mr. Ross was saying something to her.

"I didn't know there was anyone you were so serious about, Holly."

She realized how little she had said to him in this conversation, how little she had ever told about herself. "My parents were killed in a tornado yesterday," she said. She pictured them, dying together. She would not know otherwise until she went home to Kansas. It had taken her parents dying there for her to call that place home again, for her to think of it as that. "I'll have to go home," she repeated.

"Will you be alone?" he asked.

"No, I have two sisters in Kansas. Rose will meet me at the station. Rose will be there. I know she will," Holly assured him although he had asked for no guarantees. It was she, not Arnie Ross, who needed them, she realized. "Rose will be waiting for me," she promised herself.

And Rose was waiting. Holly saw her standing, seemingly in the same spot where she had stood and waved goodbye to her five years ago. Rose was the last one she had seen then. Now she was the first. They embraced at Rose's instigation. She looked the same, Holly decided. Rose was thinking that her sister had changed. The years spent apart caused a silence after their first greetings. Holly carried the old brown valise. Seeing it, Rose said, "You kept it."

"Yes," said Holly, tightening her grip on the cracked handle. "It was Daddy's."

"I remember."

Holly looked at her sister. Rose smiled. There was so much that they shared, an entire childhood. Holly reached out for her hand and pressed it. They shared the loss, too.

"I thought we would walk. It's not far," Rose said.

"Are you still in the same apartment?"

"Yes," she answered. "Everything is pretty much the same around here."

Holly detected a bitterness in Rose's voice that she had never heard before. She looked more closely at her sister and realized that Rose had aged.

"Don't look so hard at me, Holly. You look so hard at people sometimes. It makes them feel funny, you know."

"I didn't . . . know that," Holly said.

"I'm sorry I snapped at you. Don't pay any attention to me. I've been half out of my mind since it happened."

Holly wasn't ready to talk about it yet. She stared up the empty street. At the end stood a great brick building.

"Straker's," she said.

"I told you, everything's the same. They have a big army contract now. No more shirts. They make uniforms."

"Uniforms. I don't see too many around here. You sould see Los Angeles. It's one solid mass of soldiers, sailors, marines . . . uniforms everywhere."

"Sounds interesting," Rose said.

"Does it?" Holly asked.

"Yes. And working at a movie studio. Do you know any stars, Holly?" she asked, showing some excitement for the first time.

"No, I don't know any stars."

"But you must see them all the time."

"Seeing isn't knowing, Rose. I work for a man named Arnie Ross. He's about the farthest thing from a star that there is."

"Is he married?" Rose asked.

"No."

"Is he interested in you?" Rose took the edge from her inquiry with her old grin.

"No," Holly answered. She didn't smile.

"I thought you'd be different. You look different, but you're not really."

"Disappointed?" Holly asked.

"No," Rose said. "Is there anybody that you date? You never say in your letters."

"There's no one."

"Well, when is there going to be? What are you waiting for? Holly, you're twenty-three years old."

"You sound just like . . ." Holly said no more.

Both sisters thought of their mother. Neither spoke for a while.

"What about Clark Gable?" Rose asked suddenly.

"What?" Holly asked, thinking that her sister was suggesting she date him.

Rose started to laugh. Holly joined her. Her laughter was impossible to resist. Rose managed to say, "I meant have you ever seen Clark Gable."

"He's at MGM. I'm at Warner's," she said speaking of the studios as if they were different countries. "He's in the service now anyway."

"I guess you can't call him for a date then," Rose joked.

"I guess not." Holly smiled. "How's Clyde?" she asked.

"Clyde's in hog heaven," Rose said. "I've never seen him so happy. He's what's known as essential to the war effort, a guy who's not in uniform surrounded by a lot of girls sewing uniforms for guys a long way from home. Loneliness is a lot stronger than loyalty, Holly, did you know that?"

"Rosie, are you happy?"

"No."

"Why haven't you come to California to visit me?"

"I don't know. I wanted to, but I just never seem to be able to leave. Here we are."

They entered the apartment. It was here that Holly always visualized Rose, but she had thought of her happy here. Seeing her sister now in the small room, it had the look of a cell to Holly.

"Want some coffee?" Rose asked her.

"I'd love some."

Holly set the valise by the door. She followed Rose into the kitchen.

"How are Lily and Poppy?" she asked quickly, knowing she should have asked sooner.

"Lily is Lily. You'll see what I mean. Poppy, poor kid, is in pretty bad shape. She's at Lily's. The farmhouse was completely destroyed. . . ."

Holly smoothly interrupted. "I tried to locate Iris, get word to her, but I didn't have any luck."

"You wrote that she came to see you once."

"That was three years ago, Rose. Three years and not a word since."

"Well, that shouldn't surprise you. She never called or wrote any of us here, not Mama or Daddy. That's Iris."

"How close are any of us, Rose? We're sisters. Shouldn't that mean something more than it does? It's all of us, not just Iris."

"How did she look?"

It struck Holly that Rose asked how Iris looked and not how she was, then she realized that her own most vivid memory of their meeting was the way Iris had looked. She recalled very little of what she'd said.

"Beautiful, more beautiful than ever."

"That sounds right," Rose said. "Do you want to have coffee in here or in the living room?" she said.

"In the living room," Holly answered, thinking of her mother sitting at the kitchen table drinking cup after cup of coffee.

"Go on. I'll bring it in."

Holly went into the living room. Rose spoke, strangely detached from the kitchen.

"You know the first time that Clyde was unfaithful to me was with Iris."

She walked in with a tray.

"He told you that?" Holly asked.

"I asked him," Rose said. She set the tray down. "Cream or sugar in your coffee? I should remember," she apologized.

"Black."

"That's right. You and Daddy took it black," she said. "I guess I always suspected something. Clyde told me about a year ago."

"Do you believe him?"

"Yes."

"Rose, why do you stay here?"

"I don't know. I told you, I just can't seem to go."

"Rose, what happened? You and Clyde were so happy together."

"We were. We really were happy once. It's hard to remember that sometimes, but we were. Weren't we, Holly?" She moved through the degrees of doubt swiftly.

"I thought so."

"I did, too, and I think Clyde did. It was after we lost the babies that things began to go sour, I guess. But maybe it was before that even. Even before the first baby was born . . ."

"Yes." Holly tried to urge her past that.

". . . born dead," she continued. "It was when I was pregnant with the first baby that Clyde and Iris . . ."

"Yes," Holly said again.

"He told me all about it. It was in the summer. They would meet by the river. I figured it out, I must have been about eight months along, big and bloated and fat, when they started going swimming together. Clyde swore that it was innocent at first. Then when he went one day she was already in the water. She was naked. Don't you know how she must have looked, that beautiful bare body of hers. I was so ugly and all that I could give him from my ugliness was a dead baby."

"Oh, Rose."

"When you saw her she was more beautiful, you said?"

"Iris looked . . ."

". . . more beautiful, you said, more beautiful than ever," Rose insisted.

"Yes."

"I'm glad you couldn't find her, Holly. I'm glad that Clyde won't see her again."

"You should leave him."

"Should I?" Rose's store of anger, contained for years, broke through. "You're a great one for shoulds, aren't you? Well, what do you know about it? You've never lived with a man. You've never had a man, have you, Holly?"

Holly's face tightened. She did not answer. Rose moved toward her and put her arms around her. Holly did not pull away but allowed herself to remain stiffly in her sister's contrite hold.

"I'm sorry. I'm so sorry."

"It's all right, Rose."

The door opened and Clyde entered. Coming upon the sisters as they were, he assumed that they were mourning their parents. He could not have guessed that they mourned themselves.

Clyde had borrowed a car so that he could take Rose and Holly out to Lily's that night. He drove them there, calculating the time so that he could still manage to take his girlfriend Dottie riding later. At the sound of the car's approach several children came running from the house. Rose was the favorite aunt of Lily's children. They hung back and stared shyly at Holly who was a stranger to them. Holly felt herself a stranger not only to the little boys and girl but to her sisters Lily and Poppy also. She studied their faces. Both were as pale as ever. Lily was rigid with control and Poppy appeared stunned and tear-stained. Holly remembered what Rose had said to her about scrutinizing people and she dropped her eyes to her hands, watching them nervously twining. They all stood awkwardly on the porch. Workman and Clyde went off to the barn on the pretext of fixing the tractor. The sisters and children went into the house.

"The funeral will be tomorrow," Lily announced, plunged in, without preamble of any grace, the oldest sister in charge. "The Reverend Fallon is coming from Wichita," she told them. She seemed very pleased and proud."

"But Lily, Daddy was a Catholic," Holly said. She was aware of the looks that Lily, and Rose, even Poppy focused on her. She realized that she must have committed some breach. "Shouldn't we have a priest for Daddy?"

"There will be no Papists at my mother's funeral," Lily stated flatly.

"Lily, Daddy was . . ."

Rose interrupted. "Holly's right as far as she knows, Lily. You can't blame Holly. It's been a long time since she was home."

"I think we all know how long it's been since Holly was home," Lily said.

"I mean that she doesn't know. She couldn't know."

"Know what?" Holly demanded.

"Daddy stopped going to Mass, Holly. Besides, he couldn't really be in the Church after he married Mama. Mama wouldn't convert. You knew that," said Rose.

"Yes, I knew that, but Daddy always went to Mass. I used to go with him," Holly said, remembering early mornings, dark and beautiful and smoky, in big high-ceilinged churches kneeling beside her father.

"I remember that very well, Holly," Lily told her. "But our father stopped attending the Catholic church years ago."

"How long ago?" Holly asked.

"About the time you left," Rose said. "Do you still go, Holly?"

"No."

"The Reverend Fallon is coming at my request and it's a great honor that he's doing us."

The men came in from the barn. Clyde was anxious to be going. He didn't say that he was, but his impatient shiftings and gestures were a clear signal to Rose. She took up her purse and walked to the door. The goodbyes were mercifully quick.

When they were in the car Holly made a request.

"Clyde, I guess you're in a hurry, but I'd like to ask a favor."

He turned his pleasant, still boyish face to her. "Anything I can do, Holly, you know that."

"Would you drive over to the farmhouse? I want to see it."

"I'd be glad to, but there's not much to see. The house is flatter than a pancake."

"I'd just like to see it, Clyde."

"Okay."

It took only a few minutes to get there. Holly got out of the car. The darkness tempered the devastation. She stepped carefully over the scattered debris. Not knowing that Rose was behind her, she jumped when her sister spoke.

"You should see it in the daylight," Rose said.

"It's terrible enough right now."

"They found Mama in the kitchen, what had been the kitchen," Rose told her, gazing over in that direction.

"And Daddy?" Holly asked. Her voice shook.

"Daddy wasn't in the house, Holly."

"Where was he?"

"He was in the car a few hundred yards down the road."

"But I thought that . . ."

"That they were together?"

"Yes."

"I did too," Rose said. "I knew you would. They weren't together, Holly. Daddy was trying to get away."

"Without her?"

"I guess he left her behind in the house," Rose said, not condemning, only answering.

"She wouldn't have gone with him. She wouldn't have gone at all," Holly whispered.

"What did you say?"

"Nothing. Let's go. This is terrible."

They walked back to the car where Clyde waited with the engine running.

"Lily looks a lot like Mama, don't you think?" Rose asked.

"Yes, some. Rose, who is this Reverend Fallon?"

"Nathaniel Fallon. He's a preacher. Came through here about three years ago."

"He's not one of those with the flatbed truck and loudspeakers?"

"Yes. Big, kind of good-looking, dresses in a long black frock coat. He's a real spellbinder. Talks a lot about the end of the world. Armageddon and all that. I think he likes scaring people."

"You've heard him then?"

"Lily took me to one of his revival meetings. She acts like he was Jesus Himself. He's baptized all the kids."

"In the river?" Holly asked.

"Yes."

They were standing beside the car. Clyde rolled down his window and called out to them.

"Can you two gab when we get home?"

"Yes, Clyde," Rose said, deferring to him.

The weather had gone back to winter. It was April but there was new frost on the ground. The graveside harangue of the Reverend Fallon was filled with doom and went on endlessly.

Finally his arms fell to his sides. He bowed his head and the
words ceased. Lily had not once taken her eyes from him. The
two coffins were lowered into the cold earth, side by side. Poppy
sobbed loudly. Rose held Clyde's arm tightly. A thin line of
townspeople and neighbors began to file past, grasping the hands
of the sisters and speaking low and meaningless words. Holly
shivered in her thin gray suit and although she received the same
sympathetic attention as her sisters, she felt somehow shunned.
She was the dark outsider. She had not been one of them when
she lived among them and she was not now in grieving return.

Holly took the first available train back to California. She
managed to obtain a window seat in the crowded car. She sat
looking out through the faintly dirty glass and thought of her
father. This land that she was passing over, that they had
traveled together, that he had loved and hoped to leave some
trace upon, brought him fiercely back to her. At the funeral there
had been nothing of him or his life. There had been only wrong
words rained down like clods of earth onto the boxes of bones,
and she had been chilled and numbed by them. Now she could
remember him and feel the intensity of her loss. He was gone. He
would be gone tomorrow and the day after that. For all the rest
of her life she would be without him. Daddy was dead. Mama,
too. His death left an aching void, but her mother's she did not
feel. Her memories of her mother were of a haunting, ice-white
harridan. They did not dispel the Reverend Fallon's howling or
the cold aura of the grave but instead enhanced them. It was late
in the day. The sky was cloud-streaked and on the ground below
was Holly's reflective, silver-streaking, westbound train.

Chapter Ten

The sedan screeched to a stop, bumping wildly up onto the shoulder of the road. The driver looked into his rearview mirror in disbelief. He watched as the slender figure ran toward his car. When he'd first seen the sailor with the outstretched thumb standing on the embankment, he'd decided to pass by. He wasn't unpatriotic, only in a hurry. He had to be in Portland before five o'clock. He had a long way to go yet. This green Washington countryside extended forever. He hadn't time to pick up the young sailor, but something in the stance had made him look again. The way the uniform draped the body, the set of the small profile, made him halt. He was sure now. The sailor was running toward his car and long blond hair was escaping from under the hat.

Iris opened the car door and smiled in at him. He was a big-bellied, balding man, but not old. He wasn't wearing a jacket and puffy arms came from his short-sleeved shirt. He dazedly returned her smile and said, "Hop in, swabbie."

Iris laughed. "Thanks for the lift."

"Say, couldn't you get into trouble wearing that?" he asked.

She was beside him, the door shut. "I don't know. I thought it'd be fun," she said.

She was a gorgeous girl, he was thinking, and the uniform only made her more attractive. She'd look great in a satin negligee, no doubt about it, but that white sailor suit, the fit of it, and the incongruity of her in it was a startling and irresistible combination. He could almost feel the stiff starchy material against her soft warm skin.

"Where're you headed?" he asked her.

She smiled at him. "Where you headed?"

"Portland," he answered.

"So am I," she decided.

"Well now, that's just great," he said. "Name's Lewis."

"Is that your first or last name?" Iris asked.

"Any way you want it, honey," he told her and put his fat, dimpled hand on her knee. "What's your name?"

"Iris."

"Pretty name." He moved his hand up her thigh. "For a real pretty girl."

"Thanks, Lewis." She placed her hand over his, stopping its progress. She turned it upward and caressingly scratched his palm with her long red nails, nails painted to the moons and then left pearly white and bare on the crescents. "It's a long way to Portland."

"You asking me to slow up a little?"

"I love it slow, Lewis. How about you?"

"Any way you want it, honey."

"I want it in Portland. I've never had it there before," she said, and smiled, scratching harder up his fleshy arm.

"You're some little hellcat, aren't you?"

"You'll find out. In Portland."

He jammed his foot on the accelerator. He'd been in a hurry before, but now hurry wasn't the word for it. He couldn't get to Portland fast enough. He was figuring. He'd drop off the papers at Fidelity Trust by five and then get a motel room. He might not even have to buy her dinner.

Iris curled up in the seat and closed her eyes. He looked over at her. She breathed through slightly parted, moist red lips. Her chest gently rose and fell. He pictured her walking into the room that he would get for them. She'd pull her jumper off over her head. He could just see her breasts, full and firm, perfect handfuls. He couldn't wait. He reached over and rubbed across them. She opened her eyes.

"Portland," she murmured and closed them again.

They reached the city limit at four-forty-five. By ten minutes to the hour he had parked in front of the Fidelity building.

"Honey," he said. "I've got to make a quick stop here."

She yawned and stretched. "Are we in Portland?"

"Yeah," he answered. He was riffling through some papers stacked in the back seat. "I'll be right back. I've got to have these at the office before they close today."

"When do they close, Lewis?"

"Five o'clock. Soon," he told her. "And if I don't get these papers up there I'll lose my job."

"Oh, they wouldn't fire an important man like you, would they?"

"Well . . ." he hesitated, caught between pride and truth.

"Give me a kiss goodbye," she said slowly.

He dropped the papers and lunged for her. His tongue was soft and thick. She sucked it deeper into her mouth. He groaned, greedily moving his hands down her body, unbuttoning the front of her sailor pants.

"Shouldn't you get going?" she whispered to him.

"No . . . no."

"But your papers . . . your job."

He drew back from her.

"Yeah, that's right." He picked up the papers. "Geez, I hope I can walk. Look what you've done to me." He hitched his trousers.

"Hurry back," she said sweetly.

"Don't you move, honey."

She watched his fast waddle into the building and she smiled, knowing he'd be too late.

He went to the bank of elevators and pressed the button. He waited. No car came. He listened for the sound of cranking cables. Nothing. He hurried over to the stairs. The office was four flights up. He started to climb. Panting for breath, he rushed down the hall to the door marked Fidelity Trust and turned the knob. It was locked. He wrenched at it. He checked his watch. It was a quarter after five. He'd lost his job. But when he thought of her waiting for him, he didn't mind. There'd be other jobs. There'd never be another girl like this one.

Out on the street he couldn't see her in the car. He thought that she might have gone back to sleep. Oh, how he'd wake her up. He was breathing heavily still. She wasn't in the front seat. He looked in back. She was gone. He threw down the papers and the wind scattered them along the street. What did he care now, he thought. He'd lost his job and he'd lost her, too. She'd played him for a sucker, taken him for a ride to Portland, and more than that, he felt. She wanted to make a fool of him. Somewhere she was laughing at him. He slid heavily in behind the wheel. It was a company car. It'd be taken from him. He puffed and wheezed, held his heart. Iris. Iris, he thought. She'd been a dream. A dream and a nightmare.

Iris had gone into a nearby drugstore. She went to the ladies room there and changed into the dress she carried with her. She brushed her hair out before the mirror and admired herself. At the fountain she drank a Coke from a straw and swung her legs from the high stool. The soda jerk was young, only sixteen or seventeen, but cute, Iris thought.

"Would you like anything else?" he asked. "A sundae or something?"

"I'd love a sundae." She paused. "But I don't have enough for one."

"It's on me," he ventured.

"Oh no, I couldn't, really. I couldn't let you." She stammered slightly and blushed.

"Aw c'mon. Chocolate or vanilla?"

She looked down. Then, from under her long lashes, she gazed up at him adoringly. "Do you have strawberry?"

"Sure."

"You're so sweet," she said.

Iris noticed that his hands shook when he brought her the ice cream. He stood back smiling. She took a spoonful and licked the excess from her lips, running her tongue slowly, then pouting prettily.

"It's so good. I'm just going to hate it when it's all gone."

"I can get you more," he said.

"You can? Really? Oh, you're so sweet."

Iris had the faculty of reflection. She could mirror a gross and lascivious man like Lewis, be the embodiment of his prurient fantasies, or become the pure, almost unattainable, pin-up girl for this boy named Danny. Iris personified men's desires. Whatever they wished, she could be. She realized their dreams and she took from them what she needed. During the last two years in Washington many men had left money by her bed, given her jewelry or clothes. Sailors had bought her drinks at bars and brought her strange trinkets from the ports where their ships docked. She'd drained Seattle dry, reached her end there, she knew. She decided that she'd stay in Portland for a few hours and make a trade with Danny for his strawberry ice cream. She'd bartered for more, but she liked the looks of this boy. She ate the last dripping mouthful and sucked the spoon, meeting his eyes.

"Could you stay until I get off?" Danny asked.

"Maybe," she said. "Maybe not," she teased, the consummate vacillating virgin.

"It's only an hour," he told her. "Please," he begged.

Iris liked that. His eyes were dark and soft, like Holly's, she thought. Funny that she'd think of her sister now. When she was finished with Danny she'd head straight for Los Angeles, she decided. She couldn't have said why, but she wanted to see Holly again. "Okay, I'll wait," she told Danny and she stopped spinning on the stool.

Holly had been back from Kansas for a week. On the surface her life easily resumed, falling into its usual pattern, but beneath that she was deeply affected by what had happened within her family, far more deeply than she realized.

At the studio a John Garfield movie had started production. She began going daily to the sound stage where it was being shot. Arnie Ross wasn't in the office much and he didn't miss her. No one on the stage seemed to mind her presence. She was unobtrusive. She kept back but watched Garfield unceasingly in a way that made those who noticed her smile. They assumed that she had a crush, that she was one in a long line of star-struck secretaries, but if they had given her more than a quick indulgent glance they might have judged otherwise. Holly wasn't infatuated with the actor. He reminded her of her father. He had the same small stature, the same deeply sensitive and darkly sad, almost tortured, face. There was one man who observed Holly as closely as she observed the star, but she was completely unaware of him. He leaned his long frame against a wall or sprawled in a tall director's chair, smoked, and stared at her. He appeared to have no function on the set. He didn't operate a camera or a crane. He didn't pull cables or push scenery. Yet he gave the impression of belonging. Holly fascinated him. When she came on stage his gray eyes altered. When she left, he slumped and seemed to sleep. He spoke to no one and no one spoke to him.

After several days of watching, he decided he would approach Holly. He had done some investigating, learned her name, who she worked for, her age, and other vital statistics from her personnel file. He couldn't get her off his mind. What he knew about her wasn't enough. He wanted to hear her voice. Curiously eager to see what might be in her eyes when she looked at him, he had planned how he would walk over and speak to her, but all his plans were for nothing. She didn't show up on the set. It was the first day she had missed in a week. When she didn't appear the idea of going to look for her occurred to him. He had grown so used to the sight of her, and had come to expect, anticipate, her arrival. His feeling of disappointment surprised him, she didn't even know of his existence and now she never would. The thought of it stabbed at him. The chance of meeting her had slipped away from him. Angrily, he stubbed out his cigarette and immediately lit another. He wouldn't go searching for her, and if she came back tomorrow would he take the chance then and approach her? Probably not. He was hopeless, and hopelessly he raged at himself.

Holly had no idea that she would be missed. She hadn't gone to the set as she usually did because of a phone call she'd received just before lunch. The call was from Iris. Her voice had come over the wire to Holly, rare but instantly recognizable. She said that she had called the school first and someone there had told her that Holly Calder had taken a job at Warner Brothers. Holly had asked Iris if she was in Los Angeles. The connection had sounded close. Iris said she was at a phone booth on a corner in Hollywood. Her bus for San Diego was leaving in two hours. Holly told her she would meet her, that she had something to tell her. Iris incuriously agreed and gave the intersection where she was. Hollywood and Highland, she had said, and hung up.

Holly pleaded a headache to Arnie Ross and got the rest of the day off. She took a bus to Iris's corner, saw her standing there, and thought for a moment of not getting off, of riding past. Her sister wore a short white dress that displayed her long legs, accentuated her small waist, and outlined her full bust. Holly reached up and pulled the cord. The bus stopped. Iris was still impossible to resist. She waved at Holly and came bouncing, swishing, toward her, turning every head on the street.

"Hi, Hol. Long time no see."

"Hello, Iris."

"Will you buy me lunch, big sister?"

"Yes, of course I will."

"I'm starving. I saw a restaurant just down the street."

"Lead the way," Holly said.

"Swell."

They walked the half-block to the restaurant and received three whistles from passing cars before they were inside. They were seated at a small table by a window. Iris looked out at the traffic for a time and finally shifted her gaze to Holly. She didn't speak. Holly had the strange sensation that it was her turn, and just as she had when they were children and she was given a chance to play in a game, she began too quickly.

"Iris, there's something I have to tell you. I'm afraid it's bad news," she said.

The waitress came to take their order. Holly asked for coffee. Iris chose the blue-plate special. When the waitress had gone Holly expected that Iris would ask what the bad news was, but she didn't.

"It's very bad news, I'm afraid," she said. "Iris, Mama and Daddy are dead."

"Dead? They're both dead?"

"Yes. They were killed in a tornado. It was over a week ago. I tried to call you. All I knew was what you'd told me three years ago, that you were going to Washington, but you never wrote. I made call after call. To Seattle and even Tacoma."

"I'd been in Seattle but about a week ago I started hitching south," she said smoothly.

"I'm sorry that I couldn't reach you. It's terrible that you didn't know and couldn't get to the funeral. I'm sorry. I'm sorry," she kept repeating it, thinking that saying it would make it so, but she didn't feel sorry because she didn't feel that Iris was.

"It's too bad about Mama and Daddy, but, Hol, you know how it is, how it's been with me. I hadn't seen them or talked to them in what? Four years? Five? Who can keep track? It's too bad, it really is, but what am I supposed to do? Am I supposed to cry? I don't know. I don't feel like crying."

"Then you shouldn't, I guess."

"Did you?" Iris asked.

The waitress arrived with the food. Iris began to eat. Holly drank some coffee. It was scalding hot and it burned her tongue. She felt tears rising to her eyes.

"I figure it this way, Hol, we're a lot more alike than people might think. We both got out of Kansas just as soon as we could. I sure didn't spend any time looking back. I don't think you did either. So I'm not crying now," she said and stopped. Then she asked again. "Did you cry?"

"No, not when I was there, not at the funeral. I didn't feel much of anything until I got on the train to come back here. On the train I cried."

"I'll tell you, the only way that you'd get me back to Kansas would be for my own funeral. I'd have to be dead to go back there. I mean, I'd have to be shipped in a box. And even at that it'd be a rotten trick to play on me. I can think of a lot of other places I'd rather be buried."

Holly almost physically flinched at her sister's callousness. There wasn't a person on earth that she felt less like than Iris. It disturbed her that there might be any such similarity as Iris had suggested. She wanted no more talk of the past.

"So you're going to San Diego?"

"Yeah."

"Why there?" Holly asked.

"I might have a job there."

"What kind of job?"

"Singing with this band."

"You did some singing in Washington then?"

"No, I didn't get around to it up there, but this guy, this sax player I met in Seattle, he told me about this band in San Diego. It's not real great. I mean, it's not the Dorseys' or Goodman's. They travel around California in a bus. This guy, this sax player, he says he can get me in. We'll see."

"Well, good luck, Iris. I hope it works out."

"Yeah," she said. Her plate was clean. "That was good. I was hungry."

"Iris, if you need some money . . ."

"I can always use a few extra bucks."

Holly opened her purse. She handed Iris some bills.

"Thanks, Hol."

Holly had hoped to avoid the subject, but she was compelled to put the question to her sister. Much as she wanted to, she couldn't let it go unasked.

"Iris, there's something . . . something that I . . ." She didn't know how to frame it, put it neatly. It was such an untidy topic, the sort that she disliked most. "There's something I want to ask you," she said, but she didn't really.

"Yeah, what is it?"

"When I was back in Kansas . . ." she started. God, she'd put them back in Kansas again, she thought. "Rose told me . . . something."

"Good old Rose. She's still there, huh?"

"Yes. And Lily. And Poppy, too."

"Yeah, it figures they would be. I wonder what kind of pie they have here. I'd love some cherry pie."

"Iris, Rose told me that you and Clyde . . ."

"Clyde? Who's Clyde?" Iris asked. She was searching for their waitress. She caught her eye and motioned her over to the table. "Do you have cherry pie?" she asked.

"Yes, miss," the waitress said.

"I'd like some, a real big piece with ice cream."

"Anything for you, miss?" the waitress asked Holly.

"No, thank you."

The waitress left.

"Clyde is Rose's husband," Holly told Iris.

"Oh yeah, Clyde. I remember Clyde. We used to go swimming together," she laughed. "That's not all we did. Yeah, I remember him now. He was a lot of fun. Is he still with Rose?"

"Yes, I guess you'd say he was."

"I know what you mean," she smiled. "Clyde wanted me to run off with him. He wanted that in the worst way. He cried like a baby when I told him I wouldn't."

"Why didn't you? Because of Rose?"

"Rose? No. It was just that Clyde couldn't have taken me any-where that I couldn't have gotten to on my own."

The waitress came and set the pie down in front of Iris. She put the bill on the table, too, nearer to Holly. Iris took a bite of pie.

"Oh, that's good," she said. "You should have some."

"I don't want any."

"That's how you stay so thin. I like that suit, Hol. When you're thin you can wear those tailored, shoulder-pad numbers. How do you think I'd look in it?" Iris asked.

"Wonderful, I'm sure."

"Yeah? Well, maybe I'll get myself one like it."

Holly sat and watched her sister devour the pie. Soon all that was left were a few crumbs and a small pool of melted ice cream marbled with thick red cherry syrup. Iris touched her finger into the ice cream, pressed it wetly on the crumbs, then licked it. She looked at Holly.

"Hey, did you want to ask me something about Clyde?"

"No, nothing."

Iris shrugged. Silence ensued. Holly picked up the check.

"Time to go, I guess," Holly said.

"Yeah."

After they left the restaurant they stood on the street saying goodbye like two people who would be seeing one another tomorrow or like strangers come together for a brief time who would never meet again.

Iris walked away, letting the encounter go, and did not think of it again. Holly could not forget it. She was frightened. She had realized at last that her sister had no feelings. She was aware of her own avoidance of emotions, but she believed she possessed them. Still, if she hid from them so well, how different could she seem from Iris who had none?

The next day Holly didn't get over to the Garfield set until late in the afternoon. The stage was chaotic, in upheaval. There were no actors visible. The scenery was being struck. She took in the activity and wondered what it meant. She was about to leave when someone spoke to her.

"Hello," he said. He wasn't sure why he'd waited, but he had and she'd come. He felt no reluctance toward her, none of his normal reserve. Her appearance was like a reprieve. "You're not going already?" he asked.

He was a very tall, blond man. She thought that she must have seen him before. "Yes," she said, but then asked, "What's happened?"

"They're moving to Stage Eighteen," he told her. "If you'd been here yesterday you would have heard about it."

"How did you know that I didn't . . . that I wasn't here yesterday?"

"I watched for you . . ." He started to use her name, but thought better of it. "I'm Paul Sorenson."

"Holly Calder."

Two stagehands pushing a huge antique sideboard brushed close to them. Holly backed up and tripped over a cable. He took her by the arm to steady her.

"It's a little hectic in here. Why don't we go outside, Holly?"

"I was leaving. I'll just be going now," she said.

"I was leaving too," he said. "I'd decided I couldn't wait any longer for you."

They walked outside together. It was bright and quiet after the wild hustling darkness of the sound stage. Holly took a deep breath. He was standing very near her. He was even taller and blonder in the sunlight, she thought.

"Were you really waiting for me?" she asked.

"Yes. Do you have to go back to your office?" he asked her.

She thought he might offer to walk her there. "No," she answered.

"Arnie Ross is certainly no slavedriver," he said.

"How did you know I worked for him?"

He smiled at her. "I've made inquiries about you."

"Why?"

"I saw you on the set day after day. You interested me."

"I see."

"Are you angry?" he asked.

"No."

"It's difficult to tell with you," he observed. "Is John Garfield a favorite of yours?"

She didn't answer the question, but said, "I hope I didn't bother anyone on the set."

"Of course not," he told her. "Is he?"

"What?"

"Is John Garfield a favorite of yours?"

"Yes, I guess he is. He reminds me of someone."

"Boyfriend?" he asked.

She looked down at her hands.

"Army? Navy? Marines? Air Force?" he asked.

"No," she said.

"What are you answering no to?" Paul asked. "Is this fellow in the Coast Guard?"

"No, I don't have a boyfriend."

"Good, then he's not the John Garfield lookalike. I'm glad," he said. "Would you have dinner with me?"

"Tonight?"

"Yes, right now. Is it too early for you?" he asked.

"No, but . . ."

"Great, let's go. My car's right over here."

"Wait, I don't even know you."

"What do you want to know? What kind of knowledge is required before Holly Calder dines with someone?"

"I think I'd better be going."

"No, really. I'm serious. What do you want to know about me? I don't make that offer to everyone," he said. "My name is Paul Sorenson. You know that. I'm a writer."

"Paul Sorenson, of course. You wrote the script for this film. I read it."

"Did you like it?"

"Very much," she said.

"That answer entitles you to a free dinner."

She looked up at him and laughed. She liked his face and she wanted to go with him. The thought of getting into his car, riding beside him, sharing a meal with him, appealed to her. Suddenly she couldn't face going home alone another night, sitting and listening to Laurette Sparks click past.

"All right," she said. "Let's go."

He paused. "Are you sure there's nothing else you want to know about me?"

"I think I know enough."

He drove to a very beautiful French restaurant in Hollywood. It looked like a miniature château, Marie Antoinette's Trianon, nestled among the more obvious, tinsel attractions on Sunset Boulevard. There were only five tables in the dining room. As soon as they were seated at one of them, Paul asked her a question.

"If John Garfield doesn't remind you of a boyfriend, who does he remind you of?"

"My father," she answered. It was easy to answer him, but difficult to ask him any questions.

The dinner was elegantly and elaborately served to them. With each course they seemed to find less and less to say. The conversation lagged. Holly felt him staring at her. She was uncomfortable. She sipped her brandy, swirled the liquid in the crystal snifter and watched the candlelight leap through it. Paul sensed her feelings, shared them. They didn't linger long in that lovely place.

They were walking the block to his car when a young soldier staggered up the street toward them. He halted, working hard to focus.

"How come you're not in uniform, buddy?" he asked Paul. "How come, I'm asking you?"

"I don't think that's your concern," Paul said reasonably. "You're in uniform and that's what should matter to you, soldier."

The soldier grabbed at the lapel of Paul's tweed jacket and missed. "You're a lousy rotten draft dodger, that's what you are!"

Paul took him by the shoulders. He towered over the soldier, whose head was bobbing loosely from side to side. He turned him back in the direction he had been going, handling him gently.

"You'd better be moving on now. Don't let the MPs see you."

"Lousy rotten draft dodger!" the soldier screamed one last drunken and defiant time.

Neither Holly nor Paul appeared to hear. They didn't speak until they were inside Paul's car.

"I'm sorry that had to happen," he said. He put the key in the ignition. He rested his hands on the steering wheel and made no move to start the engine.

"I'm sorry, too," Holly said.

"Don't you want to ask me?"

"Ask you what?"

"What the kid asked. Don't you want to know why I'm not serving my country?"

"I'm sure there are reasons," she said, not wanting to ask him anything.

"Holly, how old do you think I am?"

"I don't know."

"Will you ask me? Will you say, 'Paul, how old are you?'
Will you do that for me, Holly?"

"How old are you?" she asked unwillingly.

"Finally a question, under duress, but a question. Do you know
that all through dinner you never asked me one thing about
myself? I guess you really meant it when you said you knew
enough about me. Do you care how old I am? Before I answer,
I'd like to know, do you care?"

"I don't know what you want from me, Paul."

"I'm not sure I know either. I know that I want something
and it's the first time I have in a very long time. I'm forty, nearly
twenty years older than you, Holly. I'm old enough to be your
father. I'm old enough to have been that soldier's father. You
must know that you're the reason that kid said what he did."

"I was the reason?"

"Yes, I had a girl and he didn't. That uniform of his was supposed to get him a girl. So what was I doing, a civilian, with you?
He was the one who was supposed to have you. And do you
know what? He's right, absolutely right. You should have been
with him tonight, Holly. Not me. You shouldn't have been with
me. You'd rather have been with him, wouldn't you?"

"No," she said. Her next words came rapidly. She couldn't
have stopped them if she'd wanted to, and she didn't. It was a
relief to say them, to say all that she had held inside herself,
things that she never thought she would say to this man or anyone else. "Everywhere I go there are little boys like that one,
sailors and soldiers, all the little boys in their uniforms. They call
out to me. They ask me to go dancing. Some of them even
follow me down the street. They are so sweet and sad and they
scare me so much. I can't touch them. I can't. I know they need
to be touched, but I can't. And I can't let them touch me. There
are lots of girls for them. There's Iris. And Laurette. Lots and
lots of girls. But I can't. Don't they know that? Can't they see
that? Don't they know what I am? What I'm not? . . . I'm not
for them."

There was no movement, not he toward her, not she toward
him, but they were in each other's arms.

PART FOUR

❀

POPPY

❀

Chapter Eleven

❀

Kansas, 1943 . . .

It had been two months since the tornado swept down upon the farm of Clay and Jane Calder, killing them, each in the same but strangely separate way. Poppy, the youngest sister, seemed most orphaned. At first Poppy had grieved in passive acceptance, but as the weeks passed after the funeral a disbelief born of dispossession and sharp loneliness had taken hold of her. She began mentally to deny her mother's death. Staying at Lily's she was kept superficially occupied with the care of the children and the house during the days, but at night, after Lily had finished reading from her Bible and everyone else slept, Poppy would go searching for the only true companion she had ever known, her mother. And in the darkness, amidst the destruction, she had faith that she found her. Poppy ceased to mourn, becoming convinced that she had not been left alone and deserted. She told no one of these visitations, these nocturnal communions with her mother who was dead to all but her.

Poppy was pitied by those living around her and hugely misunderstood by them, too. While she wandered sleepless in denial of death, they thought that she was slowly but steadily abandoning life and living. Lily feared that her sister was allowing demons to take possession of her. She believed she had witnessed this before. Lily had never forgotten Jasmine's death and the events surrounding it, Poppy's nightmares of the flaming-faced man and the first of her fits. She spoke often of that time to Poppy, who could not remember it. Lily was certain that the Devil had come to her family then. She had been chosen to be saved and she felt now that she was all that stood between Poppy and an end like Jasmine's. Life was cruel, Lily had learned, but it must be suffered. Only God could grant surcease. God had taken their mother and father, leaving Poppy to her care, Lily believed. She intended that Poppy know this and begin a life free from sin. Her demons would be exorcised. Lily was merciless in the pursuit of her sister's deliverance.

Poppy was washing the dishes from breakfast. Beneath her always moist eyes were heavy half-circles, dark rainbows colored black, purple, and deep blue. She stared down unseeing, wearily inconscient, into the dishpan. The reddened hands that worked there were her own but she did not recognize them. Lily entered the kitchen. Only from her zealot's viewpoint could this pathetic girl be seen as a child of the Devil. She had to say her name three times before Poppy heard.

". . . Poppy."

"Yes, Lily," she answered belatedly but obediently.

"Poppy, the Reverend is coming tomorrow," she said. Lily called the preacher named Fallon simply "the Reverend." There was such fealty in her tone that the title was almost redundant. "He will be baptizing Matthew."

Matthew was Lily's youngest child, fat and fair, barely past babyhood. He was very attached to his Auntie Pop. He loved her and if there was anyone that Poppy could possibly have loved in her sister's house, it was Matthew. Still, he was slightly unreal to her, not like a little boy but a big and breathing doll.

"Tomorrow," Poppy said, knowing that Matthew feared the coming day. "Saturday."

"Yes, tomorrow is Saturday," Lily affirmed impatiently. "I think it would be wonderful if you were to be baptized then, too."

Poppy could see the dishwater now. Its surface had turned shiny with grease. All the white suds had evaporated, crushed by the heavy iron skillets. Lily was forever talking baptism to her and it frightened her more than it did little Matthew. She could feel the panic rising up inside herself, a pure and pulsing dread. Sometimes she did not hear Lily, but this morning she was hearing and she was afraid.

"I . . . I don't want to," she said.

Lily took her sister's refusal as proof of her demonic affiliation. "You should be baptized. You know that. You should beg to be. You should go down on your knees to the Reverend and beg," she told Poppy. The Reverend Fallon was a Jehovah-like figure to Lily, the dominating presence in her obsessed world. For many years religion had been her boon and backbone, her mainstay, but with the death of her parents and the advent of the Reverend, Lily had become sealed in zealotry. "You should beg the Reverend."

"I don't . . . want to," Poppy whispered.

"You're going to burn," Lily told her. Her voice did not change. She might have been saying that there was a spot of egg yolk missed in the washing of a dish, so quietly and harmlessly did she deliver her deadly speech. "You'll burn. When you die you'll burn for all eternity in the fires of Hell. Just like our sister Jasmine. She's burning right now, Poppy. And you will, too."

"Don't say that to me, Lily," Poppy pleaded.

The water was cold and brown, slippery, clinging to her hands. She couldn't wait to fling it out in the yard. She wanted to do that now, but Lily blocked her path. She couldn't get past her sister. Poppy had no wish to be baptized, to be thrown backward into the dark green water of the river. From her mother's stories she knew that her grandmother had died in that flooding river water. She had nearly died there herself the night the bridge had collapsed. She had been running away from Lily's that night. Lily had never understood her fears. She couldn't tell Lily of her terror.

"Mama wanted you to be baptized," Lily was saying. "One day last winter we were sitting in the kitchen and I think Mama had some vision, a notion that she was going to die soon. She was worried most about leaving you, Poppy." The bitterness in Lily's voice was imperceptible. "I told Mama I wanted you to be saved and she said to me that she wanted that, too." Lily saw nothing sinful in using their dead mother to get Poppy to the river. It must be done and she would use any device to accomplish it. She would even have lied. And she was lying.

Poppy wiped her hands on the dishrag. "Mama wanted me to be baptized," she repeated after her sister.

"Yes. Oh, Poppy, the glory of it, the way that you will feel!"

"How will I feel, Lily?"

"You'll be cleansed." Lily believed devoutly what she was telling Poppy. She wanted her to be imbued with the spirit of Jesus Christ as she herself was. She wanted her to be blessed as she believed she was. "You will know then the true meaning. You will be able to see, so clearly. You won't be lost any longer. You can begin again, a new life, purged, free from sin. You can be reborn, Poppy. And you'll be so happy. You'll be happy, I promise you. Mama wanted it. She wanted you to know Jesus. She wanted you to love Him. And He will love you in return. He'll never leave you. He'll be with you always. You will be His child, Poppy."

"I'm Mama's child," Poppy said and knew that she shouldn't have.

"Mama is gone. You're no one's child now." Lily told her, knowing the raw and tender place where pressure could be applied to hurtfully persuade her. Lily was crusading to save her sister from the Devil, to snatch her away and bring her to the Lord. "You belong to no one, but you could be His. Jesus will guide you and protect you and love you all your days on this earth and beyond. He will."

"Yes," Poppy said, wanting to stop Lily's words, to be away from her, and to take the filthy dishwater outside. She thought she would talk with her mother in the night. For now, she would say yes to Lily. And tomorrow she could say no if Mama told her to.

"You will then?" Lily asked. "You'll be baptized on Saturday?"

"Yes," Poppy answered and she lifted the dishpan. Some water sloshed over the rim onto her hand. She hated the feel of it. She already regretted saying yes to Lily, but Mama would make it right. She always had before.

That night she could not find her mother. She walked the miles to the dark wreckage of the farmhouse and went through the destroyed rooms, thinking this was the porch, this the parlor, and this Mama's room, and this was her own, but her mother was nowhere to be seen. There was no moon that night and it was very black. She stumbled over the ripped pieces of wood and crushed mortar. She came to the kitchen, cleared a small space on the floor, and sat down to watch for her mother. She had begun coming here at night just after the funeral. She hadn't been able to sleep at Lily's and she'd felt closer to her mother here. One night Mama had appeared to her and had spoken to her, not as some terrible apparition with a declaration from the grave, but as her mother, lifelike, softly answering her questions and comforting her. She had kept at a distance, though, and when Poppy had gone too near she had retreated into the ruins and faded from sight. Poppy missed so much being held in Mama's arms. She had hoped each night that it would happen, but it hadn't, and now she could not even see her. There was no pale presence beside a far and caved-in wall, no whispery words so hauntingly difficult to hear. There was only silence and debris. She waited and waited for her, wondering if her mother was angry with her. A loose brick fell. Poppy jumped at the sound. Mama came noiselessly, she knew. She was alone. And the day of her baptism was dawning.

It was one in a long daisy chain of Kansas summer days, white-hot, yellow-centered, humid, melting, and stubbornly enduring. The Reverend preached his sermon from the river bank. The congregation listened and sweated, oozing faith and damp reverence from their pores. Several people were to be baptized that day and they were gathered in a group apart. Poppy stood with them and held tightly to Matthew's hand. The little boy watched round-eyed as the man in the black suit evangelized, waving his arms, shouting out words. Matthew could see his family, his mother, brothers, and sister. Only his father was not there, but the big man who spoke reminded Matthew of him. He looked like him, tall and towering, his face so far up in the sky like a thunder cloud, but his father never raised his voice as this man did. Matthew could barely recall his father speaking at all.

Reverend Fallon concluded his preaching. He removed his jacket. His white shirt was wet through and it clung to his undershirt and the flesh of his arms and shoulders. Poppy was aware of the way his chest bulged and how his black hair crept thickly up his broad neck. He was rolling up his shirt sleeves, showing hands and arms covered with that same dark hair. He walked over to their group and Poppy prayed that he would not choose her first. She was terrified of him and of the water where he would take her.

He selected an older woman who wore a heavy dress, floral-patterned, red hibiscuses with bright green pistils spreading all across her body. They waded together into the river. The current was slow and sluggish. The water was to the woman's waist but only just past the huge holy man's knees. He took her by the shoulders. She faced him, without will, totally given up to him and to God. He guided her down and held her under. He said words, lowly for the first time, and Poppy could not hear them, but she knew what the words were. He lifted the woman, who emerged spewing warm water. They embraced, it seemed, and she came from the river saved, wringing the water from her red dress.

Matthew cried when the Reverend approached him. He grasped at Poppy. They were the last two. The little boy wailed and burrowed his face against his aunt's legs. Poppy stood, not holding him and not pushing him away either. The Reverend took him up in his arms. Matthew struggled, sobbed, fought to be free. Once in the water he calmed. He let himself be baptized with no comprehension of the ritual. He submitted in childlike fashion and afterward, shaking water from himself like a hose-sprayed pup, was joyously reunited with his family, but he looked for his Auntie Pop.

It would end with Poppy. The Reverend stood before her. He waited while she removed her shoes and short white socks. It felt good to her to have them off, but she was embarrassed to leave them behind. He was leading her to the river, into the river, and the water was the same temperature as the still air, warm, like blood. Her dress was floating up around her and she modestly pressed it down to her sides, but it would rise up again where she did not hold it. The water was wetting her panties, seeping up through the cotton, a soft but insistent invasion. The Reverend took her deeper than he had the others. He appeared to her to be in a trance. His eyes were unfocused, glazed black and blank. He seemed not to see her, but he touched her. He placed his hands upon her. The wet skirt of her dress rippled up around his fingers, waveringly, timidly tempting. He brought his hands down, caressing her, cradling her narrow hips beneath the water where no one could see. She was dizzily falling backward. Forever he held her under with only his hands solidly supporting and restraining her. In this murky liquid realm his hands were her salvation and they were treacherous stricture, too. Then she was upright, breathing air and viewing sky. His stare was focused now, upon her, her heaving chest and her nipples erect against her river-wet dress.

It came upon him quickly, as it usually did, a great and surging irreversible wave. The damp and milk-white skin of her throat, the tiny and hard twin apophyses showing through her sodden bodice, aroused him. He had experienced this feeling many times and long ago had reconciled himself to it, made it an extension of his faith and his mission. His past apprehension of woman parishioners and his present desire for this one were part of his piety. It was not apostasy, but devout duty. He turned from her now, for the moment. She followed him from the river. She was so easily led.

With the baptisms done the crowd was rapidly dispersing. The river side was transformed from sacred carnival to deserted country dusk. Lily and the children were hurrying back to the farm to make preparations. The Reverend was coming for supper that evening, Lily's honored guest. They had called out to Poppy several times before they left. None of them had noticed where she'd gone, but they expected she'd be coming along behind them. Only Matthew really missed her and wanted to wait longer for her, but his mother had hustled him homeward.

Poppy had run to the old abandoned boathouse around the river's bend. She hadn't planned on stopping there but it was so quiet and peaceful that she had. She'd pushed open the rusty-hinged door, looked all around, and stepped inside. She thought she might sleep. She felt exhausted. There was none of the joy that Lily had promised. She did not feel like Christ's child, but terribly alone. Her mother had not come to her and she was afraid that she would never come again. She was more lost than ever. She curled up on the floor in a corner and closed her eyes. She shivered and shook, tried to find refuge in sleep, not even hoping for pretty dreams, but wanting only blind and numb slumber.

The door creaked and thin streams of twilight penetrated the shadows where she lay. She opened her eyes.

"Who is it?" she asked, knowing. Some part of her had expected him.

"It's Reverend Fallon," he told her. It was very dark, but he could discern her, white, wet, and palely amorphous, waiting for him. "Is there anything the matter, child?" he asked and crossed to her corner.

She saw that he carried her shoes and socks. She had forgotten them and now she drew her bare feet up under her, hiding them. "No," she answered. She slid back further. "I only wanted to be by myself for a little," she said. It was true and it was not.

"That's fine. Fine," he said and set her shoes and socks down beside her. "This day you began anew. Time for reflection is needed. I know what it meant to you to be baptized."

"You do?" she asked. And she wanted to ask him what it had meant, what it should have meant to her. Of all the ceremony she remembered best and felt most his hands. There were things in his touch that she did not understand but that moved her. He and the ritual drowning he had perpetrated were muddled and mixed, inseparable and unfathomable both. She was shaken and stirred, ignorant of the forces claiming her.

"I know," he said. He kneeled down and pushed back a wet strand of hair from her pale and vulnerable throat. "I know."

"Reverend, I want to believe. I want to belong . . . to Jesus," she told him.

"I know that you do, child. That's why I'm here," he said. He ran his fingers down her throat. "You're wet still." He rested his hands on her shoulders, crushing the short lace cap sleeves. "Your dress, too."

She dropped her head and turned it, accidentally but with some unconscious purpose grazing his hand with her lips. He was nearer now than when he had held her in the water to cleanse her sins. She did not move away from him. It wasn't wrong that they should be like this, she thought. He lowered his hands to her breasts, held them cupped. She couldn't think that it was wrong, that he would do wrong things to her. She looked up into his eyes with utter trust in what he said he was.

"Reverend . . ."

"Be still, child," he said.

Soon, she thought, he would be holding her the way that Mama had. This must be what Lily had meant. This was what came with baptism, the blessed sense of belonging, of being a child of

Jesus. She was eager for it. The Reverend was unbuttoning the front of her dress and parting it, pulling it from her. She sat before him in nothing but her damp cotton panties. He touched her bare skin. It was like a healing being performed, a laying on of hands. He bent his head and kissed her. She watched his black head going from one breast to the other. He backed away. Her nipples were red and glistening from his mouth. She stared down at them. They looked and felt as they never had. He lifted her face.

"How many boys have done that to you?" he asked.

"No one ever has," she answered.

"Tell me the truth, child. I will not punish you if you do."

"I am, Reverend."

"If you confess to me, all will be forgiven," he said.

She was confused and suddenly ashamed. That this was wrong, a thing to be confessed, occurred to her. "No one . . . only you . . . ever . . ." she began.

"Don't bring His wrath down upon your head. You know what you have done and what you must do now."

"I don't. I don't know, Reverend. I don't know what you want."

"It is what He wants. Not I. I am only His tool. Tell me how many boys there have been."

She feared his anger more than God's. God was remote and kind. The Reverend was harshly near. She told him again. "No one has ever touched me this way. Only you have," she whimpered. She hunched over and tried to cover herself.

"I believe you, child," he said. He drew her up, took her hands from her breasts. "I believe you are an innocent, a true innocent," he told her. "But you must know what dangers and temptations await you. I know them and you must know them, too. I will help you to know. Do you want me to help you, child?"

"Yes. I want to be good. I want Jesus to love me."

"Yes. Yes," he chanted. "Yes, child."

He pulled her close, pressing her backward under his body. She felt that she was being baptized again. He was heavy on her. She couldn't breathe with his mouth covering hers. She felt his hands probing, taking down her panties, spreading her legs apart.

"This is what men want from you, child," he said. He was

crouched over her. "This is all that they want. They are sinful beasts. You must know what they want. Say to me, child, that you must know. Say it," he commanded.

"I must know," she said.

"Say to me, 'Help me to know, help me, Reverend.' Say it, child."

"Help . . . help me to know . . . help me, Reverend."

"You shall know."

He put her panties with her shoes and socks. She looked at this small pile of her clothing and not at him as he opened his trousers. He was on top of her. She felt a tearing pain, but she did not cry out. He rocked heavily, grunting, laboring over her. Then he rolled away from her. He stood and quickly closed his pants. He took her dress from under her and covered her with it as if she were dead. She did feel as if she had been killed and her baptism dress was her unclean shroud.

"All men are sinful beasts," he said. "Do you know that now?"

She did not answer.

"Say it," he said.

She said nothing.

He uncovered her face. She flinched. "Say it." He leaned over her, his eyes growing huge.

His eyes were all that she could see. "All men are sinful beasts," she said.

He left her then.

"Mama. Mama," she whispered. "Mama, don't leave me alone. I want to be your child. Mama, I want to be yours, please. Mama, are you here?" she cried, but there was no answer. There was no one with her. She wiped at the blood on her legs, rubbing her hands together to make the blood disappear but it congealed dark and dry on her palms. She wanted to leave this place, but she didn't know where to go. The Reverend would be at Lily's. He would be seated at the head of the table. He would eat from the best dishes with Lily's polished silver. Poppy could see just how it would be. The Reverend would take Matthew onto his lap. Lily would watch and smile. She had such faith in the Reverend, Lily did. Everything would be so gleaming clean and full of faith in the house. She couldn't go there. She was dirty and bloody. She didn't belong there. She didn't belong anywhere. "Mama,

where are you?" she screamed. "Why have you left me all alone?"
Her rage came up from within her, blotting out all else, bringing
on the old familiar blackness. And Mama was not with her.
Thrashing on the dirt floor of the boathouse, she clawed and bit
at herself.

It was far into the night before she regained consciousness. She
dressed and groped her way from the dark shed. Outside it was
darker still, but the night air was not cold. It was dense and warm.
She thought that she must have slept for a very long time. She
started toward Lily's.

When she reached the house she saw the Reverend's car. She
could not go inside with him there still. She could not look at him
and feel him looking at her. She crouched down beside one of the
acacia trees in the yard and waited. Before long the front door
opened. Lily and the Reverend came out, crossed the porch, and
walked down the steps to his car. They moved well together. The
car pulled away. Lily did not turn toward the house until the car
was gone from sight. She must be sad at his leaving, Poppy
thought. Poppy could go inside now. He was far down the road,
his car lighting the black night miles from her, but still she stayed
in the yard under the tree. She was hoping that Lily would go
directly to bed and that she could avoid her sister for a few hours
at least.

Poppy walked over to the back door and entered. From the
kitchen she could see a light on in the parlor. She stepped quietly
into the hall. If she could only get past the open doorway without
being seen or heard, she would go and lie on the floor in the
children's room. In the morning Lily could find her there. But
then Lily spoke. Poppy looked and saw her sitting over her open
Bible. She seemed to be reading aloud from it. She did not take
her eyes from the page, but she was not reading, Poppy feared.

"Where have you been?" she asked.

Poppy stood, caught and silent, in the doorway.

"Come here," Lily commanded, not yet looking up at her sister. "Where have you been?" she asked again.

Poppy did not go to her, but she answered, "I . . . I was
. . . I don't know," she said.

"You don't know where you were?"

"Yes, I do know. I . . . I stayed down by the river."

"All this time?"

"Yes."

Finally Lily looked from her Bible to Poppy. "You were supposed to come back here and help me. You care for nothing. You are unreliable. Irresponsible. And today of all days to do this. On the day of your baptism to behave in this way. This was to be a sacred day, a holy experience for you, and you've destroyed it. You are a destroyer. A spoiler. Today was nothing at all to you. Look at you," Lily said in disgust. "You are of the Devil and I wash my hands of you."

"Lily, I was so tired. I wanted to rest. I went to the boathouse, only to rest for a little bit, and then . . ." She didn't finish. She didn't have the words to describe what had happened when the Reverend had come upon her there.

"And then what?" Lily asked her.

"I . . . I fell asleep."

"You slept for seven hours?"

"Yes . . . no, I didn't sleep all that time."

"I know that you didn't. I know what you were doing," Lily said.

"You know?" Poppy asked. "Did he . . . tell . . ."

"I know," Lily cut in on her. "I've known all along what you were doing when you went out at night, but this night I believed it would stop. I believed you could be saved, but you cannot. Like all the other nights you've been with the Devil."

"No, Lily . . ."

"Yes. With the Reverend here and asking for you. What could I tell him? How could I tell him that you'd hardly dried from the river before you went running back to Satan? I couldn't tell that blessed man where you were, but I knew. I knew, Poppy."

"He . . . the Reverend asked where I was?"

"Yes. Like the good shepherd that he is, he looks after his flock. He wanted to share his wisdom and his faith with you tonight, but you were not here. You are a wayward sheep. You are filthy. Not just your dress. No. Not just that. You are filthy and you cannot be cleansed, not by the Reverend, not even by Jesus Himself. The Devil has taken you. I am done with you. You are not my sister." She spoke evenly and with low-pitched assurance. She had closed her Bible and held it out from her, not as a shield but as a sword.

Poppy sensed that somehow Lily knew what had happened in the boathouse and that she blamed her for it. She laid her head back against the door frame and closed her eyes. She gripped the wood molding until her fingers whitened.

Lily went to her. "Stop that," she said. The seizures frightened her. Only their mother had known what to do for Poppy then. "Stop that, Poppy. It's the demons in you that make you do that."

Poppy opened her eyes. Lily held the Bible and it was black, black like the Reverend's trousers.

"He followed me to the boathouse," Poppy said.

"Who did?" Lily asked.

"You know."

"I do not. I will not listen to this."

"Yes, you will," Poppy told her, astonishingly firm. "He followed me and he touched me."

"He did not. He did not touch you," Lily said. Her voice held a threat but Poppy paid no heed to it.

"The Reverend unbuttoned my dress . . ."

The blow came so swiftly that it could not be seen and could not be evaded. It was too quick to comprehend. Poppy took Lily's slap and tears rose in her eyes. She could not understand the anger and the awful fear that she saw in her sister. Lily's face looked as if she had been struck. There was pain and flushed anguish plainly upon it.

"You are evil. I have always feared it. And you are," Lily said.

"He hurt me. He hurt me, Lily," she said. That was all that she had to say. She did not know what he had done to her other than to hurt her and to make her bleed.

"It was you," Lily said.

"I didn't do anything," Poppy protested. "I didn't do anything wrong."

"You're lying."

"I'm not."

"What are you saying he did to you?" Lily demanded.

But she did not know what he had done. It had hurt and she had bled as if he had cut her with a knife. She said nothing.

"Are you accusing him? Are you saying that he raped you?"

Poppy did not answer. Lily reached for her. She was tearing at her dress, lifting it, ripping it up, laying bare her stained panties and her legs streaked with her own blood and the Reverend's dried semen.

"You did this! You!" Lily screamed. "Not he! You did!"

"Lily, what is it?" Workman's voice called from the bedroom. One of the children began to cry.

"You!" Lily threw at her and turned.

Poppy held her skirt to her. She remained by the door, braced by its frame. She heard Lily speaking to Workman, short words and curt lies. She slid down the length of the door frame and stretched rigid on the rug. It was as it had been when she lay on the dirt floor of the boathouse and the Reverend had stood over her hurriedly pushing his offending limp red flesh into his pants, throwing her dress over her. She was overcome with the same incomprehension. She did not know what the Reverend had done to her. And she did not know why her sister hated and blamed her. She lay listening to Lily's child screaming, but she could not scream. She could not move.

Lily returned after a while. The house was silent. She stared down at Poppy dispassionately and spoke softly.

"Get up. Get up from there."

"I can't."

"You must. You must leave here. I won't have you here."

"But where will I go?"

"You will go to the Devil. He will take you in. You are his."

"Lily . . ."

"Get up from there."

Poppy struggled to her feet. Lily's arms were crossed before her. She made no move to help.

"Don't make me go," Poppy begged. She cowered and cringed. Lily was driving her out. "I'm sorry if I did wrong. I didn't know. I'm sorry," she apologized. She didn't want to stay with Lily, but she wanted desperately not to go. "Don't make me go, Lily."

"I cannot have you here. Not after this, not after tonight. I don't want you polluting my children." Lily spoke the truth to her sister, her own truth. "You have given yourself over to the Devil. I did believe once that you could be saved, but you are lost. You must be cast out." She clipped her words. There was no emotion in her voice. All the earlier anger and fear had dissipated. She was sure once more. She had chosen. She was now simply speaking that of which she was completely convinced.

The Reverend was the embodiment of religion to her. To doubt him would be to distrust God. Her faith was unshakable and her vision unclouded. "I think that Straker's would be the best place for you, among those others of the Devil, those women of no belief and no morality. You will leave tomorrow. I will not have you in this house."

Poppy would do what she was told. She would go to the factory and find work. She would live in the dormitory. That was the course that had been presented to her and that was the course that she would follow. She knew only to follow, but she made one last effort, what was for her a nearly superhuman attempt to tell her sister of the day she had lived.

"He did hurt me, Lily."

Lily took her hands and examined them. "There's blood under your nails. Don't you see it? You did this thing to yourself. Never speak of it . . . never speak to me again."

Poppy looked down at the dark crescents beneath her finger-nails. She didn't know how the blood had come to be there unless Lily was right about her. Maybe she had done it to herself. She could no longer think what she should trust and what she should doubt.

"Please let me stay, Lily."

"No." Lily denied her. Poppy had forsaken God. And now it was clear to Lily that her sister must be forsaken. "No."

Poppy spent her final night at Lily's and in the morning her sister drove her into town. She was dropped in front of the factory. It didn't occur to Poppy to walk the few blocks to Rose's apartment and take refuge there. Lily had told her that Straker's was the place for her and in pathetic obedience she went through the gates. She was taken in eagerly. There was always a demand for young girls at Straker's. They passed through so quickly, grew old so fast there.

It was early and the morning shift had not yet begun. Poppy was led over to the dormitory. A bed was assigned her and she was told to report to the floor lady Grace Hilliard in the packing department at eight o'clock. She was left alone with half an hour to unpack. A woman approached her and spoke.

"Hi. My name's Jake. What's yours?"

"I'm Poppy Calder."

Jake sat down on the bed next to Poppy's. "We're neighbors," she said. She smiled. "Jake's not my real name. It's Cecile but nobody calls me that."

"Why do they call you Jake?" Poppy asked, curious about this woman with a man's name and a voice that was dappled, rough and soft together.

"Back home we had an old horse named Jake. My kid brother thought that horse and me looked just alike. He took to calling me Jake. Then everybody did. Everybody still does." She smiled again. "Cecile just didn't suit me. It was too fancy, I guess. A lace-and-ribbon name, not for me."

Poppy noticed her buck teeth, the long face, and slightly bulging, soft brown eyes. Jake's features made her brother's joke true. It was no wonder that the teasing nickname had stuck. It fit her perfectly.

"The girl who used to have that bed got married last week," Jake told her.

"That's nice," Poppy said, thinking it was the right thing to say.

"Yeah. I guess you want to get married just as soon as you can?" Jake asked.

Poppy didn't answer right away. "I don't know. I guess I do. I guess all girls do, don't they?"

"Most, but not all," she said. "How old are you?"

"Nineteen."

"That's how old I was when I came to work here."

"When was that?" Poppy asked her.

"Ten years ago."

"Ten years. That's a long time."

"Yeah. You were just a little girl ten years ago." She moved over to Poppy's bed, took Poppy by the hand and brought her down beside her. Their hips and legs touched. Jake smiled, showing her strong and faintly yellow horse's teeth. "You're still just a little girl. You're scared, aren't you, Poppy?"

"How did you know?"

"It's not hard to see." She put her arm around Poppy. "Don't be scared."

Poppy leaned easily into the large woman. Jake quickly surveyed the dormitory. It was empty. They were alone. She put her lips to Poppy's forehead, pressed at the baby-fine blond hairs that grew at her temple.

"Don't you worry about a thing. I'll show you the ropes. Jake's going to be right here to take care of her little girl. I promise, Poppy."

When some women came into the room Jake went smoothly back to her own bed. She continued to smile at Poppy, warmly and encouragingly. And Poppy returned Jake's smile.

Chapter Twelve

The bus was painted the brightest yellow and red. It obviously asked for the eyes that followed it down the rural roads it traveled. Seen from a distance, or caught quickly as it flashed past, it was a glorious-looking vehicle. Upon closer inspection it was tawdry, smoking, and mud-spattered. The cheap new paint was already chipped and scraped. Its passengers occasionally glanced out through the windows with tired and jaded perspective. Between the gaily decaying bus and its load of weary performers there was a similarity. They shared a certain blatant appeal and a pall of abuse.

The bus stopped in a town called Arcadia. It was far from heaven, but very near the artichoke fields that encompassed and sustained it. The band got off the bus and filed into the auditorium where they would play that night. Iris was followed closely by a small, dark man. His name was Frankie Skylar. The bandleader made an announcement about rehearsal and after those few words the musicians began to split off in different directions. They would not come together again until there was a reason, a performance. Frankie took Iris by the arm and spoke.

"What a dump. One dump after another," he said. An unlit cigarette dangled from the corner of his thin mouth. He was trying to quit smoking, but he struck a match finally in frustration.

Iris was, as always, unaffected by her surroundings. She wanted to soak in a hot tub and to lie down on a soft bed. It didn't matter much to her if the tub was scrubbed or the sheets laundered. She didn't care that the hall was high-school–sized and the walls a sickening shade of green. She knew what the night could be here. She was sure that once she was on stage and the crowd saw her, heard her sing, that they would think she was the most beautiful thing ever to hit their town. A bunch of hicks, and hicks were so easy, Iris thought. She smiled at Frankie.

"So what? So what if it's a dump, baby? We've got each other, haven't we?" She knew it was what he wanted to hear from her and she was still giving him what he wanted.

He looked at her. She had that cat grin on her face. He had felt lately that she had him a lot stronger than he had her. It was a novel sensation for the sax player. He had always been the taker, never the giver, in relationships. He didn't get hurt because he didn't care enough. His deepest emotional investment had been made in his sax and in his music. It had been that way with Frankie Skylar until he met Iris. He had never wanted a woman as much as he wanted her and it went far beyond the taking. She had been easy enough to get into bed, too easy, but the desire had only increased, burned hotter after he'd had her. He kept expecting his need of her to lessen, but it didn't. It built and built until he thought he'd explode, and he sometimes did. He was wild about Iris. He had even thought of marrying her. He knew what she was. He didn't want to marry the kind of girl that she was. Iris was a tramp, but he was obsessed with her. He loved the slant of her green eyes, the way she walked, her skin, and her long gold hair. He craved her. He dreamed of her even when she lay beside him in bed, even with his leg thrown across her and his arms holding her, her breath in his face so close that he could taste it, even then she was still a dream to him. All over again he had to possess her and it hounded him that she could be anyone's and that she was no one's, that he'd never really had her and never really would.

"Let's see if there's a hotel in this burg," he said.

They found a gray frame building near the train station. It was, the sign said, the Arcadia Inn. There was a screened veranda with chairs lined up evenly along it, none of them occupied but the wicker seats sagging from the weight of ghosts. The place had a faded genteel appearance. Frankie liked that. It wouldn't be likely to attract the other band members and he'd have Iris to himself. They went inside and rang the bell on the desk. It took several rings before a woman came grudgingly from a back room. She stared at them, offering no greeting.

"We'd like a room," Frankie told her.

She eyed the case he carried. It was an odd shape for a piece of luggage. If she'd had any imagination she might have thought he was carrying a gun, but she did not. Its differentness alone was enough to disturb her. She wanted her guests to have normal and square suitcases. She shifted her look to the girl. A slick blond, she appraised. They weren't married, she was sure of that.

"Don't have no rooms," she said.

"The place is empty," Frankie declared. "You gotta have a room."

"Don't have no rooms, mister."

"I say you do." His quick temper flared.

"No rooms," the woman told him.

Iris had seen hundreds like her. She'd never given one of them a moment's notice, but this one had something she wanted. Iris rarely failed to get what she wanted from anyone, old or young, man or woman. She leaned closer to the hag who stood behind the hotel desk like it was a pulpit.

"My husband and I are so tired," she began sweetly. "We've been traveling all night. We saw this lovely place and I begged to stop here. It reminds me of home. Please, we'd take even your smallest room." She turned slightly from Frankie and lowered her voice, drawing the woman in. "I'm expecting," she whispered shyly. "It's our first. Frankie's more nervous than me. That's why he got mad just now. He's not really that way."

The woman visibly melted under Iris's words and her beautiful smile. They were in a large second floor room within a few minutes. The woman showed a sudden solicitous side, lingering, raising windows, straightening lampshades. When she finally left, closing the door gently behind her, Iris collapsed into the bed laughing loudly. Frankie smiled wryly.

"You play people better than I do this," he said and set his sax down. He walked over to the bed. He straddled Iris, roughly pinning her arms down. He searched her face. "Do you play me, too?" he asked.

She half closed her eyes and then opened them wide, looking directly into his. "What do you mean, Frankie?"

"You know what I mean."

"Well, you wanted a room. I got one for you. I like to give you what you want."

"Do you?"

"Sure I do, baby," she told him. She didn't try to free herself from his grip, but his hold was so tight that her skin was starting to burn. She was well aware that Frankie was a violent man. She had received his blows. Once at a party with all the members of the band there he had slapped her because he thought she was drinking too much and flirting too flagrantly. He had knocked her to the floor but she had still left with him. That night in bed had been the best ever for her. His cruelty and his passion were different sides of the same coin, she knew, and both excited her. "Baby, you're hurting me," she said, but made no attempt to get loose.

"Am I?" he asked her.

"Yes."

"You like it, don't you?"

"I like to give you what you want," she said. She brought her face to his, her lips to his. She maneuvered indiscernibly and with infinite grace. "Tell me what you want, Frankie."

That night she sang "Dream" to a packed house. They swayed in time to her song and cheered her afterward. She was exhilarated by the mass response to her. Her excitement was beyond any she had ever felt in any bed with any man, even Frankie. The power that she held over the audience was enormous and filled her with love for them because they loved her and they couldn't touch her, couldn't reach her, but could only love, purely love her.

When the band took a break she didn't see Frankie. The piano player asked her to come out to the bus with him. He kept looking at her as if he had never seen her before.

"God, you were good. I didn't know you were that good, Iris," he said "C'mon out with me. I've got something you've never had before, I'll bet. I know you're flying, but this'll take you even higher," he promised.

Iris smiled at him. He was thin and small, his narrow face bristling with black stubble, and his eyes hooded. He appeared sensitive and sinister at the same time. The only thing of real beauty about him was his hands. They were long and pale, finely shaped. His piano playing approached genius. Iris told him she would go with him.

They made their way to the back of the bus in the darkness. He produced a strange-looking cigarette, hand-rolled with brown paper. He lit it and dragged hard. He handed it to her. It smelled strong, a deep and pungent sweet burning.

"It's marijuana," he explained.

She put it to her mouth, imitating him.

"Hold it in," he instructed her.

When she expelled the smoke she began to laugh. He laughed, too.

He inhaled again. "Isn't it the greatest?" he asked her. His voice had gone high-pitched and wheezy. He passed it to her. "Take another hit."

They finished the cigarette quickly, smoked it until it burned their fingers, took it down to nothing. They were laughing at nothing. He kissed her and she laughed at the feel of his mouth. She laughed at his ugly face and his beautiful hands. She couldn't stop laughing. Even when she saw Frankie, she couldn't stop. She only laughed harder when he tore the piano player off her. Frankie jabbed his fists furiously. The piano player doubled over and fell. Frankie pounced on him. They rolled on the floor of the bus. Iris sat on the wide back seat and watched the two men fight in the narrow aisle. Some of the other band members came and pulled them apart. The piano player held one hand in the other. His face was bloody, but Frankie's was clean and white and terrible.

It was Manny King, the band leader whose name was painted in lemon yellow on the side of the bus, who paid her off that night. After the fight had been broken up, he took her aside and shoved some wadded bills into her hand.

"Go back to San Diego, Iris," he told her.

"But why, Manny? Because of this? It was just a little misunderstanding, that's all."

"Just a misunderstanding. Didn't you hear Frankie say he was going to kill you?"

"I heard. And I've heard it before."

"I can't have it, kid. My piano player's got a broken hand. My sax player says he's going to kill my singer . . ."

"I can handle Frankie. Don't worry."

"Handle him. Don't you love him?" he asked. She looked at him as if he had started speaking a foreign language. He shook his head slightly, involuntarily. Manny King didn't like to make judgments any more than he liked being judged. "What about the others? Can you handle them, too?"

"What others, Manny?" she smiled at him and widened her eyes in innocence.

"Don't bother, kid. I'm immune," he said. "You're out."

"What difference does it make to you?" she asked.

"Look, I don't care who you're screwing. What I do care about is keeping this band together and playing."

"Are you sure that's it, Manny? Or maybe I cut in on your territory tonight." Her eyes were dead level with his now. She had dropped all pretense. "Just tell me which boys are yours. I won't go near them. I promise, Manny."

"You're more trouble than you're worth."

"But I'm good. You said so. You know I'm good. You heard me tonight. You saw that crowd. They loved me."

"Girl singers are a dime a dozen. You're good all right, but where you're best is not on the bandstand. I'll make a call tonight. Your replacement will be on her way. She'll meet us in Plattville tomorrow."

"Why don't you get a boy singer, Manny?" she struck out at him.

He only laughed, not hit. "So long, kid."

She saw him turn. "Hey, Manny."

"Yeah?"

"I sing pretty good, don't I?"

"Yeah," he said tiredly.

"And I'm beautiful, too, huh?"

He turned back to her. "You're beautiful, Iris," he said. He felt something for her then, for the first time.

Iris was back in San Diego for her birthday. In the afternoon she left the room she had rented that morning. She went first to

her favorite bar. The Grotto was decorated in Hawaiian style,
someone's idea of it, someone who had never been to the Islands.
She traded the hot August daylight for the cool and dark interior.
She sat at the bar. It was too early for the waterfall. She liked to
watch the pink lights play on the cascading water. She was about
to ask Mac, the bartender, if it could be turned on for her when
a Marine mounted the stool next to hers.

"Can I buy you a drink?" he asked. He couldn't quite believe
his luck at finding a girl like this alone, but then it was only three
o'clock. He was first and fortunate. "What are you drinking?
Let me buy you a drink." He hoped he didn't sound too anxious.

Iris recognized his urgency. She spoke slowly. "Well, as a rule
I wouldn't let you . . ."—she paused maddeningly, letting him
dangle for a moment—". . . but it is my birthday today."

"Your birthday. That calls for a celebration," he told her.

"I guess maybe you're right," she said. "Would you buy me a
champagne cocktail?" Iris asked him.

"You can have anything you want."

"Can I? Can I really?"

"Sure you can. Today's your day," he said.

Iris didn't return to her room until nearly noon the next day.
She pulled the Murphy bed from the closet the way the landlord, Mr. Hagen, had shown her. She thought of Mr. Hagen's
leer and how he'd brushed against her. He'd told her that he had
a daughter just her size who lived in Cincinnati and that he kept
some clothes in his apartment for her when she came to visit.
He'd said she could borrow any of them any time she liked, just
to come down and try them on. She could easily imagine what
Mr. Hagen's apartment and his daughter's clothes would be like.
She laid down on the bed and immediately dozed off, but woke
after only half an hour. The room was strange to her. It took her
several moments to realize where she was. She recognized the
wallpaper first, white background turned to yellow and faded
cabbage roses. It was the place she had rented the day before.
She'd paid a week in advance. This was home for seven days.
Her head felt huge and heavy. She stretched like a cat, closed her
eyes, and went back to sleep. She dreamed of Rafael. He was
dying in her dream but not as he had died in her life. He was not
shot but was burning in a fire. She dreamed the flames all around
him. He was screaming, calling her name over and over again.

Then his screams became horse's cries and she was a little girl back in Kansas. She was burning, too. She bolted from the bed. The room was dark.

She went and switched on a light. She had been sleeping for hours. Her dress was ruined. She decided that she would never wear it again. She began to take it off and noticed the right sleeve was torn. She couldn't remember ripping it, not how or when she had. She recalled drinking champagne in the afternoon with a Marine at the Grotto, but after that yesterday and last night was mostly a blur. The Marine had disappeared at some point and a sailor had taken his place. He was a chief petty officer. She knew because of the hash marks on his uniform. They were very clear in her memory, but she couldn't see his face. She kept putting the Marine's blue eyes on the sailor. They were all so interchangeable to her.

She weaved unsteadily over to the bureau and stared into the mirror. Her dress was half on and half off. She looked like a sleepy child. Her face was slightly swollen, but her skin was soft and smooth. Her eyes were clear. Her hair needed to be washed and curled. She removed her dress and threw it in a corner. Her bra, slip, garter belt, stockings, and panties quickly followed. She studied herself. Too much champagne bloated the stomach. She patted hers. It was flat and firm. She was invulnerable. She had forgotten her dream already. She'd take a long, hot bath and go out. She wanted to sing and dance tonight, and every night. It wasn't her birthday but she could still say it was. She counted them, her birthdays, twenty-one of them. She was beautiful and she would always be beautiful. Mr. Hagen had told her that the bath was down the hall and to the left. She'd go just as she was, naked, and if the landlord saw her that would be fine. Maybe he'd lower her rent, give her his daughter's clothes. They were probably ugly dresses. Probably the daughter was ugly, too, like her father, Iris guessed, but that didn't matter. What mattered to her was that she could make him give them to her, make him pay tribute to her beauty. She walked out. With her gone, the incandescence departed, it was just another unkept room to let.

Holly kept a book on her desk in the living room of her apartment. It contained dates, carefully noted, some made obsolete by death. They might have been forgotten, perhaps should have been, but they were not. Holly had written down her parent's wedding anniversary, the birthdays of her father, mother, and sister Jasmine. All her living sisters' births, the days they had married their husbands and borne children, were meticulously recorded. She felt that she held her family within these covers, controlled them in some way, all of them, the dead, the disenchanted, and demented. She knew that Iris's birthday had been yesterday, but she didn't know where to send a card. In the five years since she'd run away from the farm Iris dropped in from nowhere at times and disappeared again. There was no pattern to her comings and goings, no permanence, and no address. A card stood little chance of finding her. Holly knew exactly the sort of card she would have sent to Iris, something yellow and shiny and with a short verse. The day had passed but not without her awareness of it and that satisfied Holly. She turned the page and saw the date of Rose's birthday. It was easy to send Rose a card. Rose never went anywhere. Holly thought of the small apartment where Rose and Clyde lived. She could visualize it perfectly. It didn't change. She glanced around her own apartment. It seemed different to her. It had been altered in the last few months by Paul. He had brought a chair closer to the reading lamp. He had caused her to have two place settings at the table and milk for his coffee in the refrigerator. He had not slept in her bed but he had given his presence to the place. It was no longer hers alone. He had entered here and entered her life, too. She was happy and unhappy about Paul. She wanted him and did not. Hers was an almost atavistic ambivalence. Holly was descended from a long line of emotional evaders.

Paul would be coming soon. She closed the book of dates and went to get ready. It never occurred to her that he might have wanted once to knock on the door and have her open it breathlessly, her hair slightly mussed, a stray bead of water from her shower shining on her neck, still in her robe. She was always seated in the living room waiting for him, perfectly prepared. She did not guess that he would want her any other way.

She heard his steps and they were hurried. He was late. She answered quickly when he knocked.

"I'm sorry I'm late, Holly," he apologized immediately.

"It's only ten minutes past eight," she said, looking at her watch for the tenth time in those ten minutes. Even if he was only a minute past the time he said he would come, she thought that he was not coming at all. Sometimes a flash of hope that he wouldn't appear ran through her. It was confusing and unsettling how she anticipated his footsteps and dreaded them, too. "You said eight o'clock. It's only ten after."

"I ran into an old friend. I couldn't get away," he said.

They were standing in the doorway. She wanted to ask him who the old friend was and where they had met, where they had once known each other. She waited for him to further explain his encounter. He did not.

"Come in," she said and stepped back.

He walked inside. She closed the door.

"You look beautiful," he said. The white angora sweater set and the short beige pleated skirt she wore, the pale webbed hair-net like a spider's gorgeous work that delicately held back her dark chignon, were perfection. "Perfectly beautiful." He was thinking that she could not really be appreciated until she was very near and that she rarely ever came close enough. That first night she had. He had held her in his arms, but it was as if she had allowed, desired it, because she was certain they would never see one another again. She had even told him that, but it hadn't stopped with that night. They had continued to see each other. Now it was across the barrier that she had raised again after drop- ping it for that brief moment only. That glimpse of what she could be enthralled him. She kept her beauty a secret, letting it escape like a prisoner. She reined herself tightly. He restrained himself, but the distance that she required was becoming more and more difficult for him to maintain. Remote a man as he knew himself to be, her shielded beauty drew him powerfully to her. "The reservations are for eighty-thirty," he said. "We'd better hurry."

They arrived at the restaurant on time. The proprieties, prom- ises kept, were equally important to Paul and to Holly. They were precise, punctual, and reserved, both acutely attuned to the rules and controls of life. They were escorted to their table by André, the maître d'. He bowed off from them, contrarily obsequious and supercilious, classically Gallic André.

"Who was your friend?" The question slipped from her, sur- prising her.

Paul was surprised, too, but answered quickly. "A fellow I went to school with in the east. It was eons ago."

"I'm sorry. I shouldn't have asked," she said.

"Why not?"

"It was . . . well, it was prying. You would have said earlier if you'd wanted me to know." She hated feeling the way she did. She regretted the question. She wasn't sure why she'd asked, but as she tried to dismiss it, it grew huge with inflated importance. "I don't like to pry."

"It was a natural question, Holly. Anybody else would have said right off that it was an old school friend," he told her, disliking himself. "I wish I wasn't so closemouthed."

"No, I shouldn't have asked."

He recognized in her his own ability to self-chastise. They were two of a kind, two self-loathing and isolated people, he decided. He looked across the table at her. He was fairly certain of his reasons, how he had come to be the way he was, but he didn't know hers. He didn't know why she was so like him. "Holly?"

"Yes, Paul."

The waiter came. Paul ordered a bottle of wine. The waiter left the menus. Holly retreated behind the high and thick leather volume. Paul reached out and lowered it. She reluctantly met his gaze.

"Holly, we've been seeing each other for a while now. Not a very long time, but . . ."

"What?"

"We might just as well be on our first date tonight."

"Our first dinner was here," she said, avoiding the word date.

"Three months ago, yes. Shouldn't we know each other a little better than we do?"

"You don't think we know each other?"

"No, Holly, I don't. Do you?" he asked.

"I'm sorry if you're not happy, but this is what I am. I can't . . . I don't want to be anything else," she said. Her heart had started beating very fast. He didn't like her, she was thinking. She didn't satisfy him in any way. This would be the last that she would see of him. That was fine, just fine. She'd never asked him into her life. She could survive without him. She didn't need him. She didn't want him. Still her heart pounded and she felt on the verge of tears. She didn't cry, not anymore, she told herself. She would not cry like a hurt child. She toyed with the net on her hair, as if to straighten it, but instead she freed one fine strand with her tampering.

He watched her movements. "Holly, I didn't say I wasn't happy. I said that I thought we didn't know each other. And I asked you if you thought we did. You didn't answer."

"I guess we don't," she said.

"We seem to be stalled. We're not going anywhere." He thought of how many times women had said those words to him. It was odd to find himself saying them, but he knew that Holly never would.

"Where do you think we should be going, Paul?" she asked.

"I don't know," he said quietly. "I'm much older than you, maybe too much . . ."

"No," she broke in. "You're not too old for me."

They both knew that was true. Their problem was not any disparity. They were too much alike.

"I've led a solitary life. I see you doing that too, Holly. For some reason, I don't know why, I want to stop you. I think I love you."

The waiter brought the wine. He went through the ritual of it. Finally they were left alone with two filled goblets and Paul's words heavily between them. Holly spoke, and though it was a response to his avowal, it was indirect.

"Why did you never marry?"

He answered directly. "I was too afraid of making a mistake."

"How do you mean?" she asked.

"Can you imagine what hell on earth it would be to find yourself tied to someone you didn't love, didn't even really know?"

"Yes," she said.

There was deep empathy in her voice, an understanding of a horror that he had only feared. He went on, "How can you ever be sure? God knows, emotions are the most volatile of things. Love's not carved in stone, after all. I was afraid, Holly."

"I'm afraid, too. I've seen what you're describing. I know what it is and you're right to be afraid."

It jarred him, the idea that she might have been married, that she might have loved someone once, and that that relationship had made her what she was now. The thought of it was repugnant to him. "Not you . . . you weren't ever . . ." He stumbled at the sight of her untouched perfection suddenly imperiled. She said so little, kept so much to herself. Until this moment he had never considered that she might be hiding a past.

"My mother and father were very unhappy," she told him. She thought how mild that sounded, as if Mama had liked coffee and Daddy had preferred tea, some small and silly divergence that had caused them discontent. How could she convey what their marriage had truly been? How could she express what she had witnessed throughout her childhood? How could she ever explain to this aloof man who said he loved her the hatred and cruelty that he had some vague presentiment of but that she had lived with for years? "It wasn't a good marriage," she concluded feebly.

He was relieved that it had not been her own, but that relief was swiftly supplanted by anxiety. He was on the brink of knowing her reasons, learning how deeply she had been damaged by her parents, and his instinct was to edge back and ask no more of her. For the first time in his life his visceral reticence lost out. He asked, "Did they divorce?"

"No, they stayed . . ."—she had trouble saying the word—"together."

He waited for her to tell him what she could.

"They should have parted, but they didn't." She paused. "They couldn't and I don't know why, but they couldn't. They never, never should have met. It would have been better for everyone if they hadn't, but they did. They met. They married. They had six children. And eight lives . . . were ruined. Maybe not ruined, but terribly influenced. We all seem doomed somehow. I have to think that it comes from when we were children, seeing what we did. The way they would scream, go at one another. Then Daddy would leave and Mama would turn her screaming to me. She despised me. I was Daddy's favorite. I looked like him. All my sisters took after her. In me she saw Daddy. I think she truly hated him. She would hurt him in any way and whenever she could, but he always came back. Maybe he came back because of me. Daddy loved me, but . . ." She stopped.

"What, Holly?" he asked, not wanting to know but feeling that he must.

"No matter how she hurt him they would go into that room together, whatever room was theirs, and close the door. Even when she hurt him most they closed that door behind them, and left me, all of us, outside." Paul's stare was too intense. She feared what she had revealed to him. "They were killed in a tornado last April."

"I'm sorry." It was reflexive, polite, and meaningless. He was more sorry that he'd expressed it as he had.

"After the storm when they were found, Mama was in the house and Daddy was in the car a short way down the road. Maybe he was finally leaving, but he'd left so many times and he always came back. They stayed together for all those years, but when the tornado came for them both, they died apart."

The waiter returned to their table. Paul ordered for them both.

Holly measured the waiter's steps, making sure he was far enough from them before she spoke again. "I shouldn't have started on this. I never talk about it."

"It's a part of you. I don't care how deeply you bury it or if you never talk about it, it's there."

"I don't want to talk about it anymore. I don't remember very much anyway."

"You don't?"

"No, I don't."

"You're lying, Holly," he said.

"I don't choose to remember. That's the truth."

"Tell me what you were like as a child."

"Oh, Paul . . ."

"Tell me," he demanded, no longer willing to wait for what she was able to tell.

"I was the outsider. I didn't look like any of my sisters. They were very pretty and fair."

"You're beautiful. Don't you know that?"

"No," she said. She switched to the present tense. "No, I'm the skinny dark one. The beauty is Iris. I don't even know where she is now." She moved into the past. "It was her birthday yesterday." She went further back. "Iris ran away from home when she was sixteen." And further still. "I remember her eighth birthday. We were in Kansas then. She had a big party. She looked like a princess. Rose had made a gold paper crown for her, with silver glitter for diamonds, red for rubies, and green for emeralds. She wore a yellow dress and sat at the head of the long table out under the trees. It was very warm that day. Iris was so beautiful. Poppy, my youngest sister, spilled her punch and she cried. Mama carried her into the house. They didn't come back to the party. Rose brought out the cake with all the candles lit but the wind came up and blew them out before Iris could. After the cake came the presents. Iris tore them open, ripped away the pretty paper without even seeing it. Then everyone got up and went to play a game of tag. Iris ran in and out of the big blowing trees. She looked like a gossamer fairy, that yellow dress and her long blond hair flowing against the dark green. A piece of her wrapping paper blew to my feet and I picked it up. I smoothed the creases and folded it into a little square. I kept it for the longest time. Every one of my sisters had a birthday party, but I didn't."

"Maybe you just don't remember, Holly," he temporized, trying to ease her pain when it was he who had asked her to feel it.

"No. There was always some reason. We were moving or it was too cold or too close to Christmas. Mama always had a reason and she never gave me a party. It's not that I can't remember. I remember too well, Paul. Don't ask me for memories. I have my reasons, just like Mama, for not giving them."

He saw the tears in her eyes. He did love her. She'd said nothing, no word of loving him. Maybe she couldn't say it and couldn't feel it. He wasn't able to take her back and give her an eighth birthday party. He could only love her now and possibly that was too late.

The waiter came and set their salads and the correct, chilled forks down before them.

Chapter Thirteen

Iris rode the streetcar to the outskirts of San Diego. It grew sunnier the farther the tracks ran from the ocean. Even so it was cool for October. She checked the crumpled paper with the address written upon it. The streetcar would be at her stop next. She did not feel nervous or frightened, but eager to have it over and done with. She guessed that she was lucky this hadn't happened before. She hadn't taken any precautions. Always her luck had been enough. Until now it had been. Since her twenty-first birthday two months ago Iris hadn't been so fortunate, but she didn't feel her luck ebbing. She was a reckless gambler and unheeding of portent. Returning the paper to her purse, she began to look for her compact. She pawed past the wad of bills Manny had given her. It was not as fat as it had been. She owed rent but was successfully putting off Hagen. The dress she was wearing she'd bought yesterday, but the money that was left should cover what she needed today, she thought. The voice on the phone had said a hundred and fifty.

She sat and thought of the shoes she wanted to go with the dress. She'd have to wait for them now. She could get Walter to buy her the shoes. He would, of course, Walter would, but she was saving him for bigger things than a pair of red pumps. If only this hadn't happened she could have had the shoes and a purse and those earrings, too. Instead she had to get up at seven in the morning and take the streetcar out to the sticks and hand over the money to somebody who was nothing but a voice on the phone. She wondered if there might have been some way for Walter to have financed this, but that would have been too tough, she decided. Even she couldn't have managed that. This had to be done alone. She had to use Manny's money. It should have been Frankie's. The baby was his. She was pretty sure that it was. She resumed her search for her compact, found it, and opened it. It was cracked. She didn't know when it had been broken. She must have dropped her purse somewhere, sometime, but she couldn't think when. She looked into the mirror. The break distorted her face, coming right across her forehead and down her nose to her chin. She tried to remember. What was it? Seven years' bad luck? She flinched at her image. She looked ugly. Iris thought of a girl she had known in Washington. Eloise was her name. Eloise had been a pretty girl until some guy had cracked up his car and she had gone through the windshield. The guy didn't have a scratch on him. Eloise was in the hospital for months. When she did get out her face looked just like the shattered mirror face, but for real. Eloise had needed her face, Iris thought. That guy didn't. A guy could get along all right with scars. She'd known one once with a long white gash on his cheek. He was always bragging about it, like it proved something about him, that he was a man or something. All Eloise's scars proved were that she was damaged goods, deformed, disfigured. She remembered that Eloise had gone back into the hospital, not to have her face fixed. Her face couldn't be fixed. They'd taken her away to a loony bin, a nut-house hospital. They took her because she wore veils all the time and she wouldn't leave her room or talk to anybody. Iris never heard anything about Eloise getting out. She was probably still in there. Broken mirrors gave you seven years' bad luck. A broken face gave you a lifetime of it. Iris closed the compact angrily. She'd get a new one today. She didn't care, even if she didn't eat, she would.

It was her stop and she got off the car. The place wasn't hard to find. She walked up the back stairs as she'd been told. She stood on the landing for a minute before knocking. Down in the yard of the apartment building there were some toys, a tricycle,

a red ball, and a green hose snaking over the brown lawn to a
wading pool. The door opened. Iris saw the woman standing in
the doorway. She looked ordinary. Her dyed black hair was in
a fashionable and stiff pompadour, but she wore a white smock
over her dress. It would have been an apron if she wasn't what she
was, Iris was thinking. Beyond the woman, the room was light,
with chintz covers on the sofa and chairs, an ordinary room, but
there must be another where it was done.

"What're you stand there for? Weren't you told to knock
three times?" the woman asked.

"I was just going to."

"Were you waiting for an engraved invite?"

"No," Iris answered.

"Well, c'mon then," she said and stepped aside for Iris to enter.

Iris hesitated. Suddenly she was afraid. "Will it hurt? Will it
leave any scars?"

The woman ignored her questions. "Have you got the
money?" she asked. "The money first, then we'll talk, beauty
queen," she said.

"I've got the money," Iris told her. She was thinking of scars
and of her compact, hoping to save a little for a new one. "One
twenty-five," she said.

The woman moved back fully into the door frame, blocking
Iris. "One fifty."

They stared at each other for a moment.

"Okay, one fifty," Iris said and started to reach into her purse.

The woman pulled her inside, quickly and roughly. "Not out
there," she snapped and closed the door. She bolted and chained
it. "You're a pretty dumb beauty queen. Now give me the
money."

Iris put the bills in her outstretched hand. The woman counted
them, wetting her fingers with her tongue, riffling fast.

"All right," she said, "go into that room." She pointed to a
closed door. "Take off that pretty dress and everything else, too."

Iris didn't move.

"Go on," the woman ordered her. "Don't go shrinking violet
on me. If you were a modest little girl you wouldn't be in this
fix. So cut the crap," she said. "Go on, beauty queen."

"I'm not a beauty queen," Iris said. "Stop calling me that."

"I don't care who or what you are," the woman said without

any trace of anger or rancor. It was a flat, unfeeling, and true statement. She fanned the bills in the air and slapped them into her palm. "This is all you are to me."

For the first time Iris looked around for someone else. "Are you a doctor?"

"Sure I am," the woman answered contemptuously. "I know what I'm doing. It won't hurt. It won't scar. Just get in there, beauty queen."

"Okay, doctor," Iris threw at her, attempting a cold and fearless mockery of the woman. She headed for the closed door.

Sometime about midway in the operation Iris became aware of a scratchy recording of "Moonlight Serenade" being played over and over. She listened to it while she was in the room. She heard it as she came down the back steps of the apartment building, even in the street. Iris would forget the morning, the streetcar ride, and the black-haired woman who had done things with her cold and gleaming instruments in the second floor back room. She could and would forget it all. All but the sound of that spent record and the beautiful exhausted music.

It hadn't taken long. The woman had told her to rest, but she hadn't. She'd gotten up and walked. She wanted out of there, badly, and the look of hard-boiled admiration on the woman's face had given her strength. She rode the streetcar and staggered the block to her building. As soon as she was in her room she began to feel weak and faint. She found a spot of blood on her dress. It was that touch of red mess that caused her to fall onto the unmade bed. She didn't sleep but lay and listened to the silence, the absence of that lovely frayed music. She did not realize that it played on inside her head. After an hour she got up and took off her dress. She put on her pink chenille robe and started down the hall for the bathroom. She stopped at the telephone. She put her hand into her robe pocket and found a nickel. She took that as a sign. She needed someone cool and clean with her. She knew who it was she wanted. She got the operator and placed a collect call to Holly.

The phone rang in Holly's apartment several times. She ran from the bedroom to answer, thinking it must be Paul, and wondering why he would be calling when he was due to be there in less than twenty minutes. She picked up the receiver and heard the operator asking if she would accept charges. She said yes. Iris's sweet low voice came faintly.

"Hi, Hol," she said.

"Iris, how are you?" Holly asked.

"I'm okay."

There was a pause. Holly could hear her sister breathing, clearer than her words.

"Listen," Iris started. "We haven't seen each other in a long time. I was thinking maybe you'd like to come down here and visit me this weekend."

"How long have you been in San Diego?" Holly asked.

"Not long," Iris answered. "If you can't make it, that's okay. I mean it was just a spur of the moment thing. I guess it was kind of a crazy idea."

"No, Iris," she said. She was sure that Iris's reasons for inviting her were selfish ones. She knew her sister well, and she knew, too, that her reasons for accepting, if she decided to, would have little to do with seeing Iris. "I'll be there," she heard herself saying.

"You will? You're really going to come?" she asked.

"Yes. Give me your address." Holly said, thinking she would be able to put it beside Iris's name in her book. Next year she could send a card. The thought of the card made her say, "I know I'm a couple of months late, but happy birthday, Iris."

"You remembered. God, how do you do it? Yours is sometimes in January, isn't it?" Iris asked.

"December the tenth," she said.

"Yeah, that's it. I knew it was in the winter sometime."

"Your address, Iris?" Holly asked.

"One-oh-six Third Street. Number twelve."

"I should be able to catch the noon train. That will put me in around five o'clock, I think," she said, and waited. She went on. "I'll take a taxi from the station."

"Okay, Hol. See you then."

"Goodbye, Iris."

"Bye."

The phone clicked. Holly hung up. She walked over to her suitcase. It stood by the couch packed and ready. She bent and opened it. She wouldn't need as many things for San Diego as

she had for Santa Barbara. She removed a sweater, a dress, and a
pair of shoes. She carried them into her bedroom. The dress was
Paul's favorite. She had planned to wear it to dinner tonight.
She'd made so many plans and now she'd leaped at Iris's invitation. She must not have really wanted the weekend with Paul.
He'd pushed too hard for it. She wasn't prepared for it yet. She
heard him coming up the walk. He was early. She didn't know
what she would say to him. She wished she could hide somewhere.
He knocked. She went to the door and opened it. He kissed her
lightly. He was smiling, obviously in good humor. He remarked
on her open bag.

"What, not ready yet? Are you procrastinating? I thought it
was physically impossible for you to dawdle," he joked with her.

She went to the suitcase and closed it. She busied herself with
it while she spoke. "Paul, something has happened."

His smile faded. "What is it?" His light tone deepened with
concern. He came over to her. "What's wrong?"

"My sister Iris called me from San Diego. I just this minute
hung up the telephone." She stalled.

"And?"

"She asked me to come down."

"When?" he asked.

"Now. Today," she said.

"What's happened, Holly? Is she is some kind of trouble?"

"Not exactly."

"What do you mean not exactly?"

"She wouldn't say on the phone but I know that there's something wrong."

"What makes you think so?"

"She wouldn't have called otherwise, Paul. You don't know
Iris."

"No, I don't."

She heard the anger in his voice. "Paul, I really think she needs
me."

He looked at her and she met his eyes briefly but then dropped
away from him.

"We'll have to cancel the trip. I'm sorry," she told him.

"Are you?"

"Of course I am."

"Well, another time perhaps," he said stiffly. "Would you like me to drive you to the station?"

"Yes. Thank you, Paul. I knew you'd understand."

"I'm afraid I do."

He picked up her suitcase.

"You're taking this?" he asked.

She nodded. He walked out with it. She locked the door and followed him. He put her bag beside his in the back seat of the car. They drove away.

"What do you think the problem is, Holly?" he asked her.

"Problem?" She knew her voice sounded high and guilty. She tried to make it calmer, make it lower. "Problem?"

"With your sister," he said.

She glanced over at him. He'd meant Iris's problem, not hers, she told herself. Or had he, she questioned. She chose to believe that he wanted to discuss her sister. "I told you about Iris, didn't I?"

"The beauty," he said.

"Yes."

"She left home when she was a kid, right?"

"She was sixteen years old. She ran away with two men."

"Two men?"

"Yes, salesmen. My mother insisted that she was kidnapped by them, but she wasn't. I knew she wasn't."

"How did you know that?"

"It wasn't really very difficult. Iris hated the farm. She craved excitement. Kansas was too dull for her. I knew she'd run one day. It was inevitable. These two salesmen showed up in their big car, with their whisky flasks, their blue suits, and she went with them. She was just waiting for them."

"You seem to know quite a bit about these fellows."

"Only what I saw," she said. "I was out with them the night Iris ran away. I came home. Iris didn't. Mama blamed me . . ." she trailed off.

"So you were close to Iris then?" he asked.

"Close? To Iris?" she laughed a little. "It wasn't possible to be close to Iris. Unless you were a man. She's been close to a lot of men. Maybe not even to them. Iris loves herself. I don't think she's ever really loved anyone else. She's so beautiful. There've

been men, too many men, but for Iris it's always been Iris. She's
totally selfish. She was when she was a little girl and she's showed
no signs of changing."

"Why are you going, Holly?" he asked suddenly.

She wanted to tell him the truth, to tell him why simply and
truly, but she couldn't. She gave him an answer that did not lie
but did not answer either. "Because I'm not Iris. I'm not that
self-centered. She's my sister. I feel for her. I'm worried about
her. She sounded . . . scared . . . as if she'd gotten in over her
head."

"Like you have, Holly?"

"What?"

"This weekend of ours was a mistake. I wanted it, but I don't
think you did, not really. As long as we were just talking about
it, you were fine, but as the reality of it approached . . . well, your
sister's call was a reprieve, a last-minute reprieve. Tell me if I'm
wrong. I hope I am."

"You're not wrong," she admitted.

"If Iris hadn't called you would have found some other reason
not to go with me, wouldn't you?"

"I don't know, Paul. Maybe I would have, but maybe not. I
just don't know."

"Maybe you ought to try and find out, Holly."

They drove the rest of the way to the station in silence. Paul
parked in front.

"You don't have to come in with me," she said.

"But I will."

The huge terminal was jammed. They threaded their way to
the ticket counter.

"Do you need any money?" he asked her.

"No. Thank you."

He was only waiting until her ticket was purchased. They stood
together on the line, not speaking, inching forward. It was only
minutes but they passed like hours. Holly was at the window.
Paul watched, quietly raging, not buying a ticket, not going anywhere, but seeing her make arrangements to travel without him,
away from him. The transaction was completed. They walked
from the counter.

"Have a good trip. I hope your sister is all right," he said. He
was straining to be civil.

"Paul, I . . ."

"Yes?" he asked, trying to hold down his eagerness and not expect anything of her.

"I'm sorry," she said lamely.

A group of shouting sailors had passed by them as she spoke.

"What did you say?"

"I'm sorry," she repeated.

"So am I," he said. "Goodbye, Holly."

"Goodbye, Paul."

He walked away. She let the moments pass. She let him go through the crowd and cross the vast tiled floor, let the people and the distance rise between them. Irretrievable time, she waited. She wanted to call out to him, bring him back to her, go to Santa Barbara with him and sleep beside him. She wanted to love him, but instead she let him go. He was gone. She picked up the suitcase, its handle still warm from his grip. She went to the boarding gate.

The train arrived in San Diego an hour late. Holly had difficulty finding a taxi. When she finally did, she gave the address to the driver.

"Did you say Third?" the driver asked.

"Yes," Holly affirmed. She had been surprised by the driver's voice. It was a woman's. Now she noticed the bleached, cropped hair under the cap, and the hands on the wheel, small, but the nails unpolished and cut bluntly. She watched from the back seat as the woman maneuvered the taxi expertly through the heavy train station traffic. "I thought San Diego was a quiet little place," she commented to the driver.

"Not since the war," she shot back at her.

"How long have you been driving a taxi?" Holly asked.

"Since the war," she answered.

Her responses were as sharp as her turns. There was an edge, an animosity to her that Holly felt. It didn't seem to be a special hostility that she had sparked in the woman, but an attitude already formed and hardened. Holly said no more to her. She thought of the war, how it pervaded everything, but touched her so little in any private way. To her it was a newsreel, a *Life* cover, a crowd of uniforms, a wait in a line, a ration book. Millions were suffering and dying but it was almost impossible to imagine all those people. There was no single human being, a brother in uniform and in jeopardy, or a husband, a son, that linked her to the war and made it breathe and threaten. The war was like this taxi ride with this surly and somehow sad woman. Holly was in her power, and potent, potentially dangerous as this power was, it was impersonal, too. The taxi stopped.

"This is it," the driver said to her.

Holly paid her and got out. It wasn't the sort of neighborhood or apartment building she had expected. There were several children surrounding an old man and his bicycle cart. He sold fruit-flavored ices in paper cups. The children devoured them before they melted, but the old man himself seemed to dissolve. Age and weariness transuded, ran from him. Each ice he sold was one he would not have to pedal away with.

She went nearer Iris's building, a flat-fronted and tall place with fire escapes crawling up the side like an army of marauding black ants. She walked up the stone steps. Inside she found a self-operated elevator and gratefully passed by it. Iris's apartment was on the ground floor. She began her search down the poorly lit hallway for the door with the number twelve upon it. There was an old smell to the air, as if it had been used and reused and never allowed to escape these confines. The carpet was thin and stained, the walls, too. She knocked softly on Iris's door when she came to it. There was no answer. She hoped she was in the wrong place, but she knew that she wasn't. She knocked again, louder and harder. The door opened.

"Hi, Hol," Iris greeted her breezily. "C'mon in."

"The train was late," Holly began to explain.

Iris stretched and yawned. "Oh, was it? I've been asleep."

Holly looked around the room. It was as grim and rank and threadbare as the corridor leading to it, but Iris stood in the center radiating animal beauty and sensual health.

Iris acted as if the morning had never happened. She kicked aside a pile of clothes, the blood-spotted dress a vivid part of it, and gestured for Holly to sit down on the rumpled bed, but she was seeing the room through her sister's eyes.

"This is only temporary," she said. "I was out of town. I didn't expect to come back as soon as I did. I had to have a place fast. It's a real hole, but I'm not here much."

Holly perched on the very edge of the bed. She put her suitcase down in front of her. Iris was smiling at her, the same, wonderful, wide, sweet Iris smile.

"You look good, Hol," she commented.

"So do you," Holly told her.

Iris ran a hand through her hair. "I'm in pretty good shape for the shape I'm in." She laughed.

"You didn't sound well on the phone, Iris. I was worried, but I can see that you're fine."

"Yeah? Well, I was feeling a little blue, you know. One minute I was walking by the phone on my way to the can and the next I was calling you."

Holly watched as Iris paced. She stopped and flung herself into a chair. There were several pairs of stockings dangling from the arms. She fingered them.

"Nice, huh?" she asked.

"Very."

"There's a damn lousy run in every one of them," Iris said. "I keep snagging them." She gathered them up angrily and tossed them to the floor as if her negligence were their fault.

"Tell me what you've been doing. You were out of town?"

"I was singing with a band."

"That's wonderful."

"Yeah."

"But you're not with the band anymore?" Holly asked.

"I had to leave."

"That's a shame."

"It was pretty crummy, not like I thought it was going to be. You know the routine, a lot of little towns, different one every night, traveling on a bus. It's not all it's cracked up to be."

"What are you doing now?"

"Nothing much."

"You must have some plans, something you want to do next."

"No."

"There must be something," Holly said but even as she said it, she realized that Iris had no need or desire for a plan in her life.

"I like to let things happen. Plans get messed up anyway, so why make them. There's this guy, Walter. He says he wants to get married. Maybe I will. I've never been married before."

"Do you love him?"

"God, why does everybody ask that, especially Walter?" Iris demanded impatiently.

"I guess because love and marriage go together. They're supposed to anyway."

"You and I both know better, Hol. Did Mama love Daddy? Did Daddy love Mama? God, no. They hated each other. Love and marriage, they don't go together. I might get married because it might be fun. Who knows."

"It wasn't much fun for Daddy and Mama," Holly said.

"You're right about that, but everybody can't be like them. Can they?"

"No, I don't think so."

"Hey, I probably won't marry Walter. Are you getting hungry?"

"Yes." Holly checked her watch. "It's after seven."

"I'll bet you have a certain time you eat dinner every night, don't you, Hol?"

"I guess I do."

"You know you do. You have a plan for everything, too, don't you? Do your plans ever mess up? I'll bet they don't."

"They do, sometimes," Holly told her. She was thinking of Paul.

"All of a sudden I'm starved. This morning I didn't think I'd ever want to eat again. Just goes to show you. Everything passes. God, I'd kill for a hamburger and fries. There's a great place near Balboa Park. C'mon, let's go."

"What was wrong this morning, Iris?"

"Nothing much," she answered. She crossed to the bureau and began brushing her hair. It snapped with electricity.

"Were you sick or something?" Holly persisted.

"Kind of sick," Iris said.

"What does that mean, kind of sick? What was it? What was wrong?"

"You know I don't like to be asked questions, Hol."

"No, I don't know that. How would I? How would I know you? I haven't seen you for more than an hour since you were sixteen years old. I don't know you, Iris. I don't know anything about you. Maybe you'd like to tell me a few things. Start with this morning. I think I have the right to know since you called me and asked me to come here. Don't you agree?"

"No, I don't. Don't throw your coming here in my face, big sister. You came because you wanted to."

"I came because you asked me," Holly protested.

"Yeah, you sure that's why?" Iris asked her.

Holly couldn't answer. She didn't know her reasons. They weren't pure or clear enough to know. She sensed that she wanted Iris to need her, to be somehow obligated, and she hated that in herself. And, besides, Iris remained irresistible. Too many twisted things had brought her here, Holly knew.

"Iris . . ." she began.

Iris interrupted. "Look, I was in a little trouble this morning. I'm fine now. So let's drop it, okay?" She was putting on lipstick, a bright red that matched the sweater she wore. She smoothed her red skirt over her hips. "Let's get out of here. Unless I'm asleep I can't stand this hole," she said. Holly had given her an awareness of the place. She had never really seen it until her sister's arrival. "C'mon."

Outside, standing on the sidewalk, Holly noticed that Iris was very pale against her red sweater.

"Are you sure you feel like walking?" she asked.

"Yeah."

Holly guided her across the street. She held her hand lightly at Iris's elbow. It was their first physical contact and she felt strange initiating it. She expected Iris to reject it, to throw her hand off, but she didn't. When they passed by a park bench, Iris spoke.

"Maybe I'll sit down for a minute."

They sat down on the bench.

"Something is wrong, Iris. Tell me what it is."

"Nothing is wrong. Everything's jake."

"But just now . . . if you hadn't sat down you would have fallen. You were about to faint."

"I was just a little dizzy. Quit harping at me."

"All right, Iris."

There was a lamp post beside their bench. Just beyond the bright circle of light that it cast Holly could see two sailors. They stood by a tree in the shadows not far from them. The color was returning to Iris's face.

"If you're feeling better I think we should go," Holly suggested.

Iris had seen them, too. She smiled at her sister, and to the sailors, and to herself.

"Let's stay put," she said.

"Iris, I want to go."

The men were beginning their approach.

"I had an abortion this morning," Iris told Holly.

They stalked, sauntered toward them, two white figures coming from the darkness into the light. Holly knew she had heard what Iris had said, but she was fighting any acceptance of it. Long ago, she remembered, trying not to believe her sister when she told of setting the fires. It was happening all over again and again there were two men drawing near, attracted by Iris's lethal beauty. She didn't want to know her sister's nature, but Iris was savagely thrusting it upon her.

"I want to go," Holly said.

"So go," Iris told her.

"Why did you want me to come?" she asked.

"I didn't want you to. I just wanted to see if you would."

Finally Holly believed her. Iris didn't want or need her. She only wanted and needed to know that she could still draw her, suck her in. She had proved that she could. Now she was moving on, attracting something new. Holly saw her perfect profile as she turned to the sailors.

"I've got to go," she said, speaking to no one. She got up from the bench and began to run.

"Hey, what's your hurry! We don't bite! Hey, don't go!" One of the sailors shouted after her. "Don't go!"

Holly heard Iris's laughter. It repeated harshly like rifle shots, splitting open the night. She kept on running, away from the sailors and the sound of her sister's lashing hilarity. She returned to the apartment, not knowing where else to go, and persuaded Mr. Hagen to let her into Iris's room. With the instincts of a true landlord, he brought up the rent that was owing, smelling that Holly would pay. And she did. She gave him the money he asked for and closed the door on him, but she had the uneasy feeling that he remained out in the hall for a long time, lurking, rubbing in his hands the bills she'd given him for Iris's room. She waited through the night for her sister's return and as on that night in Kansas the sounds never came. Iris never came. At dawn Holly left. She tried to give some order to this trip, some explanation of it. She had to do this for herself. She had been fleeing and Iris had been magnetizing, each doing what she did best. She didn't think that Iris would ever stop, but she believed that she herself could. When her train pulled in to the Los Angeles station she went directly to the bank of telephones and dialed Paul's number. His answering voice sent joy and relief running through her.

✿

Chapter Fourteen

✿

Poppy sat in Rose's living room and watched her sister dial the telephone. Rose had waited until Clyde had left for work before making the call. He had said nothing about Poppy coming to stay with them, but he had surely heard the rumors at the factory. Everyone at Straker's was talking about his sister-in-law, but Clyde said nothing. He went to work toting the lunch that Rose had fixed for him and packed in his black pail. When the door closed Rose crossed to the table where the telephone sat.

She didn't want to do this. She didn't know what to say to Holly. She was afraid of saying too much or too little. It seemed like she was always giving bad news to her sister. Once, just once, she would have liked to call without the forced cheery tone that Holly never failed to spot. She wished she had something good to tell, but Rose was becoming convinced that nothing very good happened in life. She looked over at Poppy, who sat still, apprehensive, as if she were waiting for a verdict or a sentence. The operator came on the line and Rose gave her Holly's number. It would be very early in California but Rose wanted to catch Holly at home. She was thinking of the telegram that she had thoughtlessly sent to her office, the telegram with the word of their parents' death. Rose cringed now at that terrible mistake. Knowing what a private person Holly was and putting her in the position of such exposed grief was an error that Rose had no intention of making again. The telephone was ringing.

"Hello."

Holly sounded to Rose as if she were only across the small Kansas town.

"Hello, Holly. It's Rose."

"Rose, how are you?" Holly asked.

Rose thought that she sounded happy to hear from her, but there was an anticipation, a slight nagging tone of expectancy, too.

"I'm fine. How are you?" Rose answered and asked.

"Just fine," Holly told her. "It's so good to hear from you. How's everyone there?"

Rose heard her other questions—what was wrong? why the early morning call?—all of Holly's unasked questions in that one spoken one. She stared over at Poppy on the couch, who was unaware of the lag in the conversation. Neither Rose nor Holly were speaking. Rose listened to the hollow silence and couldn't think what to say to lightly, laughingly fill it.

"Rosie, what is it? What's wrong?"

Holly had finally voiced the questions. Rose knew her response but she balked at giving it.

"How would you like to have a visitor?" Rose asked.

"You? Are you leaving Clyde?"

Rose detected a mix of happiness and sorrow in her sister's query.

"No," she said. "It's not me. It's Poppy."

Poppy stirred slightly at her name.

"Poppy?" Holly asked.

"Yes. Wouldn't you like to have your little sister come for a visit?"

"Of course, yes. I would. I'm surprised, that's all. I thought Poppy was with Lily."

Rose was aware of her rushing.

"She was with Lily. Then a couple of months ago she went to work at Straker's. She was living in the dormitory there. You remember the old place, don't you?"

"I remember, Rose."

Rose knew she was handling this badly. Her lightness had
become deception and Holly recognized the change.

"Poppy will tell you all about Straker's. I thought it would be
a good idea if she came out to California to see you."

"I'd love to have her, Rose."

Rose bit at her fingernail. Holly was willing to help even if
she wasn't being told the whole story. Rose was grateful to her
sister for not asking the questions that she might have, questions
she was entitled to ask in return for her aid. Rose was grateful
and guilty. She nodded at Poppy.

"This is going to make Poppy very happy," she said to Holly
while looking at Poppy's miserable, thin, rabbity face and doubt-
ing if she could ever be happy. "I'll put her on the train
tomorrow. She'll get in on Saturday. Will that be all right?"

"That'll be fine," Holly said. "Rose, I saw Iris a couple of
weeks ago."

"You did? Where?"

"In San Diego. She's living there now."

"How is she?" Rose asked.

"You know, she's . . . Iris."

"I know," she said. "And she got hold of you?"

"Yes. She called me on an impulse."

"An impulse, huh? Pretty word. Sounds like yours, not hers."

Holly laughed for the first time. Rose was pleased at the sound.

"You're right about that. How's Lily?"

The question came suddenly. Rose wasn't prepared and she
answered bitterly, "She's saved."

"What?"

"Saved. The rest of us are doomed to Hell's fire, but Lily's
not going to burn."

"Is it as bad as that?"

"Worse. Sweetie, I'd love to talk longer but I can't."

"Oh, this must be costing you a fortune. I'll expect Poppy
on Saturday. She'll call me from the station?"

"Right."

"Paul and I will pick her up."

Rose was surprised.

"Paul? Who's Paul?" she asked.

"A friend of mine."

"A friend?"

"A good friend," Holly said.

"Tell me about him."

"I'll call you next week and we'll talk some more."

Rose felt that Holly was right to wait, that this was not the conversation in which to bring up friends or lovers, whatever he was to her, but still she'd had to mention him. That kind of casual reference wasn't like Holly.

"Well, goodbye, Holly."

"Goodbye, Rose."

Rose didn't hang up. There was something left to be said, one thing among many, but this one compelling. She paused, wondering if it would be she or Holly who spoke.

"Rosie?"

"Yes?"

"I wish it was you. I wish you were coming."

"So do I," Rose said.

The connection was mutually, simultaneously broken.

Holly sat staring at the telephone, this instrument of communication, this thing that was a miracle short years ago and now a convenience. It did provide the channel, Holly conceded that, but the people at opposite ends of the line had to say the words into it. She hadn't said the words that she wanted to say and she knew that Rose hadn't either. Of all her sisters, she liked Rose best. Rose was the most likable of them, but it was Poppy coming to visit her. She didn't know Poppy, didn't even know why she was coming. She'd known her only as a child. The last time they had seen each other was at their parents' funeral. Poppy had cried incessantly and her tears were for her mother. Holly thought at times that they had had different mothers. The loving and devoted woman who was Poppy's mother had certainly not been hers. Poppy had been Mama's baby. Now Mama's baby was coming to stay with her and what would Mama have said to that, she wondered. If only it could have been Rose. She was afraid for Rose, frightened that she'd never get out of Kansas now. Time was passing so quickly and Rose was standing still. The worst of it was the resignation she sensed in her sister. Rose would continue to say that she wished she was leaving, but she was incapable of it. She wouldn't run off in a coupe with two salesmen the way that Iris had. She hadn't enough selfishness for that sort of ruthless cruelty. She wouldn't escape into religion as Lily had done. Rose was too reasonable to immerse herself in rigid dogma. She wasn't so weak, so pathetically dependent as their little sister Poppy. Rose was resilient. She wouldn't throw herself on others. And, Holly thought, Rose had no ambition to drive her out of Kansas as Holly herself had been driven. Rose was simply nice, an even-tempered and likable girl. She had a sweet humor that was turning bitter, trapping her, but sustaining her somehow.

The telephone rang again. It startled her. It was so near. She lifted the receiver. It was Paul. She was happy to hear from him but at the same time resentful at being pulled from her thoughts. Would it always be this way, she wondered. Would her emotions be forever mixed? Would she never feel one thing purely and completely? Paul was talking but his words were mere accompaniment to her thoughts. She held the telephone. The device wasn't at fault. It transmitted quite clearly what was said into it. She could hear Paul, but she couldn't tell him what she was thinking, what she was, and this conversation was another failure. She was to blame. Blame, she thought. She took blame easily. Mama had blamed and blamed her. It was blame along with her ambition that had gotten her off the farm. Maybe if Rose had been blamed as she had been, she would have gone, too. Rose had gone a short way by marrying Clyde, but Clyde had betrayed her, deserted her while he lived in the same house with her, and slept in the same bed, sometimes. . . . Probably Clyde hadn't blamed Rose either. He had probably blamed himself and that was why he stayed with her, sometimes. Blame. Blame could hold a person or drive a person out.

"Holly? Holly, did you hear me?"

Paul was asking if she'd heard him and she had. She had heard. Only she didn't know what he'd said.

"Holly?"

"I'm sorry. What did you say, Paul?" she asked him.

"You're preoccupied this morning," he said. "You're a million miles away."

"Only a few hundred," she confessed. "I had a call from Kansas this morning."

"Who called?"

"My sister Rose."

"Are you all named for flowers?" he asked.

"Yes. It was Mama's idea. We moved around a lot. She could never keep a garden. So we became her garden. That's what she used to say, that we were her garden that she could take with her anywhere."

"That's a lovely thought."

"Is it? I guess it is." She paused. "What were you saying before, Paul?"

"Tell me first about your Kansas call."

"No, not now. I'll tell you about it later," she said. "You were asking me something, weren't you? What was it?"

"I asked if you wanted to go to Burt's party tonight."

"Can we decide later?" she asked. She wanted to postpone deciding, answering, everything.

"Yes."

"I've really got to go. I'm going to be late for work."

"We can't have that."

"Don't be angry, Paul."

But he was. She slipped in and out of his reach. She was maddeningly elusive. He never knew from one day to the next if she'd let him near or dart off like a hummingbird, flashing iridescent wings at him as she flew away. He loved to hold her, feel her feathery skin and beating heart, but her flight was beautiful to him, too. He could only watch her in angry fascination, unsure if she would stay or go, and unsure which he wanted of her.

"Goodbye," he said.

"Goodbye, Paul."

She gratefully hung up the telephone. And in a moment she was sorry that she had.

It was Saturday, the day of Poppy's arrival, before Holly told Paul about her sister's coming to California. She explained to him that she was setting aside Sunday to talk with Poppy. She planned the time of reacquaintance with her usual care, but that day, and many after it, passed with few words and little intimacy between the sisters. They could not seem to grasp one another.

Poppy had been at Holly's for a month, living there quietly and as unobtrusively as possible. She had taken a job at an aircraft factory immediately. She worked the graveyard shift and returned to the apartment about the time that Holly was leaving for work at the studio. They saw one another in passing.

To Holly, Poppy appeared content. She was hardly aware of the girl's presence. Poppy was neat. There was never a dirty dish or a ring in the bathtub to remind Holly of her sister's existence, but neither were there any pleasant traces, not a vase of flowers or an open book on a table. Poppy kept everything she owned in her suitcase. She did not unpack it. She even wrapped her toothbrush in tissue and replaced it after she had used it. Holly attributed this behavior to the loss Poppy had suffered. She guessed that her sister had trouble believing in the permanence of anything now. Since the death of their parents she had been shifted from Lily's to Straker's to here. Holly realized all of this and wished that she was better able to help Poppy, allay her fears, and support her more solidly, but she was frightened of being consumed by her little sister's needs. So she let herself believe that Poppy was happy or at least comfortable. The suitcase stayed packed and a kind of desperate silence was maintained. Then finally, after some weeks, it was broken.

Holly was having breakfast when Poppy came in from her night at the plant. She wore her uniform, a pale blue jumpsuit. It flattered her slight figure, Holly thought. Poppy didn't speak but smiled at Holly and went directly to the coffee pot. She poured herself a cup and sat down at the table.

"Won't that keep you awake?" Holly asked.

"No. Nothing would this morning."

"Tired?"

"Yes. It was a long night. Some are longer than others," Poppy said.

"You do look worn out."

"Oh, I didn't mean to complain."

"Do you like the work?" Holly asked.

"I don't mind it."

"Is there any chance you could change shifts?"

"No, not for a while. All the new girls start on graveyard. I really don't mind. I never slept much at night anyway."

Holly moved past that comment. "Maybe I could get you something at the studio," she offered, feeling a little guilty that she'd not volunteered before this.

"No. I'm not smart enough. I'm not smart like you, Holly. Besides, you've done enough for me."

"I haven't done anything at all. And you're very smart, Poppy," Holly said and she tilted her head to try and catch her sister's eye, but Poppy stared down into her coffee cup. "Poppy?" She didn't look up. "Maybe you'd be happier back in Kansas. Back at Straker's, maybe." Holly knew as soon as she'd said those words how Poppy would interpret them. She wanted to grab them back when she saw the expression on her sister's face.

"If you'd like me to go . . ."

"No, Poppy." She wanted to reach out and take Poppy's hand, but the small round table was suddenly so wide she couldn't begin the gesture of love and reassurance. "I don't want you to go. It's just that sometimes you look so sad. I thought you might be homesick. It wouldn't be wrong for you to want to go home."

"I don't have a home. Home was blown away. I don't have any place to go home to anymore. And I couldn't go back to Straker's, even if I wanted to."

"Why, Poppy?"

"Things happened . . . they said things about me there."

"What sort of things?"

"Things about Jake and me. Oh, awful things."

Finally Holly thought she understood, that she had solved the mystery of Poppy's visit. She knew what Straker's was. She'd worked there the summer before she left for school, her last Kansas summer. She knew how vicious the gossiping could become. There'd been more scandal manufactured than shirts during the few months she'd worked there. She'd escaped the slurs and rumor-mongering, but she remembered that Lily had not. She recalled Lily's return to the farm from the factory. She'd been too young to understand at the time, but the pieces fit easily enough now. Lily had met a man at Straker's and maybe loved him. He had gotten her pregnant and left her. So Lily had married Workman Banner to legitimize her baby and quiet the Straker tongues. It was obvious to Holly that something similar had happened to Poppy, but Mama was no longer there to arrange matters as she had for Lily. Maybe, too, Kansas was running short of lonely and willing men like Workman Banner. Poor Poppy, Holly thought. She might even have done what Iris did. An abortion. It was terrible to think that this thin girl, little more than a child herself, had been forced to undergo that. But then, it might not have gone that far. Poppy was so vulnerable and weak. The words and the stories alone might have broken her. It might have all been lies. Holly knew that most of the Straker tales weren't true. They were casual and brutal fabrications, born of the cruel tedium, the endlessly insignificant lives that the factory foisted upon its workers.

"Was Jake your boyfriend?" Holly asked her sister.

"No," Poppy answered.

"They just thought that he was? Said that he was?" Holly questioned and prompted her simultaneously, convinced she had guessed correctly.

"Jake is a girl. Her name's really Cecile."

"A girl?"

"Yes. She worked at the factory with me. Her bed was next to mine in the dormitory. Jake was good to me. No one understood. They said . . . things about her . . . and me. Jake was like Mama. She knew about me like Mama did. Jake knew what I was saying when I told her about the Reverend. Lily didn't. Lily didn't believe me, but Jake did. Jake would listen to me. I could tell her things and she'd rub my head like Mama did. She'd let me get into bed with her or she'd get into bed with me, but when they found us together like that they said these things about us. Jake had to leave. They made her go away. They said it had happened too many times before. I was all alone there after Jake left. I was all alone all over again. Then one night . . . I don't remember . . . but they told me that I started tearing all the beds apart and that I ran through the dormitory screaming, that I hit some of the girls and scratched them . . . they said I did that."

"But you didn't?" Holly asked.

"I don't remember. I don't know if I did or not. They said I did. I must have, but I don't remember."

Holly remembered. She remembered Poppy's seizures. No medicine that any doctor had ever prescribed had helped; not even their mother's potent love of Poppy was sanative. Such total and violent loss of control had terrified Holly as a child. It terrified her now. Poppy must suffer from those seizures still. Poppy was a sufferer. She was susceptible to horrible inflictions, abuse by others, because of this horrible inner affliction of hers that knew no external cure. Holly thought of the woman named Jake and of

Poppy's cryptic reference to the man called the Reverend. She looked at Poppy and saw her now as sane—sad and confused, but reasonable and contained. Yet her sister was not far from the wild and writhing child that Holly remembered.

"What about this man? The Reverend?" Holly asked.

"I can't . . . can't . . . can't . . ." Poppy stuttered.

Holly was disturbed by this crack in her sister's composure. "It's all right, Poppy. It's all right if you can't remember," she soothed. "But I thought you said that you'd told your friend Jake about him."

"I did tell Jake. I do remember," Poppy said, calming. "But I'm not supposed to . . . I mustn't talk about it."

"Did you tell Rose?"

"No," she answered. "Rose knows about what happened at Straker's, but not the other," she said. She spoke as if all her short and luckless life was knotted together, tangled in a way that no one knew, not even herself. Only bits and pieces were known. And she was judged by others who thought they knew when they didn't. They didn't know anything at all. Mama might have known. Jake had tried to know. But no one else knew. She'd wanted to tell Lily. Lily. She remembered now Lily's words. "Lily said I must never tell about the Reverend."

"But you told Jake."

"Jake wasn't . . ."

"Wasn't what, Poppy?"

"One of the family. She wouldn't have been shamed by what I'd done."

"What did you do?" Holly asked.

"Lily said I must never, never tell."

"You can tell me. I think that I'll be able to understand," she said. But Poppy needed more than that, she knew. "I know that I won't feel the way Lily did," she told her. She was sure she could safely promise that. "Was it the Reverend Fallon?" she guessed.

"Yes," Poppy whispered. "It was."

She began with Matthew's baptism. Holly listened silently until Poppy reached the point in her story where she returned to Lily's and watched the Reverend and Lily walk to his car, then she stopped her.

"Poppy, were they close together?"

"Yes," she answered.

"Very close?" Holly asked, unintentionally leading her the way that her own thoughts were running.

"Yes. And Lily touched his face with her hand. It was dark, but I saw it. I know I did."

"What happened then?"

"The Reverend got into his car and he drove away. Lily went into the house."

"There was nothing else that you saw . . . between them?"

"No."

"Then you went inside?" she asked.

"Yes. I hoped Lily wouldn't see me, but she did. She started in on me, asking where I'd been, scolding me for running away like I did. She said she'd needed me to help. She said I didn't care about anything and that I was of the Devil."

"She said that to you?"

"Yes."

"And did you tell her what had happened with the Reverend?"

"I did. I told her how he'd hurt me. How he had come to the boathouse and hurt me . . ."

Holly realized that these were the same words Poppy had used in describing the incident to her. She kept saying she'd been hurt. It was all that she knew to say, Holly thought.

". . . and Lily slapped me. She started tearing at my dress, pulling up the skirt . . . she saw me and I was all bloody and she said that I had done it. She said I had done it. One of the children . . . Matthew, I think . . . was crying then, crying and crying. Lily went in to him. When she came back she was so white and quiet. She said she didn't want me in her house, that I couldn't stay there anymore. She told me I would go to the Devil. The next day I went to Straker's."

Holly retained a vivid image of the Reverend Fallon. She could still see him whipping himself into a frenzy at her parents' graveside. It had been bitter cold that day of the funeral, but his face had been hot and red and wet from his exertions. He was a tall man, she remembered. Poppy's halting words had conjured in her mind a starkly shocking scene in the boathouse. She could feel and smell the damp and musty mildewed darkness of the place. He had come upon Poppy there. He had taken her and she had had no defense against his strike. And Lily. Pious Lily.

What was the Reverend Fallon to her? What was he or what had he been? Lily had been a jealous and grasping girl, Holly remembered. This faith of hers had given her a dangerous strength. From the time of her birth Poppy had been Mama's favorite. That had hurt Lily most. To Lily Poppy must have threatened her again as she had in childhood. First she had taken Mama's love from Lily. And then it was the Reverend Fallon. Holly felt sorry for them all, all of them, tangled and strangling from the union of Mama and Daddy. She included herself.

"I shouldn't have told," Poppy was saying.

Holly was suddenly aware of how silently she had received most of Poppy's story and what her silence must mean to her sister.

"No. No, Poppy. You were right to tell me."

"Do you believe me?"

"Yes."

"I was so afraid that you wouldn't," Poppy said.

"I believe you, Poppy. You've been wronged, terribly wronged, by that man Fallon, and those girls at Straker's, and by Lily, too. You have to know that. You have to start believing that. You did nothing to be ashamed of, Poppy."

"But the worst I haven't told you."

"What is it?" Holly asked.

"Mama stopped coming." Poppy was beginning to cry. "I must have done wrong because she stopped coming to me."

"What do you mean Mama stopped coming?"

Poppy felt encouraged to speak. "After the tornado Mama would come to me at night and talk to me, but when I told Lily that I would be baptized Mama never came again. Lily said it was the Devil that came, but it wasn't. It was Mama. I know it. But why would she have stopped coming, Holly? Why would she?"

Holly couldn't face Poppy. It was worse, far worse, with her than she had imagined. Maybe it was madness for Poppy to believe that their dead mother came and spoke to her, but it seemed to Holly to be a harmless and self-preserving fantasy. What was abhorrent was the reality and attendant guilt that had killed the dream, made Poppy feel unworthy of her mother's cherished visits. Poppy was crushed without Mama. The pieces of her were scattered for anyone to pick up. For all her life she would seek a replacement, a surrogate mother. These substitutes would use what portion of her they wanted, making no attempt to put her together, and then leave. Like Fallon. And Jake. There'd be another and another. Holly could see no end to it. She recalled her mother's many insane cruelties, but this, she decided, was the cruelest of all. This thing she had done to her best-loved child was the most hideous and hateful crippling of all. What Mama had done to Daddy and to herself, Daddy's child, were mere pinpricks compared to this.

"Don't cry, Poppy."

Poppy took her words as a Lily-like reprimand. She rubbed at her eyes.

"I'm sorry. Don't be mad, Holly."

"I'm not mad. Well, maybe I am, but not at you. I just don't like to see you cry, that's all."

"You've been so nice. Lily said . . ." She stopped without completing the sentence.

"What did Lily say?"

"That you wouldn't . . . she told Rose that you wouldn't take me. She won't talk to me anymore, she says I'm not her sister. But she told Rose that. She said you were too selfish to care what happened to anyone else. Lily says the whole family's cursed. Do you think we are?"

Sometimes she did think so, but she said, "No, I don't. What does Rose say?"

"She laughs. It makes Lily so mad. You know how Rose is, always laughing and joking."

"She's still that way?" Holly asked doubtfully, thinking of Rose's letters.

"Yes. She laughs a lot, but not like she used to."

"How do you mean?"

"Oh, I don't know. She laughs when things aren't funny and it doesn't sound the same anymore."

"I'm afraid Rose isn't very happy."

"Maybe we really are cursed, like Lily says."

Holly gave advice that she wished she herself could always follow. "Don't you believe it, Poppy. Believing it puts you half the way there."

"I guess you're right." She paused. "Holly?"

"Yes?"

"Do you think Mama might come and talk with me again soon?"

Holly hesitated. "I don't know." She was hedging.

Poppy felt that Holly didn't believe her about Mama. Her doubt was only softer than Lily's, kinder, but it was still suspicion. She was all alone. Holly really didn't understand.

Holly stood. "I have to get to work," she said. "You should get some rest, Poppy. Don't sleep on the couch. Use my bed." She was gathering her purse and sweater, a pile of scripts, in her arms. "And Poppy?"

"Yes?"

"Please unpack your bag. There are two empty drawers in the bureau."

"Those drawers are for me?" Poppy asked.

Holly realized that Poppy had seen them but never thought of filling them or even asking for them. "They're yours," she told her. She knew she'd have to guide her sister, take her by the hand and lead her. Poppy was her responsibility now. She started for the door.

Poppy followed her. "Thank you, Holly."

"You're welcome," she said. "Didn't you mention something about a USO dance tonight?"

"Yes, some of the girls from work are going. They asked me along."

Holly shifted under the burden of her sister, trying to get used to the weight. "You should go to that dance, Poppy," she advised strongly.

Poppy did go to the dance. That night at eleven-thirty she came running into the apartment to change into her work clothes for the midnight shift. Holly was sitting up reading a script.

"Hi," Poppy said excitedly.

"Hello," Holly greeted her. She saw that Poppy's usually pale face was flushed.

"I went to the dance like you told me to. You were so right, Holly. I had the best time. I'll tell you all about it in the morning. I've really got to hurry."

"I think you're going to be late." Holly glanced at her watch. "How many blocks do you have to walk?" she asked.

"I'm not walking with Betty tonight," she said.

"You're not?"

"No, I've got a ride with Deke."

"Deke?"

A horn honked outside.

"That's Deke. He's waiting for me. I've gotta go."

"Can't you tell me a little about him now?" Holly asked.

Poppy looked at her sister. She thought that Holly held her script in the same way that Lily held her Bible. "I will in the morning, Holly. Is that okay?"

"Yes, of course."

No, not like Lily, Poppy decided. "Bye," she said.

"Goodnight. Poppy, you look very pretty tonight."

"Thank you." She opened the door. "Deke asked me to marry him."

"Poppy, wait . . ." Holly began, but Poppy was gone. She'd just begun to take her up and now she was gone.

Deke's horn blasted impatiently.

PART FIVE

❀

HOLLY

Chapter Fifteen

September 1944, Kansas . . .

Clyde was hurrying. Rose knew that he was. He didn't need to say anything to her. Words weren't necessary. She knew he was eager to be somewhere else. Rose didn't want to know where. He drove the truck wildly, bumping crazily along the road out to Lily's. When they reached the signpost that marked the path to the farmhouse, Rose spoke to her husband for the first time since they took their positions beside one another in the stifling hot cab.

"You can stop here," she said to him.

"What?" he asked. He had a habit of pretending that he hadn't heard what she said to him. It gave him time to decide what he should answer. He answered Rose carefully these days. She was so touchy. Well, he supposed, she had the right. He knew that she did.

"Stop here. Let me out. I'll walk the rest of the way," she said.

"You want to walk?" he asked.

The truck was already stopped.

Rose knew that Clyde knew she didn't want to walk. She wondered why she still tried to make things easy on Clyde. Why did she accommodate him and try to please him? Everything they'd ever had together was gone. All that was left was a deep and glass-topped reservoir of resented knowledge. They knew one another. Too well. Still, she attempted to make him laugh and make him happy, and she didn't know why.

"I'll walk, Clyde. I know you don't want to see Lily. I don't want to see her either, but I have to. You don't. Just come back in two hours. I'll wait for you right here."

"Okay," he quickly agreed.

Rose climbed from the truck. She didn't hesitate for that moment. She didn't linger for him to kiss her goodbye because she didn't want to be disappointed. She started down the dirt path and all that she heard from Clyde were the spinning wheels of his truck. She'd made him happy. She'd turned him loose. Had there ever been a time, she wondered, when being with her had made him happy? There had, but it was like a dream, that time was, like a dream, not like anything that had ever really happened. She trudged on through the dust. Her legs rubbed together, the skin burning and chafing. It was such a hot day. Her dress was drenched by the time she got to Lily's. She stopped and took a handkerchief from her purse. She mopped at her face. Her breath was coming hard. She was wheezing, fighting for air, like a fat lady, she thought. She looked down at herself. She was fat. When had she gotten so fat? Was she like this yesterday? She must have been. And the day before. And the day before that. Rose guessed that she'd been fat for years.

The children were playing in the yard. When they saw her they rushed to her. They flung themselves upon her and the touch of them was good. They were cool and stalky, reedlike, these children that loved her were. She was so glad to see them. She wished she saw them more often but when Lily appeared, stepped out onto the porch, dressed in a long and heavy gown with a cross on a chain around her neck, Rose knew why she saw the children so seldom.

"Hello, Lily," Rose called to her.

"Rose."

The children went back to their game and Rose walked to the porch.

"Can we sit out here, Lily?" she asked.

"Too many flies. Too light," Lily stated flatly.

She went back into the house. Rose reluctantly followed her. The house was curtained, close and closed. Lily had gone to the kitchen. Rose stood in the doorway and watched her sister pour black, thick coffee into a cup.

"I'll have a glass of water," Rose said.

"Suit yourself."

Rose went to the sink and ran herself a glass. She took a drink but seeing Lily swallow her coffee made the water go hot in her throat.

"Lily," she began. She sat down at the table. She listened to the shouts of the children and she wished she were out there with them, anywhere but here. "Lily, Poppy is getting married."

Lily said nothing.

Rose continued. "She and Holly called me this morning. I wanted to come and tell you. I thought you'd like to know." She stopped. She waited for some response. There was none. "Poppy sounded good. I got the feeling that Holly might have wanted her to wait a little, but she's not going to do it. He's in the army. He's being shipped out soon. I guess there's no holding them. Maybe they're right. Holly can be too cautious sometimes. Don't you think so, Lily?" she asked, trying to draw her out. She swirled her water in its glass. Finally she drank it down. Now it was merely tepid. She spoke again. "Lily, what do you think about all of this? Do you have anything to say?"

"No."

"Lily . . ."

"Poppy is no longer my sister. That's all," she said.

"All right, Lily. That's fine. Just fine."

Rose took her glass to the sink. She was thinking of the two hours that she had before Clyde would be coming for her. And Clyde would be late. He was always late when he came for her. When he left her, he left early. Two empty hours. What to do with them? But then, her days were filled with empty hours. She was used to them.

"I'm sorry you feel the way you do, Lily," she said. "I'm going out to play with the children."

"The Lord be with you." Lily dismissed her from the kitchen.

"Lily, for God's sake, what's happened to you?" she asked, unable to go without asking, but not expecting to be answered. She had turned away and her hand was on the back door knob.

"Do not take the Lord's name in vain in my house," Lily said.

"I'm sorry," she told her. She was poised to go through the door, to walk from this hot and dark place out into the day where the children breathed the summer air and she could, too, but she felt she had to finish this. "His name in Deke Cody. He's twenty years old. Poppy says he's handsome and nice. I'm glad for her, Lily. I don't think she should wait. I think she needs someone real bad. I'm happy she's found Deke Cody. We all need someone to love."

"You mean a man, don't you?" Lily asked.

"Yes," Rose answered.

"The love of Jesus is more fulfilling than the love of any mortal man," Lily preached.

Rose spun slowly around. "Is that so?"

"Yes."

"Don't you love your husband, Lily? Don't you love your babies? Yours and his?"

"I love Jesus. My love for Him sustains me. It fills me and covers me . . ."

Rose interrupted her. "It's eating you up inside."

"No, I am filled with the love of Jesus."

"There's no love inside you. Not for Jesus. Not for anyone. My God, Lily."

"You blaspheme. Leave my house."

"Don't you care about Poppy?" Rose asked. "Don't you feel a little happy that that poor lost child has found someone to love and who loves her? Poppy's getting married. Lily, can you hear me?"

"I hear you."

"I don't think you do."

"Leave me, Rose. You've told me what you came to say. It is my hour of prayer. I will pray for you. I will pray for us all."

"Poppy, too?"

"Yes. I fear it is too late for Poppy but still I will pray for her."

"Why do you say that? Why is it too late for Poppy?" Rose asked.

"She has gone the way of Jasmine."

"Jasmine?" Rose questioned her sister. It had been so long since she had thought of Jasmine. The name was strange to her. "Our sister Jasmine? Is that who you mean?"

"Yes. Poppy is of the Devil. She has gone Jasmine's way."

"You believe that Jasmine was of the Devil?"

"Was and is. Poppy, too."

Rose couldn't speak.

"Rose, will you pray with me?" Lily invited her.

She couldn't answer. She watched Lily slide to the floor. On her knees, her eyes closed, and her face lifted to heaven, she began her supplication. Rose was revulsed by her sister's pious demonstration.

"I don't think that I will," she told Lily.

Lily did not hear her refusal. She was deep in prayer. Rose left her. She went out and sat on the porch steps. The children ran around the yard, laughing and shouting. Hope walked up to her aunt.

"Aunt Rose, do you want to play?" she asked.

"No, I'll just watch," she said. She put out her hand and touched the child's soft cheek.

"Don't you want to, really? We're going to play hide-and-seek. It's a fun game."

"Yes, I know it is. It used to be a favorite of mine."

"Then come play. Don't old people ever play, Aunt Rose?"

"No, old people don't have much fun. You go on. I have to be leaving soon."

"Will Uncle Clyde be picking you up?"

"Yes."

"Here?"

"No, out on the road," Rose told her.

Hope gazed at her, saying nothing, looking for answers, not listening for them. Old people's faces said more than their words, especially Aunt Rose's, the little girl decided.

Rose was beginning to feel uncomfortable. "Go on, Hope. Go on and play. I'll watch for a while," she said.

Hope ran off to join her brothers in the game. Rose leaned back against the top step and waited, waited for the sun to go down and the heat to ease, waited for the time when Clyde would be stopping at the roadside to get her. The little boys had all hidden themselves away. Hope, with her eyes closed, stood in the center of the yard counting to one hundred. Rose could still see Lily kneeling on the kitchen floor. She had closed her eyes, too. Rose thought of all the things, being the seeker in hide-and-seek, praying, sleeping, kissing red-haired boys, all the things that closed the eyes. Hope called out.

"Here I come! Ready or not!"

Hope began to hunt. She searched behind the trees. Rose watched her. She came past, looking under the porch, and smiling at her aunt, asking no hint where the boys had hidden. She would find them herself. One after another Rose heard the shouts and she knew that each little brother had been found by Hope. They straggled back to the yard. Finally only Jonathan was left still in hiding. The sun was setting. Rose stood and waved to the children. She started down the road, hoping she would find Clyde waiting for her. She was tired of always being the one who waited and waited. She paused and over her shoulder took a last look at Lily's place. She saw Hope enter the barn.

Hope had found Jonathan up in the loft. She knew he would be there. She had saved his finding for the last. She came up the ladder and saw him lying on his back. She lay down next to him.

"I found you," she said.

They stretched out beside one another. They could see the clouds gathering in the east, framed by the tall barn window. From the white masses they made pictures. They never said what they saw. They always saw the same things in the clouds. They didn't need to tell each other. Hope rolled her head to the side and Jonathan had looked from the clouds to her at the same moment.

"Will we always be together?" she asked him. It was the question that she always asked, knowing what he would answer. "Even when we're old?"

"Yes," he said. "We'll have a big farm and we'll raise horses."

"How many horses will we have?"

"Stables full and pastures full," he told her.

"And what colors will they be?"

"Chestnut and bay, black and roan and one golden horse with a golden mane and a golden tail."

"Whose horse will that be?" she asked.

"Yours," he answered.

"Mine," she said dreamily. She smiled at him. "I want to see it, Johnny. Show it to me."

He unbuttoned the bib front of his coveralls. They had played this game often. Hope watched his movements. She was fascinated by this thing that her brother had and she did not. All her brothers had one. Only she didn't. She wished sometimes that she did, that she was like the rest of them. Johnny showed her his and he let her touch it and that was nearly as good as having one of her own. He held it tenderly in his hand now. She reached out and stroked it. The skin was soft and pinker than the skin on his arms or his legs. The color was why they had begun calling his thing Pinky.

"Show me your hole," Johnny said.

They had found it together, her hole. A long time ago, early one morning, under the covers of the bed they shared, Johnny had put his finger in it. She had wanted to know where the hole went, if it stopped somewhere inside her, but Johnny said that it didn't stop. He said that it must go on and on, right up through the middle of her. And she thought that she was like the hollow chocolate Easter bunnies that came in their baskets, the ones that they sucked until the candy melted in their mouths and the rabbit was gone. She must be empty inside like that and her brothers were filled with something that she didn't have. They were full. They had little soft and pink things that they held tightly or gently and she didn't. She had a hole that went straight up inside of her. She undid her coveralls, pulled them down, and then her panties too. Johnny watched and held Pinky. Pinky was hardening, swelling, and reddening. She looked down at herself, the folds of skin that hid the hole. Johnny put his finger in it.

"Can't you feel where it stops, Johnny?"

"It doesn't stop."

"It has to stop somewhere. I want it to stop," she said.

"But it doesn't."

"Pinky's longer than your finger."

"So?" he asked.

"Put Pinky in the hole and see if you can feel where it stops. I want it to stop. I don't want to be hollow like a chocolate bunny," she told him.

"Okay," he said.

They didn't hear the creaking of the ladder up to the loft. Johnny was straddling Hope and Pinky was pressing against her bare stomach. They didn't hear the faint creaking but they heard their mother's screams.

"Vile! Evil! Vile!" Lily screamed.

Neither of the children moved. They stayed as they were, looking at her, not understanding why her face was so white and her mouth was opened wide and black in a scream. They were still and staring at the screaming hole in their mother's face.

"Evil!" she said again. She was tearing Jonathan off Hope. "Abomination!"

"Mama. Mama, don't. You're hurting Johnny." Hope was crying.

Lily dropped the boy and struck at Hope. She began beating her daughter, landing blows heavily everywhere that she could. Jonathan jumped on her and tried to stop her. Lily flung him off and he nearly fell down the ladder. Hope was wailing.

"Put on your clothes," Lily ordered them. She had gone suddenly quiet. "You will be punished for this."

"What are you going to do?" Jonathan spoke up.

"You will be punished by God," she said. "Get dressed. Cover your evil nakedness. Evil. Evil. Evil," she murmured.

They buttoned themselves under Lily's eyes. Hope wiped at her tears, but Johnny did not cry. When they had passed from the dusty darkness of the barn out into the yard, Lily started to speak.

"God save this accursed family," Lily whispered as if in prayer.

"What, Mama? What did we do?" Hope asked her mother. "What was wrong?"

Lily slapped her to the ground.

"Evil! Evil!" the screams exploded once more.

"I hate you!" Jonathan shouted at her. "You're not my mother and I hate you!"

Lily took him by the shoulders and forced him to his knees in the dirt beside Hope.

"Pray!" she cried in command. "Pray for your immortal souls!"

The children did not pray. They wished. They wished that they were grown and living on their horse ranch. They wished that they were away from here and her. They wished that they could hold one another's hand.

Clyde drove the truck more slowly on the way home. And Rose talked.

"And do you know what Lily said then?"

"What?" Clyde asked without interest.

"She said that Poppy wasn't her sister. She's pretty far gone, Clyde. I feel sorry for the children. It's like they know somehow. They stay among themselves. Workman's never there. He's out in the fields or he's asleep."

"Poor guy," Clyde said with some feeling.

Rose looked at her husband. She started to say something but stopped. It was much easier to discuss Lily's domestic situation with Clyde, much easier than discussing their own. "I swear I don't know what happened to Lily. It's like she took on all the bad things about Mama and none of the good."

"Yeah, it's too bad." Clyde had gone neutral again. He had no real sympathy for Lily or Lily's children. He felt sorry for Workman, the man who was trapped in a life of labor and rest from the labor and nothing more. He didn't plan on getting stuck like that. He was going to get out before he was in that deep. He thought of the stillbirth and Rose's miscarriage, how sad he'd been at the time, but maybe they'd been a blessing.

Rose switched from Lily to a happier subject. "Couldn't we go to Poppy's wedding?" she asked.

"What, in Los Angeles?"

"No, I told you it's going to be in San Francisco. Deke's being shipped out from there. They'll only have two days for a honeymoon. It's so exciting and romantic. Don't you think, Clyde?"

"Yeah."

"Why don't we go?"

"Rose, you know we can't go to California."

"Why not? We could even move there." She was saying finally what she had been thinking of for so long. "You could find work. There'd be work for you anywhere. You're such a good mechanic. Why don't we go? Why don't we give it a try?"

He stared straight ahead. He'd thought of going, leaving Kansas, but not with Rose. He and Ginny had talked about going west. Ginny was young and fresh. She was eager to be moving somewhere new. He wanted to take Ginny away with him. Now Rose was talking about their going. Why had he been in such a hurry with Rose? Why had he married so young? Why hadn't he waited for Ginny? He should have known that he'd find her one day. Somehow he should have known that. Someone should have warned him, told him to wait a little. Out of the corner of his eye he saw Rose raise her plump freckled arms up over her head. Ginny had beautiful slender arms, white and soft, without a mark on them. Rose was spotted like a Dalmatian dog, an over-fed one. Why hadn't he seen that before? Why hadn't he guessed that he'd get tired of this blotchy and laughing girl? Rose's laughter grated on him. He hated her jokes. Ginny didn't laugh much. She just looked at him with those big green eyes, looked at him and moistened her lips with her tongue and begged him without words to kiss her.

"It's still so hot," Rose was saying. "Clyde, why don't we go to California? What's holding us here anyway?"

He couldn't tell her that she was what held him. He couldn't tell her. It was her. How could he say that she was the trap and he wasn't about to cart that trap with him to California? If he was going to escape he'd have to cut his chains, not drag them along with him. Rose was the chains. She was what was choking him. He could be happy with Ginny in Kansas or California or anywhere, but with Rose he couldn't be happy anymore at all.

"What put this bee in your bonnet?" he asked his wife.

He didn't want to go, she was thinking. She could read his tone. She knew why he had chosen that silly, slighting little phrase, bee in her bonnet. She knew him well. He didn't want to go to California. He didn't want to go with her. She knew it but she fought knowing it. "I've been thinking about this for a long time. Today at Lily's, I don't know, it kind of clinched it. I don't think there's anything in Kansas for us anymore, Clyde. It's old here, old and tired, like an old woman waiting to die. We need something new. We need to start all over. We were so happy when we first got married," she said. She was trying desperately to reach the sweet and sincere red-haired boy who loved her once. This man beside her wasn't a stranger. She knew him. She knew this man and she wanted the boy he had been back again. "We were happy, weren't we?"

"Yeah."

"Maybe it could be like that again in California. Why don't we go to Poppy's wedding? Why don't we see what it's like out there?" She was aware of the pleading note that had come into her voice, but she couldn't make it go away. She was pleading, pleading for her life.

"Will Iris be there?" he asked.

Rose wanted to scream. She wanted to hit him. But she laughed. She laughed until he spoke.

"What's so funny?" he asked her.

"Nothing, Clyde. Nothing is funny really."

"Why are you laughing then?"

"I don't know. I didn't know what else to do, I guess."

"You're always laughing about something," he told her, obviously disapproving.

"I'm sorry, Clyde."

"Look, Rose, what happened between me and Iris is ancient history," he defended himself angrily.

She looked at him in disbelief. How was it that he was always able to turn it around and make her feel to blame? Now he was threatening her with his anger. She was to blame for making him angry and she mustn't do it again. Well, she would, she thought defiantly.

"Maybe you'd like to talk about something or someone a little less ancient."

"No, I wouldn't."

"Why did you have to ask about Iris? Do you still think about her?" she demanded.

"I just asked, that's all."

"Do you? I want to know. Do you still think about her . . . about Iris?"

"Yeah." His anger had turned sullen. "I do, sometimes."

"Holly told me that Iris said she was coming to the wedding. Do you want to go now, Clyde?"

"No."

"Neither do I anymore."

Clyde's truck bounced down the dusty road, leaving a rising trail of dried Kansas earth behind it. Rose pushed back her hair and rubbed at a freckle on the back of her hand as if to make it go away. Poppy used to try and count her freckles when they were children. Now Poppy was getting married. She wouldn't be there to see it, but Holly would. And Iris would, too.

Iris was sitting on a bench in the bus terminal. She was listening for the call for the San Francisco bus. This wedding of

Poppy's might be fun, she calculated. There might just be a good time to be had. A sailor sat down beside her on the bench.

"Hi," he said.

She smiled at him. "Hi."

"Where you going?" he asked.

"San Francisco," she told him. "How about you?"

"Oh, I'm not going. I just got in."

"You'll like San Diego. It's a fun town."

"Yeah, so I've heard," he said.

"So how come you're hanging around here?" she asked. "There are lots of good places to go, better than the bus station," she said.

"I saw you," he said simply. "And I couldn't leave without saying something, anything, to you. I had to talk to you. You're the most beautiful girl I've ever seen," he said. "I mean it."

He had a wide and innocent face. There was no guile in it. She liked the look of him. She especially like the way that he looked at her. Clean adoration was becoming a rare thing lately.

"I could show you lots of places, lots of fun things to do," she said. "I could if I wasn't going to San Francisco."

"Don't go."

She wondered how many times she could make him say that to her, beg her not to go.

"I have to go," she said.

"No. It's foggy in San Francisco. I know, I've been there. You don't want to go there. You belong in the sunshine."

She liked that.

The call for her bus came. "That's mine," she said.

"Don't. Please, don't go."

"It's my kid sister's wedding. I said I'd come," she told him.

"Do you like to swim?" he asked suddenly.

"I love to swim."

"We could go to the ocean."

"I know a beach, a cove, where no one ever goes," she enticed him.

"That's swell," he said. "Let's go."

"Do you have a car?" she asked.

"No, but I could get one. I've got three hundred bucks. We could get a car for that, couldn't we?"

"Sure we could and have a little left over for a bottle."

"It sounds swell," he said.

"Let's go find us a red convertible."

"Yeah," he enthused. "And when I'm shipped out you can have it. You'd look swell in a red convertible. You'd look swell in anything."

They heard the last call for her bus.

She teasingly tested him. "I really should get on that bus and go to San Francisco."

"Please don't," he begged.

"Okay, I won't."

"Swell!" he said.

"Let's go get that car."

"Yeah, let's go."

They started to walk from the station.

"Say, what's your name?" he asked her.

"Iris," she told him, but she didn't ask him his. There had been too many names.

"I guess they'll miss you at the wedding. Does it bother you a lot?" he asked her.

"No," she answered. "I can't remember what she looks like even."

"You can't remember what your own sister looks like?"

"No," she said, and she couldn't. She had attempted briefly to recall Poppy, but all that came to her was a faint image of a scrawny and scared-eyed little girl. "I'd rather be with you," she told him, using her smoothest honey tone. She didn't notice how strangely the sailor was looking at her.

She was beautiful, the most beautiful girl ever, and she was going to show him a deserted beach. Maybe she'd let him kiss her, he was thinking. He couldn't let this chance slip, but still there was something about her, something behind the green eyes, something beneath the satiny skin, that he didn't like. She was kind of scary, he thought, but too beautiful not to be chanced. Was her sister who was getting married like her, he wondered, but he'd never know. Iris couldn't tell him. She didn't know. Poppy's wedding was happening in another world, not Iris's. The bus left for San Francisco without her.

A cold wind was blowing from across the bay, making the city wildly and vividly clear on Poppy's wedding day. Everyone's thoughts and plans had gone only up to the moment of the ceremony. After the justice of the peace, wheezing with a sinus condition exacerbated by the wind, had pronounced Deke and Poppy man and wife, they all stood for a time, uncertain what to do, what happened next, except for the snivelling magistrate who sneezed violently three times and collected his fee, putting it in the same pocket as his saturated handkerchief. Paul suggested that they celebrate with a wedding luncheon. It was late in the afternoon and no one was really hungry, but they all leaped at the first course of action presented to them and away from the awkward inactivity in the drafty living room of the JP. They piled into Paul's car and drove to one of the city's landmarks, an elegant restaurant perched atop a lovely old hotel.

They were seated in the nearly deserted dining room. All of San Francisco was just beyond the window, spread before them proudly, gloriously. Poppy commented first and somewhat breathlessly.

"It's so pretty here," she said.

Holly had to agree. "It's very beautiful, Paul. I'm so glad you thought of it.

Deke was ill at ease. Holly sensed his discomfiture. There was an odd quality about this young man who was now Poppy's husband, Holly was thinking as she watched him. He was good-looking, but his eyes flicked from object to object constantly. It was impossible to make contact with him. He wouldn't focus long enough. He seemed incapable of a sustained visual encounter. His speech was similar. He spoke rapid-fire, nervously skittering from subject to subject.

"Yeah, nice joint," Deke said. "Expensive, I'll bet."

"Worth it, I think," Paul commented softly.

There was an obvious strain between the two men, a friction caused by a deep difference in natures and maybe more than that. Holly was very aware of it.

The waiter came to their table and Paul ordered champagne. Deke twisted restively. Before the waiter was gone, he spoke up.

"Will you bring a beer along with that?" he asked.

"Yes, of course, sir," the waiter replied.

"I didn't think they'd let me have any liquor," Poppy giggled and whispered.

"They wouldn't say a thing to you, baby. You're my wife. You can have anything I say you can," he swaggered verbally and put his arm around Poppy's thin shoulders.

Poppy smiled up at him. Holly flinched. Paul studied the menu.

"I don't know what could have happened to Iris. She said she was coming," Poppy was saying. "Oh, Deke, I wanted you to meet Iris. And I haven't seen her in so long but I remember how beautiful she is. Iris is the most beautiful of us all."

"I'd like to have met your sister, baby, but she couldn't be any prettier than you."

"Oh, but she is. Isn't she, Holly? Isn't Iris the most beautiful sister?" Poppy asked.

"Yes, she is," Holly agreed. "Iris is the most beautiful."

Holly avoided Paul's eyes. She could feel him looking at her. She stared down at the pale peach-colored linen napkins and the white mums in the crystal vase, the heavy silverware with the intricate pattern and the large thread-thin water goblets. She didn't want to look at Paul. The waiter came with the champagne and the beer.

The lunch progressed smoothly. Not much was said. Poppy and Deke held hands, kissed, and ate little. Holly and Paul watched them for a while and then began talking of San Francisco. Paul had lived in the city when he was an young aspiring novelist, he told Holly lightly. He had turned that passage in his life into a series of clever and entertaining anecdotes, but Holly perceived his disappointment in the lost dream.

"You never told me that you wanted to write novels," she said to him.

"I did write novels. Four dreadful unpublished novels."

"Just because they weren't published that doesn't make them dreadful," she said. "I'd like to read them, Paul."

"That would be impossible," he said.

"Why?"

"They were burned," he told her. He answered her inquiring look. "I burned them."

Their casual lunch talk had turned serious. Deke intruded.

"It's getting kind of late," he announced.

Holly checked her watch. "It is," she said. "Where are you staying?" she asked suddenly. "The city is jammed. I hadn't even thought of it until now. Where will you go?"

"I got a room for us in a place down on Market," Deke said.

"Market can get a little rough, Deke," Paul said. "I may be able to help. I used to know the manager of this hotel. Of course that was nearly a century ago," he smiled. "But he may still be here. Would you like to stay here?"

"Oh, it's so pretty. I'd love it," Poppy said.

"We've got a room," Deke told her. "Maybe it's not so fancy, but I got it."

Poppy's lip quivered. Both Holly and Paul noticed.

"Thanks anyway, Paul," Deke said. "C'mon, let's get out of here."

Deke reached for the check. Paul stopped him.

"This is my party, Deke."

"No."

Holly saw for the first time a straight and solid look from Deke. It was directed at Paul, a glowering and glazed belligerent stare. It frightened her.

"I insist," Paul told him.

With one swift sweep Paul laid several bills across the check, summoned the waiter, and the bone of contention was gone.

"You're pretty slick, aren't you?" Deke leaned forward across the table. "Let me tell you something. I can pay for my wife's and my meals. And I can get our hotel room, too. I don't need your help, slick guy. Okay?"

"Deke . . ." Poppy placed a hand on his arm.

He threw it off and glared at her.

"Stay out of this," he warned her menacingly.

Tears began streaming down Poppy's face.

"Deke, I wanted to make this my wedding gift to you. I should have let you know that. I wasn't trying to grandstand. I hate check grabbers as much as you do." Paul spoke smoothly, soothingly.

Holly was reminded of their first evening together when that drunken boy had approached them. Was he a soldier or a sailor? She couldn't remember now, but he'd been young and in uniform and he had called Paul a draft dodger. Paul was reacting now the same way that he had then. He was handling Deke, calming him.

"The next one will be on you, Deke. I'll tell you what, when this war is over we'll all go out for a big steak dinner and the tab's all yours," Paul continued sanely, almost sweetly.

"Okay," Deke responded. "Sounds good to me." He laughed tightly, edgily. "With me going over there, the war's gonna end a lot sooner, a helluva lot sooner. I'm gonna take on plenty of Japs."

His bravado was pathetic, terrifyingly pathetic, Holly thought. Deke and Poppy walked out of the restaurant first. She and Paul followed. She spoke in low tones to Paul, afraid of being over-heard, and more afraid of what she was saying.

"There's something very wrong with him, Paul."

Paul nodded his head slightly. "I'm sorry to say so, but your little sister is in for some big trouble with that boy."

"Is he crazy?" Holly asked. She paused, thinking maybe he was only young and proud and insanely patriotic, volatile and violent. The streets were teeming with boys like that. Maybe Deke was one of those. "Or am I?"

"Well, we know you're not. About Deke, I'm not so sure."

Holly put her arm through Paul's. She felt relieved. She was not alone in her assessment of Deke. She worried about her opinions, thinking them harsh and wrong sometimes, but Paul was agreeing with her. She experienced a closeness to him, a shared view of the world that she had only vaguely sensed was between them before. He pressed her arm lightly. She looked at him, seriously and lovingly. She did love this man, she realized at that moment.

"How can I tell Poppy?" she asked him.

"You can't," he said. "And I wouldn't suggest trying. If she didn't see it the first time she looked in his eyes, I'm afraid she's doomed to suffer it when it escapes from behind them. There's madness just behind his eyes."

"She should know, Paul."

"Holly, she adores him, that's obvious. It's for Poppy to find out what he is, not for you to tell her, and certainly not for you to warn her. Maybe for Poppy he'll be something other than what we see."

"How can you say that after seeing how he reacted to her at lunch, how he lashed out at her? She's the perfect victim for him."

"Maybe that's why they're together."

They were nearing the car. Poppy and Deke had reached it already. The gap between the two couples was narrowing.

"Maybe so," Holly said.

"You won't say anything then?" he asked, trying to confirm her discretion, pin her down to prudence in this matter of her sister and her sister's husband.

"I'll only wish her well, that's all."

"That's enough, Holly."

"I just wish I could reach her. I wish I could have reached her before she did this. I think I could have saved her some pain."

"I doubt it. We make our own pain. We create it and either survive it or it destroys us."

"Paul, I want to stop in Monterey," she said. Their plan had been to drive through the night back to Los Angeles, but the way that she felt toward him now made that scheme wrong. "I've always wanted to see it. I don't want to drive past it in the darkness. I want you to show it to me. Will you take me there?"

They were at the car now. Deke and Poppy were close, within earshot. There was much that he wanted to say, but he could only answer.

"Yes, Holly."

They drove Poppy and Deke to the hotel on Market Street. Holly hated to leave her sister there, but there was nothing else that she could do. She knew that Paul was right. They took Poppy's suitcase from the trunk of the car. It was the same suitcase that she had left packed for so long at Holly's apartment.

The young couple stood out on the sidewalk until Paul's car was far down the street. Poppy waved and waved.

"C'mon, baby," Deke said. "I want you to see the room I got for us."

It was a small, light room, clean and plain, a place of passage. The first thing that Deke did was go from window to window pulling down the shades.

"I like it sunny. It's nice." Poppy said.

"No," he told her.

One of the shades slipped from his hand and snapped loudly upward. Poppy jumped at the sound. Deke pulled at it furiously and it got away from him again. He battled with the shade while Poppy watched. Finally he ripped it from the brackets on the wall and threw it across the room. Then he turned on Poppy.

"Why are you looking at me like that?" he asked her. "What're you scared of me or something?"

"No," she answered, but she backed away a little.

He came forward and took her by the shoulders. "I'm your husband," he said. "You can't be scared of me."

"I'm not scared, Deke," she told him, but she was. She was terrified.

He kissed her, not gently as he always had before, but roughly and quickly as if to get the caress out of his way. He began to unzip the back of her dress. He swiftly stripped her clothes from her. She stood finally like a bare and stiff doll.

"I have such a pretty lace nightie. Holly gave it to me and . . ." she said, starting to tell him about her tiny trousseau.

"Yeah," he interrupted. "Holly's the lace-nightie type." He paused. "How long have she and that guy Paul been seeing each other?"

"About a year, I guess," she said. She didn't understand his question. "Why?"

"A year and I'll bet he's still not screwing her," he said. He was taking off his uniform. "I couldn't wait a year for you, baby. I wanted to screw you the first night, but I knew you weren't that kind of girl. A guy has to marry a virgin, I figure, but there's a difference between a little girl like you who's never done it and a cold broad like your sister who just doesn't want it. You're gonna want it all the time, baby, once you've had it you will, but you're gonna have to wait for me to come home. 'Cause I swear if I ever found out you'd been with another guy I'd kill you, baby. I swear it."

She wasn't hearing his threats. She was thinking about Holly. "Holly's not cold," Poppy defended her sister.

"Forget her. Go get in bed," he commanded her.

She went quickly and crawled under the covers. From behind the edge of the pulled-up sheet she watched him remove his socks and shorts. He was naked now and walking toward her. He tore the covers off her. She curled up in a little ball.

"Don't do that," he said. "Don't be scared. I told you, don't be scared of me."

He pried her from herself and spread her out on the sheet, arranged her. She did not resist. She did not respond. He lay down on top of her. He whispered hoarsely.

"I gotta break you open, baby. I gotta do it. I gotta break you."

He was pushing inside of her. He moved himself in and out of her for a longer time than the Reverend had, but finally it was the same, the same low moan and gushing wetness, the same soft and satiated retreat. She lay very still. He seemed to be sleeping, but he spoke.

"You're my wife. You belong to me. No other guy has ever had you and no other guy ever will." He was reciting her history and her future, her own life to her.

"Deke, back home in Kansas, there was a man, the Reverend Fallon . . ." she began, and in her true innocence she did not even know that she was destroying the image of purity that her young husband had made for her. She had no idea of her destruction or the destructive forces that she would be unleashing in Deke. ". . . this man, he did that to me," she said.

"What are you talking about?" he demanded.

"He . . . he did what you just did," she said.

His face took on the same expression as when he had fought with the defiant window shade. He grabbed hold of her and started to shake her.

"Deke, don't . . ."

He slapped her.

"How many times? How many times did he do it to you?" he was shouting at her.

"One time," she cried.

"You're lying. I'll bet you two did it every Sunday," he said, and in his mind he saw pictures, horrible pictures forming. "After service, after everybody was gone, he'd take you behind the pulpit and he'd pull up your pretty white Sunday dress and he'd screw you with his big holy cock, didn't he? Didn't he?"

"No, Deke."

He struck her again.

"Don't you lie to me," he said.

"Don't hit me, Deke, don't hit me anymore."

"I can do whatever I want to. You're my wife. You belong to me. I thought you were a virgin, but it looks like I married myself a whore. You're my whore wife and I can do anything I damn well want to you."

He began beating her. Then he was heaving on top of her again, savagely striking within her. Her mouth was bleeding. She could taste it. The Reverend had made her bleed, too, but not at the mouth. That must be what men were about, she thought, bleeding fear, and if there was no fright and no blood from a woman then she was cold, like Deke had said that Holly was.

The inn was beside the sea. It was dark when they drove up to it and the lights in the windows did not penetrate far enough to illuminate the nearby water, but the sound of it and the smell of it was strong, irrevocably the sea. Holly and Paul had coffee and brandy in the dining room. Neither of them wanted dinner. Their desires were perfectly meshed. They even left the same amount of brandy at the bottom of their snifters when they departed the dining room and climbed the stairs to the second-floor suite that they would share this night.

Paul lit a fire in the grate. They sat down before it in twin, winged chairs and looked alternately from the flames into one another's eyes. They did not speak. Still without a word between them they rose from their chairs. They walked to the high, ancient, canopied bed and slowly began to undress. It was as if they were performing the steps of a flawlessly plotted ballet. They seemed to dance, glide together. After hours of tender lovemaking they slept, blissfully spent, in one another's arms. The fire was ash and a sea-gray sky was lightening to dawn, but the lovers lay in their sweet, flushed flesh.

❀

Chapter Sixteen

❀

Poppy returned to Los Angeles in the middle of the week, the honeymoon at an end. Holly couldn't meet her train. She and Paul had stayed longer in Monterey than they had planned. Her first day back at work was the day Poppy was coming home. She didn't feel that she should ask Arnie Ross for any more time off, even though she knew that her slack and reprobate boss wouldn't have cared. She didn't like the sly remarks he had been making about long weekends. She didn't want him thinking that her life was anything like his, that he might possess any salacious knowledge of her. Poppy would have to find her own way from the station, she was thinking as she typed synopses of scripts for Ross.

Holly expected to find her sister at the apartment that evening and Poppy was there. She was asleep in the living room. Holly entered and saw her lying on the couch. One arm was flung across her face, fending off something, bad dreams maybe, Holly thought. She looked at Poppy and saw the little girl she had been. This was still a child sleeping here, she observed, but a married child. She'd read of child marriage and it had seemed barbaric to her. Holly was pursuing this mental abstraction when Poppy stirred and waked. Holly could see her face, the face she had been masking in slumber, and she felt a sickening coiling of her stomach at the sight. With her words Holly put up her own protecting arm.

"Welcome home." It was a normal greeting and a deep evasion.

Poppy rubbed at her eyes. They were red and swollen. There was a discolored swelling at her mouth and nose too, an awful mottled mass of blood beneath the skin.

"Hi, Holly."

It was the same softly sad and slightly muddled voice.

"How are you?" Holly asked her, a pleasantry and not a probe.

"I'm okay. I think maybe I slept too much."

"How long have you been sleeping?" she asked.

"I don't know," Poppy said groggily. "What time is it now?"

"Five-thirty," Holly told her.

"The train got in at eleven. I guess I've been asleep since about noon."

"Poppy, what happened to you?" Holly asked, unable to keep back the question any longer.

"What do you mean?"

"Your face. What happened to your face?"

Poppy put her hand to her face. "What's wrong with it?"

"Well, Poppy . . ." Holly started impatiently and stopped. She thought of how she might soften her comments so that she would not scare her sister into silence, or worse, tears. "It's all puffy and . . ."

"I've been sleeping, that's why," she explained.

Holly wondered if she should accept this, but she knew that she could not. She knew that she could not pretend not to see the terrible bruised look of her sister. Poppy had been hurt, wounded. She could not gently ignore the abuse.

"Poppy, did Deke do this to you?"

"Oh, Holly . . ." and the tears started.

Holly went to her and knelt down by the couch. "What happened?"

"I don't know. I don't know," she sobbed out repeatedly. "It wasn't the way I thought it would be."

"What wasn't?" Holly asked.

"Nothing was . . . nothing."

"Poppy, I want you to stop crying and tell me what happened. Can you do that?" she asked her.

"It just wasn't . . . wasn't the way I thought it would be," she stammered and cried, resaying and saying nothing.

Holly tried a different tack. "How did you think it was going to be?"

Her tears subsided somewhat. "I thought it would be like . . . like our lunch was, so pretty and fine, but it wasn't like that."

"How was it?" Holly asked, seeking specifics to confirm her fears.

"Deke got so mad and he was mean. He wasn't nice to me like he used to be. He wasn't nice at all. He was mean and mad all the time."

"Why was he angry?"

"I . . . I don't know. He just wasn't the same . . . not like he used to be."

Holly was thinking that Poppy spoke as if she had known Deke for a very long time, as if she had had years of sweetness from him and suddenly he had changed. But she'd only known him a month and she didn't really know him at all. Poppy knew nothing about him. She had quickly married a stranger. Now she was tied to him. He was gone but he'd be back some day, and then what? Holly tried to think of some solution for her sister. Could Poppy just pretend that none of it had ever happened? But it had happened. There were records. Legal bonds had been forged. A divorce then? Should she suggest that to Poppy? No, she decided, she'd wait, but something had to be said now to comfort this confused, crying child on her couch.

"Poppy, it will all work out somehow. You'll see," she said. She patted her sister's arm awkwardly. Touch was still a foreign thing to her, but she was beginning to use it. Words were no longer her sole form of contact. "Did you and Deke argue?" she asked.

"No, it wasn't like that," she answered and seeing Holly's eyes focused on her mouth she put her hand to it to hide the hurt.

"But something happened," Holly persisted.

"It's not like you think . . . he didn't mean it . . . I don't think . . . he meant it. He just got so mad, but it's not like you think."

"I don't think anything. You're not telling me anything. I don't know what to think. Now what happened to your face?" she demanded to know.

"Deke hit me."

"He hit you?"

"He was mad because of what I said."

"What did you say?" Holly asked.

"I told him about the Reverend . . . but he . . . he didn't understand."

"And so he hit you? Oh, Poppy."

Swiftly she was defending him. "It made him mad. Jealous, I guess, but doesn't that mean he loves me, Holly? Isn't that what it means?" she pleaded to know.

She chose her words carefully. "I'm sure that Deke loves you, but I don't think hitting you proves that. Do you?"

"I don't know. I don't know anything. I'm just so stupid."

"You are not."

Now the words flowed from her. "We were in bed. Deke had done to me what the Reverend had done. You know . . . we were naked and . . ."

"Yes," Holly said, suddenly very uncomfortable.

"When I told him about the Reverend, he said that the Reverend and I must have done it lots of times. I said only once, but he started hitting me and he kept on hitting me . . ."

As Poppy revealed these violent intimacies Holly began to regret her tender ones with Paul. Shared secrets, joint acts of love or hate, this thickness, brought a vulnerability with it. Paul could hurt her now as Deke had hurt Poppy, but he wouldn't. Paul wouldn't, Holly protested inwardly, but still it didn't matter that he wouldn't. He could. And that mattered. It terrified her that he could. Poppy was continuing.

"I tried to tell him how it was, but he wouldn't listen. I spoiled everything and I love him so much."

"You don't want to leave him then?" Holly asked.

"Leave Deke? No."

"Maybe you made a mistake, Poppy," Holly ventured gently.

"No," she said, becoming very sure and adamant. "I love Deke and he loves me. It's not a mistake."

"All right, Poppy," Holly said. She had misjudged, she decided. She had believed her sister's tears and bruises, but Poppy bruised easily. She cried easily. She put too much meaning into Poppy's suffering. "It was just that you seemed so hurt and unhappy. I thought you were sorry that you'd married Deke."

"No, I'm not sorry. I wish he'd been nice like he used to be, that's all. I love Deke."

"Do you know who he is?"

"What do you mean? He's Deke Cody," she said. "He's Deke."

Holly realized that she was only further confusing her sister. She tried to make herself understood, speaking simply. "Yes, but what do you really know about Deke? Where did he grow up? Is he from a big family? That kind of thing. If you know those things about a person, about their past, then it's sometimes easier to understand and know them now, in the present. Do you know what I mean?" she asked.

"I guess so," Poppy said weakly.

"What about Deke's parents?"

"His father is dead. He told me that. His mother raised him. She lives on a little ranch in New Mexico."

"New Mexico?" Holly asked.

"Yes, that's what he told me."

"So Deke's mother lives in New Mexico?" she asked.

"Yes." Poppy answered.

"Maybe you should go and visit her. She would like to meet her new daughter-in-law, don't you think? She could tell you all about Deke, what he was like when he was a little boy. She'd help you to understand him, what he is now."

"Oh, I don't know."

"Why not, Poppy?"

"Maybe Deke wouldn't want me to," she said.

"I think he would. I think he'd love it if you went to see his mother. It would make him happy, Poppy, I know it would."

"Maybe so." Poppy had already submitted. She'd always been guided or driven. Holly was showing her the way. She'd expected that it would be Deke to lead her now that they were married, but Deke was on a troop ship out on the ocean somewhere. And Holly was here. And she was strong. She was telling her to go to New Mexico and meet Deke's mother. That must be the right thing to do, but she was afraid. Still she knew that she would go, fearfully. What else could she do?

"You should go," Holly advised.

"Well, okay . . . will you help me write a letter to her?"

"Of course," Holly said. She got up and started for her desk. She asked, "What's her name? Deke's mother?"

"He wrote it down for me, but I think I can remember. It's a funny name . . . it's Zara. That's it . . . Zara Cody. Deke was kind of funny about her . . ."—she vacillated—". . . not funny, but well, maybe I shouldn't go there. I'm scared to go, Holly. I'm afraid she won't like me."

"She'll like you, Poppy," Holly assured her. "She'll love you," she said as she was returning to the couch with paper and a pen. "Don't worry."

"Okay." Poppy gave herself over to her sister.

Holly looked at her and realized once again how easy it was to press Poppy into moves and shapes. She was like soft butter, Holly thought.

"Paul is coming soon. Will you have dinner with us tonight?"

"Oh, no," she said. "I wouldn't want him to see me like this." She touched her face. "Let's write the letter and I'll go mail it before he gets here."

"If that's what you want."

"Yes."

"All right," Holly agreed readily. She was anxious to speak with Paul alone, share her thoughts with him. That desire was marbled with revulsion. She feared her need of him.

They started on the letter. Poppy wrote in her rounded hand the words that Holly said. They finished it quickly. Poppy sealed and stamped the envelope. She had it in her jacket pocket and was nearly out the door when Holly felt she should ask her one more time.

"Are you sure you won't come to dinner with us?"

"No, I couldn't," she said. "I'll see you later.

"Goodbye," Holly called.

It was with guilty relief that she watched the door close. Poppy might not physically join them tonight, but Holly would bring her sister along. She would bring Poppy to hide behind.

Paul's reaction was not the one she had anticipated. They had eaten dinner and driven out to his house at the beach. She had saved the subject, waited purposely. They were sitting on the terrace. The surf was high and broke whitely in the night. This sound of the sea would forever be interlocked with Paul for her. She listened, loving the wild peace of this place that was his. All that was here belonged, except maybe herself, Holly was think- ing. Paul was not disturbing the time with a single word, but he too had a subject that he had been saving all evening. She spoke, turning toward him even though she could not see him in the darkness.

"Poppy came home today," she said.

"I thought this was the day," he said. "How is she?"

"When I came home she was sleeping on the couch. She looked terrible."

"How so?"

"Swollen . . ." She hesitated. ". . . beaten."

"What do you mean, beaten?"

"Exactly that. He'd hit her."

"Were you surprised?" he asked.

"No," she said. "She and I talked. I thought that she'd want to end it now . . ."

He interrupted. "But you were wrong, weren't you?"

"Yes. She says she loves him. She says he loves her."

"And what did you say to that?" he asked and his voice had taken on an intensity that was not there moments before.

"I said I was sure that was true, but . . ."

He interrupted again. It was as if he needed to say it before she did. "But, you told her, they should part. That's always your answer, isn't it?" he asked.

She was glad that she could not see his face. She did not want to see the expression that might match his tone.

"No," she answered, "I didn't tell her to leave him."

"What did you say?"

"I said that she didn't know him."

"What did Poppy say to that?" he asked.

"The same. She loves him. I suggested she visit his mother, try and find out just who this man is that she married."

"You suggested?"

"Maybe it was a little stronger than suggestion," she admitted.

"It was excellent advice. You're very wise, Holly."

She detected something close to contempt in his words. "What's the matter, Paul?"

"What makes you think there's anything the matter?" he asked.

"There's nothing wrong?" she asked.

They were fencing. They hadn't had a conversation like this since before Monterey. This was an exchange from their past, not the distant past, but the past. They had crossed a line during those days in that lovely coastal town. Neither thought there would be any going back after Monterey, but they seemed to be regressing tonight. The tide was going out swiftly. He wanted to stop it and so did she, but the momentum had subtly shifted backward. He reached out and took her hand, but only that, took hold of it and nothing more. She allowed his grasp.

"You've been waiting all night to talk about Poppy, haven't you?"

"Yes, I guess so. I was eager to speak with you about the situation," she said. She hated the formality that had crept into her words to him, but she couldn't stop the stiffening of her voice.

"All of tonight, all of our time together, you've been waiting through, to get to this, to get to Poppy, poor pathetic little Poppy and her crazy husband," he said. His resentment was clear.

"You're angry and I don't know why, Paul."

His tenseness eased, mitigated by resignation. "No, you don't, do you? I'm sorry, Holly. I had other things that I wanted to discuss, a different idea of what this night would be," he said.

She thought of how Poppy had said over and over that nothing had been as she thought it would be. Now Paul was saying the same thing. Expectations were dangerous. They seemed to lead inevitably to disappointments. She heard Paul continuing.

"You want to talk about your sister. You're concerned about her. Let's talk about Poppy," he said.

Just as she had felt compelled to extend Poppy one more invitation to dinner when she really didn't want her to come, now she asked Paul what she didn't want to know.

"What did you want to talk about?"

"I wanted to ask you something," he told her.

"What? Ask me," she said, still not wanting to hear.

"No," he said. "Another time."

She accepted this. "All right," she agreed to his newest evasion, realizing his was only echoing hers. "Poppy's going to New Mexico," she resumed. "That's where Deke's mother lives. I helped her write a letter to her tonight. Poppy was out mailing it when you came. She didn't want you to see her . . . her face."

"Unfortunately I've seen beaten wives before," he said.

"When? Who?"

"Not anyone I even knew, Holly. You've seen them, too. Maybe you tried to think that you didn't, but you have. We all have. All of a sudden you are aware of a woman beside you in an elevator or a bus and there's a pain about her that's palpable, her eyes are blacked, her mouth like pulp, and with a sickening kind of thud it hits you, hits you like she's been hit, pummeled, in the name of love probably, in the sanctity of marriage," he said. The irony of the moment was not lost on him. He had intended to ask Holly to marry him tonight, but somehow this other course had been charted. Deke's and Poppy's tragic union had brought them to this. It occurred to him that Holly might have unconsciously wedged her sister between them on this lovely dark night that should have been perfect for a proposal. He wondered if she could have possibly known his intentions. Holly was capable of expert defensive escapes. He remembered that she had once used her sister Iris in such a way when she feared he was coming too close to her. She used her sisters. Their mistakes, their follies, would not be hers; by sharing in theirs she could avoid her own. Her sister Poppy was in trouble. She could turn that, twist it into an excuse for flight from him, he knew. He must be very careful with her now, he was thinking as he sat with her hand in his but exerting no pressure upon it.

"I have seen women like that," she said. "Poppy looked just like that." She felt Paul's exquisite understanding and still she was afraid of him, feared the bloody mess of entanglements that even his fine love of her might perpetrate. "It's a terrible thing."

"Yes," he bitterly assented. "It is."

The night was lost, both Holly and Paul knew that. What they could only guess was how much more than an evening might be draining away from them. Neither knew how to stop the slippage. They did not go back into the house but left by the steps from the terrace. He drove to her apartment. He did not turn off the engine when he pulled up out front of the building, but let it idle.

"I'd ask you in, but with Poppy . . ." she began justifying herself.

He swiftly broke in on her excuse, not wanting to hear it, and hating her need to say it.

"That's all right, Holly, I understand."

"I'm glad that you do." She sounded anything but glad.

"Goodnight," he said.

"Goodnight, Paul."

There was an interminable moment of words unspoken, gestures unadvanced, a connection unraveling. She opened the car door, but lingered, trying to wait through the awful, awkward fault she was feeling.

He was aware of her hesitation and thought, hoped, that she was waiting for something from him. He wanted to make it right, melt this night with a word or two.

"I'll call you tomorrow," he said finally.

She was sorry he'd said that. If it was ending, and she felt inexplicably that it was, why politely prolong it? She didn't know what to say in return. Perhaps there was no need of a response, she thought. Anyway, she had none to offer. All that she might have said was that she was sorry. She might have attempted an apology for this aversion that was sweeping through her. She was sorry. She truly was, but she said nothing. She left his car without a word. In her apartment, once again, she came upon Poppy sleeping. She was careful not to wake her.

Within a few days there was an answer from Zara Cody, a short and curt letter written on brownish, brittle paper. It stated that Poppy could visit the ranch if she liked. There was nothing in the letter that showed any desire on Zara Cody's part to see her daughter-in-law. If Poppy wanted to come, she could. There was no welcome extended or even an invitation, but only a grudging acknowledgment of the relationship, and brusque permission to travel to the ranch.

Holly strongly urged Poppy to go. She didn't know why she was driving her sister, but she was. After bouts of indecision and counterattacks of conviction, it was arranged that Poppy would leave on a Sunday.

Holly and Poppy went to the station together. Poppy's train had the loveliest name. It was called The Desert Blaze. As Holly watched it pull out, she wondered what New Mexico had become, if it was still the way that she remembered it or if it had changed beyond her recognition. She felt sudden envy of Poppy's going there, letting it surface now that the train was moving. Perhaps that was why she had pressed the journey on her sister. Perhaps she had wanted to go there herself and was satisfying that desire through Poppy. Still it was right that Poppy went. She had good reason to go. She might find some answers there. Poppy

was traveling with the hope that somewhere on the desert ranch
of Deke's mother she would find the key to her mysteriously
violent young husband's character. Holly had given Poppy that
hope, but Holly herself had nothing to find in New Mexico.
There were no answers to any of her own questions there, Holly
believed, and she strained for a last look at the departing train.
Why then, she asked herself, did she want to be going? But she
didn't want that. She didn't. She repeated her denial to herself
over and over. She left the station, needing a fate, a destination.
West. To the ocean. To Paul's. That was it. That was where she
wanted to be, she decided. That was the direction she would take.
She was headed for the white cottage that was Paul's. She was
headed for him and the sea. That was what she wanted. There
was nothing for her on the desert. Poppy was the one with a seat
on The Desert Blaze.

The train moved Poppy through the night and into the morning, sunrise, and then hour after hour, mile after mile, of unyielding desert daylight. She arrived at noon. Deke's mother waited
for her. Zara Cody was a taciturn woman. She had lived alone
long and it showed. The isolation was in her eyes, but Poppy did
not see it. She saw only an older woman with a tanned and
wrinkled face, long gray hair in a braid down her back, and a
mouth that was set like Deke's. That was what she saw when she
got off the train.

The two women had little trouble recognizing one another.
They greeted briefly and Poppy followed Deke's mother to a
wood paneled old vehicle, battered, rusted, and warped. Poppy
was accepting of circumstances and of people. She was still what
she had always been, a docile and pliant child. She watched out
the window as Zara drove through Santa Fe. The one quick look
at Zara at the station was enough for Poppy. She studied no further the face of Zara Cody. She had accepted her as her mother-
in-law. Instead she carefully took in her surroundings. There was
a vaguely familiar feeling to the place. She guessed that it was
like many towns in New Mexico, bigger maybe, but like the one
that she had lived near when she was a child here with her family.
She spoke to Zara.

"There are so many young men on the streets and none of them in uniform," she commented. She was so used to Los Angeles, the multitude of soldiers and sailors milling there. "Isn't that kind of funny?" she asked.

"Funny?" Zara questioned.

"Well, strange," Poppy amended.

"Plenty of folks around here would agree with you. I don't pay those young men much mind. They started coming about a year ago. There's lots of stories about why they're here. There's always lots of stories when folks start in speculating about a thing."

"Oh," Poppy said. She stared after a group of young men dressed in boots and cowboy hats. Their clothes didn't seem to suit them. They looked as if they were at a masquerade party, almost clownish. "I thought they might be ranchers."

"Ranchers," Zara snorted. "A ham-handed bunch of ranchers they'd be. They're from the city." She spoke of the city as if it were one place, one awful place. "Some of them don't even speak English and they ain't Mexicans nor Indians neither. I know their lingo. No, they sound like Germans to me. There was a German had a farm next to my pa's. Name was Hoffmann. I remember the way he sounded. They sound just like him. Germans, they are, and nobody's going to tell me any different."

"Could they be spies?" Poppy asked. She had read the posters at the factory about saboteurs. Pictures of men as snakes and rats with dynamite sticks, the fuses lit, were nailed on all the walls and they had made a great impression on her.

"No," her mother-in-law told her.

They were out of the town now. The road veered west and then northward.

"They're not spies?" Poppy asked for reassurance.

"No. They're something else."

"What?"

"They're building something," she said.

"What are they building?"

"Some folks think they're building a factory to make windshield wipers for submarines. Some say it's a nudist colony or a home for pregnant WACs," she said. She looked at Poppy and Poppy smiled at her. Her tightlipped mouth curled slightly in a grin. The girl's sweet softness was hard to resist. She understood her son's sudden marriage, looking at his wife, she did. "But they're not doing any of those things."

"What are they doing? Do you know?"

"I've got a guess," Zara said.

Poppy waited, but no more was said. They were traveling a narrow dirt road with trees on either side. Through the willows she could see pastureland and beyond, huge burnt-red mesas.

"We'll be to the ranch soon," Zara told her.

"What is the name of this place?" Poppy asked.

"The Parajito Plateau, that's what we're coming to," she said. And because Poppy had not asked she returned to the subject of the mysterious builders. "This is near where they're working, the foreigners and the others."

"On the factory?"

"Ain't no factory, no ordinary kind. I've seen it and it's got barbed wire all around and guards with pistols."

"Is it a prison?"

"No. They're building something there, all right," she said. "They're building something about the size of a breadbox, small, but it will blow up the earth. The end is coming. They're building it right up there . . ."—her eyes were fixed on the steep, pumice-stone canyon walls. "Up there on Los Alamos Mesa."

Poppy twisted to get a view of this place.

"It's an evil world and the end of it is near," Deke's mother declared.

It was the first ominous hint given by Zara Cody of her character, the true nature of it, the potential for madness that her son had inherited from her, suckled from her, somehow ingested, but Poppy did not hear it. She was trying to imagine the world ending. She thought of Lily. Lily was always talking about the end of the world. It didn't seem to Poppy that the end would come in a fiery explosion. She believed it would come quietly, like sleep, just like falling asleep and never waking. It did not seem so very terrible to her.

"Mrs. Cody?" she asked.

"Yes?"

"Would it be all right if I called you Mama?"

She looked again at Poppy. From her life spent in the desert sun she had a perpetual squint. She regarded all with a sort of slitted scrutiny, but especially this girl beside her. She was judging her authenticity, studying her the way she would a stone, assaying the mineral, the mental makeup of her. The composition of her was simple and true, she reckoned. "You can if you like," she told Poppy.

"I lost my mama almost a year ago. She was killed in a tornado. I miss her so much," Poppy said.

"That's too bad," she said. Zara Cody felt a thing for Poppy that she had not felt in a very long time or perhaps ever. She pitied the girl, though she was a pitiless woman. Deke's mother had either been born or grown early into a pitiless woman. She turned off the road to the ranch.

Poppy thought the place was the loneliest-looking spot she had ever seen. There was a silence, a stillness, that pervaded everything. She sensed it but could not penetrate it. It enveloped her but she could not touch it. She took the ranch as she did the woman who lived upon it. In her sheerly childlike way she believed that her mother-in-law was simply a lonely old woman whose home was a lonely old ranch. Poppy never really saw Zara Cody, what lay beneath the skin, the sun-baked surface of her. She lived in her house for three weeks, ate breakfast, lunch, and dinner with her, listened to the green-glowing radio at night and the silence that came with the switching off of the machine, but she did not guess what Deke's mother truly was. Even if Poppy had been granted a more complete awareness, she could not have comprehended, could not have interpreted, the signs that would have warned her what Zara Cody was and what she had made of her son. Poppy did not recognize the woman or her offspring any more than she had recognized the Reverend Fallon. She was an innocent, frightened and weak, without will, the perfect prey of madness.

After nearly a month Poppy returned to Holly. She had gained no knowledge of her husband. His mother had not spoken of him and Poppy had been afraid to ask the questions that she had brought with her. She carried them still, unanswered, and carried something else, too. She had begun to be sick in the mornings. Her third week back in Los Angeles she went to a doctor and learned that she was pregnant.

When Poppy told her sister, Holly said little. She appeared to be calm, even cold, in the face of Poppy's announcement. Since Poppy's return from New Mexico, Holly's precise and measured movements, her efficient exterior, had been covering an emotional upheaval. Holly had been canceling dates with Paul, drawing back, away from him, and into the center of the strange storm that raged within her. This news of a baby further convulsed her already unsettled spirit, but to Poppy she presented a perfectly composed front.

"That's wonderful. A baby. That's just wonderful," she said, showing a false enthusiasm that she believed would look true. A baby, she was thinking, Poppy was having a baby. Mama had had babies, one after another, a chain of them. Lily, too. Would Poppy produce babies as they had? Or would she lose her baby like Rose? Be rid of it, have it scraped from her, like Iris? Poppy was having a baby. She too could have one. Paul could give her one. He could plant the seed within her the way that Daddy had told her long ago that it was done. Daddy. Daddy. She thought of him. She wanted no babies. She wanted to be his baby. Daddy's baby. That was all she'd ever wanted. She did not want Paul and the babies he could give her. Holly stared at Poppy. She should look different, Holly thought. She was changed, but she was the same. Poppy was the same child, but now carrying another.

"I'm going to write Deke tonight," Poppy was saying.

"Yes, you should do that," Holly said absently.

"Maybe I will right now."

"Yes."

Poppy went over to the desk. Holly watched her hunched in effort, pen tightly gripped, but no words being written.

"What's wrong?" Holly asked.

"I don't know how to say it. Will you help me?" Poppy pleaded.

Holly did not move. She knew that if she walked to the desk with her words it was the beginning of her involvement in Poppy's pregnancy. She dreaded it, but it was inevitable, unavoidable, Holly felt. Poppy couldn't do it alone. Holly went to her.

The next day Paul walked into her office. She hadn't seen him in weeks. Arnie Ross happened to be coming out his door at the

exact moment that Paul entered. Holly was caught between the
men, their looks and their greetings.

"Paulie, kid, how's the best hack on the lot?" Arnie effused.

"Hello, Arnold," Paul said. "Holly."

"Hello, Paul."

Arnie glanced from one to the other. Arnie Ross's glance was
a leer, always. "Looks to me like you two kids want to talk. I've
got a lunch date, Holly, and if I get lucky I won't be back today. Why don't you take the rest of the day off."

"There's a pile of scripts that I have to read, Mr. Ross."

"Get her, will you? Still calling me Mr. Ross and won't take
her nose from the grindstone for even a couple of hours. The kid
scares me sometimes, you know. Conscientious kid. But looking
a little pale these days. Wan. Is that the word, Paulie? I always
check with Paulie. He knows all the words," Arnie jibed. "Take
the rest of the day off, Holly. You're too good. You make the
rest of us look bad. Be a little bad this afternoon." He winked at
Paul. "Bye."

He walked out of the office.

Paul smiled slightly after him. "A lout, but an observant one,"
he said. "You do look pale. Are you all right?"

"Fine," she answered.

"Will you have lunch with me? I happen to know you have a
free afternoon," he said.

"I really should go home and check on Poppy. She's the one
who isn't feeling well."

"I know. She told me she was going to have a baby."

"When?" she asked sharply. "When did she tell you that?"

"Last night. I called, but you weren't home."

She went around this mild accusation of his. "She must have
forgotten to tell me."

"Would you like to drive out to the beach?" he asked.

She was caught off guard. "Yes . . . no . . ."

"Which is it?" he asked.

"No," she answered.

"I want to talk with you, Holly," he told her. "Would a light,
loud, crowded restaurant suit you better than the beach? You
are afraid we'll make love, aren't you, if we go to my house?"

She said nothing.

"C'mon, I know the perfect restaurant."

Paul always knew everything, she was thinking. They had gotten as far as his car and he was opening the door for her when she quailed.

"I can't," she said.

"You can't even talk with me?"

She shook her head. "I can't."

"Holly. Holly, what are you doing?" he asked sadly.

"I don't know. I wish I did. I've been avoiding you. We both know it. You deserve an explanation, but I can't give you one. I can't give you anything, Paul. There's something terribly wrong with me. It's better, I think, if I'm alone. Then I don't disappoint anyone. You. I don't want to disappoint you. I should be by myself."

"Right now or always?" he asked.

"Always, I think," she told him.

"Holly, I'm stepping off this merry-go-round."

"I'm sorry. I wish . . ."

"Don't tell me what you wish," he said, and for the first time anger replaced the quiet sorrow in his voice. "Holly, this baby will be Poppy's, no matter what you do, not yours. It will be your sister's baby. It's Poppy's life, not yours. You're not going to have any life of your own if you don't stop this."

"Stop what?"

"Living through your sisters," he said.

"Is that why you came to see me today? To tell me that?"

"No, I didn't come to tell you anything. I came to ask you something, but I can see it would be pointless. Futile," he told her. "Tell Poppy I said hello."

Holly nodded numbly. "Goodbye, Paul."

"Goodbye."

She turned from him. He knew he couldn't chase after her. He couldn't even shout after her. He had never shouted, never cried out at her inadequacies, but tried to understand and allow them. He had found her briefly and beautifully. Now he had simply and sadly parted from her, but it was she who walked steadily away.

Chapter Seventeen

The war had been a long one and Poppy's pregnancy short. It was May and there was a victory being celebrated, a partial winning to be blessed. Battles were still being fought in the Pacific, and men were dying, but on the day that the war and the killing ceased in Europe, Poppy gave birth prematurely to a tiny baby girl.

Holly saw the infant through the glass in the nursery before she went in to Poppy. She felt in a very compelling way a part of this birth, almost as a father would have felt. She had lived through the months of carriage with her sister, vicariously suffering and enjoying all the moments. She had overcome her initial terror and dread at the idea of a child and experienced the pregnancy as if it were her own. She gazed at the sleeping baby and she was hers, too. Holly knew that she was somehow tied to this child and always would be. It came to her most powerfully as she stood there separated from this new small life by the windowed partition, but feeling so close, so very close to it. Only once before, with her father, had she known this kind of bond. Daddy, she thought, here is another little girl that holds some of Daddy within her. But she would call someone else Daddy, this child would. Holly thought of the role that Deke had played, and it seemed so small, a fleetingly minute but essential act in the creation of the baby. The war was over in Europe, but Deke was in the Pacific. How long would it be before he returned and claimed his rights, his parentage, Holly wondered. Suddenly she resented the young soldier and questioned his stake in this infant who now yawned and stirred in her swaddling bands. The possessiveness that she felt was wrong, she knew, and she must purge it or at least hide it, for it would bring only pain to her.

Holly walked away from the nursery reluctantly and went down the hall to Poppy's room, a ward with seven women in beds, her sister one of them. She saw Poppy propped up on pillows. Holly had grown so accustomed to a swollen and ponderous Poppy that this pale and thin girl was a stranger until she smiled. That weak, rather crooked gesture was familiar. Holly drew up a chair by Poppy's bed and sat down.

"How are you?" she asked. She had planned to hug her, touch her in some way, but Poppy's frailty caused a kind of sympathetic revulsion in her. And she sat in her chair with her hands folded.

"I'm okay," Poppy answered. "The doctor says the baby is fine. Is she really?" she asked.

"She is. She's perfect, Poppy. I just saw her. She's the tiniest baby in the nursery and the prettiest. Truly she is."

"I was so scared. It all started happening so fast."

"I know."

"I want to see her, Holly."

"They'll be bringing her to you soon. I'm sure of it."

"Did you call Rose?" Poppy asked.

"Yes. She's all excited. She's knitted a dress for the baby."

"What color?"

"White. She said that she'd tell Lily the news."

"That's good," said Poppy. "I guess Deke won't know for weeks. Maybe even months."

"No. The Red Cross is going to get word to him as soon as possible. I spoke to a very nice lady there and she promised me."

"Thank you, Holly. Thank you for everything. It's not enough just saying that. It's not enough for all that you've done," she said and tears trickled down her drawn face.

"You're tired. You should sleep. I'll come back in a few hours. How does that sound?"

"Good."

Poppy obediently closed her moist eyes. Holly left without telling her of the other telephone call that she had made. She walked from the room thinking that it was some sort of miracle that she had managed to contact Iris. And Iris had told her that she would come up to Los Angeles, but Holly was afraid of disappointing Poppy. She didn't trust Iris's promises. She didn't believe her anymore. Yet she had called her. She had felt a need to communicate this birth to Iris. Holly found herself back at the nursery. She stared for a long while at the baby, oblivious to the officious nurses, the fond fathers, the proud grandparents all around her. Finally she forced herself away.

Out on the street there was an impromptu parade passing by. She watched its wending. On the people's faces she saw restrained joy. It was like a daylight, springtime New Year's Eve, a warm and bright striking of midnight. There was cause to celebrate, but there was still reason to fear. It was a mixed rejoicing. Holly could almost hear the strains of "Auld Lang Syne" though no one was singing. Ghostly lyric . . . should old acquaintance be forgot . . . how to forget all the old acquaintances, the old loves, the young boys who had been lost, and might yet be lost, Holly wondered. She joined the crowd, allowed herself to be jostled and moved by these subdued celebrants. It was the sort of conflicting cheer, the reserved happiness, the quality of incomplete jubilance and unfinished triumph that Holly had experienced all of her life. She was well-suited to this VE Day assembly. She traveled with it for a time.

When she returned to her apartment she thought of calling Paul. She knew that he would like to hear about Poppy's baby, but what else had she to say to him? If she could call him with the news of their child, her desire to have their child, then it would be right to dial the number, but her feelings, her fears, had not changed in regard to them, what they were capable of having together. She missed him, but she was afraid to have him. She feared returning to his bed, wonderful as it had been. The consequences, the aftermath of bed, she could not govern. Going past the telephone, she walked to the lovely white bassinet with the arched lace canopy that she had purchased for the baby. She had bought it months ago and they had maneuvered around its emptiness. Now there was a baby to fit it beautifully. She fingered the soft cloth and imagined her sleeping on the cushions piled within.

In the afternoon Holly went again to the hospital. Poppy was looking better. She had seen the baby and was finally convinced of her well-being.

"You were right. She's so pretty," Poppy told her.

"Didn't I tell you so?"

"Yes," she said. "What are we going to name her?"

Poppy had been asking that question for months. Neither she nor Holly had been able to come up with a name that was right.

"Now we really do have to decide," Holly said.

"I kind of like Judy," Poppy put out, but waveringly. "I know that you don't."

"She doesn't look like a Judy," Holly started, and stopped. It was like Poppy to pick a popular name, a well-reinforced choice. There'd be hundreds of Judys and this baby shouldn't be one of them. She was unique, but she was also Poppy's, Holly told herself. "But Judy is a nice name."

Poppy ventured uncertainly, "I was thinking maybe Judy Jane Cody."

Holly said nothing. Of course, she thought, Poppy would want to name her baby for the mother she'd loved. It was Poppy's little girl and if she wanted to name her for Mama, then she should, but Holly could hardly bear to think of the small and beautiful baby carrying that name.

"I think you have a better one for her," Poppy said.

The name had never consciously crossed Holly's mind in all the months of searching for one, but it came to her now so swiftly, so smoothly, that she realized while the baby had lived namelessly in Poppy's body she must have christened her in her own heart long ago. She said the name.

"Jasmine."

Poppy simply nodded.

"You're going to call her that?" Holly asked incredulously.

"Yes. She's Jasmine."

They spoke no more of names after that.

A nurse came and announced that afternoon visiting hours were over. Holly departed, telling Poppy that she would be back in the evening.

The florist shops were filled with the jonquils, violets, and lilacs of spring, but Holly had to go to three different ones before she found a single sprig of jasmine to take to Poppy. She walked to a drugstore a block from the hospital and picked out some magazines that she thought might interest Poppy. She also bought a pretty tin of chocolates. As she wandered the aisles killing time, she tried not to think of Iris and whether or not she would show as she had promised she would. Holly was nearly certain that she would not. It was the small trace of hope that surprised her, that she resented and wanted to drive out. She decided she would go over to the fountain and eat some dinner.

While she was eating she read through all the magazines that she had purchased for Poppy. She was just finishing, gathering together her things, and preparing to leave when an older man sat down beside her. He smiled at her.

"It's a grand day, isn't it?" he asked her.

For a moment she didn't know what he meant. She had forgotten about the victory in Europe. Europe was far away and the birth of Jasmine was close and consuming. Then she remembered and realized that he was speaking of the war's end.

"Yes, it is," she agreed.

"I only wish it had come a month sooner," he said and his smile was gone.

Holly was thinking that Jasmine had come a month sooner than she should have. She did not question the man, only looked at him without really seeing him, absorbed as she was in her own thoughts.

"If peace had come a month sooner . . ." he was explaining pitifully when she had asked for no explanation. ". . . I might still have my Edward, my son. It happened on the outskirts of Berlin . . . a sniper."

Holly heard him now. He spoke of death while she was thinking of birth. "I'm very sorry," she told him.

"Just one month," he was continuing mournfully. "One month late."

A month late and a month early. Death and birth. Perhaps, Holly thought, this man's son and her niece Jasmine had touched in passing, souls in transition, and now there was this drugstore-counter contact between herself and this grieving old father.

"I have to be going now," she said.

"You're probably going to meet a young man. There's probably a party, many parties tonight," he said and he was smiling again, smiling in polite farewell to her.

He had told her of the death he had suffered and now she felt that she must speak of the birth she had enjoyed. "No, it's not a party and it's not a young man. I'm on my way to see my sister and her new baby daughter."

"A baby," he said. "Babies are a blessing."

They had said all that they had to say to one another. It was one of those rare, brief, but complete encounters. Holly left.

For the first time that night she saw Poppy and Jasmine together. She arrived a little early and the baby had fallen asleep on Poppy's breast. The nurse came to take her to the nursery, place her back behind glass.

"Isn't she the most wonderful . . . the prettiest and sweetest thing?" Poppy asked.

"She is," Holly answered.

They sat quietly for a moment. Holly held the gifts forgetfully in her own hands, failing to present them. She looked down and noticed. She held out the sprig of jasmine first. Poppy took it and sniffed at it.

"It's jasmine," Holly told her.

"It's Iris," Poppy said.

Holly thought for a moment that Poppy was saying the flower was an iris and then she realized what was happening. She turned and looked toward the door. She saw their sister. Iris. Her entrance was like something from a movie, Holly thought. A movie set would be the ideal place for Iris, a world where nothing was real, all was mobile and make-believe. There she could shimmer and shine, only pleasing, never paining. In the fantasy environment of a cavernous sound stage, properly lit and posed, Iris could be the dream, the ultimate dream, without the intrusion of any harsh or cruel reality. She was wearing a tight gold satin evening dress. Everyone in the ward, new mothers, mothers-to-be, and their visitors, was watching her. She swayed over to Poppy's bed. She held in her arms a giant stuffed bear with a bright pink ribbon around its neck. And she was not alone. Two sailors followed behind her, totally in tow, never taking their eyes from the satin-swathed, undulating flesh of her body.

"Hi," she greeted them.

"Iris, how did you know?" Poppy asked. She was astonished at the appearance of her beautiful sister. She hadn't seen Iris in years, but she'd never forgotten her.

"Hol called me," Iris said.

"You didn't tell me that," Poppy said to Holly. It was a hurt accusation.

"I wanted to surprise you," Holly explained. She was the one who was surprised, shocked that Iris had really come.

The two sailors stood back a little but followed the exchange among the sisters.

Holly was acutely aware of their presence. Iris saw her looking at them.

"Guys, these are my sisters," Iris said. "Holly and Poppy. This is Skip and . . ." She smiled at the one she had forgotten.

He supplied his name and removed his white hat at the same time. "Donald."

"Yeah, Donny," she nicknamed him. "I'm parched. We drove without stopping from San Diego, and Skip, the bad boy, drained the bottle in Oceanside. I could sure use a drink."

Holly was prepared. She didn't expect Iris to ask Poppy how she was or to make any inquiries about the baby, but she knew that Poppy wasn't braced for Iris's selfishness. She could still be hurt by it, Holly feared. She interrupted the slurring monologue of their sister.

"Have you stopped by the nursery yet?" Holly asked.

"Yeah," Iris answered. "All the babies looked the same to me. I couldn't figure which was which. Geez, I never knew they were so ugly, all red and wrinkled, bawling their lungs out. You know, this place stinks. Really stinks. God, I hate the way hospitals smell."

Poppy seemed to be listening avidly but the question that she asked was unrelated to babies, hospitals, or smells. "Iris, why didn't you come to my wedding?"

"I meant to. I mean, I was at the bus station, but something came up. You know how it is. Things come up sometimes," she said. It was as close to an apology as Iris had ever made.

"Oh, I know." Poppy was eager to excuse her. "Things happen. But I wish you could have been there."

"Yeah, so do I," Iris said. As an afterthought she threw out. "So how are you doing? I mean, are you feeling okay?"

"I'm fine. It wasn't as bad as I thought it would be. The baby came early and I was awfully scared," she said. She glanced shyly at the two sailors standing at the foot of her bed. "It hurt but it wasn't so bad."

The sailors, Skip and Donald, moved restively. Skip said to Iris.

"Hey, me and Don are going to get us a drink. We're gonna leave you to your girl talk. We'll meet you out front in half an hour, okay?"

"I want a drink," Iris told him.

"You've already had enough vodka to float our destroyer," Skip observed roughly.

"You buy me another bottle for the road," Iris wasn't requesting favors, but demanding tribute. She ran her hand along Skip's arm. "Don't be a bad boy. Get me a bottle and I'll show you what a good girl I can be," she said. She seductively controlled, sensuously ruled.

"Sure thing, honey," Skip responded. "C'mon, Don."

They backed off from the sisters, Donald with his hat still in his hand and Skip's pushed forward to his eyebrows.

"Real nice guys," Iris said to Poppy. She had directed none of her words to Holly. "I told them my little sister had had a baby in Los Angeles and like a shot they said they'd bring me up to see you. Real nice guys."

"You look so beautiful, Iris. Just like I remembered you," Poppy said.

"Geez, you haven't seen me since I left Kansas. How many years is that?" she asked.

"Six," Holly answered.

Iris turned toward Holly, addressed her directly for the first time. "Same old Hol," she said. She only thought of the passage of time when reminded of it as she was now. She was twenty-two years old, she was thinking, momentarily aware of her age. "Got it all figured out to the minute I bet."

"No, not really," Holly said defensively.

"So what have you been doing, Iris?" Poppy asked. "Holly said you were singing with a band. That's so exciting. I guess you're really wonderful. I keep expecting to hear you on the radio someday. Have you made any records or anything?"

Holly knew that Iris was enjoying this. She could see her basking in Poppy's adoration. She felt sure that Iris would lie to maintain and increase the admiring attention. Holly waited for the falsity, the imagery, that Iris practiced so well.

"Well, I haven't cut a record yet, but I've had lots of offers. I'm waiting for the right song, you know, the one that was written just for me. I'll make that song my trademark and it'll make me a star."

"I always knew you'd be famous, somebody special, Iris," Poppy said. "Remember the duets we used to sing together?"

The image of two blond children in flimsy costumes with white-powdered faces sprang into Holly's mind. She looked from Iris to Poppy now. They'd changed very little, she thought.

"Yeah, when we were kids. I do remember," Iris said.

Poppy began to sing quietly, her weak and whispery voice trilling a song sung in their childhood. Holly felt her throat tighten. It was painful, unbearably sad, to her, seeing Poppy and hearing her. Then Iris joined in. Her low and sweetly vibrant voice extinguished Poppy's as it always had before.

Now Poppy and Holly were Iris's audience and the rest of the ward was, too. Iris was performing. She was, Holly realized, a pure performer. She sang to no one and to them all. And she glowed. The light in the hospital room changed from stark and bright whiteness. Iris was bathed in warm amber. The color came from within her. It was impossible to tell where the soft and lustrous gold satin of her dress left off and her skin began. When she finished the little child's song, applause broke out. With a potent mixture of grace and greed she gathered it to her, lovely lust.

"Sing another!" someone called out. It was a man's voice.

Iris smiled. There was more applause and she waited for it to swell and then subside. It was silent. She lifted herself up onto the iron footboard of Poppy's bed. She stretched there, lounged, almost lay full out. The slit of her dress revealed completely her long and tawny silken legs. She began to sing "You Made Me Love You." The throaty, velvet *a cappella* voice raised goose flesh on its listeners. At that moment Iris was totally sincere. She meant every word that she sang, even though she had never loved in all her life. When the love song ended there was sustained and stunned silence.

"Iris, why don't you come with me to the nursery? I'll show you Jasmine," Holly said.

Holly's words broke the spell. There was a roar of approval, and calls for more erupted. Iris slid from her perch, a golden songbird.

"That's it for tonight," she told them. She loved leaving them hungry. She looked back to her sisters. "Jasmine. So that's what you called her?" she asked Poppy.

"Yes. It was Holly's idea," Poppy said.

"I'll just bet it was," said Iris.

"Shall we go see her?" Holly asked.

"Sure, Hol, let's go."

"You'll come back, Iris, to say goodbye?" Poppy begged her.

"Sure I will," Iris told her.

Holly and Iris left Poppy clutching the stuffed bear tightly to her. Out in the white corridor, Iris spoke.

"Poppy's a nice kid," she said.

"Yes, she is."

"Geez, this place stinks. Can you smell it?" Iris asked as she walked beside Holly.

"It's the antiseptic," Holly said.

"I hate it." Iris did not connect the smell of the hospital with that of the black-haired woman's upstairs backroom. She did not remember. She only felt sick at the smell that assaulted and should have reminded her.

They arrived at the nursery window.

"That's the baby. That's Jasmine. The third from the left," Holly told her.

"Yeah. Well, I've got to say she looks better than the rest of them. She's awfully small, isn't she?"

"She was a month premature," Holly told her.

"Well, she's real cute."

"I wish you'd tell Poppy that."

"Maybe you'll tell her for me. I've got to get out of here, Hol. I can't stand this place."

"You said you'd be back. That you'd tell her goodbye. She'll be disappointed."

"No, she won't. Not if you explain for me. You explain things real good."

"I can't explain you, Iris."

"Nobody asked you to. Just tell Poppy I had to leave, that's all."

"You can't go back there for one minute and say goodbye to her?"

"I don't want to," Iris said.

"But she's waiting for you."

"So what? I told you, I want out of here. Geez, you're always pitching, always pushing, aren't you? Trying to get people to do the right thing, what you think is the right thing. Who ever said you were always right, Hol?"

"I don't know what you mean," Holly said stiffly.

"There it is. There's the voice. That cool princess voice. Holly, the little fixer, Miss Perfect, always arranging everything."

"Just because I feel some responsibility and I'm aware of the consequences of what I do . . . just because I don't live my life like some wild animal, going at things like a bat out of hell like you do, Iris, that makes me a terrible person. Is that right?" she asked. She was shaking with emotion and anger. "Is that right?" she asked again and her question was high-pitched and quavering.

"You're mad." Iris sounded surprised. "You're really mad. I've never seen you like this. Back at home when we were kids . . ." She started haltingly, pulling long ago times from within her that she wasn't even aware she remembered. ". . . and Mama would start in on you, I used to think, why doesn't she get mad? But you never did. You just took it from her and then you'd walk away, go off by yourself. Now you're mad. How come I can make you mad and Mama never could?"

Holly looked at Iris. She wanted to tell her that her anger came from love. She did love her. She knew her, the terrible, cruel, and thoughtless things she had done, the hurt she had caused in others, but she loved her. She knew she couldn't tell Iris. She was afraid of her knowing, afraid of how Iris might use her love for her against her. Holly hadn't loved their mother, not in life, and not in death. She had hoped that death might temper her feelings for Mama, but it hadn't. "I never loved Mama," she told Iris. She revealed herself in that circuitous way, feeling that Iris wouldn't penetrate her love for her then, and still she had indirectly voiced it, faced it.

"I've got to get out of here," Iris said.

Holly didn't know if Iris was fleeing the hospital or her love. "Go then! Get out!" Holly said and she heard her near-screeching tone. It was like Mama's. She glanced around and lowered her voice. "Just go, Iris."

"Afraid somebody might have heard you, Hol? Afraid somebody might have been looking? Seeing you? You really are scared to death of that, aren't you?"

Holly didn't answer, but asked, "And what are you afraid of, Iris? Scared that your sailors won't wait for you?"

"They'll wait."

"Scared they might drink all the vodka? You need some pretty badly right now, don't you?" Holly cruelly probed. She was angry. Iris was one of the rare few who could bring her to anger. Her words were barked with feeling. "Don't you?"

"I drink vodka because I like it, not because I need it," Iris answered her.

"Is that why you sleep with so many men? Because you like them? Or because you need them?"

"They like me. They need me. Crave me," she told her. She looked once more into the nursery. "It's a cute baby. Tell Poppy I said so. Bye, Hol."

She started for the elevator.

"Iris!" Holly called after her.

Iris stopped and turned.

"How old would your baby be now, Iris, if you hadn't killed it?" she asked.

Iris didn't speak. She smiled, that perfect, feral showing of teeth from behind red painted lips. She moved on toward the elevator in smooth strides, a remorseless and catlike parting.

Holly stood regretting her words, rooted in the responsibility of them. Again she thought of Iris on a movie sound stage and wished that her sister could be isolated there. She should be kept behind the heavy rolling doors. The red warning light should flash for Iris. There she could play in safety and in illusion, and not bring havoc to the lives she touched. Holly loved Iris and she hoped and prayed that no one else ever would.

Chapter Eighteen

For a summer, the summer of 1945, there was fighting still in the Pacific. In August the hostilities ended. The war was completely won. There was victory on all fronts and the news of it caused riotous demonstrations throughout the country. Gone was the reserve of the VE Day rejoicing three months before. All stops had been pulled. There was total abandonment to the complete triumph.

On the studio lot in Burbank a massive party was in progress. There was a surging conga line of howling humanity weaving through the more sedentary celebrants. Among the crowd was Paul. Holly was there, too. Without their knowledge they were coming closer and closer together. Paul felt her presence before he saw her, before she was mashed to his chest by the wildly happy throng. She held her arms in front of her, trying to make some small space between herself and the man she took to be a stranger.

"Hello, Holly," he said.

She looked up at him. "Paul," she said and her hands went to his shoulders.

"How are you?" he asked.

"What? I can't hear you?" she shouted.

He put his arms around her waist and began to guide her along. They were dancing. Everyone was dancing. Holly followed him willingly. They found an open sound stage and an empty corner of it. They stopped, but for a long moment the embrace that had been thrust upon them by the crowd they let linger and lengthen. They stood in one another's arms and finally released.

"How are you?" he asked her again.

"I'm fine," she answered.

They paused. The time apart, months, since long before Poppy's baby had been born, waited to be bridged by them.

Paul didn't form the words in his mind. They slipped from him, from some involuntary part of him. "I've missed you," he told her.

It was so good to see him, to be with him, standing quietly and out of the madness of the mob, she thought.

"I've missed you, too, Paul."

"If we missed each other so much, why didn't we get together? Why didn't you call me? Why didn't I call you?" he demanded, showing as much impatience with himself as with her.

"I thought of calling, so many times. I'd pick up the phone and . . ."

"Oh Holly, why didn't you?"

"I didn't know what to say. I felt I didn't have the right things to say to you," she said.

"All that you had to say was what you just did, that you missed me. That's all I would have needed to hear."

"I guess I wasn't ready to say that until today, Paul."

"You're the strangest girl I've ever known, the most resistant to feeling, the most guarded and reticent . . ." He stopped his tender tirade and stared silently at her. "I love you, Holly."

A group of singing men and women careened into their corner and it was no longer a quiet haven. Paul and Holly escaped. They fought their way across the lot, against the jubilant tide, to Paul's car. It and all the other cars had been festooned with paper streamers, red, white, and blue ones. He started to remove the patriotic decorations.

"Please don't," Holly asked of him. "I like them."

The one that he had already taken off before she made her request he took now and draped around her neck. She smiled at him. He cupped her face in his hands. They kissed. The afternoon sun was brilliant, hot, and blaring. Her lips were cool, but they heated swiftly at the touch of his. From a distance the celebration could be heard, the muted shrieking, the laughter, and singing. Holly and Paul, apart from the revelers, on the spot where they had separated months before, were rediscovering one another, finding again the feeling that they had shared, the love, the passion. It was reverie and reunion both. Heedless of being observed, they stood on the heat-drenched pavement of the parking lot and kissed and kissed.

"I want you to come home with me," he said. "I want you to come with me right now."

"Yes," she said and that was all.

They drove toward the ocean. All along the way cars were honking their horns in commemoration of the day, the victory. Paul returned the salutes, honking his horn playfully, and the paper streamers were blown from his car by the wind. They left trails of them on the Pacific Coast Highway. When the last one had been lost to the road, Holly took the red streamer that Paul had placed around her neck and let it slide from her hand out the window. She watched it fly in the air briefly and then begin to drift downward, sinking to the asphalt. Something stirred in her, some memory that she could not quite catch hold of, but she knew that she had made this gesture before. This had happened before, she felt. Then she remembered the red sash from her Easter dress and the Sunday that she and Daddy had escaped across the desert. Daddy, she thought. She and Daddy had run away and left Mama screaming in the sandy dust. Dry and hoarse, screaming and screaming.

A convertible passed them. It was filled with soldiers and girls. The girls were screaming. Screaming. Their screams whipped past them on the wind, but these were happy, delirious screams. They were not like Mama's had been that Easter, Holly thought. She looked back to find the red streamer, but it was gone from the highway, gone anyway from the retreating section of the highway that she could still see. She wondered about her sash, if someone had picked it up or if it had disintegrated, turned by the elements into nothing.

Paul put his arm around her, brought her closer to him, just like Daddy had done. Holly nestled, but watched to see his face go tight, his forehead knot, and his hand on the wheel clench white.

She waited for him to gently push her from him. She waited for her moment to allay the guilt and say that it was hot, too hot, to be so close. Holly waited and watched, but Paul did not let her go.

She could not believe that it was the light of the moon coming through the blinds and streaming across the bed. Paul was sleeping. She ran her fingers along his shoulder, up his neck, and traced his profile. He opened his eyes.

"I love your touch," he said softly. "It's like no one else's. Light. It almost can't be felt. To feel it I have to concentrate on the sensation and it's magnified a hundred times. I have to think of it to feel it. You make thought and feeling come together."

"I love you, Paul," she said.

"Will you stay with me tonight?" he asked.

"It's morning now. It has to be nearly three o'clock."

"I want to sleep beside you. I want to wake and find you next to me. We'll walk on the beach at dawn."

"I can't stay. Poppy's at home and she'll be expecting me. She'll be worried. I'm sure she is already."

"Call her and tell her."

"I can't do that, Paul."

"Why?" he asked.

"I can't tell her that I'm staying here. And besides she hates to be alone at night. She gets frightened, just she and the baby alone in the apartment."

"All right," he conceded. "But don't run away yet. I want to lie here with you and talk. God, how I've missed talking with you, Holly."

"I've missed our talks, too," she told him.

His next words showed how well they communicated, how well he could trace her thoughts.

"Tell me about Poppy's baby," he said.

"Her name is Jasmine," she began.

"It is a girl then. Somehow I knew that it would be. I didn't think that Poppy would have a boy. Was Deke disappointed?"

"From his letters it's hard to tell what he's feeling or thinking. Poppy reads them to me. She seems to get a great deal of satisfaction from them, but to me they're pretty shallow stuff. I am fine. How are you? That kind of thing. He's an awfully vacuous character or at least his letters are, but Poppy loves them."

"She loves him."

"Yes. Well, he'll be marching home soon enough now. It's hard to believe that the war is really over. I guess it's too new yet, the end, I mean."

"It's true. I keep thinking of the party on the lot today."

"Yesterday," she corrected him. "It's morning."

He didn't want her to sepak of going yet. He didn't want to hear about the morning. He swiftly continued. "A lot of those people are going to wake up hung over. They're going to feel low and lousy. And they'll blame the celebrating, but I don't think that will be the real reason."

His ideas fascinated her. And he had caught her with them, was holding her not only in his arms but with his thoughts. "What do you think the reason will be?" she asked.

"I think that many people are going to be sorry and sad in a strange way that the war is over."

"How could anyone be sorry or sad about that?"

"The war created an atmosphere for all of us. No matter how far we were from the actual fighting of it, the war made us feel close to death. Because of that life became very precarious and precious, something to be enjoyed to the fullest, experienced to the hilt, grabbed and devoured before it was taken from us. With the war over that feeling will disappear. We won't be living on the edge any longer. It will be back to business as usual, normal and mundane. Some of us just aren't going to be able to go back to that, I don't think. It was all too exhilarating. A lot of people are going to look back on these war years and believe they were the best times they ever had. Young people, with a whole life ahead of them, are going to see a long future that will pale in comparison to the brief and exciting past. Times like the ones that we've lived through will never come again. Maybe we should thank God for that. And maybe some of us will miss them, wish them back again."

She hadn't thought of it, but he was right. Two people came immediately to her mind. She said their names. "Deke and Iris."

"Yes," he agreed.

"Iris has always lived that kind of life, but the war must have made it easier for her, a perfect cover. She'll miss the war, but she'll go on as always," Holly said.

"What about Deke?"

"I don't know. I only know that I'd be very afraid of him without his uniform as an excuse."

"What do you mean?" Paul asked.

"Maybe excuse is the wrong word. I guess what I mean is that it seems to me that being a soldier is Deke's reason for existing. Where will he go, what will he do, without the army to tell him? They took him as a child and trained him to fight. The fight is finished. Now what does he do?"

"Comes home to his wife and baby?" Paul suggested.

"I don't want him to," Holly said and she looked at Paul, realizing that he had been leading her to this admission. He had felt her disturbed state of mind and he had prepared her gently for revelation. "Paul, I'm afraid of his coming. I dread it. I don't want him to take Jasmine from me," she said. She told him what she had never said to anyone else. "I think of her as mine. Not all the time, but sometimes I do. I never intended that this would happen. When I first found out that Poppy was pregnant I didn't want any part of it, but somehow I became a part of it and that baby became a part of me."

He held her cradled to his chest. "Holly, do you want a baby of your own?" he asked her.

"No," she said quickly.

"When are you going to stop living through your sisters?"

"Let's not start that again," she said.

"It's true and you know it," he told her. "I want to ask you something."

"What?" she asked and there was apprehension in her voice.

"What happened between you and Iris that time you went to San Diego? You never told me. You just came back to me. That was enough then, but now I want to know what drove you back."

"What happened? Only what had been happening between us since we were children. A repeat performance. That's all," she said. She knew that Paul deserved more from her. "Iris had had an abortion. One more of her destructions."

"You're doing the same thing, Holly."

"What?"

"You're destroying at a different stage, a little earlier than Iris."

"That's not true, Paul," she said. And then condemning and confessing too. "It's not fair."

"I love you. I want to marry you and have a family."

"Oh, Paul, please."

"You were afraid I'd say these things, weren't you?"

"I know what you want from me. I'm afraid I can't give you that. I love you. Believe that, I do. But, Paul, I . . ." She hesitated.

"What?"

"I don't think my love is enough, my kind of love. You said it to me earlier. I'm reticent and resistant. I can't help it. I've tried. I tried to change for you. We've come so close, you and I, but there are some things, some parts of me, that I can't seem to release. I can't let go."

"I know. I've felt you holding back, banking something. God, Holly, I've done it too often to too many people myself not to recognize it. I've held back, but not from you, never from you. It's strange, in a way I feel that I'm being paid back for my silences and my restraint with yours."

"I'm sorry."

"You're about to leave me again, aren't you?"

"I have to go now."

"And will you be back? Will you avoid me for months and then come walking back into my life?"

"I'm afraid I'll always come back to you if you'll let me, Paul."

"Will you?"

"Yes, unless it hurts you too much and then I'll try my very best not to."

"I told you the last time that we said goodbye that I was getting off the merry-go-round," he said.

"Yes, I remember."

"I can't do it. I can't find my way off, Holly. I can't stop caring for you," he admitted to her, knowing his extreme vulnerability, but he trusted her innate decency. She had to know that he loved her as he had never loved. "I'll drive you home now," he said.

It was almost four o'clock in the morning when they reached her apartment building. About the place there was an aura of disorder. Something was wrong, Holly sensed this immediately. She

had not yet noticed the square of light that fell onto the courtyard from her living room window, but still she felt the waves of
wrongness, disturbance, in the atmosphere. She heard Paul com-
menting on the light.

"Is that light coming from your apartment?" he asked.

It was. She saw it now. "Yes," she answered him easily.

"Could there be anything wrong? Poppy wouldn't still be up,
would she?" he asked.

"No," she told him, averting his involvement. She didn't know
what had happened, but she was certain that something had. When
she forced him from her life, its details and its intimacies, as she
was doing now, she hated herself. It was this aspect of her nature
that she could never truly explain to him or anyone, but, she
knew, Paul needed no explanation. "Well, possibly she was up
with the baby and forgot to turn out the light." She excluded him
and evaded the trouble and fear that she felt at the same time.
Jasmine had slept through the night from the time that she had
first come home from the hospital. She was such a good baby,
but she might be sick, Holly was thinking, tormenting herself.

"I want to see that baby sometime soon."

"She's a lovely thing to see," Holly said distractedly. She was
glad that for once Paul did not seem to be reading her thoughts,
penetrating her mood, but then he asked.

"Are you all right, Holly?"

"Yes. Just a little tired," she said.

"Shall I wait and make sure everything's all right?" he asked.

"No, there's no need," she told him. "I'm sure everything's
fine." She listened to her lies, but she told herself they weren't
really false. She didn't know that anything was wrong. She
wasn't hiding any reality from Paul. It was only a feeling, but it
was strong and sure. She knew that she should voice it, tell Paul,
but she could not. She wanted to be out of his car and in her
apartment confronting the thing that lay beyond the abnormal
shining square. That light was a beacon, warning of danger, and
she wanted to meet the trouble squarely and alone . . . without
Paul beside her. He gave an extra layer, another dimension to the
confrontation that she did not need.

"Goodnight, Paul."

He leaned over and kissed her. His mouth was the same mouth
from the afternoon of encounter and the night of blissful reple-

tion, but it was morning now and she needed to be free of his kisses and of him.

"Goodnight," he said. "Will you remember?" he asked her.

"Remember what?"

"Yesterday. And how much I love you."

"I'll remember. I remember everything. Too much."

She got out of the car but put her face back through the open window.

"I do love you, Paul."

He stroked her face. She could see his smile. He dropped his hand from her. She was going toward something terrible, she knew, and dear as he was to her, she could not tell him. She was holding back again, and fearful that this loving man might recognize this as he said he could, she was thrusting her love of him forward. It was that emotion that she usually reserved and now she was using it as a kind of smokescreen. She was hoping to hide her tracks from him as she walked toward the bright and knife-edged shape cast upon the dark ground.

Poppy was sitting in the living room. Holly saw that her face was tear-stained. That could mean anything, Holly knew. All the catastrophes that might have occurred ran through her mind in the seconds before Poppy spoke. Deke might have been killed, a last-moment war casualty. That would mean a telegram. She saw none lying anywhere. There could have been bad news from Kansas. That would come over the phone. She strained to hear any residual ringing, the remnant of a jarring late-night call, and there was some trace of that in the room, she thought. And then, she shied from this, it might be the baby. Something could be wrong with Jasmine. She looked toward the closed bedroom door. Behind it was the white lace bassinet. Did Jasmine sleep peacefully within it? Or not? She heard Poppy's thin whine.

"Where have you been? Oh, where have you been, Holly?" she wailed. "I was all alone and . . ."

"I'm sorry. It doesn't matter now where I was. What's happened?"

"It's Iris," she told Holly.

Holly was relieved. She hadn't even thought of trouble connected with Iris and, of course, she should have. That should have been her first thought. She considered what might have happened to Iris. Living the life that Iris did, anything could have happened. Holly couldn't summon much sympathy for Iris anymore. Iris had abused her sympathy too often. Poppy's flowed freely, like her tears her ruth came.

"What happened?" Holly asked. "Did one of her sailor friends beat her up?" She made no effort to keep the bitterness from her voice. She was bitter but resigned to the brutality, the destructive wantonness of Iris's existence. Maybe someone had finally reversed the action and made Iris the target. Even so, Iris would rise up just as beautiful and as cruel as ever, as insensitive and wildly selfish, a gorgeous and glowing cold phoenix from the ashes, from the bruises of any man. Holly was convinced of Iris's invulnerability, even her immortality. She was not afraid for her. She was not sorry for her.

"Iris is dead," Poppy said.

The moment froze. Everything whirled, spun, and stopped. Iris was dead. It wasn't possible for Iris to die. Iris was going to live forever and thousands would die for her, hundreds from her, but she couldn't die, Holly thought.

"They called at about midnight. She was killed on a motorcycle. A Marine died too. He was driving. She was riding behind, they said. They were on a road in a place called Torrey Pines up above San Diego. She's dead, Holly. They said she was dead. Iris is dead."

"Poppy . . ." She had to halt the words. "Stop saying that," she commanded softly. "There's been a mistake. Iris can't be dead. Not Iris."

"But they said . . ."

"I don't care what they said. It's all a mistake."

"They want someone to come and identify her body," Poppy said.

"You see, they're not sure. They don't know if it's really Iris."

"The girl who was killed was carrying Iris's purse. Her identification was inside. But maybe . . ." Poppy was swallowing Holly's hope. She had accepted the phone call and Iris's death, but now she was taking in her sister's refusal, making it hers. There was some doubt. If Holly said so, then it must be true. Maybe it wasn't Iris who was killed on the highway with the trees down the center of it, Poppy was thinking. They had told her there were trees down the middle of the road and that the Marine and the girl on the motorcycle had been playing in-and-out-the-window through them, but they had lost control of the bike and crashed into one of the trees, one of the tall pines. They told her that, but maybe they were wrong. They were wrong. It wasn't Iris. It was another girl, some poor girl who was carrying Iris's purse for some reason, but it wasn't Iris.

"It wasn't Iris." Holly echoed aloud Poppy's thoughts.

Poppy didn't know why Holly was so sure that Iris wasn't dead, but she willingly and eagerly accepted that surety.

"It wasn't Iris," she repeated after her sister.

"I'll have to go to San Diego," Holly said.

"You mean you'll have to go and look at that poor dead girl and tell them it isn't Iris?" Poppy asked.

"Yes, that's what I'll have to do. I'll have to tell them that it isn't Iris," Holly said.

But it was. It was Iris. The room was cold and white. A man pulled out a long drawer from the wall. He folded back the coarse sheet. Holly looked down and saw Iris. Iris, hideously smashed, beautiful Iris finally held accountable, answering for her life with her death. And it must have been a terrible death. Her white naked body was covered with deep gashes. Her right arm and leg had been torn away. She was gouged and battered. It was inhuman, but it was Iris. It was undeniably Iris. The sickness that had started in the foul-smelling taxi cab on the way to the train in Los Angeles overwhelmed Holly now. She silently nodded her head in affirmation of the horror and then ran from the room. In the corridor she vomited into the gleaming white enamel drinking fountain. She heaved and retched until she thought that she would spill out her insides into that bowl. Finally the convulsing ceased. She let the water run to wash away her mess and then took a handful and splashed it to her face. Someone touched her shoulder. The man who had escorted her to the body was standing near her. He had stayed discreetly back until her sickness had passed. How could he be so squeamish, his sensibilities so delicate, she wondered, when he looked daily upon the horror that she had just seen? To be the guide, this morgue's boatman, to grotesque death and then to wait until vomit was washed from sight in a sink, seemed a profound contradiction to Holly. But then perhaps he was considering her and not himself. Perhaps he didn't want her to be embarrassed by his presence, his witness of her grief.

"I'm sorry," he said to her.

She could only look at him, wipe at her mouth and look at him.

"She was your sister?" he asked.

Holly nodded as she had over the corpse.

"She must have been a lovely girl."

Holly was sure now that he was trying to be kind to her. In an attempt to respond and show her appreciation, she said, "Yes, Iris was beautiful, very, very beautiful."

"We have her things for you," he said.

"Her things?"

"Valuables. Personal possessions," he explained. "If you will come with me down to the office, there are some forms that have to be signed."

"Yes, of course," Holly said, pretending to know the procedures of a morgue.

He placed a cold and white helping hand to her elbow. She drew her arm away. She guessed that now she would have to say what was to be done with Iris. Iris's body. She could have it shipped to Kansas and buried beside Daddy and Mama, but that seemed a terrible course to take, to condemn Iris to the Kansas earth that she had hated. The thought of cremation occurred to Holly. The burning would cleanse and eradictate the damage done the beautiful body. Cremation would be best, she decided. Her thought process was remarkably clear and dispassionate. She was functioning and she was standing back watching herself do it. She felt hollow from being sick. She was detached and empty, walking these white halls with this white-coated man.

Holly carried the paper bag that held Iris's property from the morgue. Now she must go to Iris's room. She thought of the landlord. Mr. Hagen. She would have to get the key from him. She had hoped that she would never again see that man. Their meeting was only moments away. She walked up the steps of the building. She entered and knocked on the door of Mr. Hagen's apartment. A woman answered.

"I was expecting . . . I mean I wanted . . . is this Mr. Hagen's apartment?" Holly faltered.

"Yeah," the woman said. "I'm his daughter."

Holly noticed the resemblance and pitied the woman.

"What do you want?" the woman asked.

"My name is Holly Calder. I'm Iris Calder's sister."

"Yeah, I know that one."

"There's been an accident. Iris was killed last night," Holly snapped out the sentences. "I came for her things," she said, using the morgue man's phrase.

"She's dead?"

"Yes. If you could let me into her room or give me the pass key . . ."

"There's rent owing on her room, you know," the woman said.

The similarity to her father went deeper than a simple ugly facial one, Holly thought. "How much?" she asked.

"Thirty bucks."

Holly took three ten-dollar bills from her wallet and held them out to the woman. "May I have the key?"

They exchanged the cash for the latchkey, a wary and eye-locked trade.

Holly walked away, feeling the woman, the Hagen daughter, standing at the door watching her just like Hagen had done at Iris's door that night. She was at Iris's door now. She paused and then put the key in the lock. She stepped inside.

The room was as she recalled it. It was the same squalid place, but now without Iris to ameliorate the squalor. Holly cleared a chair and sat down. She opened the bag given her at the morgue. Inside she found Iris's purse and her shoes. Her dress and under-things had been disposed of, the man in the white smock explained, because they were badly torn and bloodied. Holly emptied the purse onto her lap. There was a compact with its mirror cracked. There was a tooled Mexican leather wallet. The plastic holders for pictures were empty. There was no money. A social security card and a driver's license that had expired three months ago were paper-clipped together. A package of Lucky Strike cigarettes that was crumpled, its contents smoked, only the smell of tobacco lingered. Several matchbooks with the names of different bars, nightclubs, and restaurants embossed on them, mostly in red letters, revealed a string of Iris's haunts. There were three lipsticks. Not knowing why, Holly read the paper spheres on the bottoms of the gold cylinders. Passionate Plum. Everlasting Rose. Wine Kisses. There was a brush, the bristles choked with strands of Iris's long blond hair. And that was all that there was. She put the objects in the bottom of the bag.

She got up and walked in circles around the room. Iris had not accumulated much. Hanging in the closet was a chenille bathrobe. The gold satin dress she had worn to the hospital was thrown on the bed. A white sharkskin suit was dumped in a pile on the floor. In one drawer there was a tangled wad of stockings, garter belts, bras, and panties. Holly tried to remember if she had ever seen Iris wearing the same thing twice. She hadn't, but then she had seen her so infrequently. She couldn't have known that it was a pattern of Iris's to wear a favorite article of clothing until she got tired of it and then throw it away. Iris had rarely ever possessed more than three outfits at one time. Having too many things impaired her movement. Usually she had gotten men to buy her a dress that she liked. She would go directly to a public restroom and change into it, discarding the old dress in the trash or simply leaving it on the floor, but Holly had no knowledge of any of this. She did not know how Iris avoided memories or anything, even a scarf, that might invoke the past. Anything a moment old had been ancient to Iris, the long-ago past of yesterday. Holly gathered the few clothes and folded them into her bag. She searched for any photographs, mementos, but there were none. There was a scrap of paper with a telephone number on it, but no name. She took that, too. She started to leave, but stopped at the yellowed vanity mirror. She reached into the bag and took out one of the lipsticks. She rolled it open and the imprint of Iris's lips was clear. It had been worn down to the shape of her mouth. Ceremoniously Holly painted her own lips. She pressed them together and they felt strange and heavily bright. She looked at her reflection and, this homage paid, she left the room empty of Iris.

At the hall phone she dialed the number from the piece of paper. She awaited an answer anxiously, not knowing what she would say, but the operator came on the line and told her that the number had been disconnected. Disconnected, Holly thought, like Iris's short and random life.

She then placed a long-distance call to Rose, thinking she could make the call brief under the circumstances. She felt able to have only quick contact with her sister. She knew that Poppy would

not have called Kansas. She would be the first to tell this, to shock
with it. The phone was ringing.

"Hello," Rose answered.

"Hello, Rosie," Holly said.

"Holly! How are you?" she asked.

"Not good. Rose, Iris has been killed."

Rose was too stunned to make note of the fact that for once
it was not she who was the bearer of bad tidings, but she would
think of it later.

"Oh no. Oh, Holly. How? When?"

"Last night. It was a motorcycle accident. I'm in San Diego
now. I can't talk long. I'm at a pay phone in her apartment building. I just came from the morgue."

"Oh God, Holly."

"Rosie, I know how you're feeling and what a terrible shock
this is. You don't need to say a word, and I can't. I'm standing
here with a bag of her clothes trying to believe it. I just want
to get home, but I wanted you to know, Rosie. Really I didn't
want you to know. I wish none of us had to know. I wish it
hadn't happened."

Rose was remembering a gorgeous fair-haired child with a
voice like ringing bells. Iris's death had erased other, harsher
memories.

"She was so beautiful," Rose said.

"Yes, she was," Holly said, but she knew that she would never
again see Iris's beauty, not even in remembrance. For all her life,
from this time forward, when she thought of her sister she would
see the betrayed and lacerated form laid out upon a frigid slab.
For Rose and so many others Iris would always be beautiful, the
most beautiful, but for Holly, Iris was a monster. What Iris had
done, how she had lived, the beast within her, had been released
at her death and had shown itself. In life Iris had given Holly
glimpses, but it was difficult to penetrate the lovely veil. Now the
image was unmasked and horrible and real. To the sisters, except-
ing perhaps pious Lily, she would be beautiful Iris forever,
beyond death, an object of envy and emulation, the heroine of
an exciting flash, a lightning-bolt life. To Holly she would be a
bitterly beloved *monster*. Again she was alone with the truth and
with death. She thought of the cold desert night and how the
little girls had gathered on the couch and cried, all her sisters,

save the one they wept for, Jasmine. She had stood apart. She, alone among them, had looked upon the violent ending of a life. Now she was once more the sole witness.

"I'll call you when I get home, Rosie. Goodbye," she said, and she did not wait for Rose's goodbye, but hung up.

Then she picked the phone up once more, one last time. She was calling Paul, but there was no answer. He was on the beach, she guessed. He couldn't hear her call, but she would go there and find him. She wanted him now.

She put the key on the fraying doormat of the landlord's apartment. She wanted no more of the woman within, but as she walked from the building and down the steps she had the sensation of the Hagen daughter's narrowed, hating eyes on her back.

PART SIX

❁

ROSE

❊

Chapter Nineteen

❊

Kansas, 1947 . . .

He sat in a chair on the front porch. He might have been
asleep. His straw hat was slanted down over his eyes and whether
they were opened or closed could not be seen, whether they were
seeing or not could not be seen. A small and pale fly, not the fat
and shining-black summer variety but a starved and cold, nearly
lifeless, winter one, crawled along his arm. The insect's climb
would have tickled skin with sense, but there was not a twitch of
flesh. He did not explode, swinging and slapping, assaulting the
fly in small rage or large irritation, but remained motionless. He
could have been cat-napping in the afternoon, resting in the last,
thin wintery sunshine of the day, but sloth was contrary to the
man. He was a hard worker, a constant laborer. He had been that
until he was demolished. He was not a man at rest or at peace. He
was seething silently within a wasted shell.

Workman Banner had suffered a massive stroke three months
before. They had gone out looking for him when he had not
returned home at sunset as was his lifelong habit, and they had
found him, lying rigid, living, but barely, in his darkened fields.

It had happened at harvest. And Workman Banner had reaped ruin, his own. They had carried him home and now he was shifted from his bed to a chair in the parlor to this chair on the porch. He was fed like an infant and his pants changed like diapers, but he did not fret or squall like a baby. He was a large and silent mass of human flesh that lived, but from which any spark of life had either fled or been hopelessly trapped when he was stricken. The eyes beneath the hat were open, staring at nothing. He was, appeared to be, a breathing dead man.

Hope came up the road from school. She was alone. The boys had stayed behind to play ball. She was as good a player as any of them, but she had not been asked to join the game. She was a girl and she didn't belong. So she walked the road alone. Hope would turn fourteen this year. She was not pretty, but appealing. She had Lily's beautiful and yielding mouth but little else of her mother's looks or nature. She saw her father on the porch. She went to him, gently pushed the hat back from his face, and patted his cheek. There was no response, but she seemed not to take notice. She sat down at his feet and smiled up at him. She began to speak as if she believed she could be answered.

"Hi, Daddy. How are you feeling today?" she asked. She stroked his hand that had not felt the sun of the fields upon it in three months but was still brown, tanned from the exposure of years. "It's warmer today, isn't it? Spring is teasing us. It won't be coming for so long. There'll be snow again before it comes."

She felt that he heard her. She continued.

"Daddy, I'm feeling bad today. The boys wouldn't let me play ball with them. Jonathan wanted me, but not the others. He said he'd leave with me, but I knew he wanted to play. I told him to stay. Daddy, why is this happening? It used to be we all played together, but not anymore. What's changed? Something has. Me, maybe. I don't feel the same."

She brushed the fly from his arm.

"I don't know what I'm supposed to be. I feel so funny and kind of sad sometimes, like I don't belong anywhere. Except with Jonathan. It's always good to be with Johnny. Daddy, I love Johnny the best. I want to love the others as much, but I don't. It's different with him and me. Is that because we had different mothers, do you think? Gee, I wish I knew the answers. I've got so many questions, Daddy. And Mama, well, you . . . you know

Mama. I can't ask her. I can't talk to her at all. Today Auntie Rose is leaving for California and Mama won't drive into town to say goodbye. I wanted to say goodbye. And Auntie Rose is Mama's own sister, but she wouldn't. You would have driven me, wouldn't you, Daddy? If only you could . . . if only you hadn't gotten sick."

The screen door opened and Lily stood listening.

"Get up from there. You're getting your school dress dirty. Go in the house and change. There are chores for you to do."

Hope rose and dusted the back of her dress with her hands.

"I was talking to Daddy," she told her mother.

"He can't hear you."

"Mama, I think he can. I . . . I feel that he can. He likes it when I talk to him. I know he does. He does hear me."

Lily reached out and yanked her daughter by the arm.

"Stay away from him."

"But Mama . . ."

Lily slapped her across the mouth, the mouth she had given her, pouting and offending mouth. Hope reeled. Workman sat impassively, but there was a straining that could almost be heard emanating from him, a humming hatred and despair at his impotence, his utter helplessness. There was awareness draining from him like pus. Within this pitiful, sightless, senseless body there was something, a soul perhaps, that could see and feel but could not communicate through the inert corpus.

"Get in the house," Lily said to Hope. "This is God's work and will. God made him this way and only God can help and comfort him. Your Daddy can't hear you. He can't feel it when you touch him. Don't you be touching him or talking to him anymore. Leave him be. Leave him to God."

"But Mama . . ."

"Do you want a beating?"

"No, Mama."

"Then get!"

Hope rushed past her mother and into the house. Lily called after her. "Change out of your school dress. And don't be spending too much time in the bathroom. Leave the door open. I don't want you standing in front of the mirror primping. Vanity is a sin. You are a vain and sinful girl. Leave that door open. Do you hear me?"

"Yes, Mama."

Hope's voice came faintly.

Lily stared down at her husband for a moment. She pulled the hat down over his face and went back into the house. The fly returned to his arm. It lit upon him, sat as unmoving as he. It died there. Workman Banner's lungs involuntarily sucked in the fast-chilling air.

Rose went through the empty apartment making sure that they were leaving nothing behind, nothing that they wanted to take. She looked in the cupboards and the closets. She checked the drawers, running her fingers into the far corners of them. She and Clyde were leaving nothing in Kansas. She was sure now. They had sold or given away most of their furniture. The few things they were taking were piled and tied in the back of the truck. Clyde was gunning the engine, jamming his foot on the accelerator pedal over and over again as he waited for Rose.

Rose walked from the place without regret. She was glad to be going. She was only having trouble convincing herself that it was really true, that she and Clyde were actually leaving, going west to California as she had dreamed for so many years that they would. She had nearly given up the dream and now, suddenly, it was real. She heard the angry-sounding, staccato snorting of the truck as she approached. She told herself that Clyde was only impatient, eager to be going.

Clyde was trying not to think of Ginny. Ginny, his sweet little girl, had run off and married Axel Jorgenson last month. She hadn't even told him she was going to do it. When he had managed to get her alone and demanded to know why she'd done this thing, she'd told him that she couldn't wait for him forever. Ginny said she was afraid she was getting old. She was twenty-two. Twenty-two. Ginny wasn't old. She couldn't be because then he would be, too. She was older than she'd been that first time he'd kissed her behind the shirt bins at the factory. She was older now than when she'd first let him touch her small, ripe, seventeen-year-old breasts. She was older, but she wasn't old. Now Axel Jorgenson had her. Well, Clyde comforted himself, he'd had Ginny when she was best, when she was fresh and wild, not afraid of anything, sure not afraid of getting old. She'd age fast enough now, he thought.

Rose got into the truck beside him.

"What took you so long? What the hell were you doing in there?" he asked her.

"I was just making sure we hadn't left anything."

He looked in the rearview mirror and saw the lumpy collection in the truck bed. "I wish we'd left it all," he said. Most of all he wished he could have left Rose, but for some reason he couldn't. In California he would, he promised himself. He'd go as far as that with her. He guessed he owed her that much. But, he thought, as soon as they reached the land of sunshine and orange trees and movie stars, he was gone. He was going to start out new and on his own, footloose and fancy free.

"Let's go," Rose said.

"You're sure you're ready now?" he asked.

"I'm sure, Clyde," Rose told him. She squeezed his arm. "I'm ready. California, here we come."

He didn't look at her. He put the truck in gear and they drove down the street away from Straker's, away from Kansas. Away, Clyde was thinking, from the new Mrs. Axel Jorgenson.

"Pinch me, honey. I think I must be dreaming," Rose said. She laughed. "Is it true? Are we really going?"

"It's true," he said.

Rose pressed herself close to him.

"I'm so happy," she said. "Are you?"

"Yeah."

She kissed his cheek, kissed down his neck. He hunched his shoulder and twisted away from her.

"Rose, I'm trying to drive."

"I'm sorry." She withdrew. "I'm just so excited. California. Holly's going to be so happy." She'd told her sister so many times that she was coming and she never had. She'd thought of not telling her, but at the last minute, when everything was sure, she'd wired Holly they were on their way. She'd wanted to surprise her as much as she was surprising herself, but she knew that Holly liked to be prepared and so she'd sent the telegram. "I can't wait to get there. I can't wait to see Holly's face," she told her husband's profile.

Her loving talk of dreams and happiness was nothing more than jabbering to Clyde, like the jouncing of their things in the truck bed it sounded to him. He said nothing. Soon Rose grew quiet. They made their noisy and silent way west.

Holly was peering down into a tidepool. She would sit for hours or as long as the ocean allowed and study the watery environs, the elusively beautiful inhabitants. Paul came quietly up behind her. She could have caught his leaning reflection in the pool's smooth surface, but she was looking past the mirrored top, deeper, down to the bottom where the shy sea creatures lived their mysterious lives for a brief and shallow time.

"Hello," he greeted her.

She started.

"I'm sorry. Did I scare you?" he asked. He lifted her hair and kissed the nape of her neck.

"I didn't think you'd be finished so soon," she said.

"Soon. Do you know what time it is?"

She gazed around. "The sun is setting," she observed, astonished at the swift passage of time.

"You look golden in this light," he told her.

"How's the chapter coming?" she asked, diverting attention from herself.

"It's finished."

"That's wonderful, Paul."

"Read it and then tell me that," he said ruefully.

"I'll be happy to. Right now?"

"Right now," he said.

He put his arm around her shoulders and they started back to it and he brought her up and to him.

"How did I ever let you talk me into this?" he asked.

"Into what?"

"This novel-writing business. I'm not a novelist. In the words of our friend Arnie Ross, I'm just a studio hack," he said, seeking her denial, wanting her reassurance.

"You're so much more than that," she told her.

"I gave up writing novels in my youth. I couldn't do it then. Why am I trying again? Now?"

"Because your time has come," she said. "You're a wonderful writer."

He stood and extended a hand to help her to her feet. She took the house. The setting sun was turning the sea to molten gold and Holly's tidepool had disappeared in the onslaught of rising surf.

She settled on the couch by the bay window with the new pages of his manuscript. She could feel Paul watching her and she guessed that he was nervous about her response to his work. After reading the same sentence four times over she looked up at him and smiled. As gently as possible she told him.

"Go away, Paul."

"What?"

"I can't read with you staring at me. I know how eager you are to hear what I think, but it'll go much faster if you'll leave me alone with it."

"It's odd, but I wasn't even thinking about the book."

"You weren't?"

"No. I was just looking at you, thinking how right you are in this house. Out on the beach you were golden. Inside you're silver, but everywhere you're beautiful. You are happy when you're here, aren't you, Holly?"

"Very happy."

"Come and live here with me."

"Paul, I . . ."

"Don't say no. Please, don't say no again. When you leave here there's an emptiness, such an emptiness. You belong here, Holly. You know that you do."

"I love it here."

"And I loathe the thought of you going back to that apartment."

"Paul," she paused. "I'm beginning to dread it myself. Without Poppy and Jasmine there it's like a tomb," she admitted to him. "I can't make myself believe it was the right thing for Poppy to take Jasmine and go to Deke in Japan. I'm worried about them. And . . . I miss them." She had grown accustomed to her sister and her niece, their presence. And she fearfully realized that she could not go back, there was no returning, to the life she had lived before they had entered her life. Looking back on it now,

it seemed to her to have been a terribly lonely existence, although
she had obstinately and pathetically protested that it was what she
wanted. It may well have been what she wanted then, she thought,
but she didn't any longer. Poppy and the baby had unfitted her
for solitude. Still, she was very afraid of deepening the relationship with Paul. It was comfortable here with him, but she fought
that easy and pleasant ambience. She swung wide, back and forth,
on the subject of Paul and herself, but the apartment was hateful
to her now and she had to confess that to him. She hoped she
had not encouraged him too much with what she had said. She
was far from convinced that she was ready to trade that rented
place, stark and silent but still all her own, for this shared sea
house.

"Don't go back there," he said.

"Today?"

"Ever," he said.

"Paul, I don't know. I still don't know. When are you going
to get tired of me and my everlasting reservations and uncertain-
ties? I'm tired of me. And of them."

"I can wait them out. I can wait you out, Holly," he told her.

"Are you sure of that?" she asked.

"Yes."

"Let me read this, will you?"

"Yes."

Holly did return to her apartment that Sunday evening. Paul
reluctantly let her off and she walked slowly through the courtyard to her door. The newspaper had been thrown by the boy
onto her porch. She carried it inside with her.

It was beginning to rain. Suddenly it was showering in torrents,
a downpour. She wished she had stayed with Paul. She was concerned about him driving in this storm. She went to the table and
checked her watch. It was eight o'clock. At nine, she told herself, strapping on the timepiece, she would call him and make
certain that he had gotten home safely. She went through the
rooms turning on lights. She wanted no shadows tonight.

She sat down with the newspaper. Opening it, she read the
black headlines about the Black Dahlia. She wondered when it
would stop, when people would have enough of the girl's grue-

some murder. The paper had been full of it for days, covering every awful angle, and yet she began to read the story of the newest suspect. The young man had admitted to spending the night with the Black Dahlia, but he claimed he sat up in a chair in the hotel room. He protested his double innocence. He hadn't loved her and he hadn't killed her. What kind of girl had this Black Dahlia been, Holly wondered. A drifter. An aimless, wandering girl with black hair in a black dress, wax filling the cavities in her teeth. A girl looking for what? A good time? And finding horrible death. Holly shuddered. She was thinking of Iris. How easily this might have been Iris. The Golden Iris. Holly folded the paper and set it aside. She went to wash the black print from her hands.

The sounds of the water running in the sink and the rain falling outside mingled. Holly soaped her hands over and over again, not aware of the repetition. She might have gone on for hours if the knocking on her door hadn't roused her. She jolted into consciousness and dried her hands. She couldn't imagine who was at her door. It might be Paul, but she doubted it. She called out.

"Who's there?"

The voice that answered was dear and familiar. She threw open the door. Rose and Clyde stood in the wet yellow glow of the porch light. Rose began to laugh at the expression on Holly's face.

"You look like you swallowed a gnat," she said. "Didn't you get the wire or didn't you believe it?"

"I got it, but it didn't say when you'd be arriving," Holly said.

"Surprised you, huh?" Rose smiled.

"Surprised isn't the word," she said. "Come in. You're getting drenched out there"

They stepped inside.

"I thought California was sunny," Rose said, and laughed again. She threw her arms around Holly. "Are you glad to see me?" she asked. Rose looked to Clyde who was standing in the still open door. "Us," she corrected herself, pulling Clyde closer and shutting the door.

"I'm so glad," Holly said. "Rosie, I can't believe it's true. Clyde," she said and took his hand, trying in her turn to include him. "Come in and sit down. I'm just trying to believe that you're really here."

Rose and Holly sat side by side on the couch. Clyde slumped into a chair.

"How long are you staying?" Holly asked her sister.

"We've come for good," Rose told her.

"You've left Kansas? You're going to live here? Permanently?" Holly asked incredulously.

"Yes. Yes," Rose piped enthusiastically.

Clyde was saying nothing at all. Holly turned to him and asked.

"Clyde, was this your idea?"

"No. It was your sister's," he said sourly.

Holly looked away from him. She met Rose's eyes and then dodged the contact, what she saw there.

"Rosie, I am so glad that you've come. You'll love it here. I know you will."

"I know I will, too."

Clyde had closed his eyes. He appeared to be dozing. Rose began to excuse him.

"He's been driving for ten hours, Holly."

"Ten hours. He must be exhausted." Holly joined Rose in the apology, the conspiracy to explain Clyde.

"Yes," Rose said.

"I'm still trying to make it real, believe that you're actually here," Holly said. "Now you and Clyde will take the bed and I'll sleep on the couch."

"No," Rose said.

"What do you mean no?" she asked. "I'm used to the couch. When Poppy was pregnant I slept on it and it was fine."

"We've already checked into a motel."

"You didn't do that. I want you to stay with me."

"No. It's a real nice room. Clyde was all for staying there and waiting until morning to come over, but I wouldn't have it," she said, glancing over at him. He was sound asleep. She had lain awake watching him too many hours into too many nights not to know when he slept, really slept. "I just couldn't stand to think of being only a mile away from you and not seeing you. I couldn't wait until morning. I know he's tired, but I couldn't wait," she told Holly. It was strange to her, not deferring to Clyde as she always did. "I told him that I'd walk in the rain if he wouldn't take me."

Holly was imagining the scene in the motel between Clyde and Rose. She felt an intense dislike for Clyde. He treated Rose badly, she thought. Rose deserved better than the sprawled man in the chair. His snoring was a relief after his surly behavior. Holly realized how much it must mean to Rose to see her. It was rare that Rose crossed Clyde, she guessed. It appeared that things went mostly Clyde's way, but he had said that coming to California was Rose's idea. Perhaps Rose let the small decisions be made by her husband and saved her will and strength to decide the large ones. Holly couldn't be sure. She remembered Rose and Clyde as young lovers and then newlyweds. She'd seen them so little as adults, only the time she'd gone back to Kansas for the funeral, and Clyde had been more obliging then, accommodating, perhaps compensating, but distant. He was still removed, and angry now, too, but he had come to California and he had brought Rose with him. Holly thanked him for that. Her sister, she was afraid, would never have left alone.

Rose had picked up a silver-framed photograph from the table. It was one of several recent pictures that had been added to the two old ones in Holly's apartment. They were scattered everywhere and they were all of the same subject. Rose held this one, looking closely at it, and smiling.

"Jasmine," she said.

"Yes, that's Jasmine. She was a year and a half when that was taken," Holly said, gazing at the plump blond baby in a slightly askew sunbonnet.

"I wish I could have gotten out here before she and Poppy left."

"So do I, Rosie."

"You miss them," Rose said. It was a statement without question.

"I had a letter from Poppy last week."

"How does she like Japan?"

"She seems to like it well enough," Holly answered vaguely.

"Why do you suppose Deke wanted to stay on in Japan? Why would he join the regular army? You'd think he would have had enough, that he couldn't wait to get out, get home."

"Yes, you'd think that, but then it's hard to know about Deke."

"You've met him. What's he like?" Rose asked.

It occurred to Holly that she had seen Poppy and Deke as she had seen Rose and Clyde years ago, in the early stages, the days of discovery, when they were new.

"He's good-looking. Very young. He's an unusual boy, Rose."

"You don't think he's right for Poppy, do you?"

"I guess I don't, but who am I to say? Who knows why any two people get together?" Holly said, and she couldn't keep from looking at Clyde who stretched comatose in her reading chair.

Rose followed Holly's stare to her husband. "Or stay together," she added her own concern.

Holly jumped to a safer subject, less emotion fraught. "So tell me your plans. Are you going to settle in Los Angeles?"

"I'm not really sure, Holly. It's just so damn good to be out of Kansas," she said.

"Yes." Holly thought of that state. Only Lily remained now. "How is Lily?" she asked.

"It's terrible, Holly, terrible to see. You know that Workman had a stroke?"

"Yes, you wrote to me about it," Holly said.

"He just sits. He can't move. He can't talk. Lily thinks it's a punishment from God. She's started taking him to faith healers. Nothing. Nothing happens. And that farm. God, Holly, going to that farm is like visiting a grave. Those poor kids, trying to grow up in the middle of that, but they're doing it. They're all so big now, and just waiting for their time to run. Hope will go first, I think, probably wind up at Straker's."

"That's becoming almost a tradition," Holly said.

"You're right."

Both Holly and Rose thought that factory was an awful legacy.

"Well, you're out of Kansas anyway, Rose," Holly said.

"It took me long enough."

"You're here now and that's the important thing," she told Rose. Daddy had hated Kansas, Holly was thinking, or had it been the staying in one place he'd despised? Anyway, they'd all fled, all but Lily. She liked to believe that Daddy had won in that. He'd had too few victories and too many defeats. It was a contest. She thought of Daddy and Mama pitted against one another. Daddy and Mama. Who could ever know why two people came together? She asked that question again, this time within herself.

And Rose's question reverberated in her thinking. Why did two people stay together?

Rose was replacing the picture of Jasmine on the table. Clyde twisted in the chair, trying to find a comfortable position.

"We should go," Rose said to Holly. "He'll wake up with a crick in his neck and be a bear."

"It's good to have you here, Rosie."

The rain hadn't stopped. Holly heard it still falling. When Clyde and Rose had gone she would call Paul. Suddenly she didn't want to be alone, not with the rain still falling.

Chapter Twenty

Poppy had her first view of Japan through a bus window on her way from the airfield to Tokyo. Over the blond head of her child who slept in her lap, she was given the truest and the most searing image of the country that she would ever receive, but Poppy did not know what she saw. She was looking at a land of defeat and devastation. The bus jounced past the farmland villages to Yokohama, sharing the narrow highway with American army trucks and jeeps. The thatched roofs of the houses were in need of repair. The farmers and their families, seen only fleetingly, appeared to be shabbily dressed and thin, but their utter hopelessness, despair, and hunger were not apparent to a speeding observer, a passing intruder and foreigner like Poppy. Theirs was a subtle but no less terrible destruction. The fifteen miles between Yokohama and Tokyo showed more clearly and starkly the ruin visited upon the vanquished. This section had been fire-bombed incessantly toward the end of the war. It was ash and rubble, a black and flattened skeletal stretch of earth. Seeing it from her bus, Poppy could not have known that once this had been a gentle sweep of fragile and beautiful wood and paper houses, homes where human beings had once lived. Not aware of the past, Poppy was spared speculation on the present and the future.

She did not have to wonder what had become of those who had dwelled here. To her it was simply what it was now, an ugly and barren place. She did not know it was a graveyard. She could not see the death because she had never witnessed the life that had thrived before the war had come and the bombs had fallen from American airplanes. Now American buses loaded with the American wives and children of American servicemen whirled victoriously over the razed earth in American arrogance or ignorance, but without a ripple of resentment from the Japanese.

She did not realize that the Americans had built their own city within Tokyo, and that that was the destination of her bus. When she saw the new and clean apartment complex for military personnel, she was happy. It seemed a totally American island, a protected haven, set down in the midst of this strange foreign place. Deke was waiting for them and she followed him willingly, eagerly, into the freshly plastered and thin-walled cubicle that was their new home and her deathtrap.

Days, weeks, and months passed in nightmarish succession. Deke was still the violent and volatile soldier from their honeymoon, and Poppy thought daily of running away from him, but he had many ways of holding her, devices laced with love and hatred, cruelty and complaisance, ways so widely disparate that they contained only one common element, his madness.

It was late in the afternoon of the first day of her tenth month in Japan and Poppy was bathing Jasmine, preparing for Deke's return home. He liked to have the baby clean and sweet-smelling. He would play with her, tossing her in the air, catching her and holding her to him, squeezing her too tightly, and then hand her over to Poppy. He expected the little girl to go right to sleep. Then he wanted his dinner. He liked Poppy to look a certain way, too. He hated the big shirts and slacks that she was most comfortable wearing. He wanted her in a dress. He liked these things. And he demanded them.

Jasmine was dawdling in the tub and Poppy could feel the time passing. He would be home soon. She had so many things to do still. There was never enough time. She tried to hurry the little girl out of the water, but Jasmine, feeling her mother's urgent coaxing and testing her will, slowed. She was a good-natured but stubborn child, and she wanted her way. Poppy was surrounded by those who wanted their own way. So she gave, yielded, handed over pieces of herself, trying to please everyone and becoming utterly lost in the process. Her accepting and sacrificing nature might have found a home on this Eastern archipelago. If ever there was a people in harmony with Poppy it was the Japanese, but she was isolated, kept from them, held within this American army compound, buffered by her nationality and hideously protected by her husband and his uniform. He would be walking through the door too soon, she knew.

She had dried and powdered Jasmine. She was buttoning her into a yellow piqué sunsuit when she remembered the stew she had cooking on the stove.

"Wait right here. Mama will be back in a minute," she told Jasmine, thinking how sweet she looked, how pleased Deke would be with her tonight.

She ran to the kitchen. The stew was bubbling nicely. The warm and savory scent of it was filling the room. She stirred it. It was Deke's favorite. Everything was going to be perfect, she was thinking, and she hurried back to the bathroom. Jasmine had overturned the open jar of talcum powder, covering herself and the floor with it. She was licking the powder from her arm.

"Jasmine!"

She stood looking at her mother in pure white innocence.

"Don't eat that. It's nasty," Poppy said.

"No. Good," the child told her.

"It is not. It's not to eat. Don't." Poppy pulled at her, wiping and brushing her off. She coughed as she inhaled the fine dry substance. "Oh, Jasmine. Why did you do this? We're late now. Daddy'll be home and he'll be mad."

While Poppy was cleaning the floor Jasmine continued to dip her fingers into the container and eat the powder that had not spilled. Poppy looked up and saw her.

"I said no." She snatched away the jar. "No. No."

Jasmine began to scream. Poppy carried her to the bedroom and put her in the crib that stood beside her and Deke's bed. The bed had not yet been made. The sheets were twisted and the blanket trailing on the floor. She could smell something burning. It was the stew. She turned and caught her foot in the rumpled bedspread, nearly falling. She recovered her balance, coming upright in front of the dresser mirror. She stared, trying to recognize herself. There was a girl standing there with a thin and pale face, her hair tied in a blue checkered bandana, wearing a too-big red plaid shirt and baggy trousers, white socks and loafers. She didn't know who she was. She heard the door open and Deke enter. She began to tuck the girl's shirt into her pants.

Deke followed the sounds of Jasmine's screams into the bedroom. He saw Poppy looking at herself in the mirror and the baby wailing in her crib. The smell of burning stew was strong all through the apartment.

"What the hell is going on around here?" he shouted.

"Deke, please don't yell. You know they can all hear you," she said, referring to the other tenants separated from them by only thin, hastily constructed walls.

"I'll yell if I damn well please. Christ, anybody would yell. Look at this place! Look at her!" He pointed at Jasmine who had gone ugly and red-faced with her screaming, almost in accompaniment to her father. "Look at you! You look like a damn Jap in those baggy pants."

"I'm sorry," Poppy said.

"And what the hell is burning?" he demanded to know.

"The stew," Poppy said and she ran past him out of the room.

He came after her. He stood watching her try to scrape the charred mess from the pan into the sink.

"That's great. That's just great."

"It was so good. It was going to be so good. I just checked it and it was so good," she said.

"Yeah," he said disgustedly. "Well, what now? What am I supposed to eat for dinner? I'm hungry."

"I'll make you a sandwich."

"I don't want a damn sandwich. I want dinner. I want a wife who can run a house, who isn't such a dummy that she can't do a damn thing right. You can't do anything right!"

Poppy started to cry.

"And I'm sick and tired of you crying all the time!"

"Deke, they'll hear you," she pleaded.

They did hear. They'd heard it all before. His shouts, the blows, and her screams came nightly through the walls, but no one did anything but gossip about it. No one asked Poppy what was wrong or if they could help her. They listened and whispered behind their closed doors, but no one tried to stop the domestic violence. It was a common occurrence and a fact of life, grisly and ordinary.

Jasmine stood at her crib railing, hiccupping, her cheeks damp from tears, and heard as the neighbors heard what was happening in the kitchen. But it was her mother and father she heard and not two young strangers muffled by mortar.

"Deke, don't. Please, don't, Deke. Deke . . ."

His name became only a shrill shrieking cry.

"You're going to learn! You're going to learn to do what I tell you to!"

He swung his arm into her body and she thudded to the tile floor. He dragged her to her feet only to knock her down again. The sounds of the blows repeated for an hour and then there was silence. The front door slammed. Deke had come home and gone again. Poppy crawled from the kitchen into the living room. She pulled herself up by the table's edge. She took several deep breaths, trying to smooth out the jagged gasps that came from her. She retied the scarf on her head and wobbled to the room where her baby was. Jasmine was still standing in her crib. She had not moved. Poppy went to her and put her arms around her, lifted her over the railing. She lay down on the bed with the child cradled close to her. Poppy whimpered softly and rocked silent Jasmine until they both fell asleep.

Deke came in at three in the morning and found his wife and daughter huddled together in the center of the bed. He picked up Jasmine, handling her gently, pressing his lips to her face, and he thought that she slept but she was limp with fear of him. He put her in her crib. She watched through the bars as he undressed. Naked, he straddled her sleeping mother. She woke and they rolled and writhed on the bed, but there were no more screams. Tears trickled from Jasmine's eyes. She was afraid her mother would be hurt again. He hurt her all the time and he hurt her in so many ways. The baby closed her eyes to keep from seeing him.

The next night was different and yet it was the same. Deke had MP duty and had told Poppy he wouldn't be home until nine o'clock. She had accomplished much in the few extra hours. The apartment was shining clean. There were candles and a white cloth on the table. A roast was cooking slowly in the oven. Jasmine had been asleep since seven and Poppy had spent careful time on herself. She had curled her pale hair. When she turned her head it swung around her shoulders. She had applied lipstick and even mascara. She was wearing her best dress, a pink, full-skirted taffeta. She looked her best when Deke entered.

He kissed her. He had flowers for her. She put them in a vase on the table. She served the meal while Deke went into the bedroom and unstrapped his service revolver and MP armband. He removed his shirt, too. He came in to dinner wearing only his trousers.

"Everything's ready," Poppy announced.

"It looks swell," he said.

He started on the food.

"How is it?" she asked.

"It's great," he told her. "This is how it always should be."

"I know and I'm sorry it's not. There just doesn't seem to be enough time to do everything."

"You have all day," he said. Between bites he told her. "You've got to get organized. Hubba-hubba. It's all organization, that's what my sergeant tells me."

"Jasmine takes so much of my time."

"Too much. You spend too much time with her. She's old enough to entertain herself. You're spoiling her rotten. She's too attached to you."

"I'm her mother," Poppy protested faintly. "She's supposed to love me." She was defending the one solidly happy thing in her life, her baby.

"Yeah," he said. He was jealous of the attachment and bitter about what his own mother had been to him.

He poured more wine into Poppy's glass.

"Drink up," he told her. He drained his glass and refilled it. She hadn't touched hers. "Drink up, I said."

She took a sip. She thought that now might be a good time to bring up the subject. She had tried so many times to speak to him about it. It always ended badly. She was hoping that tonight would be different, that he would listen to her and agree with her.

"Deke," she began.

"Yeah?"

"Deke, I was thinking. Maybe Jasmine and I should go home."

"You know what I've told you about that."

"But I want to go home," she said.

"You are home. Home is where your husband is, where I am. I want you here and you're staying. You're not leaving me. End of discussion."

"But Deke . . ."

"I said that's the end."

"But Jasmine and I wouldn't be leaving you. We'd be leaving Japan. I don't like it here. I'm not happy."

"Poppy," he said and he reached across the table and gripped her wrist in his hand. "You will do what I tell you to."

"Yes, Deke." Her voice was mild and weak, but she was experiencing a powerful surge of anger. She swallowed it down. She felt as she had the night that Lily had tried to hold her, had tried to keep her from going home to Mama, the night of the storm when the bridge had collapsed.

"What's for dessert?" Deke asked, unaware of what was passing behind the pallid face of his wife.

"I made a peach cobbler," she answered him quietly.

"Swell," he said and he released her arm. "Go get it," he ordered her.

She went into the kitchen and was at the sink putting the cobbler into a dish for him when he came up behind her. He took her around the waist and moved his hands up to her breasts.

"You look real pretty tonight," he told her. He was pulling down the front of her dress, unhooking her bra, and rubbing her small breasts. "I want you here with me. Save the cobbler . . . c'mon."

He led her from the kitchen into the bedroom. He finished removing her dress. She stood in her full, white lace petticoat and she spoke the wrong words to him.

"If we only went home for a few weeks . . ."

"You're not going. You're not leaving me."

He tore at her slip and then her panties.

"Don't, Deke," she said.

"You're staying right here." He pushed her back onto the bed. "With me." He unzipped his trousers. He spread her legs. "You're mine." He stroked between her legs, penetrating her with his fingers. "This is mine. All mine. Nobody else's. You're not going back to the States so you can screw somebody else," he said.

"Deke, I wouldn't. I'd never . . ."

"Shut up," he told her and he continued to manipulate her with his hand. "It's getting wet. It drips so fast. How many times did you do it while I was gone?" he demanded to know.

"I didn't, Deke. I never did, not with anybody," she answered. His words were so angry and his hands so tender. He had asked this of her before and she had failed to convince him. When he didn't believe her, he hurt her, punished her as he remembered being punished. She hoped that he would believe her now. She desperately repeated herself. "I never, never did."

"Are you telling me the truth?" he asked.

"Yes, Deke."

"Why do you want to go back to the States?"

"I'm homesick."

"I told you, this is your home now."

She made a mistake. "It's not home to me."

He took her face in his hands. She could smell herself on his fingers.

"Who is it you want to get home to screw?"

"Nobody. There's nobody but you, Deke."

"You're lying to me," he said. "I don't like it when you lie to me."

She raised her arm to protect her face, anticipating a blow.

"I'm not going to hit you. And I'm not going to screw you either. I'm going to leave you all wet and lonely until you tell me who the guy is you want to get home to."

"I just wanted to go home for a visit, that's all," she said. "I don't like it here. It's sad here. I don't like it. Why don't we all three go home?" she suggested.

"I'm never going back there. There's nothing there for me," he told her and he was thinking of the ranch on the desert, how the heat shimmered and the cold pierced, and his mother binding his hands until they bled. "I'm staying here and you're staying with me."

"You mean we're never going home?"

"No."

She tried to get up from the bed but he held her down.

"Where do you think you're going?"

"I want to get up."

"No."

"But Deke, I have to go to the bathroom."

"No," he said.

He had her pinioned, restrained beneath his body. She fluttered slightly like a butterfly on a pin, but she did not struggle. He stared down into her face, his own white and taut in the darkness.

"Go right here, now," he commanded.

"No, Deke."

"Go. I want to see it wet the sheet and run down your legs."

"No, please don't make me . . . please . . ." she begged and she could feel the tingling sensation between her legs.

"Go," he told her.

The warm urine rushed from her. He remembered his mother beating him until his skin was raw for wetting his bed. In the night he would feel the hot release and in the morning when it was cold he knew that she would come and whip him.

"I'm watching you," he said. "Don't try and leave me. You'll be sorry if you do. Don't you ever try and leave me."

He lay beside her on the damp sheet and they slept. Poppy dreamed. Her nightmares carried her backward to Kansas. She tossed and turned, moaned and cried out. Deke did not wake, but Jasmine did and she watched her mother from her crib. She saw Poppy's body arch like a cat's, a great white cat in the darkness. The child followed her mother's every move. Poppy got up from the bed. She passed by the crib, close, and Jasmine could see her eyes. Her mother's eyes were not like she had ever seen them. They were opened, but blank, not registering any outside images, only seeing and being guided by some interior force, deeply driving. Poppy circled the room. She hit into a wall, continued to bang her head against it, but she showed no feeling of pain. She crossed to the dresser where he had left his pistol. Poppy picked it up and it was heavy, the weight of it pulling her thin arm downward. She walked to the bed. Jasmine watched. She saw her mother lift her arm and hold it straight out, her hand ending in his gun, its barrel aimed at his sprawled and unconscious form. Poppy fired the gun. The sound was loud and Jasmine covered her face with her small hands. Five more shots came.

Poppy awakened to find Jasmine being carried away by a strange woman. All the lights were on in the apartment. She was standing in the living room and she could see the table with the dinner dishes still on it, the flowers Deke had brought to her, and the candles burned down to the copper holders. The front door was ajar and there were people out in the hallway. They were staring in at her. Instinctively she started to move her arms in front of her to protect and hide herself from them, but she couldn't. She felt something hard binding her hands, holding them together at her back. Her head felt swollen. She was dazed and confused. Two soldiers with MP armbands like Deke's approached, flanked her, and began to guide her out of the apartment.

"What are you doing?" she asked. "Where are you taking me?" Coming from down the hallway she heard Jasmine's cries and she remembered the woman carrying her baby away. "Where is my little girl being taken?"

The soldiers did not answer. They nearly lifted her feet from the ground as they escorted her out and through the crowd of robed and puffy-eyed, gawking neighbors.

"Please close my front door," she said to the soldiers. "Don't leave it open like that. Deke doesn't like it when it's left open. I forget to close it sometimes and he gets mad. Please, close the door or Deke will get mad."

They took her in a closed truck to a cell. She was locked inside. She sat up in a chair, never thinking of trying to sleep on the cot that was there. No one spoke to her. A guard passed by every fifteen minutes, but he did not even turn his head slightly to look at her. She sat and waited for what would happen to her next. Sometime early in the morning her cell door was opened and an army officer walked inside. He removed his hat. Since she occupied the only chair he sat down on the edge of the narrow bed where she had not slept.

"Mrs. Cody," he said. "I'm Captain Harris. I'm your attorney."

"I don't understand. What's happened? Why was I brought here? Why do I need an attorney?"

"Mrs. Cody, I'm here to help you, but you're going to have to tell me the truth. Otherwise there's nothing I can do for you."

"I don't know what you mean, Cap . . . Captain." She struggled over his title, intimidated and frightened by it. "All I know is that they brought me here last night and they took my little girl away. A woman I've never seen came and took her. You're the

first person who's talked to me. Please, if you'll call my husband
. . . have him come for me. Deke will come. I know he will.
He'll come and take me home . . ."

"Mrs. Cody, are you trying to tell me, do you expect me to
believe, that you don't know what's happened to your husband?"

"What's happened to Deke?" she asked.

He searched her face for some hint of deceit, any trace of
treachery, but there was none. He believed her and he knew that
he was about to deal her a smashing blow. He told her as gently
as he could. "Mrs. Cody, your husband is dead."

"No," she said. "No, he can't be." She remembered how they'd
gone to bed last night. They'd both fallen asleep. Could Deke
have gotten up and gone somewhere, she wondered. He did that
sometimes. Had he done it last night? "Was there an accident?
Was he hurt?" She refused to believe that he was dead. She could
and did accept so much, but this she could not.

He realized that he would have to present her with the bald
and brutal facts. He had come to her cell expecting to find a
woman accused of murder, a woman either repentant or defiant,
but he had not anticipated this pale half-child, lost, a confused
innocent who had killed and did not even know that she had. He
felt that the truth, terrible and cutting as it was, might not penetrate her haze, but being a lawyer, her lawyer, he had to try and
believe in the power of words, the influence of decree, and the
strength of justice. He had to inform her of her guilt and then
prove to her judges her innocence.

"Mrs. Cody, your husband is dead. You shot him last night."

"No," she said loudly, then softly. "No. No."

He checked his notes and resorted to cold, hard, and legal
jargon. "A neighbor, Staff Sergeant Whylock, heard several shots
at approximately three A.M. this morning. They came from your
apartment. He went to your door and when he got no response
by knocking, he broke in. He found you, Mrs. Cody, standing
over your husband with his gun in your hand. Corporal Cody
was lying on the bed. Sergeant Whylock ascertained that he was
dead. He had been shot six times."

"I shot him?" Poppy asked.

"Everything indicates that you did."

She looked at the sincerely worried, clean-shaven face of the
captain, and she knew it was true. With the acceptance came the

tears. "Deke is dead. I killed him," she confessed to the man on the cot who was here to defend her, and to herself, too.

"I want you to tell me everything that you can about last night."

The tears flowed steadily, making her vision wavering and watery. She could barely make out the captain. And the night before was as unclear through her tears as he was. She could remember very little.

"I can't remember," she told him.

"You must try, Mrs. Cody."

"But . . . but I can't."

"It's vitally important that you do. Your life depends on it."

"I can't remember," she said.

Poppy thought of Jasmine. "Where is my little girl? Where did they take her?" she asked him. She could think of her baby daughter taken from her but not of her husband killed by her.

"She's with a family in your building," he told her.

"Do they have children, these people?"

"Yes, I think they do," he answered.

"Then she'll have someone to play with. That's good. Are they kind people?"

"Yes," he assured her, not really knowing.

"What's going to happen to me?" she asked him.

"You'll be put on trial."

"Back home?"

"No, here, in Japan."

"By the Japanese?" she asked in fear, thinking of the hordes of small and impassive people she had seen in the streets.

"No, by the army. A court-martial."

"But I'm not in the army. My husband is . . ." She stopped, and seeing the expression of the captain, said, ". . . was . . . was in the army."

"Here in Japan you are considered part of the United States Army, Mrs. Cody. You are under its protection and its jurisdiction. You will be tried by the army," he explained to her. "I've been assigned by the army to defend you. I want to give you the best possible defense. I need your help to do that. You must help me to help you, Mrs. Cody."

"You believe that I . . . killed . . . killed Deke?" she asked, hoping for some shred of someone's disbelief.

"There's very little doubt that you shot your husband. Sergeant Whylock's testimony, even though he's not an eyewitness, will be very damaging to you, very convincing to the judges. What is of utmost importance now is why. Why did you shoot him? You did shoot your husband, didn't you? You're not saying that there was an intruder or . . ." He halted, not able to think of another alternative.

"No, it must have been . . . me . . . but I don't remember . . . I . . . don't . . . know . . . why . . . but it must have been me. I must have done it . . ." Her words weaved and repeated incoherently.

He attempted to draw her back to lucidity. He was desperate to understand, to penetrate, this muddled and endangered girl. "Tell me about yesterday. Begin in the morning and tell me, very slowly, about yesterday."

She thought of the day, tried to piece it together, Deke's last day alive, the last day that she would ever see him, and it was through him, every event related to him, that she had experienced and would now recall the day.

"Deke left very early and he told me that he would be home late. He had MP duty. I spent the day cleaning the apartment. Jasmine cried in her crib, but I had to keep her there because I can't get anything done when she's always under my feet. I wanted everything to look nice. I took her out in the afternoon for a walk so that she would be sleepy. There was a man selling funny little toys. They were made of straw or something and they had a string attached so that you could bounce them . . ." She made a gesture, moving up and down, with her hand to show how the doll jumped. ". . . up and down . . . up and down . . ." She drifted, watching her hand.

"And then what happened, Mrs. Cody?" he questioned, urging her back to reality.

"I bought one for Jasmine. She liked it. She took it to bed with her. When I went in to check on her she was holding it to her neck and she was asleep. She'd been asleep for hours when Deke got home. He had flowers for me, pink ones. It was all so nice, but then I spoiled it. I made him mad."

"How? What did you do?"

"I told him that I wanted to go home."

"Back to the States?"

"Yes."

"You told him that you were leaving him? Did you ask for a divorce?"

"No. I only wanted to go home."

"And he didn't want you to go?"

"He told me I couldn't. He thought that I was . . . that there was someone else, another man."

"Is there?" he asked.

"No. Never. I told him that. I told him, but he wouldn't believe me."

"Then what happened?"

She was silent.

"Mrs. Cody?"

"We went to the bedroom . . . to bed. He held me there. I said I had to get up, but he wouldn't let me. He held me . . . held me down . . . and I said I had to go to the bathroom. He wouldn't let me go. He made me . . . made me . . ."

"What?"

"He made me wet the bed. He told me he was watching me . . . he wanted to see me do it . . . he was watching me . . . and not to ever try and leave him . . . he told me . . . he was watching me and I did it and the sheet was wet underneath me . . . and then I fell asleep. I must have fallen asleep and Deke did, too. When I woke up the apartment was all bright and there were lots of people and two soldiers were taking me away . . . here . . . and the woman took Jasmine. I could hear Jasmine crying, but no one would talk to me, tell me what had happened."

"That's all you can remember?"

"Yes."

"Did your husband ever strike you?"

Again she was silent.

"Did he? This is vital to your case, Mrs. Cody. You must try and save yourself now. Did your husband ever strike you?"

"Yes," she answered.

"Often?" he asked.

This man didn't understand, she thought. No one could. She couldn't. She didn't understand Deke, but she'd loved him. And she'd killed him. Now she was being asked to betray him, tell his secrets to save herself.

"Mrs. Cody, please answer me. I don't think you fully realize the trouble that you're in. I think I can help you if you'll let me," he said. He knew where he must press, where this weak girl was weakest and strongest, too. "Your little girl is without a father. Do you want to leave her without a mother, too?"

"No," she whispered.

"Did your husband strike you often?"

"Yes."

"Is there anyone who can corroborate this?" he asked.

She didn't know what he meant. Seeing her puzzlement, he spoke, attempting to clarify his words.

"Could anyone else testify to this? Is there anyone who witnessed your husband's abuse of you?"

"No," she said. "Well, yes, someone did . . . Jasmine, my little girl saw. I never wanted her to, but I know that she saw . . . she saw . . . maybe even watched when I fired the gun. She was in the same room . . . the same room."

My God, he was thinking, was he going to have to use the child? "How old is Jasmine?" he asked.

"She's two. She'll be three soon."

Too young, he thought, too young to have seen what she had, and too young to tell of it.

"Your neighbors, could they have heard some of your arguments?" he asked her.

"They did. I know they did. I always told Deke that they could hear us," she told him sadly, ashamed.

But the army lawyer was glad. For the first time he saw some hope. "All right, now we're getting somewhere," he said and he closed his notebook. "I'm going over to your building and talk with some of the other tenants."

"What will you ask them?"

"What they heard," he told her.

"I don't want them to say what they heard."

"Mrs. Cody, this is your only chance. I have to establish the sort of relationship that you and your husband had. He abused you. He drove you to what you did. The plea will be momentary insanity. It's all we've got. I have to have the neighbors' testimony. I'm on my way there right now," he said and he stood.

"Cap . . . Captain?"

"Yes?"

"Will you check on my baby? Will you make sure that Jasmine is all right?"

"Yes," he told her. "Guard!" he called.

Poppy was left alone in her cell.

She was tried swiftly, judged by soldiers for killing a soldier. Most of the proceedings flashed by unperceived by her. Poppy sat mute with her hands folded in her lap. The neighbors who came to testify in her defense told of the fights that they had heard coming from the Cody apartment, but about Poppy herself they could say little. She did not recognize most of the faces of those revealing her domestic turmoil on the witness stand. And that was the impression left by these strangers. They were strangers. Poppy Cody did not mix. They did not know her. She had spent most of her time in the apartment with the little girl, they said to her judges. She was unknown to them, but they did know that her husband had beat her, and that they were here because she was accused of killing him. Captain Harris did not even try to claim self-defense. Poppy could not or would not give any word to substantiate that plea. He had decided that Poppy herself was her own best defense. She was an American girl, far from home, lonely and unhappy in a foreign country, abused by her husband, driven by him to the point of madness. It seemed easy enough to believe, but the military tribunal was not convinced. And they were not compassionate.

Poppy was convicted of first-degree murder and sentenced to life in prison. The entire trial took one week. Justice was quick and punishment total. For taking her husband's life Poppy was condemned to live out her own behind bars.

Captain Harris came one last time to her cell to explain where she would be taken. He took his accustomed seat on the edge of the cot. Poppy faced him from her chair. The young lawyer was changed. He looked haggard. He had lost sleep, and would continue to, over Poppy. She was too faint, passive, and pale to linger, to burn into his or anyone's brain, but her fate was horrible enough to keep the captain sleepless for a lifetime of nights.

"Mrs. Cody, you're to be flown to Hawaii tomorrow. From there you will travel by ship to the States."

"They're sending me home?" she asked.

"Yes," he said. "You'll be taken to a federal penitentiary in Washington."

"Washington?"

"There's an island, a prison, in Puget Sound. That's where you'll be . . ."—he had started to say living, but said instead, ". . . sent."

"And Jasmine? She won't be left in Japan? Captain Harris, they wouldn't leave her here, would they?"

He had lied to her. Every day he had lied. He had not told her the truth. He was afraid to tell her, but he knew he could no longer omit or avoid. She had to know what had been done.

"Mrs. Cody, your daughter was flown out of Japan three weeks ago," he said.

"But you've been telling me every day how she was. You said that you saw her, every day," she said. She had eaten his words like food, thirsted for them like water to quench a parched throat. She had taken what he told her and imagined Jasmine in their building still, happy with a family there. Every moment she had tried to know, to visualize in her mind, what her child was doing and feeling. And Jasmine had been torn away, gone for weeks. This man had lied to her. She had trusted him, but he was like all the others, all the other men. They had all lied and hurt, abandoned her. They had taken Jasmine from her.

"Where? Where is she?" Poppy asked.

"Corporal Cody's body and your daughter were taken under military escort to New Mexico."

"No," Poppy's voice rose. "They didn't take my baby to her, not to Deke's mother! No! No!"

"It was decided that that was the best thing for the child."

"Who decided? How do they know? They don't know. His mother . . . she did things to Deke, terrible things . . . he told me that she did. She'll hurt Jasmine. She'll do to her what she did to him. She can't take her. I want my sister Holly to have Jasmine. My sister Holly . . . not Deke's mother . . ."

"The army has decided . . ."

"No!" she screamed it. "No!"

The captain saw her eyes turn up into her head. She slid to the floor and began thrashing. She pounded her face to the hard concrete, bloodying it. He tried to restrain her. She bit at his hands. He called for the guard.

They bandaged his hands at the infirmary. He thought of how he had witnessed his plea for her become reality. She had gone insane, perhaps momentarily, perhaps forever. If the men at her court-martial could have seen what he just had, there would have been no doubt, but what would have changed, he bitterly wondered. She would have been confined to an asylum instead of a prison. She would still have lost her child and her freedom. She was, probably always had been, and surely always would be controlled by others. She was powerless, a helpless and maddened victim. He looked down at the bandages. In a week they would be removed, but he would carry the scar of Poppy Cody's futile rage all the rest of his life. Her raised red teeth marks would fade, lighten to white, the color of her hair, but they would never completely leave him. He would never forget her wasted life, her decreed fate.

Poppy, heavily sedated, and surrounded by soldiers, was taken to the Atsugi Airfield the next morning. It was on this strip that the kamikaze suicide pilots had been trained during the war. Poppy was an American sacrifice, a drugged and burnt offering. She was led to the waiting plane, headed home at last.

Chapter Twenty-one

Paul stood by while she packed. He claimed to understand perfectly the postponement of their wedding, but Holly felt his close scrutiny of her movements and she wondered if he was questioning her motives. His understanding of her, the depth of it, no longer surprised her, but his entrenched tolerance continued to amaze her. His love was soft, gentle, and rock-solid. And even she did not fully realize how much she depended upon it and upon him. While Paul was there with her, and strong, he could not be missed. She was going away, not for long, and not from him, but, still, she was leaving him behind, and she tried to imagine what it would be like without him. She looked at him and couldn't know what the lack of him, the want, would be.

Thoughts of the journey she was about to make began to crowd out all other speculation. It was a terrible trip, she was thinking, to travel to a prison to visit a sister who was sentenced to live out her life there for the crime of murdering another human being. Poppy, poor little Poppy. Of all the ends that she might have met, Holly would never have guessed this one. Poppy had always been the victim, the eternal sufferer, but she had pointed a pistol at Deke while he slept and fired six shots into him. The army

said she had done this. They had convicted her. Holly did not
doubt the event. She only wondered how many faces Poppy's
husband's sleeping face had worn when she killed him, how many
others from her traumatized past she had been murdering when
she brutally ended Deke Cody's life. Looking at it now, after the
fact, it was as if Poppy's whole harmed life had been spent in
preparation for this one moment of release and killing retribu-
tion. Holly knew that Poppy had done this thing, though it had
seemed more likely that Deke would have killed Poppy. Once
again Holly was confronted with the image of a sister being
murdered. She remembered thinking how easily Iris might have
been slain, becoming a splashy and sensational newspaper head-
line. Now she thought of the murder of Poppy rather than seeing Poppy herself as the perpetrator, the murderer. Murdered
sisters, she thought, and yet none of them had been. Long ago
Mama had believed that Jasmine's life had been taken, but Holly
felt that her sister had taken her own life. In a way, both her
sisters who had died, Jasmine and Iris, had killed themselves.
Even Poppy who still lived on had ended her own life, stopped
the true living of it anyway. Holly remembered how Jasmine
had hated the idea of leaving the desert and moving to Washington . . . Washington . . . Washington. It echoed within her,
ominously, hollowly repeating. She dropped the skirt she was
folding. It fell noiselessly to the carpet. She was shaking.

"What's the matter?" Paul asked her.

"Washington," she said. She had not meant to say it aloud.
Washington. "Poppy was born there and now she's going to be
locked away there forever." Holly stopped speaking, her voice
escaping her, trembling like her body was.

"You know it's perfectly reasonable for you to be reacting like
this," he said.

"Like what?"

"You're spooked. You should be. Anybody would be. This is
a horrifying experience. It's not the sort of thing that's ever
expected to happen. It's the stuff of tabloids . . ."

She spoke over his quiet and sane voice. "Paul, did I leave the
sweater that matches this skirt at your house?"

He followed her. "You may have."

"Could we drive out and see?" she asked. "They match, the
sweater and skirt do, and I'd like to wear them together," she

told him. "I always wear them together. I don't know how they could have gotten separated. I hope the sweater's at your house. I couldn't have lost it. I hate to lose things. I hardly ever do. I'm careful, you know, not to lose anything because I just hate it so when I do. It has to be at your house. I couldn't have lost . . ." She knew that she was speaking in crazy, endless, and meaningless circles. She wanted to avoid thinking of the oddly linked pattern, the strange circle, her family had made in Washington. So she compassed and covered with her words, her talk of her skirt and lost sweater.

"Let's go and see," Paul said.

"What?" she asked him. "What did you say?"

"I said let's go see." Her look was disoriented, spinning from her circles. "Let's go see if your sweater is at the house," he carefully explained to her.

"Yes, all right," she agreed, recovering.

When they got to the house they searched everywhere but couldn't find the sweater. They even emptied a large closet on the sunporch. They sat amidst the piles of old and slightly musty, sea-damp clothes, and the cool gray air seeped through the screen. She touched a wool jacket of Paul's. It was made of dark blue, wonderfully coarse cloth. She rubbed her cheek against it. She had never seen him wear it, but it seemed so suited to him. She could visualize him walking on the sand and the collar of this coat turned up to keep the wet winds from him. She put it on. It was much too large for her and she sank down into it.

"Why don't you ever wear this?" she asked.

"I do, sometimes," he said.

"I've never seen you wear it."

"Actually it's not mine," he told her.

"Who's is it?"

"It was my father's. He wore it when he sailed."

She knew so little about Paul's past. It was hers, always hers, that they navigated. Shoallike, her past was patently dangerous, but his remained uncharted.

"You've kept it all this time because it was his?" she asked.

"It was the most tangible thing I ever had of him," Paul said.

"What was he like, your father?"

"He was . . ."—he chose the word carefully—"distant."

"And your mother?"

"Was not . . . distant."

Holly sank down further into the coat. Her face was half hidden in the collar.

"Did you love your father?" she asked Paul.

"I didn't know him. He didn't let me know him."

"You loved your mother," she said, not asking.

"I loved her."

"I wish that I'd loved my mother. Even now I wish I could love her, but I can't. She's dead and I can't find even a memory of her to love. That's a terrible thing, isn't it?" she asked.

"It's very sad."

"Still, I had Daddy. Daddy loved me enough for both, for Mama and himself."

She wasn't aware that she had switched from her feelings for her parents to their feelings for her, but Paul noticed.

"You loved him very much, didn't you?"

"More than anyone . . ." She stopped. "He was the most important . . ." She broke off again.

He watched her conceal herself. Only her eyes could be seen above the collar of his father's coat. He moved closer to her. He parted the coat and pushed it down off her shoulders.

She felt as she had the first time he had seen her naked. She felt naked. He kissed her. He pressed his body to hers.

"Here?" she whispered.

"Here. Now," he said.

They made love and the coat was their bed. She felt Paul deep inside her. Her bare skin rubbed upon the fibrous weave of the coat. She was touched by this man loving her and touched, too, tingling from the contact of the rough cloth, by her father's coat. Paul's father. Not hers. Not Daddy's. Daddy's. Daddy. Daddy. It nearly came from her, that cry for him, but she was silent through Paul's surging.

They discovered later, back at her apartment, that she had already packed the sweater they had gone seeking. They'd found something else, but they spoke of the sweater.

"I can't believe it. I never do things like this," she said when she saw it neatly folded in her suitcase.

"I'm glad you did," Paul told her. "Very glad."

She smiled at him.

"I'm going to miss you," he said.

"I'll miss you, too." This feeling and admission of loss was coming more easily to her now than it ever had before.

"Holly, no more delays. As soon as you get back we'll be married."

"Yes," she agreed, but even as she said it she was beginning to feel that familiar slipping sensation. She was sliding away from him and toward Washington. And she wanted to go back to the beach, wrap herself in his love and his father's old blue pea jacket, but she could not. She had to leave him again.

Holly had stood alone over Jasmine that night on the desert when her sister had convulsed madly and died. She had gone alone to San Diego to identify Iris's beautiful smashed body, but Holly was not going to Washington alone. Rose had left Clyde in the tiny duplex, a twin of their Kansas apartment, where they'd been living during their first months in California, and joined Holly. She was sitting beside her on the train that sped north up the coast of California, through Oregon, toward their haunting and verdant destination.

"Why do you think she did it?" Rose asked. It was the question she had wanted to put to Holly for hundreds of miles. Now they had nearly arrived and she decided she should not and could not wait any longer.

"I don't know," Holly told her. She had expected the question sooner, all the long way; through three states she had anticipated it, and within minutes of their destination, when she thought she had escaped, it came. She had no answer. She didn't know if there was one.

"Do you think that he hit her? Or there might have been other women? Or maybe he drank?" Rose guessed.

Holly realized that these were reasons from Rose's experience. They were actions that her sister could understand, things she had seen or known.

"Maybe Deke did drink or run around or beat her, one or all of them, but Rosie, you don't shoot someone because of that. You leave," she said, and even as she said it she knew that Poppy couldn't have left. "I mean there isn't any sane reason or sensible explanation for one person's firing a gun into another person, is there?"

"You think Poppy's crazy?" Rose asked. "Is that what you're saying?"

Holly looked into her sister's open and concerned, frowning but still comical face. That face, spotted with freckles and simple sincerity, stared back at her. How could someone like Rose fathom insanity, the horrifying and murky quicksand of it, the way it sucked and pulled its victims under? How could anyone but passive and abused, mad Poppy know what had made her do what she'd done? Holly doubted that even Poppy herself knew what terrible outrage had waited, accumulated hideously inside her.

"I don't know," she said to Rose again.

Rose seemed to accept this. She asked no more questions.

When they pulled into the tiny terminal that was their journey's end, Rose followed Holly off the train. The station was an open platform and across the street from it was the town square. There was the usual bronze statue, aged to green, an orator with lifted arm, and a bandstand for outdoor summer concerts. People were gathering there. It could have been a Memorial Day celebration or the nucleus of a July Fourth parade. There were flags everywhere and men in uniform. The white steepled church of the town rose up behind, a righteous fortification and backdrop of probity for the festivities. The two sisters looked on. They stood with their bags in hand and the perfect, small-town tableau of patriotic camaraderie unfurled before them, but they were outlanders, here for very different reasons from the crowd across the street, or so they believed.

"What do you think is going on?" Rosie asked.

"It's not a holiday," Holly said, always certain of her dates.

"Maybe it's a local shindig," Rose suggested. "It looks like fun," she said, the sociable and joyful part of her wishing that she could join the group and not go where she knew she must.

The station master came up beside them, tilted his hat back, and hoisted his leg up onto the railing. He was chewing tobacco ruminatively.

Rose smiled at the man and asked pleasantly, "What's the party for?"

"No party, miss, far from it," he said.

The grin had gone from his face. He had taken on a rock-hard, angry look, his lips locked into a grim seam.

"There's a woman coming into town today," the man told them. Holly edged back from him. A warning sounded within her.

"Come on, Rose. Let's be going," she said.

Rose looked from the station master to her sister and then across to the seemingly amiable crowd of townspeople.

"Is this woman a movie star or something?" she asked.

The man stared at her for a moment. "She's a killer is what she is."

"Come on, Rose," Holly said, her words tugging at her sister's arm.

"A killer?" Rose persisted, still not understanding, not yet seeing, not associating her presence with the gathering flag wavers. She couldn't recognize the link, the woman who had killed and who bound them all together.

"That's right, a killer," the man continued. "And we've got a little reception committee lined up to meet her. The army's bringing her through town on her way out to the prison on Dukhobors Island . . ."

Now Rose realized. She turned to Holly. The group from the square was filing down the street. Among the flags and the uniforms, unseen until now, there were crudely lettered placards. Rose read them, mouthing silently, her lips trembling with the words. MURDERESS. HUSBAND KILLER. BURN HER. HANG HER. KILL HER LIKE SHE KILLED HIM. NO MERCY.

The signs, held high, passed. A small boy of eight or nine in short pants trudged along behind the rest. He carried a bucket of red paint. It sloshed down his bare legs. Seeing him, Holly thought the paint looked like blood, as if the boy were bleeding. It hit her that it was intended to appear that way. The paint's purpose was to masquerade as blood. It would, she guessed, be thrown upon her sister, Poppy, the husband killer, the woman that this lovely little town wanted both to burn and hang.

"Bringing her through in about fifteen minutes now, going down to the wharf. The prison launch is waiting for her and we'll be waiting for her, too. Maybe you'd like to go down and see for yourselves. The wharf's just . . ."

"No," Holly interrupted him. "No, I don't think so," she managed to say.

Holly practically pushed Rose down the stairs to the street. Rose seemed stunned to paralysis by the station master's words. Holly guided her eastward toward the Jefferson Hotel where they had a room reserved. Once away from the man, Rose came to, as if regaining consciousness after a blow.

"How can we stop them?" she asked.

"We can't," Holly said. She knew that there was no stopping this mob that they had mistaken for a holiday bunch. "We can't stop them. All that we can do is not watch," she told her sister's antic-featured but grief-stricken face.

The crowd had arrived, milling and pressing, at the wharf. They were waiting for the rumbling sound of the army vehicle on the wooden planks. The children among them played, chased after one another, all but the little boy with the paint. He was solemn and apart, almost sacred in his duty, like an altar boy. Before the crowd heard the heavy rolling of the wheels, they felt them, the vibrating approach, and they tensed as one in anticipation, in tight union. They were melded in faith and hatred and expectation, all eyes strained in a single direction. The prison launch rocked on the water in sickening rhythm, waiting, too, for Poppy. The large, gray unmarked car pulled up and stopped. A soldier was driving. He did not move, remaining within. Poppy sat in the back seat. A man in uniform was on either side of her. The crowd craned for a better look at the woman they had come to revile.

They were surprised to silence by Poppy as she got out of the car. They had envisioned, wanted to see, a monster. Poppy wore a plain pale gray dress with a pink sweater over her shoulders. The sleeves of the sweater swayed empty. Her hands were manacled behind her. Her hair was pulled away from her face. She did not wear a hat. Her pitiful and lost expression was naked and unmasked. She did not see the signs that the people held. She accepted the presence of the crowd as one more unexplained event, a circumstance thrust upon her. The small boy with the bucket came forward through the parting and quiet patriots. He was a child and he had been given a task. Poppy's appearance had not done to him what it had to his elders. He had no expectations and he'd suffered no disappointment or shock. He had no new sympathy or old hate for Poppy He was blandly obedient. He had his instructions. He was a simple child with a cruel mission. He would come to Poppy innocently and in innocence, un-suspectingly, she would meet him. The two guards were moving her along quickly toward the boat. The little boy had to break into a trot to catch them. The paint was escaping from the bucket, running in rivulets down the sides.

"Wait!" the child cried out.

Something in the high-pitched treble reminded Poppy of Jasmine and, thinking of her baby, she turned toward the voice. She and the boy stood face to face, not more than a yard from one another.

"Killer!" he shouted and swung the pail at Poppy.

Most of the paint splattered to the wood planks of the wharf, seeping into the splintered and uneven surface. A few splashes of bloodlike stain marked Poppy's gray dress. One wetly red streak slashed across her white cheek.

The boy ran back into the crowd, not looking at Poppy but to his father. The man who wore the cap decorated with medals and ribbons gave his son the approval he sought. He crushed his compliant child to him.

The guards were moving faster now. The townspeople had begun to chant. As she was pushed along, Poppy stared down at the paint on her dress. She could feel it on her face but was unable to lift her bound hands to wipe it away. Then she was in the small boat and the songlike screaming was growing distant, coming across the choppy black water faintly, less fiercely, and finally not at all. She sat, chained, and it was quiet on the Sound. She had not comprehended the commotion on the land. One of her guards took out a handkerchief and gently rubbed the paint from her face.

"Thank you," she said.

Her guard said nothing. He was fighting to reconcile his feelings with his duty. He pitied her and he was angry with her for making it so difficult to despise her as he believed he should.

Rose and Holly waited for what they feared and knew to be happening to be finished. They sat in their room at the Jefferson Hotel. Holly followed with a fingertip the pattern of her Martha Washington bedspread. Rose, natually, was the first to end the abiding silence.

"I think we should have tried to stop it," she said.

"How?" Holly asked.

"I don't know. Couldn't we have called the police, the sheriff, or someone?"

"The sheriff was probably leading that parade," Holly said. "What we have to do is get out to the prison as soon as possible and make sure that Poppy is all right."

"The army told us she was being transferred yesterday. What do you think happened?"

"Some kind of paperwork snarl. Maybe they were giving these people here time to properly prepare their demonstration."

They were taken out to the island prison on the same launch that had carried a paint-spattered and confused Poppy that morning. Now it was late afternoon. Most of the day had been consumed with obtaining permission for this visit. They had been told that they could have half an hour with Poppy.

Once within the high-walled stone prison complex, Rose and Holly were taken to a small room that was divided down the middle by a wired glass partition. There were chairs on either side. Both halves of the room looked the same but between the two there was the difference of freedom and imprisonment. One side was for inmates and the other for their visitors. Poppy was brought in. There was a faint familiar resemblance, a vague sort of connecting tissue, among the three young women. The slender, dark-haired girl with the quietly elegant gestures and presence, and the freckled, plump redhead whose face was congealed in laughter but shadowed with sadness, sat beside one another facing the pallid blond who had a guard posted a few feet from her. She was the guilty one, the accused and condemned. The other two were innocent guests in this place; their guards, bars, and chains were elsewhere, and their guilt, too. They talked through a small circle cut in the glass.

"Are you all right?" Rose asked Poppy.

"Yes," Poppy answered. "But I'm worried about Jasmine."

"She's with Mrs. Cody," Rose said. "Didn't they tell you?"

"Yes, I know," Poppy said. "I . . . I don't like her being there. I don't want her there."

"Why?" Rose asked.

"It won't be good for her there," she told Rose. She looked to Holly. "I want her to be with you, Holly. You love her as much as I do."

"I do love her, Poppy, but . . ."

In her weak voice she spoke over Holly. "Jasmine should be with you."

Rose mediated. "I'm sure she's fine with her grandmother, Poppy."

"No." Poppy's tears were starting.

"What if I went to see Jasmine? If she's happy where she is, she shouldn't be taken away, not by anyone." Holly spoke of stability for the child, but she was thinking of other things. Poppy's words had sparked a sudden panic within her. She was frightened of the little girl she loved dearly. The responsibility of her affection made her afraid. She continued to speak of Jasmine's security and not her fears. "Jasmine's life has been disrupted, her world turned upside down. If she's settled in with her grandmother it would be very wrong to move her." Holly knew that Poppy would feel guilty. She disliked using that weapon, but it was too effective to set aside. "Jasmine should be allowed to be happy. She's been through enough."

Rose was watching Holly. She hated what she saw and what she was hearing. She looked at Poppy, listening for her response, sadly sure what it would be.

Poppy was crumbling, capitulating, and crying. "My poor baby. It's all my fault." Then she caught herself and a strength she'd never shown materialized. She would not give way, could not give up, on her child. "But I don't think it's good for Jasmine there. I know things . . . things that nobody else does. You promise that you'll go and see her?" she asked Holly.

"Yes, I promise," Holly said. She wondered what things Poppy knew or thought that she did. She wondered, but she didn't really want to know.

Poppy was being led away. At the barred door she stopped and raised her hand in silent goodbye to her sisters. The door was opened and closed behind her. She was swallowed up into a world that those who walked free could not even imagine.

"Goodbye, Poppy," Rose said, though Poppy was already gone and on her way back to her cell. "My God in heaven, let's get out of here."

They left the prison confines and the launch returned them to the mainland. They stayed that night at the Jefferson and the next morning took the morning train out of that brutal and pretty place. Just as the station master had reduced Rose to crippled disbelief, so she remained dumb while in the town's territory, but as their train began to move she began to talk.

"It's like a nightmare. I keep thinking I'm going to wake up and none of it will be true. I can't believe that Poppy is in that awful place. And she'll be there for the rest of her life."

"I know," Holly said. "I really can't think about it. Rosie, will you come to New Mexico with me? To see Jasmine?" she asked.

"Holly," she began. She took a deep breath. She thought of how Holly had manipulated Poppy, how she'd made her feel to blame for everything that had happened. Maybe Poppy was guilty, but Rose feared that Holly had used her guilt to try and escape. She had thought that she knew Holly but now she wasn't sure. She had seen a side of her sister, cold and forbidding, that she was afraid might be her core. "I'd like to go with you, but I can't," she said.

"Why can't you?" Holly asked.

Rose spoke the truth, but it was an easier truth than the one of her thoughts and fears. "Clyde didn't want me to make this trip. I know he won't agree to another one so soon."

"Why should Clyde mind?"

"I don't know, but he does," she said and added sadly, "I thought he'd be glad to be rid of me."

"So that's it then? If Clyde doesn't want you to go, you don't?"

"That's right. I'm holding on to this marriage by my fingernails."

"Rosie, I don't know why you're holding on at all."

"I didn't think you would, Holly. I wonder if there's been anybody you wanted to hold on to, ever, since Daddy. How long are you going to keep Paul dangling?"

"I'm not keeping Paul dangling."

"All right, if you say so," Rose said. "This is your trip to make, Holly. Poppy wanted you to go, not me."

"I'll go," Holly told her. "Alone."

"That's the way you like it, isn't it?" Rose asked.

Holly gave no answer. Between the two sisters there was a strain. A tension had surfaced. Each was wondering, as she sat beside the other, how long it had lain dormant and why it had sprung up now.

Paul was at the Los Angeles station waiting for them. They drove Rose home. Rose was looking to see if Clyde's truck was parked out front. It was not. She wasn't disappointed. She was hurt and she had expected to be.

"Would you like to come in?" Rose asked, a polite offer without enthusiasm.

"I'm awfully tired," Holly said.

"So am I. Well, call me tomorrow if you get a chance," Rose said to Holly. "Thanks, Paul." Her natural warmth beamed briefly.

"You're welcome. Goodnight, Rose," Paul said.

"Goodnight," Rose returned.

Holly said quietly, "Goodnight."

Paul waited until Rose had opened the door of the duplex and stepped inside before he drove away.

"What's wrong?" he asked Holly immediately.

She told him about Jasmine and Poppy's fears for her daughter. Then she recounted her exchange with Rose on the train, but she omitted Rose's mention of him. She didn't tell him what her sister had said about their father either. They were at her apartment by the time she was finished. They entered and Holly snapped on the lights.

"Would you like some coffee?" she asked him. "Or brandy?"

"Coffee, please."

He followed her into the kitchen.

"Holly, I know how much you care for Jasmine." He thought of the times he had seen Holly and the little girl together, how many times he had pretended that the child was theirs. The pictures that lined the apartment were proof of Holly's devotion and he was almost jealous of that love, but he saw it as a breakthrough for Holly, too. And he was grateful to Poppy's daughter. He hoped that Holly would come to want one of her own.

"I love Jasmine." She spoke as if she had been accused of not loving the child.

"I think I might have a solution. I agree with you that Jasmine needs security. We could give her that," he said. Perhaps Jasmine was the small wedge he had been looking for, he was thinking. "Let's get married right away. We'll adopt her. We'll be a family."

Holly was carefully spooning coffee into the tin basket of the percolator. She hated to get grounds in the water. She continued spooning deliberately.

"What do you think?" he asked.

"Paul, I'm so tired I can't see straight, much less think about something as important as this. Can we talk about it tomorrow?" she asked, certain he would say yes.

"I don't think so, Holly," he said.

She was rinsing the spoon under the faucet. She looked up at him in surprise.

"Too many times we've waited until tomorrow. We have tomorrows, you and I, stacked up to the stars," he said. Suddenly he felt he couldn't wait any longer. "Tell me now, Holly, yes or no."

"Paul, I'm torn up over Poppy. I'm disturbed about Rose. And then there's Jasmine to consider. It's all too much. I'm tired. Please, don't pick this moment to deliver an ultimatum."

"I didn't think it was an ultimatum. I thought I was offering you a solution, I hoped a welcome one."

"Tonight I want to say no to everything and everyone. I want to crawl away and just be left alone, can't you understand that?"

"No, I can't," he said. "You don't want to get married? You don't want to adopt Jasmine? You're telling me no?"

"Paul, please, can't we talk tomorrow?"

"I'm afraid not."

He walked from the kitchen. She stopped him at the front door.

"Don't go," she said.

"Give me a reason to stay. I've run dry of them. Do you have some new reason to give me?"

"I love you," she said.

"That's not new, is it?" he asked.

"No, I've loved you for a very long time."

"Will you marry me tonight? We'll drive to Nevada. Will you?"

"I . . . I don't know, Paul."

"That's not new either. It's getting a little old, in fact. If you don't know now, I'm afraid you never will."

"What's happened to you? Where's the patient and understanding man . . ."

"Fool, not man," he corrected her. "Patient and understanding fool. I'll tell you something, Holly, patience and understanding and even foolishness have their limits. I've reached my limits. I can't reach you. You hold yourself just out of my reach, Holly."

"Why tonight, Paul?"

"I don't know. Maybe I'd gotten used to you shutting me out, but to see you closing yourself off from Jasmine, the little girl that you supposedly love, I guess that did it for me."

"I'm not doing that. I'm going to see her."

"I know, because you promised Poppy you would. And you never break a promise. You only make empty ones," he said. "I'm more tired than I realized. Goodbye, Holly."

With his usual civility and grace, he left her.

She went back to the kitchen. The coffee was perking loudly. She was grateful for the noise. She could listen to that and not for Paul's returning footsteps. When the coffee was ready and darkly quiet, she turned on the radio. The program was the Chesterfield Supper Club and Perry Como was singing sweetly. But the music ended. The coffee went cold. And Paul did not come back.

PART SEVEN

❀

JASMINE

Chapter Twenty-two

New Mexico, 1948 . . .

Most everywhere it was the week of waiting, that time of festive abeyance that prevails once a year. Christmas had been celebrated and now began the short span of lame-duck days to be lived out until the much heralded arrival of the new year.

Zara Cody's ranch had not been decorated for the season. Her daily routine went on unaltered and untouched by the occasion. Here there was small evidence of Christmas and no trace of New Year's anticipation, no sense of an ending or a beginning, but a suspended and sinister, a solitary timelessness. Yet she was no longer alone on the place. Jasmine was with her, but only the spare old woman could be seen hoeing her barren garden on this morning after the birthday of the Savior.

Holly and Rose had sent holiday packages and cards to their niece and these had been opened with cautious joy by the child, but the large box that came from Washington had been disposed of by Zara before Jasmine could see it. It was intercepted and thrown away just as the weekly letters that Poppy wrote to her daughter were. The little girl had nearly forgotten her pale and gentle mother. Jasmine was not even four years old and the months passed without Poppy comprised an enormous portion of her life. She still had a hazy memory of a soft voice and white loving hands, but the reality of her grandmother was stronger, harsher. Zara Cody was the all-powerful and malevolent force in Jasmine's world now. It was exactly as the imprisoned woman who wrote letters that would never be read had feared.

Jasmine was trying to twist free, at least loosen the knots, but they were tied too tightly. She stopped that struggle and lay back, looking up, searching, for any cracks of light, but there were none. She'd been bad again. She hadn't meant to be, but when she was, her grandmother carried her here to the hole, bound her, and put her in, then placed boards closely, without gap, over the top. This morning Jasmine had spilled her milk at the table. She was being punished for the accident. She would be confined in the darkness for the day. She had spent many days this way since she came to live with her grandmother on the ranch. Sometimes in the night she would wake and think that she was in the hole. Even in the daytime when she was outside playing with the old dog Jess, a blind border collie, and the desert sun was bright, it would seem to disappear from the sky and everything would darken. Jasmine would feel that she was lying in the hole, unable to move from the blackness and the dirt. When she was not actually there she was either dreaming or fearing it. The hole was with her constantly. She would sit and pet the dog's head, trying to think how it was for him not being able to see. To be blind was to be in the hole, she would think. Now she was in it again, sightless and in terror, in the hole her grandmother had dug years before for her father.

Jasmine at her early age was experienced in certain techniques of survival. Things she had seen that were too terrible to remember, she had totally blocked. She had no memory of Japan, her father's brutality, or his murder. She had learned to forget. Now she used another device, one acquired in defense of her life on this desolate ranch. She drew mental pictures on the black sides of the pit, her prison. She didn't become crazed as she might have but sprung her trap with beauty. She called up from her mind the images of the cards she had received for Christmas. Aunt Rose's was funny, with little elves dancing around a tree, and Jasmine smiled thinking of it, but it was Aunt Holly's that she loved. She could see every detail of the card. The paper was thin and shiny, blue and silver. There was a snow princess holding a white fur muff and wearing a crown of diamonds. Doves flew about her head and she was wishing peace and joy to all the world. Aunt Rose's elves paled beside this beauty. Jasmine fantasized that her Aunt Holly was the princess and that one day she would come and take her away with her. They would run from the desert to a place where it snowed in flakes like lace and they would be happy. Jasmine painted her wishes on the low dark walls and the day went by. Night came, but it was perpetual night in the hole and she was lost in her dreams so she did not know of its coming. She heard her grandmother's steps and then she knew. One board was pulled aside. Jasmine could see stars overhead in the dark dome of sky.

"Are you going to be good?" her grandmother asked.

"Yes, Grandma. I'll be good."

The rest of the boards were removed. Zara climbed down and untied the child. They both crawled out from the hole and walked to the house. Supper was waiting on the table. Zara undid her checkered apron as she had Jasmine's bonds.

"Go and wash your hands," she told her granddaughter.

Jasmine dutifully went to clean them. The grime under her fingernails had not collected in child's play, but from being buried alive for a day, and yet she went to wash like a normal little girl. Jasmine came to the table, her hands scrubbed. She was very careful with her glass of milk. She tried to do everything as her grandmother wanted, but she was waiting all the while for rescue. For her snow princess to come. For Aunt Holly.

"Holly, come in here."

Arnie Ross tossed the command as he passed by her desk and went through the door to his office.

She allowed a moment, then stood, and followed him. He sat with his head in his thick hands, a weary and pensive pose, odd for this easy, ebullient, thoughtless man. Holly was surprised at him. She waited uncomfortably for him to see her.

"Sit down," he said.

She sat down.

"I've been with Herlick for the last three hours," he said. He ran a hand through his thick, oily hair. A large diamond flashed on his finger. "The bastard," he added.

Holly thought of Sidney Herlick, a newly created vice-president, amorphous still, his powers unknown, gray, like the man himself, his flesh and his suits. She had guessed his realm to be numbers, grosses, budgets, and salaries. She was well aware that her boss's metier was people. Arnie Ross knew who was sleeping with whom, who wanted to be sleeping with whom, who gambled, won, and lost, who drank and whether gin was their muse or bourbon their demon. He knew the cheats and the liars and the players and he wielded his knowledge ruthlessly and well. She couldn't imagine what these two men would have to talk about for three hours or even three minutes.

"What were you discussing?" she asked, unable to resist her curiosity.

"You," he answered.

"You were talking about me?" she asked.

"That's right, kid," he said. "I'm leaving, you know."

"I'd heard some talk, Mr. Ross," she said.

"Yeah, jungle drums, the old grapevine. Well, it's true. I'm starting my own agency. It's been in the works for months. It's finally jelled."

"That's wonderful. You'll be wonderful at it," she said, and she meant it.

"I'll tell you something, you scare the hell out of me. You always have. You're a scary broad. I told Herlick that you should have my job."

"You recommended me?"

"You're doing the job," he said. "You have for years. We both know it. Why not have the title?"

"What did Mr. Herlick say?"

"He doesn't want you."

"Oh," she said, but the rejection slammed her hard. "Why?" she asked calmly.

" 'Cause you're a broad . . ." He looked at her and noticed for the first time that she stiffened at that word. "A lady," he said and grinned at her. "You really are a lady. Herlick's afraid that you'll go off and get married, have babies. I told him, not this kid. I said you weren't the wife and mother type."

She didn't like him judging her, believing that he knew her when he didn't, but she couldn't deny that she had given him every reason to think of her exactly as he did. He wasn't wrong about her, but he wasn't right either. She didn't want to be a wife and mother, but she did. She did want his job, but she didn't. She was ambitious but her ambition, she knew, was filling some need, some gap inside of her, and she couldn't begin to explain all that to Arnie Ross.

"Do you think you convinced Mr. Herlick?" she asked.

"That's what took three hours but I think I've got him where I want him. You do want the job, don't you, kid?"

"Yes," she answered, not showing any hesitation that she might have felt.

"You're not going to run off and get married, are you?"

"I'm not planning on it," she said.

"You don't do anything you don't plan on, do you?"

"I try to see where I'm headed, that's all."

"Yeah," he said. He examined her as if she were some rare species of animal he'd never seen before. "Yeah, the only guy I thought you might have had a thing for was Paul Sorenson."

She didn't speak.

"Old Paulie's doing all right for himself with his book. They say it's going to be a best-seller, another *Gone with the Wind* or *Forever Amber*. Cold bastard, that's what I always thought of him, but then that makes the best kind of writer. Most of the writers I've ever known were nothing as people. It all goes into the work, you know. I'm going to have to look Paulie up and see if he's properly represented. He could use a good agent. And I'm going to be the best," he said, lapsing into visions of his bright future.

"When do you think Mr. Herlick will make a decision?" she asked.

"What's that, kid?"

"When will I know about the job? Whether it's mine or not?"

"It shouldn't be long now," he answered vaguely.

Holly left him wreathed in foul cigar smoke and deep in his sweet dreams of power and wealth. And she thought that she had seen him as she never had before, the vulgar man gone vulnerable.

That evening Rose dropped by her apartment. They had seen little of each other since the Washington trip. They did not talk often and when they did nothing was said. In the months since their visit to Poppy in prison, Holly had time after time postponed going to New Mexico as she had promised. Something always happened to keep her from leaving and at each deferment Rose drew back further from Holly. Still, she had appeared tonight, remembering what they had once shared, thinking of the letters that Holly had written to her in Kansas and how they had been her salvation then. Rose was in need of her sister, hoping that she might be saved again, but beginning to doubt that it was possible.

They were standing facing each other just inside the front door.

"Have you eaten?" Holly asked. "I just finished dinner, but there's some fish and a little salad left. Are you hungry?"

Rose laughed. "Always," she said. She looked down at herself. She had gained forty pounds since coming to California. She had arrived plump and hopeful. Now she was fat. The features of her sanguine face were lost in flesh and lost too were her illusions of happiness. "Fish and salad, huh? Do you have any ice cream?"

Holly shook her head. "No. How about some coffee?"

"Sure, that's fine."

Rose followed Holly into the kitchen. Holly went to the coffee pot. It was nearly empty. She was drinking too much coffee lately, she thought. Maybe that was why she was sleeping so poorly. She poured some for Rose and drained the rest into her own cup. She came over to the table where Rose had sat down.

"Wouldn't you rather go into the living room?" Holly asked.

"I'm fine here," Rose said.

Holly reluctantly drew back a chair.

Rose noticed. "What's the matter?"

"It's silly, I know, but sitting in the kitchen reminds me of Mama. She was always at that kitchen table. I can see her there, sitting, drinking cup after cup of coffee," she said. She pushed her cup away.

"Mama liked her coffee and her kitchen," Rose said. "Do you want to go into the living room?"

"No, it's all right."

"You sure you don't have any ice cream? Or cookies? Something sweet?" Rose asked.

"No, I don't, I'm sure."

"No wonder you're so thin," Rose commented bitterly.

"Rosie, you've got to stop."

"I know I'm fat, Holly. Don't start on me. I get enough of that from Clyde."

"How is Clyde?" Holly asked.

"The same," she answered. Her unhappiness, so close to the surface, emerged suddenly and swiftly. "The same. Why did I think he would be different when we got here! I guess I thought Kansas was causing all our problems and California would solve them. Pretty dumb, huh?"

"No, not dumb. You're not dumb. You're just full of dreams."

"Not any more, Holly. I stopped dreaming. Clyde's still running around . . . and I think . . . now . . . that he's really serious about some girl."

"You mean he's fallen in love with someone else?"

"I think he thinks he has."

"How do you know?" Holly asked.

"It's easy to know. What's hard is trying not to. Clyde's always on me about being fat. I know I'm fat. He doesn't have to tell me all the time, but he looks at me and he says, you're fat, Rose, and I think to myself, who's he comparing me to? Who's he been with who's got a good figure and who's younger than I am, and prettier? I think, who's he wishing he was with while he's looking at me and saying I'm fat and ugly?"

"Oh Rosie, why don't you . . ."

Rose spoke over her. "I know. Leave him. You think I should have left him years ago. I know what you think, Holly."

"What do you think?" Holly asked her.

"I don't know. I can't imagine being without Clyde. All my life I've been with Clyde, it seems. I was just a kid when I met him."

"I remember. It was at Lily's wedding. I remember you two dancing together."

Rose smiled. This was a glimpse of the sister she loved, the sensitive treasurer, the careful watcher and keeper of all their lives, but quickly the remote and judgmental woman returned.

"You should leave him," Holly told her.

"Clyde will be the one to leave. I can't walk, Holly," Rose said. "Have you talked to Paul lately?" she asked.

"No," Holly said, wondering what connection, what association had been made in Rose's mind that she would ask her this.

"The last time I saw him was the night we came home from Washington. I guess you'd say we argued." Even as she said it she knew it hadn't been anything as simple as an argument. "I haven't spoken to him since."

"When are you going to see Jasmine?" Rose asked suddenly.

"Soon," she said reflexively.

"You're been saying that for months."

"I said I would go and see Jasmine. I will."

Holly hoped this would finish it.

Rose wouldn't let it go. "When? You've cancelled how many times? Six? Seven?"

"I've been very busy."

"With work?" Rose asked.

"Yes."

"Your work is awfully important to you, isn't it?"

"It's the one thing I can rely on. I know I do my job well. And it looks like I'm finally going to get some recognition."

"Recognition?" Rose asked.

"Yes, I'm being considered for a promotion. I may be getting my boss's, Mr. Ross's, job."

"I'd be happy for you, Holly, but I don't think they'll ever give you that job."

"Why would you say that?"

"Because it's a man's job."

"No man could do that job as well as I would," Holly said.

"When has that ever made any difference? It's a man who'll decide if you get the job or not, right?"

"Yes, that's right."

"He'll chose another man. Not you."

The next day Holly discovered that Rose was either a prophet or a realist and she'd never thought of her sister as either one of those things, but she remembered Rose saying that she'd stopped dreaming. Arnie Ross arrived late in the morning and asked her once again to come into his office. She hardly had time to sit down before he began to talk.

"I'm sorry, kid. Geez, I try, just once in my life, to do something good, nice, and it turns to shit. I'm sorry. Herlick told me this morning that they've hired somebody's brother-in-law for the job. The guy just graduated from Yale or some place: Ivy League, you know the type. An English Literature major. He was with Herlick in the office today. That's what really steams me. They had this guy all along and I'm recommending you and they're laughing up their sleeves. Geez, I'm glad I'm getting out of here," he said. He looked across his desk at her and again he apologized. "I'm really sorry, Holly."

"I guess I shouldn't have expected to get the job." She was using graciousness to cover her disappointment. "Anyway, I know I can help the new man a great deal. What's his name?"

"Get this, will you. Geoffrey Ornsby III. The third. Geez, they should have stopped at the first."

"I'll do whatever I can for Mr. Ornsby."

"Aren't you mad, kid? Aren't you mad as hell? You should have gotten the job. It should have been yours, not some little prep-school prick whose sister married a studio executive. Why don't you yell or something?"

"I'll be all right," she said.

"I haven't told you the worst, kid."

"What?"

"This Ornsby guy, he wants to bring in his own assistant."

"You mean that . . ."

"I mean he's scared shitless of you. He wants you out. Herlick was good enough to offer to let you go back to the typing pool."

"I can't do that," Holly said. She was too stunned to say anything else. "I can't do that."

"Listen, I want you to come to work at my agency."

She wasn't hearing him. She was remembering what she'd said to Rose the night before. She realized what a fool she'd been. She felt that there was nothing she could depend upon here or anywhere. She was completely alone, but someone was speaking unintelligible words. She could hear the sounds but they meant nothing to her. She felt sealed in her aloneness. She tried to listen, tried to focus. She could see Arnie Ross's face, a satyr's, unapologetic and unashamed of its appetites, but now marked by genuine concern. The thick lips moved, speaking to her.

"I want you to come with me. I would have asked you before but I didn't think you'd come. We'd make a great team. Come with me, kid."

Yesterday she'd seen it and now it flashed again, his vulnerability. She was suddenly sorrier for him than she was for herself. Still, she answered him coldly.

"Thank you, Mr. Ross. I appreciate your offer."

"But you're not coming with me?"

"No, I'm not. I've been with the studio nearly seven years. I suppose I thought that I'd always be here."

He misinterpreted her. "Listen, there are plenty of guys around here who'd snatch you up in a second. You wouldn't be in that typing pool long. You know that. I can put in some calls to some guys right now. You probably wouldn't have to go to the pool at all. You could work for any of the guys around here," he told her.

"Thank you, but I don't think I want to work for any guys anymore."

"Hey, it wasn't so bad working for me, was it?" he asked defensively.

"No," she said. "I'm going to take some time off, Mr. Ross."

"A vacation. That's a great idea. Leave for a couple of weeks. Let things settle down. When you come back you can pick and choose where you want to be around here."

"No, I won't be coming back. I made a promise and there's someone waiting for me," she said, and thinking of Jasmine she felt a little less alone.

Ross watched her leaving his office. He'd never understood her. He didn't even like her much, but he respected her. Never in his life had he respected a woman. Women, to him, were to be made use of, but not this one. She was different. He let her cryptic statement pass unquestioned. She was at the door. He wanted to say something to her.

"Holly?"

She turned to him.

"Yes, Mr. Ross."

"Good luck," he said.

"Thank you. The same to you."

She started out of the office.

"Holly," he stopped her again. And again she turned to him. "Wish me luck again," he asked of her.

"Good luck, Mr. Ross."

"No." He wanted this small intimacy. "Say good luck, Arnie."

"Good luck, Arnie."

Arnie Ross's last day at the studio was Friday and Holly made that hers, too.

Chapter Twenty-three

Holly came awake in the motel room. It was dusty-bright and warm. The window was open and a hot wind blew through the ragged screen, billowing the curtain inward and then strongly sucking it back, flat to the rusted wire mesh. She had had the dream again, the same one she'd had every night for months. Jasmine, the beautiful baby she remembered, came to her on wobbly legs and began to feel her face with an infant's soft exploring touch. Awake she could still feel the small hands upon her, moving across her skin, over her faintly fluttering closed eyelids and her parted lips, a unique handling of pure innocence.

Today she would see the real Jasmine, not the constant dream, but the child, substantial and possibly grown beyond recognition. The two, the chimeric remembrance and the projected reality, vied for Holly's feelings and her loyalty. There was someone else in her dreams and her memory, someone who had resurfaced in her consciousness since her coming to the desert. The other Jasmine, the first, her dead sister, struggled with her niece for possession of Holly.

She reached for the glass on the bedstand. Her mouth felt parched, but before she drank she saw floating atop the water a thin coating of dust, accumulated in the night, and she set it away from her in disgust. Her skin must be layered with it too, she thought. She scanned the room. The rusted faucets of the wash basin seemed no source of thirst slaking. This room was as arid as the desert that lay beyond it. She swallowed, trying to create some moisture within herself, but she was desiccated. There was only a slight sleep-soaked wetness at the back of her neck, and she rubbed at it, then brought her dampened hand to her mouth. She was thinking of Daddy and this dry land, how he'd hoped to change it and how he'd failed. There wasn't enough water on earth to turn this place to paradise, she decided. Daddy's had been a futile dream. Dreams. Jasmine came to her again. It was time to let the dream of her go and face her actuality.

She'd written Zara Cody that she was coming but she hadn't waited for a reply. She should call before going out to the ranch, she thought. She wasn't even sure if there was a telephone there. She remembered Poppy's description of isolation and remoteness. She should probably have waited for a return letter, but for some reason she had dreaded getting one of those coarse brown envelopes with the same sort of pages within and the same sort of words upon the paper. She sensed that the texture of Zara Cody's voice would be coarse and brown, too. Still, she didn't want to just appear at the ranch. She thought that she should announce her arrival. Why she should feel the need to be stentor and give warning call of her coming, she did not know.

There was a movement on the periphery of her vision. She looked to the window, thinking it was the blowing curtain, but the wind had died and the drape was hanging limp. She could see a lizard on the screen. It moved again, its long slender body creeping bonelessly. It was a sandy umber color, not as beautiful as Jasmine's lizards had been, Holly thought. She remembered the lizards in the box and how they would line up by the numbers her sister had painted on their backs. The memory came up so clearly. It was the most vivid recollection yet. She was so near here in New Mexico. Jasmine had lived and died here. She was buried on this desert. Holly continued to study the lizard. Calmly she watched it, but then her heart began to pound. She realized that it was not on the outside of the screen as she had supposed but within the room. She was frightened, not of the harmless animal, but of its shocking nearness to her. It was so close. The lizard crawled upward. She got up from the bed and went to

the window. She slammed it shut. Now she was safe. It was barred
from her and it wouldn't be harmed. It could go out the way it
came, through one of the many tears in the screen, and be free.

Free, she thought. She had freed it just as she had the others,
Jasmine's lizards. She remembered the rage she'd felt and the loss
when Jasmine had set herself free. She recalled the day that
she'd kicked at the lizards when they lined up for her and not her
sister who was dead and being buried. She'd hated them because
she did not know the riddle, the secret, that Jasmine had known.
She frightened them into fleeing, into freedom. She'd ruined all
of Jasmine's touch in one stroke of anger and incomprehension.
Holly watched through the glass, her barrier, to see that the lizard
would escape and it did. It slithered through the flawed screen
and was gone. It could have come into the room in the night
while she slept, Holly was thinking. It could have slid silently
to the bed and crawled across her body. Her skin tingled at the
thought. She was too close to too many things here. She hated
this place, the fine-blowing and destructive dust, the primal creatures, and the proximity of unknown things, unthought things,
and unremembered, until now. She would go out to the ranch
today, see Jasmine, and leave here. She wanted to be gone from
here, swiftly, gone before the lizard grazed her flesh and it all
came back too acutely, graphic and afflictive.

Zara Cody did have a telephone and her voice was like her
letters. The tone of the written and the spoken was the same.
Holly had been granted leave to come out. She drove with a
blond doll for Jasmine as her passenger. It sat in the seat and its
blue glass eyes stared blankly at the desert scenery. It was a
winter landscape, wasteland winter, unending gray stretches, red-
tinted and sun-baked. What trees there were stood starkly revealed, no leaves to hide them, their branches like bones, bare
bones. Holly envied the doll's impassive and inanimate response.
She wished she could be as vacant as it was, but she was stirred
by and filling up with the desert. She arrived at Zara Cody's
ranch.

A little blond girl was seated on the porch steps. There was a
dog lying at her feet and she petted its mangy flanks. Holly knew
that this was Jasmine. She had tried to anticipate the child but
some part of her had still expected the baby from her dreams, the
baby that Poppy had carried away to Japan. She had known there

would be a change, but knowing it in her mind and finding it so solidly before her were two very different things. Jasmine stood at the sight of the car. Her legs were long and thin like a colt's. Holly remembered when her own legs looked like that and how she used to run on them, but Jasmine did not run from the porch steps. She stood waiting. Holly stopped the car and got out. She walked to the still child.

"Hello, Jasmine," she said. She did not climb the stairs. She and Jasmine were at eye level with one another, equals. "Do you remember me?" she asked.

Jasmine shook her head slightly. She did not remember but she knew who this was. It was Aunt Holly, but she wasn't holding the white muff or wearing the diamond crown of the snow princess. Jasmine had believed that her aunt would appear this way when she was told that she was coming, coming at last. "Aunt Holly," she said. "Grandma said you'd be here soon."

She spoke in a clear and quiet voice, remarkable for her age, Holly thought. "Yes, I called your grandma this morning. Have you been waiting all this time?" she asked. She realized that the hours must have been like days to the child.

Jasmine gazed at her. She wanted to tell her aunt how long she had been waiting for her to come, longer than just this morning, but she didn't have all the words to express her thoughts. "I've been waiting," she said simply.

The level look of the little girl standing on the top step disconcerted her. She turned her attention to the sleeping dog. It was dreaming, running, and its legs made the motion of it in the stillness of sleep.

"Is that your dog?" she asked Jasmine.

"That's Jess," Jasmine said. She did not claim the dog, not knowing if it was hers or not, never having thought of it before. Jess was part of the place. He just belonged here and not to anyone.

"He's dreaming of chasing rabbits," Holly said. She smiled at her niece.

"He can't see. He can't chase rabbits anymore. He doesn't run. Mostly he sleeps."

"And dreams," Holly added.

Jasmine continued to stare at her aunt. She wasn't wearing what the snow princess wore and she didn't look like her either. "Why isn't your hair like mine? Why is it black?" she asked.

"Some people have dark hair and some light. You have hair like your mother's," Holly told her. She nearly reached out then and gathered a few of the pale strands in her hand. "Blond, like your mother's hair."

The door opened and Zara Cody came out. Holly felt as if she had been listening to what was being said and that she had chosen this time, at the mention of Poppy, to interpose herself between the child and her visitor.

"Hello, Mrs. Cody," Holly greeted her.

"Hello," she said.

The three froze awkwardly. Only the blind dog moved in blissful oblivion, chasing after rabbits it could still see in its dreams.

"Jasmine, I brought you something," Holly said, chipping at the ice-cold moment of meeting. "It's out in my car. Why don't you go and get it?"

Jasmine glanced at her grandmother, who nodded solemnly. She skipped down the steps toward the car. As she passed by her, Holly realized how small she was. Jasmine opened the car door with some difficulty and disappeared behind it. She emerged embracing the beautiful doll. She stroked its fair hair, thinking that the snow princess had come after all. She cradled it gently and smiled toward the porch. It was the first smile Holly had seen from Jasmine.

"How is she doing, Mrs. Cody?" Holly asked. It was difficult enough to speak with this remote woman, but to bring up the subject of Jasmine's well-being was particularly hard. The little girl's state of mind was bound up with what she had witnessed in Japan, the murder of her father by her mother. And it was this woman's son who had been killed. It was Holly's sister who had shot him. The links were tortuous. Jasmine was the embodiment of those two people, Poppy and Deke, and all that they had done to one another in their brief and harrowing time together.

"She's fine. You can see she's fine," Zara said.

The bright child holding the doll in the sunlight did look fine.

"She's happy?" Holly asked. She wanted to make other inquiries. Did Jasmine have nightmares? Did she cry often? Did she ever ask for her mother or her father who had both been wrenched from her one night and had never returned? These were the questions she had come to find answered, but instead she found herself asking the easiest one, the one that would require the easiest one-word answer. She balked at knowing the uneasy answers to the disquieting questions now that they were so near.

"She is fine. You can see," Zara said.

Holly searched the woman's face. If it could be seen that Jasmine was fine, what was there to be seen in Zara Cody, she wondered. She thought of what Poppy had said, that Deke had had things done to him by his mother. What sort of things had she done to him? What might she be doing to Jasmine? Holly looked but she saw only a stolid and aging woman standing in the eaved shadow of her house. She did not ask of her what she should have. She saw Jasmine returning to them. Zara Cody spoke, not in reluctant response, but, for the first time, bringing forth words of her own.

"She doesn't remember. Not any of it. A merciful God washed the slate clean. Praise be to Him. She doesn't ask about her mama or her daddy. And I don't say their names. I don't speak of them to her."

Holly felt the warning from the grandmother. She was being cautioned not to speak of them either.

"But Poppy writes to Jasmine, doesn't she?"

Jasmine was at the porch steps and Zara held up a large and tanned admonishing hand. She did not answer. Was she protecting Jasmine, Holly questioned inwardly and silently, but she did not voice her doubts.

"What do you say to your Aunt Holly for that pretty thing?" Zara asked Jasmine.

She clutched the doll to her, looking up over its golden head to her towering grandmother, up from the sunny yard to the darkness of the porch. She turned to Holly who was part in light and part in shade, the slanting roof cutting her in half, sharply.

"Thank you, Aunt Holly."

There should be more than this, Holly was thinking. She'd driven hundreds of miles. She'd spent months of agonizing avoidance, battling with herself over coming here, and for it to climax with the delivery of a doll and a few words spoken standing on a sand-dusted stoop was not enough, but she couldn't seem to carry it further. Discontented, and eager to escape, she said.

"I guess I'll be going now."

Zara Cody did not react and her granddaughter, watching her closely, mimicked her dry and stoic silence. Holly felt that she was being turned away. She sensed the power of the shadowy woman. This was her place and her will was done here. Holly was the intruder, an unwanted guest, and she did not possess the conviction or the courage to press her presence, it seemed. She had been allowed to come here, but any true entry into this world was denied her. And she had not asked it because the life that was lived here, Zara Cody's life, made her afraid. She wanted no part of it. She did not want to cross the porch and step inside the house, into this hostile and forbidding existence, but she was struggling with the knowledge that her niece was living here, maybe suffering here. Yet Jasmine appeared to be all right. Holly was incapable of delving deeper. She couldn't ask the child. The child couldn't tell her. Zara Cody's tenancy, her temper, loomed large and ominous. She dominated and decreed here. Holly, aided by her own ambivalence, was being moved along, away. She started down the steps.

"Goodbye, Miss Calder," Zara said, dismissing her.

"Goodbye," Holly returned. She was going, but her feeling for her niece and her sense of fairness were too strong to leave without disobeying Zara Cody. It was a small disobedience but vital. As she used to circumvent her mother, she went around this force, this forceful woman, now. "Walk with me to the car, Jasmine," she said and she took one of the child's hands from the doll and led her away with her.

The grandmother's eyes glittered from the darkness of the porch like a cat's. The blind dog woke from its dreams of sight and running rabbits. It caught the scent of a stranger. It slowly rose up and trailed, stiff-haunched, after Holly and Jasmine. Holly stopped and stood near the car, away from the house and its ruler. Jess came sniffing at Holly's legs and lay down at her feet.

"What will you call your doll, Jasmine?"

"Snow," Jasmine answered without hesitation.

"That's a beautiful name for her. Have you ever seen snow?"

"No," Jasmine said. Along with everything else she had forgotten the snow of Japan and how she'd seen it collect on sacred mountain peaks.

"Would you like to see the snow someday?" Holly asked.

"Yes," the child said. "Could we go now?"

Holly tried to weigh this request. Was it the usual desire for immediacy typical of children, youth? Or was Jasmine anxious to be away from here? Was it snow that she wanted to see? Or did she want to run? But why would she want to flee, Holly wondered. Zara Cody was a strange and set woman, but she seemed to care for the child well. Jasmine looked happy. Holly convinced herself.

"I don't think we could go right now, but sometime we could."

Jasmine tightened her hold on the doll. Aunt Holly wasn't going to take her away today. She was leaving without her, leaving her with Snow, beautiful Snow, and—Jasmine looked toward the house—with her grandmother. Tears came to her eyes. Tears were one of many things that she had learned to forget. The little girl was surprised by the wet flow of them.

Holly saw that she was beginning to cry. She thought of Poppy and her constant weeping. Jasmine was like her mother, Holly decided. She needed to believe that there was nothing really wrong here, nothing to cause the child's tears. She needed to believe and she did.

"I have to go now, Jasmine," she said.

The little girl bit at her lip. She held her doll and didn't speak.

"I'll be back," Holly told her.

"When?" Jasmine asked.

"Sometime soon," she answered evasively.

Jasmine backed away from her. Fresh tears pooled in her eyes, sparkling on her lids, but these did not fall. "Goodbye, Aunt Holly," she said.

Holly spoke, focusing on the doll's sere and insensate eyes. She couldn't look at her niece. "Goodbye, Jasmine."

She nearly ran to her car. At the sound of the whirring engine Jess stirred and stood. The last look Holly had of Jasmine was framed in the chrome square of her rearview mirror. It was flat and fixed like a photograph, like any one of those in her apartment, a moment captured and yet lost. Jasmine held up one hand in a still wave, the doll Snow was cradled to her, and the blind dog beside her.

It was with incomparable sadness and an overwhelming sense of inadequacy that Holly left the ranch. She would have liked to have blamed Zara Cody and certainly she'd played her part, but Holly wondered if she herself was not the one more responsible for the unfulfilled and deficient encounter. She couldn't shake the feeling of incompletion. She'd have to return, she knew, but before she could there was some unfinished business elsewhere. And she didn't know where or what that was. She wasn't certain if it was Jasmine's or Poppy's life that had to be pieced together. Perhaps it was her own. Thinking of this and not her driving, she made a wrong turn onto the highway. After a moment she realized that she was heading east. She was not on her way back to California, out to California, but pointed inward. Kansas. She thought of Kansas as she drove toward it, but that was the wrong direction, she told herself. She had vowed at her parents' funeral that she would never again return to Kansas, but she continued to drive the road that led to it. She knew that she could turn around at any point, but she did not. Holly realized at that moment that there are two roads, the one of plan and intention, the one she had always taken, and another she had never traveled, an unconscious course, a fated route she had resisted too long. The desert that she was now fleeing was an unresolved, an insoluble place still, but Kansas was dead. There was nothing there for her that had not been dispatched and put away long ago, she felt. There was no missing piece to be found in Kansas, not for Poppy or Jasmine or for herself, but it drew her. She was being called, pulled, up and in, to the center, the gut of the country, to Kansas. For some reason, unknown to her, she had turned east. It wasn't an accident, a mistake, as she wanted to believe. She was being guided, and for once, unquestioningly, Holly allowed herself to be.

For two days she drove, was driven, held to the highway, stopping only to eat and for a few hours sleep in the night. She arrived at Lily's late in the afternoon. Why she had come, had to be here, she didn't know. Her arrival and her anxiousness were inexplicable. She got out of the car and her legs were cramped and stiff. She walked cumbrously and she was reminded of the blind dog on Zara Cody's place and of her father, how he had walked after his accident. One crippled moment. She wondered what a lifetime of it would be. She was nearly to the house when a large truck pulled up. The back of it was filled with children, big and boisterous boys, but there was one girl, Holly saw. Lily was driving and her husband was her passenger, her load and burden. Her cross, Lily would have said, her cross to bear. The boys scrambled from the truck before it came to a complete stop. They were tumbling over themselves like a litter of pups. In naive and blatant curiosity they stared at Holly. She smiled at them.

"Hello," she called. "I'm your Aunt Holly."

They reacted in unison, in clumsy sweet shyness. The tallest boy and the only girl stood together apart from the pups. Holly guessed that they were Jonathan and Hope. They were smiling at her in response, the only ones with enough years to remember her or her name at least. Lily came around the front of the truck. She halted abruptly at the sight of her sister.

"Hello, Lily."

"Holly," she said. The name had not been used in years. It sounded strange and strained.

Holly walked toward them. None had made any move to her. "I came . . ." She wanted to say why, but she couldn't. "I came to see you . . . all," she said, looking at each of them, lingering on the friendliest face, Hope's. Lily's she had passed quickly, seeing its harshly uninterested expression.

"Boys, take your daddy into the house," Lilly commanded the pups.

They went to the truck cab and opened the door. Tall Jonathan joined them in the effort to lift and carry the heavy and deadened man, their daddy. Holly was aware of Lily's stare. She turned from the boys, who were straining like pallbearers under the coffinlike weight, to her sister. Lily was like Mama. Holly wanted to be gone. She wished she'd never come. She remembered Rose saying that it was like visiting a grave, and it was. She knew she must say something. She refused to spend another silent, standing time in a yard as she had in New Mexico on Zara Cody's ranch. This was Kansas and her sister's farm and it had to be different, even if it felt so much the same.

"I was visiting Jasmine in New Mexico . . ."

Lily looked at her strangely.

"Jasmine's grave?" she asked Holly.

For a moment Holly didn't understand and then she realized that Lily thought she had been speaking of their sister Jasmine.

"No, Poppy's little girl, Jasmine," she clarified. "She's named Jasmine . . . Poppy's little girl is . . ." She faltered in the face of Lily's potent disapproval.

"Was there another Jasmine?" Hope asked innocently.

Both Lily and Holly had forgotten her presence. The sisters answered simultaneously.

Holly affirmed, "Yes."

"No," Lily denied.

Hope looked from her mother to her aunt. She didn't seem to be confused by the conflicting answers, but very curious.

Holly honestly overruled Lily, not realizing what risk she took by speaking the truth. "Jasmine was our sister who died, a long time ago, when we were little girls," she told Hope.

"How did she die?" Hope asked her aunt.

"She was poisoned," Holly stated simply.

Now Lily spoke her truth. "By her own hand. A sin. An abomination. Jasmine took her own life. She burns in Hell for what she did. And Poppy's child was named for her. Shame! Shame, I say! That child carries a sin-soaked name and she's cursed by it. I disavow Jasmine and Poppy and Poppy's child. God denies them. I, by God's decree, deny them, too. They are of the Devil," Lily preached wildly.

Holly was appalled at her sister's devout diatribe, her pious insanity. She looked to Hope and there was an understanding, a sympathy, between them, wordless but profound.

"How is Aunt Rose? And Aunt Poppy?" Hope asked. She remembered both these aunts far better than the one she stood facing right now, but she felt a link with Aunt Holly that she never had with the others.

"Your Aunt Rose is fine. She loves California. You'll have to come out for a visit, Hope," she said. "And Poppy . . ." She hesitated. She didn't know if Lily had told her children about Poppy, the murder, and her imprisonment. She guessed that Lily had not, and hoping to avoid another outburst from her sister, she said. "Poppy is living a quiet life."

"Aunt Rose said that she was in Japan. She's not there anymore? She's with her little girl in New Mexico? Is her husband there, too?" Hope knew that she was asking too many questions, but she couldn't help it. It was wonderful to have someone to ask, someone who would answer and not preach. She had so many questions that had gone unanswered for so long.

"No, Poppy's in Washington. She's living on an island there."

"An island. It sounds like Robinson Crusoe," Hope said.

"It's not like that," Holly told her and the gray stone walls of the prison rose up in her mind.

"Aunt Poppy's living alone on this island?" Hope asked.

Holly thought of the cell that she'd never seen, the barred cubicle that was Poppy's home now. "Yes," she answered her niece.

The boys returned to the yard. Their father had been placed in his chair in the parlor. They began throwing a baseball back and forth among themselves. Jonathan walked over to the women.

"Aunt Holly, it's good to see you," he said.

Holly smiled at him. She calculated quickly. He must be about seventeen years old, but he looked older to her. He was over six feet tall and broad across the shoulders. She had last seen him when he was a tow-headed child. His hair had darkened to an amber-gold and he was nearly a man now.

"It's good to see you, Jonathan. You've grown." Holly looked to Lily. "All the children have grown so much, but especially these two." She glanced at Hope and Jonathan who were standing close together.

Lily eyed the boy and girl. Under her scrutiny they moved a little away from one another. To Holly she said, "You'll stay for supper."

"I'd like that," Holly said. She felt as if she'd been commanded, not invited.

"And you'll sleep on the couch in the parlor," she told her. Lily was still the oldest sister, the first Calder girl. That had not changed. Beneath her madness, her faith, there remained the instinct of kin, a proprietary, almost jealous, claim on her blood ties.

"No," Holly said. "I don't want to put you out. This was such a spur of the moment visit. I'll find a hotel for the night."

Jonathan spoke excitedly. "We've got a brand-new motor lodge. I helped build it. I worked on it last summer," he said proudly.

Holly could see Jonathan working shirtless in the sun and she thought of another young man who'd come to Kansas to labor and to build. Daddy. Daddy as full of youth and enthusiasm as Jonathan. And Mama had been waiting for him, waiting to drain him of all of that.

"Where is this motor lodge?" she asked Jonathan.

"Out on the route road," he said. "They tore down that old place. You know the one I mean," he paused, trying to think of the name. "The Bluebird Café."

The Bluebird Café, Holly thought, and she traveled back ten years or more, to her last night in Kansas. When Kansas was still her home and she was leaving it the next day, she had hoped forever. Now she had returned but the old roadhouse was gone. Iris was gone. The names of the two salesmen who had taken them to the Bluebird Café were gone, too, gone from her memory. All gone, but she was here.

Lily had started toward the house. Holly followed her. Jonathan and Hope remained outside with their brothers. Stepping into the darkened house Holly could make out the still silhouette of Workman Banner. She couldn't just pass by him without some acknowledgment of his presence, his life, shattered as it was. Lily had gone into the kitchen. Holly stopped by his chair. His hands were folded in his lap. They had been arranged that way by one of his sons. Holly thought that it must have been Jonathan. She couldn't imagine one of the other exuberant boys, any of the pups, doing it. She bent slightly and patted his hands.

"Hello, Workman," she said.

Lily had come into the doorway.

"He can't hear you," she told Holly.

Holly started to ask if she was absolutely certain of that, but she decided against it. She walked away from Lily's husband.

"How long has he been this way?" Holly asked.

They were in her kitchen now.

"Two years," Lily answered.

"It must be very hard on you."

"It is God's will. I wasn't put on this earth to question God's will."

"No, I guess not, but still it can't be easy."

Holly felt a strong aversion to this room. Lily's kitchen was like Mama's, just as she, Lily, was like their mother. Her sister moved comfortably here, taking out pots and pans, beginning to prepare supper.

"Is there anything I can do to help?" Holly asked.

"No."

Holly was stymied, unable to converse with Lily.

"I think I'll go back out, visit with the children a little," she said to Lily.

"There are things I won't have them knowing," Lily said. "This world is evil and this family cursed. My children will learn soon enough the nature of this earth and of their brothers who walk upon it."

"Lily, I have no intention of telling them things that you don't want them to know. I didn't come to Kansas to do that."

"Why did you come back? After all these years, why?"

"I don't know. Maybe I'm looking for something."

"What?" Lily asked her.

"Something that's been lost. It's somewhere. Maybe not here. Maybe it's inside me. I don't know, but I'm hunting so hard," she said, never hoping that Lily would understand what she was saying, but saying it anyway, for herself.

"You shouldn't have come here."

"You don't like me being here. Why, Lily? It makes you afraid. Why is that?"

"I don't like your ways, Holly. I never did. You were always different from the rest of us. You were like . . ."

"Daddy," Holly finished for her. "I'm glad of it, so glad, Lily. I never wanted to be anything like Mama."

Lily was glaring at her.

"Mama knew about you. She knew about you and Daddy," Lily said.

Holly felt that she had to get away. "I'm going outside, Lily. I promise I won't tell any of your secrets," she said. She hadn't intended it to sound like a threat, but she realized it was a somewhat menacing assurance.

"I have no secrets," Lily declared.

"Lily, we all have secrets."

Holly crossed the kitchen and went out the back door. The boys were still playing ball. She saw Jonathan and Hope coming from the barn. Jonathan joined the game and Hope came over to Holly.

"I'd like to go for a walk, Hope, but it's been so long I'm afraid I might lose my way. Would you want to come with me?" Holly asked.

"Yes."

They began walking. Hope waved to the boys. Only Jonathan waved back, but she had been waving only at Jonathan. Holly noticed.

"You and Jonathan are very close, aren't you?"

"Yes, I guess you'd say that. We get teased about it a lot. And Mama doesn't like it, but Mama doesn't like much of anything. I think she gives all of her love to God and there's nothing left for anyone else. That doesn't seem right to me. Does it to you, Aunt Holly?"

"No, it doesn't."

"I mean it seems to me that Mama's God makes her hate so many things and so many people. It shouldn't be that way."

"You're right, Hope, it shouldn't."

"Aunt Holly, was Mama always like she is now?"

"That's a difficult question to answer. She's the same now as I remember her, the same in many ways, but she's very different, too. Her religion. Call it her faith. That's much stronger, more a part of her."

"I know I shouldn't say this, but sometimes I think Mama's gone crazy. Really crazy. Sometimes I just want to run away from here and from her. I can't talk to her. I can't make her understand what I'm feeling. I don't understand my feelings a lot of times."

"What kind of feelings?" Holly asked.

"Well, like the way I feel about Johnny," Hope said.

"How do you feel about him?"

"I love him, Aunt Holly," she said.

"Why does that disturb you? He's your brother and you love him. There's nothing wrong with that."

"You don't think so?"

"No, I don't, Hope."

"I love him so much. I want to be with him all the time. That's when I'm happiest. When we were little kids we used to talk about having a ranch together. I still want that, more than anything, and I'm not a little kid anymore."

"You're not exactly old, Hope." Holly was smiling.

Hope said seriously, "I'm sixteen. All my girlfriends date. One of them's even married already. Mama won't let me go out with boys, but I don't really want to anyway. I don't want to be with anybody but Johnny."

"What about Jonathan? Does he date? Does he have a girl-friend?"

Hope didn't answer immediately. Finally she brought out the words. Holly could see her effort, her pain, as she spoke.

"He did, kind of, once. There was this girl. Her name's Annie Baldwin. When there was a dance at school or a party or something, sometimes Johnny would dance with her. Last summer there was a dance out at the pavilion by the river and I saw Johnny and Annie Baldwin kissing. You know what I did? I started crying. I tried to run away but Johnny saw me and he came after me. He caught up with me at the boathouse. It was dark and there was no one else around. It was wrong, I know it was, but we . . . we kissed. It wasn't like a brother and sister should kiss. I was crying and Johnny put his arms around me and then we were kissing. I didn't want to stop. I wanted to keep on kissing forever. I know how wrong it is for Johnny and me, for a brother and sister . . . it's a sin, I know."

"Has it ever happened again or was it just that once?" Holly asked.

Hope looked away.

"Hope?"

"More . . . it's happened more than once. I want to stop and so does Johnny, but we can't. And he's touched me, too, Aunt Holly," she confessed.

"Touched you?"

"Yes. One night at the end of the summer, last summer, it was so hot, and I couldn't sleep. I got up. I was just going to walk in the yard, try to cool off some. Johnny had gotten up, too. We went out to the barn. We used to always play up in the loft when we were kids. We climbed up there. I wanted him to kiss me and he did. We lay down in the hay. Johnny was wearing only his pajama bottoms. His chest was bare. His skin was sunburned and it felt hot. The air was so hot and still. It was like we were the only people on earth. There was no one else. Just Johnny and me. He slipped my nightgown down off my shoulders and he . . . he touched me. I stopped him. I said that it was wrong and I know it was . . . it is, but it didn't feel wrong. I can't help loving him, feeling the way that I do, Aunt Holly. I can't help it. I can't."

Holly was thinking of her last words to Lily. Secrets. She'd promised to keep her secrets. She had planned on skirting the subject of Poppy. She had been prepared not to speak of Jasmine, but she'd never guessed that this would be the secret she would have to suppress. She'd never imagined that she would have to keep from telling Hope that Workman Banner wasn't her father and that Jonathan wasn't her brother, not her half-brother, not related to her at all. This miserable girl who was condemning herself, hating her love, was tragic to Holly. She wanted to ease her pain, to set her world right, and it would only have taken a few words, but she had promised. She couldn't speak.

"It is wrong, isn't it, Aunt Holly? I guess I'll burn in Hell just like Mama's always saying, but I can't help loving Johnny."

"You love him, I know. He's very special to you and always will be I'm sure, Hope, but there'll be someone else someday," she told her niece. She wanted Hope to believe. She would have liked to have given Hope the truth but in lieu of that she spoke convincing and soothing words. "I know how I felt about my father. I didn't think that I could ever be as close to anyone as I was to Daddy." Lily's words were echoing. Mama knew. What did Mama know, Holly wondered. She almost forgot Hope. The girl's question jolted her.

"But it happened? There was someone you were closer to? Someone you loved better?" she asked eagerly.

After a long moment Holly answered. "Yes, there was someone."

"But you didn't marry him? You never got married, did you, Aunt Holly?"

She realized how old she must seem to Hope. To her niece she was finished. She had lived her life, exhausted all her dreams, had been given and had taken and had lost all her chances, in Hope's eyes. She was twenty-nine years old and Hope was sixteen. She must appear to be ancient to the girl and yet she felt that only now was she really ready to begin living. Holly was feeling on the brink and Hope had her over the edge.

"No, I never married," she said.

They had been walking steadily. They came to a bridge. The hemp one that had collapsed in the storm years before had been replaced with this stable and broad wood structure. On the other side was the old family farm. Holly was beginning to recognize the places where she used to run and where she used to hide. She stopped.

"This used to be a swinging bridge. It was made of rope," she told Hope.

"I think I remember it."

"Did anyone ever rebuild the old farmhouse?" she asked.

"You mean where Grandma and Grandpa used to live?"

"Yes."

"No. Somebody went there and stripped it, took away all the wood and bricks. There's not much left. It's really close. We just have to cross the bridge and then . . ."

"Yes, I know."

"Do you want to go take a look?"

"No. We should head back. Supper's probably ready by now," Holly said.

"Aunt Holly, you won't say anything to Mama? I mean, what we talked about . . . about Johnny and me? You wouldn't tell her, would you?"

"No," Holly said. "I wouldn't do that." Secrets. It was like she'd said to Lily. Everyone had his or her secret. They grew and spread like some insidious disease. Everyone was infected with the contagion of secrecy. "I won't tell," Holly promised again.

They started back to the house.

Workman was not brought to the table for supper. Holly sat in his chair which usually stood empty at the head of the table. After grace was said, a lengthy thanksgiving by Lily, the younger boys wolfed their food. Holly had no appetite. She watched rather than ate. Hope and Jonathan sat silently next to one another. Lily spoke, sounding as if she were offering another prayer.

"It is good when the family gathers. It is a blessed thing. Jeremiah," she addressed one of the boys. "Do you feel the blessing? Do you feel the grace?"

Jeremiah gulped and swallowed. "Yes, Ma, I feel it. I feel 'em both," he said and returned to his plate.

"Hope?"

"Yes, Mama."

"You're quiet tonight."

"Yes, Mama."

"Are you feeling well?"

"Fine, Mama."

Among these innocuous questions Lily slipped another. On the surface it was as harmless as the others, an ordinary inquiry, but it was not so safe. The mother put it lowly, perilously, to her daughter. "Where did you go with your Aunt Holly today?" She did not look at Holly, wanting no answer from her.

"We went for a walk," Hope told her.

"Where?" Lily asked.

"Nowhere."

"What do you mean, nowhere?"

"I mean we weren't walking to get any place special. We were just walking," Hope explained.

"Ma, can we be excused?" Jeremiah, their spokesman, asked for all the young brothers, the pups.

"Yes," Lily permitted.

They left the table, banging their chairs, and clattering their plates to the sink. The door slammed and they were gone. Hope and Jonathan remained. Lily and Holly stayed seated, too.

"What did you and your aunt talk about?" Lily asked Hope.

"We talked about the old farm, Mama and Daddy's place, and the new bridge. There's a lot that's stayed the same, but some things are different now," Holly answered for her niece.

Lily was not listening to her sister. She was watching Jonathan place a surreptitious and comforting hand over Hope's.

"Don't do that," she commanded. "Don't touch her." Lily told Jonathan. "I won't have sin in my house."

Jonathan's jaw clenched. He removed his hand.

"I'm going outside," he said and stood. He spoke to Hope, ignoring his stepmother. "I can't stay here."

"Johnny . . ." Hope said to him.

"I've got to get out of here," he said.

The women at the table knew that he was speaking for more than going out to the yard, that he was proclaiming his inability to live this life as it was any longer. The reactions to him were polar.

"Don't go, Johnny," Hope said.

"Go. Leave this house and take your evil ways with you," Lily cried. "You have contaminated her with your sinful lustings. I see. Don't think I don't. I see it all. You are a wanton. You would take your own sister to satisfy your evil cravings. Evil. I see, I know."

Jonathan walked out on her rantings.

"Lily," Holly called to her as if she were a long way off, and Lily was, far into the region of her malignant faith.

Lily turned to her sister. "This is not for you. Stay out of this, Holly. You can have no words to say on this. You, of all, should remain silent. You have sinned. You are not without sin. You don't go blameless, Holly."

"Mama, please don't." Hope wanted to defend Holly. She thought that her mother was saying that her aunt had told her things that she shouldn't have. She couldn't know that Lily's accusations went deeper than that. "Aunt Holly was only trying to help me. We did talk about Johnny and me, but . . ."

"I don't want to hear." Lily ended Hope's defense. "Take a plate in to your father. Go and feed him his supper," she told her daughter.

Hope looked from her mother to her aunt, and she began to see that there was something else being said here. It was the terrible silence between the two women that spoke so eloquently. She realized that she was no longer being discussed. She took Johnny's plate and began piling food onto it for her father. Whatever was happening now she had sparked, she knew, but she was out of it. She took the loaded dish and left them in the kitchen.

Holly asked Lily, "What did you mean when you said that I of all should not speak of this? You said I had sinned. What did you mean by that, Lily?"

"You have sinned. You know that."

"I do not. What do you think I've done?" Holly asked. She told herself that she truly could not imagine what her sister meant. She did not know how Lily thought she had sinned. She didn't. She didn't know, she kept inwardly assuring herself.

"You and Daddy. Incest," Lily condemned. "The Lord told Moses, I am the Lord and none of you shall marry a near relative. A girl may not marry her father, nor a son his mother, nor his sister, nor half-sister. Do not defile yourselves in any of these

ways, the Lord told Moses. It is written in the Bible. Defilement.
It is a sin to have carnal knowledge of your father."

"You're saying that Daddy and I . . ." She could not complete
it. It was too awful to become whole.

"You and our father."

"It's not true," Holly said. "Lily, it's not true."

"You cannot deny it now. Mama knew. Daddy took you when
you were a child . . ."

"Don't say it."

"His accident was a punishment from God for his sin. Mama
knew. She told me."

"It never happened," Holly told her. She thought of Washington, remembered leaving her bed and getting into Daddy's, but
she stopped there. She could remember no more. There was
nothing more, she told herself. She told Lily. "Never. It never
happened."

"Later, when you were older, you tempted him again. You
went whoring after him . . ."

"Stop it! Don't say it!" Holly cried. "It's all lies."

Lily's face was set and her belief hardened like stone. She
knew what she knew. "Why do you think Mama hated you so?"
she asked Holly.

Holly had no answer. She rose from her chair. Had she come
here to learn this? Was this the missing piece? Better it had
never been found.

"Mama hated you. And I hate you," Lily told her.

"Jonathan and Hope are not brother and sister." Holly said.

"They are half-brother and half-sister. It's the same. The Bible
says . . ."

Holly interrupted. "No, they don't have the same father.
They're no relation at all. Workman isn't Hope's father."

"He is."

"No, he's not."

Lily's white face went whiter still. "You were too young . . ."
she said, exposing her fear and the fact. ". . . to remember. How
do you know?"

"I know, Lily. I wasn't that young. I remember it very well,
how you came home from Straker's . . ."

"You're going to tell her. To hurt me you're going to tell
Hope."

"No," Holly said.

"You're not going to tell her?"

"Yes, I am, but not to hurt you, Lily. I don't want to hurt you. I don't hate you." She did not say that she didn't hate Lily as Lily hated her. There was no need to say it, but simply, "I don't hate you, Lily."

"Why are you going to tell Hope then?"

"Can't you see how much in love they are? Jonathan and Hope. You've made them feel guilt that is totally undeserved. They should be allowed to love one another. How any love could have come into this house and survived, I don't know, but Hope and Jonathan love. If I can make them feel clean, sinless in their love, I will."

Holly started out of the kitchen. Lily sprang up after her. An old and terrible sensation swept Holly at her sister's approach. She flinched reflexively. She was a little girl again and Mama was coming for her. Mama in a rage. Mama. But it was Lily. Holly faced her and Lily halted. She could confront Lily as she never could Mama. She had always run from Mama. Why, she wondered? Was it because she'd been a helpless child and the only course was to flee? Or was there some guilt that she'd felt that had made her twist free of Mama and not meet her? Now she met Lily squarely. She had right and truth with her against Lily, but it struck her horribly that she's always felt doubt and blame when facing Mama. Why? Mama's hatred had come from Daddy's love of her. Holly could not remember just what Daddy's love had been. How had he loved her? Could it have been an incestuous love? She couldn't remember, but she knew that she must. One day, she must. For now she was not afraid of Lily or her anger. She knew that she was right about Hope and Jonathan. Lily was stopped and she walked away from her. This would be the final and unanswerable, unrectifiable break between herself and her sister. What she was about to do would drive them apart forever, but Holly did not think she would feel the lack of Lily in her life. Lily had cruelly and harshly presented her with what could be a lie or what had been buried and forgotten but was true. Only Holly could look within herself and find the truth or the falsehood. It was unknown yet. Now she must go to Hope and give her the truth that she knew.

In the parlor Hope sat at the feet of the man she believed, had never doubted, was her father. His supper plate was resting on his knees and she reached up to feed him. As if he were her child, she fed him. Gently and slowly, with infinite patience, she waited for him to chew and swallow, not forcing him through his meal. She talked to him the whole while and Holly stood back listening to what the girl said to Workman Banner.

"Daddy, I don't know what to do. I'm sorry if I'm a bad girl. I don't want to bring shame to you, but I love Johnny and he loves me. Mama wants to make him go away. I'll die if he does. Or I'll go with him. I can't be without Johnny. Daddy, I'm sorry. Please forgive me."

The plate was empty. She set it down on the floor.

"Do you think you'd like any more, Daddy? Are you hungry still?"

He didn't answer. He couldn't. He couldn't tell her that he was full of food given by her dear hands. He couldn't tell her that there was nothing to forgive, that she was a good girl, the best girl in the world for his son. He couldn't say any of these things, but his desperate desire to speak came up through his inert flesh so strongly that it could almost be heard. Hope felt his sympathy and love.

"Hope," Holly said.

She looked around. "Oh, Aunt Holly, I didn't see you standing there."

"I want to talk to you, Hope."

"All right," she said. "I'll just take Daddy's plate to the kitchen. I'll be right back."

Hope went past Holly and into the kitchen where Lily was. Holly waited. After a few moments when Hope didn't return it occurred to her what Lily might do. Lily would brutally tear Hope's father from her, swiftly dispossess her daughter, just so that she would be the one to tell her secret. Holly ran back into the kitchen, but she was too late. She heard Lily saying.

"He's not your Daddy."

"Yes, he is. He is," Hope said.

Lily saw Holly. "This whore will tell you. Then you can be a whore just like her. Whores! Both of you! All of you! Whores!" she screamed.

Lily walked from the room.

"Is it true, Aunt Holly?" Hope asked.

"Yes, it's true. Workman Banner is not your father. Your mother was very young when she met a man at Straker's. She thought that she was in love with him, Hope. You can understand that, can't you?" Holly asked her gently.

"Yes, I understand."

"This man was already married. He didn't tell your mother. He left and she was pregnant. Workman was a widower. Jonathan was only a few months old. He needed someone. So did your mother. They got married. No one thought there was any need for you to know this until now. I wanted to tell you, Hope, because of you and Jonathan. He's not your brother. He's yours to love."

"Mama wouldn't have told me, would she?"

"No."

"She only did because of you," Hope said. "She knew you'd tell me."

"I wanted to be the one. I was afraid she'd tell you the way that she did."

"It's all right, Aunt Holly. You would have said it softer, but maybe this was better. I have to go tell him."

"Jonathan?"

"No, Daddy. I want him to know that I know."

"Does he hear you, Hope?"

"He does. I'm sure of it. He hears me and he knows me better than Mama ever could. Even after his stroke he's heard me. Even now that I know he's not my father he's more a part of me than she is. I have to tell Daddy first. I think I can still call him Daddy, don't you?"

"Yes," Holly said.

"And then I'll tell Johnny."

"What will you two do now?"

"I don't know, Aunt Holly, but whatever it is we'll do it together. We can now. And we will."

Hope started to leave but came back to Holly. She put her arms around her and kissed her.

"Thank you, Aunt Holly."

She went quickly away and Holly was alone in Lily's kitchen. And it was Mama's kitchen. Mama's and Lily's hatred was thick, as thick and as bitter as the coffee they swallowed cup after cup, day after day, year after year, sitting in their kitchens waiting.

Waiting for what? For God? For death? Holly didn't know. She only knew that she could not breathe the hot and lethal air of this kitchen. She walked out the back door. The room was abandoned but Holly knew that Lily would return soon, her strength and madness renewed, to resume the raging in her graveyard.

Chapter Twenty-four

Holly heard the two sets of footsteps approaching, the heavy thudding of thick-soled shoes and a lighter, quicker tread. She knew that Poppy and her guard were coming and she tried to prepare herself for her sister's arrival. She pushed back her hair, thinking that it might be out of place, but it was not. It perfectly framed her face in soft, waving darkness. She had thought of cutting it. Women were wearing their hair shorter now. She was surprised at herself, the triviality of her thoughts, but these trifling considerations helped ease her tension. She was frightened of this place and of being within it. The idea of the inmates, the human beings who were caged here, her own sister among them, was horrifying to her. She saw the far door open. Poppy entered. The guard walked behind. Poppy smiled at Holly and came swiftly to the screened glass partition.

Holly had not expected Poppy to look as she did. She had gained weight. Her thin face had filled out and the wan expression was gone. Poppy still looked a child but no longer a lost one. There was even the slightest rose tint to her cheeks. It didn't seem possible but it appeared that prison agreed with Poppy. Holly spoke to her through the aperture provided for words.

"Hello, Poppy."

"Hi, Holly."

"You look just . . . great."

The small smile still lingered. "I'm fine," she said. "You look tired, Holly."

"It's been a long drive," she said. She had come directly up to Washington from Kansas, not stopping in Los Angeles for fear she would settle in there and find too many reasons not to come here again. "I came straight from Kansas."

"Kansas?"

"Yes, I've been to see Lily and her family."

"Oh," Poppy said. The disappointment was loud in her soft declaration.

Holly heard it and added hurriedly. "I went to New Mexico too."

Poppy asked eagerly. "How is Jasmine?"

"She's doing fine."

"When were you there?"

"Just last week."

"And she's really all right?" Poppy questioned.

Looking at Poppy through the glass Holly thought of Jasmine as a newborn in the hospital, protected and isolated from the world. Her sister seemed to be thriving in this nurserylike prison.

"Yes, Jasmine's really fine," she answered Poppy.

"Has she grown?"

"Yes. She's nearly to my waist. I think she's going to be tall."

"Deke was tall," Poppy remembered. Jasmine was Deke's child, too. Deke was dead. So many things to remember, so difficult remembering them. She could see Deke in his uniform. He was tall. "And skinny," she said to Holly. "Deke was so skinny. Jasmine's not too thin, is she?"

"She's all legs right now, a pair of big bony knees. She reminded me of myself."

"Did she look pretty?"

"She's going to be a beauty."

"And she was happy?"

"Yes," Holly told her. "I had a doll for her, a big blond doll. She loved it. She called it Snow. She thought of the name all by herself. It was perfect."

"What about the doll I sent? Did she like it?" Poppy asked.

Holly didn't know how to answer. She hesitated.

Poppy started to explain. "One of the guards went shopping for me and picked out the most beautiful doll for Jasmine, for Christmas. She did get it, didn't she?" Poppy was troubled. Her face was clouding over.

Holly had anticipated tears from Poppy. This was the girl that she had expected and she wondered how much of a part her expectations played in Poppy's behavior. She had been calm and contented, Holly was thinking, when she entered here. Now she was beginning to tremble and cry. The lost look was returning. She had disturbed her sister, Holly knew. She shouldn't have come. She should have written a letter. It was easier to write a fable than to tell one, Holly decided. She had planned such a lovely story for Poppy, a beautiful picture of her little girl, a gentle invention. She could have written and the choice between kindness and truth would have been far easier to make. Holly didn't really know what the truth of that ranch was, but she still recognized a kindness. She could have, should have, put it in a letter. Poppy would have been able to have read it and believed, but instead Holly had come to the prison and disrupted the tenuous peace that Poppy had garnered. In trying to tell the tale she had failed. Poppy had begun asking questions that she couldn't answer. Her sister's questions were shedding light on her deep reluctance and the failure, the fragmented journey to New Mexico. The light was searching and glaring, like one of those atop the towers that ringed this place. Holly attempted to answer, to evade, to stop the weave of her story from unraveling.

"I didn't see the doll, but I'm sure that Jasmine loved it."

"But she didn't say anything about it?"

"Well, no, she didn't, but you know how children are. I was there a few days after Christmas. Three or four days is a long time for such a little girl."

"You think she'd forgotten about the doll I sent her?" Poppy asked.

She was hurting Poppy and she hated doing it. She knew that Jasmine hadn't forgotten the doll. She guessed that she had never received it. She was letting Poppy think that her daughter was a thoughtless and selfish child, and that was wrong. She didn't want Poppy to see Jasmine the way that she was painting her. The picture was a distortion. She was only doing it to maintain her story of well-being and happiness, but Jasmine was becoming a spoiled and ungrateful little girl in the process. She couldn't do that.

"She's a lovely little girl, appreciative and very understanding for her age, but she's barely more than a baby, Poppy. I'm sure she loved the doll that you sent. Maybe she didn't even make a connection between you and me. It's not an easy concept for a child to grasp. I'm her Aunt Holly but what does that mean to her? It means that I'm related to her, but it doesn't necessarily follow that I'm related to her mother."

"Did she ask about me?" Poppy wanted to know.

It would be an outright lie to say that she had. She hadn't come to tell lies. She'd come with a pretty story, not untrue, but unfinished. The omissions were getting clearer and clearer. She would either have to fill them with lies or admit her imperfection as an emissary for Poppy. She had gone to the ranch as her sister's eyes and she had closed them, Holly realized. She didn't want to open them even now, but she also didn't want to tell blinding lies. She couldn't.

"No, she didn't," she said, and still trying to mitigate, "But it's the same thing, Poppy. How could Jasmine have known that I was your sister and that I'd come to see her for you?"

"You could have told her," Poppy said.

Holly knew this without being told. Poppy didn't need to tell her. She could have and she should have, but she hadn't. She had succumbed to Zara Cody's wishes, her will, and she had said nothing of her own sister, Jasmine's mother, the unseen presence that had stood on the porch beside her, Poppy.

"Poppy, you're right," she admitted.

"There's something wrong there, Holly."

"What? What is it?"

"I don't know, but I can feel it. I don't want Jasmine there. If only she were away from there and with you, I could be happy," Poppy told her.

Holly gratefully swung away from Jasmine for the moment. "When I first saw you walk in, Poppy, I thought that you looked so well. I couldn't quite believe it, that you could be in this place and be happy, but you looked it. Are you?"

Poppy followed her sister, dropping her daughter, and speaking of herself. "It's not so bad here, Holly," she said. "It really isn't. I feel, I don't know, kind of safe or something."

"Safe?" Holly asked through the glass and she thought again of the nursery behind glass.

"Yes," Poppy answered. She wanted to tell her sister about Velma, but she didn't know how to begin it. "You know I told you about the guard who went shopping for me? The one who got the doll for me to send to Jasmine?"

"Yes," Holly added quickly, hoping to keep Poppy from returning to Jasmine. "That was a very nice thing to do."

"Yes, she does lots of nice things for me."

"She . . ." Holly looked over at the guard who stood by the door. The guard was a woman. She hadn't noticed. There would be female guards for female prisoners, Holly was thinking, of course there would, but it hadn't meant anything to her before. That was why she hadn't been aware. Now she was and Poppy's happiness was taking on a new meaning. ". . . she does?"

"Yes, she brings me special food. She comes to my cell and . . . talks with me. Her name is Velma."

Holly thought of the woman from Straker's who had befriended Poppy. It occurred to her that women had been kind to Poppy all of her life, a few strong and gentle women had loved her. Men had only hurt and betrayed Poppy. The Reverend, the boy she married, the men who'd judged her, took her child from her, and put her here. Mama had loved Poppy best. Daddy had never been to her sister, any of her sisters, what he had been to her, Holly was thinking, but she put that aside. She didn't want to think of that. That was for another time, not now.

"Velma is like Mama was to me. Nice and good to me." Poppy confirmed Holly's thoughts without knowing it.

Nice and good, Holly heard those words, and more. She heard the intent of them. Poppy was telling her that she had found someone to love her. She was safe and protected and loved. That was why she was happy. It was all that Poppy had ever wanted. Strange that she should come upon it here of all places, but she had, Holly could see that clearly. The one thing that kept Poppy from complete contentment now was Jasmine, her little girl who had been placed in other hands. And Poppy feared those hands. Holly remembered the large and dried-brown hand of Zara Cody, how she'd held it up in warning. It had been a threatening gesture and a frightening hand. Poppy was right to be afraid for Jasmine, Holly knew that.

"Velma and I talk and talk. She's had such a sad life. Her son was in the army. He was killed in the war. She had him when she was only fourteen years old. The man who was his father married her. They made him marry her, but then he ran off. She raised her little boy all by herself. She never even divorced her husband. He just was gone and she never saw him again . . ." She stopped briefly, but then continued, showing the jump of her thoughts in her words. "You were right about Deke and me, Holly. I shouldn't have gone to Japan. I should have left him, divorced him, right after the honeymoon. He hit me even then. Deke always hit . . . hurt me. I told Velma all about it and she says that you were right. You were right. I shouldn't have stayed with Deke. I shouldn't have married him. There was something wrong with Deke. Velma says there was for sure, that he was crazy, and that I'm not to blame for what I did. She understands. She knows, Velma does. She doesn't hate me for what I've done. She doesn't blame me. She nice and good . . ."

Again those words, Holly thought.

"Velma loves me, Holly. And I love her."

"I know, Poppy. I know."

"And it's not bad. It's not nasty and bad like all the girls at Straker's said . . . said about Jake and me . . . it wasn't bad . . . it isn't with Velma. It was bad what the Reverend did . . . and Deke. Deke hurt me. So did the Reverend. Men hurt, Holly, but Velma loves me and she never hurts me."

It was a scattered revelation. It should have been shattering, but to Holly it wasn't. It was as fragile and fragmented as Poppy was. She knew that she should be revulsed by it, that it should seem unnatural and abhorrent, but she couldn't keep from believing it to be the best solution for her sister. It was too right for Poppy to repel her.

"It isn't nasty or bad, Holly," Poppy concluded.

"No, I don't think that it is."

"I told Velma that you would believe me. She was afraid for me to tell you. She says that no one should know. We have to keep it a secret, otherwise they might try to separate us, like they made Jake go away from Straker's. So Velma comes in the night to my cell when no one can see us. But I told her that you would understand."

Holly had a sharp vision of the two women in darkness on a

narrow cot. A light from far down the cellblock shining on keys, silver keys, that the one woman wore on her belt, the keys that opened the door to Poppy. The silvery keys caught the light in Holly's vision and the light shined, too, on the moving white flesh, soft white women's flesh, coming together and apart finally when the light of dawn came too revealingly. The white bodies parting for the day, the keys going from silver to steel gray, and the waiting beginning, the waiting for the night to come again. Velma clanging the cell door closed on her love, Poppy. That was what Holly saw, and it wasn't ugly to her. It was survival.

"It's good that you have Velma," Holly said. "Do as she says, Poppy. Be very careful," she paused. "You must try and keep one another," she told her and she meant it.

"Velma says that a man gave her her son and she wishes more than anything that she could have saved him. Deke gave me Jasmine. I want to save her. You have to help me save her, Holly. I don't want Jasmine there," Poppy was saying.

"Poppy, what can I do?" Holly asked.

"Take her away."

"You know I can't do that. Custody of Jasmine was given to her grandmother. I'm a single woman. I can't give Jasmine a family."

"But neither can Deke's mother. She's alone. She's a woman. Like you, but not . . . not like you. She's cruel, Holly. She did cruel, terrible things to Deke. He told me. And she'll do the same to Jasmine. I know that she will . . . that she already has."

"Jasmine was fine when I saw her."

"Then you didn't really see. You didn't see enough. I know. I can feel it."

Holly had an idea. She held it out to Poppy, not really believing that it was feasible, but desperate to offer something.

"What if Rose and Clyde could take Jasmine?"

"And not you?" Poppy asked.

"I could visit her, even take her to stay with me sometimes, but Rose being married, it would be better if she asked for custody," Holly said. It was reasonable. It made sense. And she knew that it was only a ploy. She was dangling some hope in front of Poppy so that she could evade the responsibility of Jasmine. She hated what she was doing, but she couldn't stop.

"I always thought you'd marry Paul," Poppy said suddenly. "I would have liked you and Paul to have had Jasmine, but Rose and Clyde would be good, too, I guess."

"I'll talk to Rose about it."

The guard moved in on them. Their time was up. Holly searched the face that was shadowed by the bill of the peaked prison guard cap. This had to be Velma. It was not a soft face, but lantern-jawed and pock-marked, not a pretty passport in a male world. There was strength, character, and a deep decency in the eyes. Those eyes were watching her as closely as she was watching them, Holly became aware. Velma had been scarred, that was apparent, but she had lived. There was neither pride nor shame in her face, but only life lived and endured. Now Holly could put a face to the woman who wore the keys in her vision. This was Velma who nightly went to Poppy's cell and entangled herself, becoming guardian not guard. Velma was very near now. She put a hand on Poppy's shoulder. Poppy turned.

"Is it time?" she asked.

"Yes," Velma told her.

Holly wondered how many times Poppy had asked that at dawn in her cell, and how many times Velma had reluctantly answered yes and left her. Holly saw the rare softness come into Velma's eyes when she looked at Poppy. The voice softened, too, and Holly was sure of its usual hardness. Poppy stood.

"I have to go back," she said.

"Yes." Holly knew that she did and she thought that Poppy seemed relieved to be going.

"You'll talk to Rose?" Poppy asked.

"I will. I'll do all that I can, Poppy, but I can't promise."

"Please try," Poppy pleaded. "Goodbye, Holly."

"Goodbye."

Poppy reached the door and glanced back over her shoulder at her sister. She smiled slightly. Velma had not moved. She stood staring at Holly, her dark, eroding, but enduring face silently beseeching her to help her love, her child Poppy, and Poppy's child. Then she, too, turned. Velma and Poppy went through the door together. Holly listened to their double steps departing as she had listened to their arrival, but now the sounds seemed oddly fitted. Holly was happy that Velma was in Poppy's life. This

potently ugly, almost virile, uniformed woman loved her sister
and Holly could not feel sorry that she did.

On the prison launch to the mainland Holly sat rigidly erect.
The swaying of the small boat rocked her but she did not bend
to it. She fought the wake of feeling and of water, holding to the
edge of her seat, struggling for control. It was as if she were being
pursued, as if she had escaped from the prison, but no one was
coming after her. It was fear that chased and apprehension that
would finally arrest her.

Her apartment was musty, as if it had been closed up for
months instead of weeks. Holly went from window to window,
raising them, letting the stale air out and breathing in the fresh
winter warmth. She walked to the telephone to call Rose, but
hers was not the number that she dialed. Holly didn't realize what
she'd done until she heard Paul's voice. She said nothing, but listened to his repeated hellos and then the click of his receiver. She
hung up. Her heart was beating rapidly. She hadn't intended to
call him. The accidental connection caused an aching, a yearning
for him. She wondered how he was. She had bought his book,
carrying it with her and reading it late at night in motel rooms
from Kansas to Washington and down the long coastline home.
Home. Here. Was she home? She didn't feel as if she lived here
anymore. This was an empty, dusty, and stifled place. She didn't
want to be here. She'd felt more at home in the strange roadside
rooms where she'd been living, with Paul's book open in the light
and closed beside her in the darkness. He had been with her all
the long way. And now she'd mistakenly called him. But was it a
mistake? Yes, it was, she told herself. She denied her need to respond to him, to tell him what she was thinking and feeling, to
ask him what he thought and felt. She carefully dialed Rose's
number and when her sister answered she asked her to come over.
Rose said that she would.

Holly sat down to wait for her, but the empty time filled with
Paul. She took her suitcase into the bedroom and occupied herself
with unpacking. It was no more than fifteen minutes before she
heard Rose.

"Hello!" she was calling through the open door.

"Come in! I'm back here unpacking!" Holly called in return.

"Do you want me to leave the door open?" Rose asked.

"Yes, the place needs air."

Rose walked into Holly's bedroom. Holly was stacking sweaters in her closet. She piled them according to color. The stacks were neat and soft and Rose knew that they would smell faintly of Holly's perfume. She gazed at her sister, thinking that Holly was the only one of them all who had grown prettier with age. No, Rose decided, pretty wasn't the word for Holly. Holly was beautiful now. She'd been the ugly duckling when they were children, but not ugly really, only different. And in childhood difference and ugliness were the same. Rose, habitually, listed her sisters. She began a new comparison among them. Lily had been best at about age sixteen. Rose estimated that she herself had been most appealing when she was eighteen, just when she'd gotten pregnant with the first lost baby. And Iris. Iris had always been gorgeous, but she had lived too fast and too hard to have sustained it, Rose thought. Still she had accomplished a kind of perfection by dying young when she was still flawless. Rose would always remember Iris's beauty. She could not imagine her old and wrinkled. It was the same with Jasmine. Jasmine had been a lovely child. She remained a hauntingly exquisite ghost, but no one knew what she might have been had she lived. That was part of the mystique of the one among them who had been first to die. Poppy had been a pretty little girl, but she had suffered from her nearness to Iris. No one matched up to that kind of rare incandescence and certainly not poor little Poppy. Poppy was still childlike, but with the years her face had changed from piquant to pathetic. But Holly, the stranger, the dark one, had grown to beauty. Maybe because she was alone now, and mature, not surrounded by fair young sisters, but by herself, a bistered and autonomous beauty.

"Hello," Holly greeted her. She still stretched as she stacked sweaters on the top shelf of the closet. She turned. "How are you, Rosie?"

"Oh, you know. I'm all right," Rose answered. "Tell me all about the trip. You didn't spend all this time in New Mexico?"

"No." She paused. "I went to Kansas and Washington."

Rose asked in surprise. "Why Kansas?"

"I don't know. I guess I was nearby and . . ."

"Not that close. There must have been some other reason."

"I wanted to go back." She switched the subject quickly. "Anyway, after Kansas I went straight on to Washington to see Poppy and tell her about Jasmine."

"You did a lot of moving around," Rose observed.

"Yes. It's strange. We lived in all those places when we were children. A lot of memories, Rose, good and bad."

"How is Lily?"

"Lily," Holly said and she shook her head.

Rose understood. "She's the same then."

"I'm afraid I got in the middle of a family crisis."

"What happened?"

"Hope and Jonathan happened," Holly told her.

"What do you mean? What about them?"

"They grew up and they fell in love."

Rose didn't react in any perceptible way, but merely said, "Those two were in love when they were babies, little children."

"Hope didn't know. Lily had kept it a terrible secret. I thought that Hope should know that Workman wasn't her father and Jonathan wasn't her half-brother. She had a right to know, I thought."

"And so you told her?"

"No, Lily did."

"Lily?" Rose asked in disbelief.

"It was awful. I'm sorry it happened, but I'm not. It just didn't seem right to keep it hidden. When does a secret become a lie?" Holly was really asking herself and she answered. "I guess when it reaches the point where only lies will protect the secret and continue the concealment. I couldn't understand keeping Hope and Jonathan from one another when there was really no reason and they were so in love."

"I never thought love meant that much to you, Holly," Rose said. "How did Hope take it?"

"Very well. She's a strong girl."

"She was a strong little girl. So self-contained. It bothered me. I used to think about it a lot, but it looks like it was a good thing after all. Hope needed to be born strong."

"She needs to get away from that house and her mother,"

Holly said, knowing that need well. "I'm sure she'll go now. You were right, Rose. Going there is like visiting a grave."

"Kansas, all of it, not just Lily's little piece of it, is like that to me. Too many babies, and Mama and Daddy buried there. Too many dreams to even count that died in Kansas. I'll never go back there, but I'm leaving California, Holly," she said, springing it suddenly on her sister.

"Where are you going?"

"Nevada."

"You and Clyde?" Holly asked.

"Yes. Clyde's been offered a job there. He's taking me with him."

It was a peculiar phrasing, Holly thought. "Well, of course he's taking you. You're his wife."

"He was going to go alone. He said that he'd get settled and send for me, but . . ."

"What?"

"I didn't believe him. I didn't think he'd send for me. It seemed like the way he'd leave me, backing away, slowly, you know," she said. She laughed. "It's easy to get a divorce in Nevada I've heard."

Holly couldn't join in Rose's laughter though she knew Rose wanted her company. Holly knew that her sister wasn't joking. "Let him go."

"No," Rose refused.

"Does he want you to go with him?"

"I didn't say he wanted me. I said he was taking me."

"Because you asked him?" Holly asked.

"Because I begged him," Rose told her.

"Oh, Rose, why?"

"I want to be with him."

"But you think he wants to divorce you, isn't that right?"

"I was kidding, Holly."

"No, you weren't."

"All right, I wasn't. If I go to Nevada with him, stay close to him, maybe he won't leave me."

"What if he does?" Holly asked.

"I'll be there when he comes back."

"What if he doesn't come back? What if he never comes back? You could spend the rest of your life waiting for him."

"I'm going to Nevada with my husband. That's simple enough, isn't it?"

"Rosie, if you can't leave him, can't you at least let him go?" Holly asked gently.

"No," Rose said. "I thought of going. Years ago back in Kansas I thought of coming out here on my own."

"Why didn't you?"

"I guess I was scared."

"And you are still?"

"No, I don't think I am anymore. You know what I am now, Holly?"

"What?"

"Old and fat and tired. Maybe sometimes Clyde remembers me when I wasn't like this and maybe he still loves me a little then, but who could love me now? Without the memory of what I used to be, who could love me? Besides, Clyde's already done everything I was afraid he would."

"Everything except leave you."

"I can keep him. I can keep him from going," Rose insisted. "I can."

"Rosie, don't. Don't do this. Don't go with him to Nevada. Let him go alone."

"I can't."

It was clear what Rose could and could not do, and just as clearly the sorrow for her sister showed in Holly's face.

"It's not so bad, Holly. Don't feel sorry for me, please. It's really not so bad."

Holly recalled Poppy's words. They were the same as Rose's. Prison wasn't so bad. Clyde wasn't so bad. Life wasn't so bad. It was a settling, Holly thought. It was a pitiful sort of concession, a trading of self for affection and attachment. Was it so terrible to be alone, Holly wondered. It must be to most. Then that was the choice in life. Terrible and unyielding loneliness or identity not so badly lost in compromise and companionship, she was thinking. Reminded of Poppy, Holly said aloud, "You couldn't take Jasmine, could you?"

"Take Jasmine?"

"Yes. Poppy wanted you and Clyde to take Jasmine."

"I thought she wanted you to have her."

"Since I'm single, it seemed to make more sense that you . . .

you being married . . . you'd be better able to give Jasmine a home, a family life."

"Was this Poppy's idea?"

"No, it was mine," Holly admitted.

"I thought so," Rose said.

"I'm not trying to shirk responsibility, Rose."

"No? I think you are. I think you're scared to death to take that little girl, but I don't know why. You're the one who claims to love her so much. You have pictures of her everywhere." Rose looked at the three setting on the dresser. "Is that easier for you, neatly framed pictures, and not the real child?"

Holly thought of her last sight of Jasmine in her car's rearview mirror, all dimension flattened and emotion removed, as in a photograph. Rose had uncanny insight. Holly had noticed that much of her sister's humor had gone. Now she saw that it had been replaced with a sort of disenchanted intuition.

"I do love Jasmine. That doesn't have anything to do with it."

"It has everything to do with it. You have a funny notion of love, Holly."

"What do you mean?"

"Love to you is some kind of pretty fairy story. It's Hope and Jonathan now. It's Clyde and me twenty years ago. It's beautiful and doomed. You don't believe it can last. You can't stick, Holly. If it gets a little ugly or messy or too demanding of you, you run. You ran from Paul and you're running from Jasmine. You and Daddy. You're two of a kind."

"Daddy stayed with Mama," she defended him.

"No."

"Of course he did, Rose."

"Oh, he hung around, but he wasn't really with her."

"Like Clyde with you?" She was sorry after she said it, seeing the pain in Rose's eyes.

"That's right, just like that," she answered.

"I'm sorry, Rosie. I didn't mean to . . ."

"No. It's all right. It's true. Now I know how Mama felt, why she was so crazy."

"But she was the one who held on so tightly. If she was so miserable, if Daddy made her so unhappy, why didn't she let him go?"

"You still don't understand and you'll always defend Daddy anyway," Rose said.

"Lily said that Daddy and I . . ."

"What?" Rose asked.

"That Daddy and I . . ." She still couldn't say it.

Rose narrowed her eyes, as if she were squinting at a too bright light.

"I know what Lily said, Holly. She's said it to me about you and Daddy." Rose hesitated. "Is it true?"

"No," Holly answered immediately, and then, "I don't remember. I swear, I don't."

"I think you'd better try."

"I don't want to remember, Rose."

"You have to, Holly. You have to straighten it out, sort it through, in your own mind. It doesn't matter what anybody else thinks or thinks that they know, but you have to know."

"Rose, would you think it was terrible if it were true?"

"I told you it doesn't matter."

"But it does. Would you?"

"I can't tell you because I don't know how I'd feel. I'll say this. You have the best chance of any of us and I think Daddy gave it to you. You're the Calder girls' best hope."

"You still have a chance."

"No. I might have once a long time ago, but I met Clyde. And Clyde brought out Mama in me. I followed him here and I'm following him to Nevada. You don't have to tell me that it's a dead end. I know it, but I'm as trapped as he is," she said. She slowly stretched her hands and clenched them into fists. "I'm in up to my knuckles." Her knuckles were white with strain and anger. "Lily is lost. Jasmine and Iris both dead. Poppy's life is destroyed."

"Maybe not," Holly said.

"She's going to spend the rest of her life in prison."

"Poppy's not minding prison so much."

"What do you mean?"

"There's someone . . . she's met someone."

"In prison?" Rose asked.

How to describe Velma, Holly thought. "A guard. A woman."

"A friend?"

"A lover," Holly told her.

Rose didn't speak for a moment. "Her lover . . ." She left off.

"Velma," Holly gave her name.

"Do you think Velma is Poppy's lover or her mother?" Rose asked.

Holly was taken aback by Rose's insight. She remembered how Poppy had been loved and dominated by Mama. Now it was Velma. Poppy needed that soft torture and maternal immolation. She was the eternal victim and child, too, but what of Jasmine, Poppy's child? Holly didn't answer Rose's question, but asked, "You can't take Jasmine, can you, Rose?"

"No, you're the one who has to do it, Holly. You're the one among us who can," Rose said. She stood. "Well, I have to start packing."

"So do I," Holly told her.

"But I thought you were unpacking."

"I was, but now I'm not."

"Where are you going now?" Rose asked.

"I'm going . . . to retrace some steps," she answered.

Holly undid the clasp on her suitcase and opened it.

"Walk me to the door?" Rose asked.

Holly went to her.

"Rosie, don't give up, please."

"I already have, Holly, but don't you."

They walked from the room together. Holly's arm was around Rose's waist and Rose's was around hers. Holly had never felt as close to her sister as she did now at their parting.

Chapter Twenty-five

Holly had made a rushed pass through Arizona before, but now it was a destination, an objective. From childhood she remembered her father's stories of the Roosevelt Dam. Thinking of it now, it seemed to her that he had described it like a love affair. It had been his first love. This construction had started him on the life he had lived and loved, building dams and altering the earth with his hands. Farming in Kansas had never been any kind of achievement to him, she knew. For him the plow had been a snare and the tilling of the soil eternal, an endless cycle, unchanging and unceasing. He had despised his maimed agrarian existence. Clay Calder had hated his life once the dams stopped for him. Once he had told Holly that the name Calder meant rushing water. She'd never forgotten that. When he could no longer dam the rushing water, harness its flow and control it, make it conform to his will and design, then his true life had stopped. Holly recalled Rose saying that he had begun to wait to die after she left Kansas, but it wasn't her leaving. He'd wanted her to go. He had started his anticipation of his end when he fell in that craggy and ice-cut Washington coulee and his body was crushed and he could no more dam the rushing water.

Holly had come to the site of the old Roosevelt not to see the solid castlelike structure but to confront the intangible dam within herself, the invisible bulwark of forgotten experience that held back the years of flooding emotion. She walked along the top, thinking that he had helped to build this. He had been adopted by the construction crew. While he grew and the dam slowly rose these men had been his family. This place had been his home. Then he had joined with them, as one of them, not as a child mascot or pet, but a man among men. He had completed the dam with them and moved on with them. He had turned away from his birthplace and followed to the next dam site. Kansas. And Mama. But he had come back to Arizona. Holly remembered his story. She remembered sitting on his lap in the darkness of the many porches of the many houses where they had lived, and his telling of the time he had returned to the Roosevelt Dam. It had been on the day she was born. He had told her this, Daddy had, in the darkness. He had told her how he'd driven across the state on the day that she was born. He had come here at dawn and stood and thanked God for his new baby daughter. That was what he'd told her time after time and she had believed. She stopped her pacing and where she stood she hoped that he had stood. She still believed, believed him. Daddy. She thought of Lily's accusation. She knew that a part of it was not true. She hadn't tempted him when she was grown. Perhaps she had wanted him to leave Kansas with her. Yes, she admitted to herself, she did want to draw him away, but because she loved him and she knew what his life was and was not in Kansas. As a woman she'd never tried to lure him from Mama. She'd never asked his touch, brought him close to her ripened body, never. She knew that. But when she was a child . . . as a child she'd lain in his arms. It was the days of her childhood, the time when Daddy might have initiated a love that she could not have comprehended, that she had lost. She could not now recall. There were moments on porches and beside him in cars that she could conjure up. She felt a vague spreading warmth at these recollections. She tried to focus on Washington, the trip they had made alone there after Jasmine had died. She suspected that if there was any truth in what Lily had said, it would be found somewhere along the road they had traveled to Washington.

With conscious effort she remembered. Her memory reeled
back to the end of the journey rather than the beginning. She
could see her mother's white face suspended over her father's
white hospital bed. Daddy was asleep, in a kind of pained stupor,
and Mama was smiling. She forced herself back beyond that.
Mama was gone. She and Daddy were alone. They were standing
at the coulee's edge. It was deep and the sides jagged. Far down
at the bottom there was a formation of black rock that looked like
a gathering, a coven, of huge dark animals. They, too, faded, as
Mama had, and she was further back, riding through the desert
in a truck, but it wasn't the desert. It was Washington. Still it
looked like the desert they had come from. Off the road was a
tall sunflower with a black center and the image of Jasmine sprang
up beside it. Jasmine and the flaming-faced man who'd come on
the day of Jasmine's funeral and who had cried, his tears extin-
guishing the flame and her fears of him. Then Jasmine was dying.
The night she had died in agony on the desert was before Holly.
It was cold, a cold desert night, and Jasmine was writhing in the
moonlight . . . Holly stopped remembering. She'd gone back
too far. She had skipped and skidded over the times in Washington that she had to remember, had tried so hard to remember.
Still they eluded her, those memories and the answers that they
held.

Holly looked down the arching wall of the dam. She could
jump, she thought. It would take no effort at all to jump right
now. There would be no more memory, no more struggle to
remember or forget. There would be nothing, nothing at all . . .
nothing. She leaned out. A spinning vertigo, a sweeping desire to
experience nothingness, the freedom of nothingness, the libera-
tion of death, seized her. She strained toward the edge, the end.
She heard her mother's voice above the roaring of her death
stretch, but Mama was not speaking to her. Holly knew that she
was not because she heard Daddy answering.

"Stop it, Jane."

Holly heard him saying it.

"Do you think Holly would like knowing that you're a bastard?" she heard her mother asking him.

"She wouldn't even know what that was."

"But you do. You do. Do you think she'd understand that your
mother was a whore? Or maybe she'd like to know what really

happened on the day she was born and you went to the Roosevelt Dam. Would she understand that you wanted to die on the day she was born?"

"That's not true."

"It is."

"But it had nothing to do with Holly."

Standing, poised to leap, Holly heard them as clearly as she had when she had stood in the hallway outside one of their many closed doors during her childhood. She listened and she knew that Daddy had wanted to jump just as she did from the turreted top of this old dam. She and Daddy. She and Daddy. Everyone said that she was like him. Sometimes she thought that she was him. She felt the thin and empty air around her. She closed her eyes. She would now do what Daddy had intended doing, had wanted to do. She would. She would fulfill him finally, the ultimate fulfillment. She would live and die his fate. She would jump for him and for herself, too. They were the same. She was Daddy. Daddy had loved her, groomed her to become him. She was here to take his place, his part, in life and to relinquish it as he had wanted but could not do himself.

Mama's voice came to her again. She listened as a child to it. Behind her closed eyes she was standing once more in the hallway outside their room. She heard Mama, but her voice was not speaking words. There were soft cries, choking sounds, as if she were drowning in warm water. The child Holly cracked opened the door. She watched her mother and father in their bed. Mama moved to the dying noise that she made, but there was no sound from Daddy . . . no sound from him that night, only silent wavering, as she spied upon them through the gaping door . . . but the night in Washington. . . . The memory rose up effortlessly now. The night in Washington . . . the night she'd left her small bed and come to his big one . . . the cool sheets and the tears he cried as he touched her . . . touched her while he thought that she slept on the cool sheets. She hadn't slept. She was awake with her eyes closed as she was now standing on the brink and remembering it at last. Daddy was touching her, but not as she had seen him touch Mama. She was beside him in the bed and he touched her skin, stroked it, and her hair, too, but gently, so gently, not roughly, not hatefully riding her as she had seen him ride Mama . . . Mama splayed beneath him, wetly choking, and Daddy soundlessly moving himself in and out of her split body . . . it wasn't like that, not what it had been with Mama. That night in Washington he'd held her to him, but he had not entered her. He had cried and touched and loved her. He was hers . . . her Daddy, and he loved his little girl, loved her from the day that she was born so darkly like him . . . like him . . . like him.

Holly opened her eyes and backed away from the edge. It was true that Daddy had come here to die when she was only hours old, she knew that, but he hadn't died. He hadn't jumped. And neither could she. He had loved her. Her small life had saved him from death that dawn. He loved her and that saved her now. Mama had been capable of only a choking passion, a drowning love, and all her daughters were like her. All but one. Herself, Holly realized. She was Daddy's child. He had loved her. And he had saved her. They, she and Daddy, loved in a different way. This was how she would fulfill him, not by committing the suicide that he had once considered, but by loving in his manner. She would funnel the rushing water through a dam of understanding and tenderness, not obstructing or repressing any longer, but lovingly controlling. Daddy had wanted that for Mama, too, but she had been beyond control, past resuscitation, drowning and dragging under all those near her, too. She'd destroyed them all, Mama had, all but the dark sister, the stranger among them. Daddy had delivered his child, but he hadn't been able to save himself. Holly cried for him now.

And now she was able to go on. She could leave the old Roosevelt, leave it with the knowledge that had been damned and dammed within her. Once off the high structure she was astonished at the clear memory of nearly jumping. She didn't want to die. She hadn't really wanted to die when she was contemplating death from the dam. She had wanted to know. She had been tortured; wondering whether to believe Lily or to believe in Daddy. Even Rose had been suspicious. Good Rose had had her doubts. All the sisters had, Holly realized now. They were all Mama's girls, either actively or passively destructive women, unable to love a man, but possessed by an uncontrollable desire to attract men or to hold them. Iris had worked a killing fascination, her life littered with discarded lovers she had hated. Jasmine had chosen to die, to cease as a child on the desert, rather than become a woman, a bleeding monster, a Mama. Lilly, Poppy, and Rose, too, practiced unconscious, even unwilling, strangleholds with varying degrees or fluctuant power and fearful cruelty. None of them could understand what Daddy had given to her alone, Holly knew. She was different from them.

She drove her car away from the dam feeling strongly this difference. She was driving toward Jasmine, hoping that she could take her from her grandmother and raise her differently, impart and preserve this precious difference. And she thought of Paul. She wanted Paul to be a part of her life and of Jasmine's. She needed Paul. She loved him. She had always loved him, but she had always feared that along with Paul and her love of him would come the instincts and actions of Mama. How she had feared that, feared turning into her mother, grasping at Paul and destroying their love and even themselves. Mama had done that to Daddy and to herself. She had to tell Paul this. Though they had never spoken of it, she knew that she had let Paul believe that Daddy was to blame, that no one, no man, could ever be what her father had been to her. She had believed, been afraid of that, herself. She had to tell Paul that it wasn't Daddy. It was Mama. It had always been Mama. It wasn't that she'd been so damaged by Mama's treatment of her when she was a child. She had survived that. It was something else, something that she had very nearly not overcome, that she was only now realizing. It was the daily display of Mama's character that had terrified her. This was what it meant to be a woman, what Mama was, she had thought. She had lived in fear of becoming Mama. It was as simple as that, but the tangled associations and kinked memories that had grown up around that one fear had made it far more complex than it was. She had to see Paul and explain all of this to him. She couldn't let Paul blame Daddy any longer. It was Daddy who had rescued, not ruined, her. She had to go to Paul, but she knew that he might not be there for her. She might have lost him to her years of reticence and fear. Paul might be gone. He might turn away from her as she had turned away from him so often in the past. It was painful to think of Paul cold toward her. How many times she had been cold toward him, she knew, but there had been flashes of warmth. She could only hope that those brief flares had been enough to sustain him and his love for her, but she couldn't depend upon that. She had to prepare herself for the loss of him. Still she couldn't believe that Paul had stopped loving her. She had never stopped loving him. If only she could go to him immediately and show him the things she had found today, but Jasmine had to come first. She had to try and take Jasmine. The child was the key. She wanted Jasmine as much now as she wanted Paul. They came together for her. She loved them both. Jasmine would be her proof to Paul and to herself, proof that she could love without the possessive loathing that was Mama's legacy. Holly was joyously disinherited. She would take Jasmine and go to Paul. He would be waiting. He had to be. She drove faster. Soon she would cross from Arizona into New Mexico.

This time she did not call before arriving at the ranch. She came unannounced and found Zara Cody out in her garden. The old woman hoed the ground where nothing grew. Nothing had been planted there. The stony and porous earth was raked but never seeded. Holly stopped the car and got out.

"Hello, Mrs. Cody," she called to her.

Zara Cody stopped her work. She planted the skeletal digits of the rake in the ground, leaned on the long wooden handle, and glared at the intruder.

Holly approached but did not come too near. "I came to see Jasmine," she said.

"She's taking a nap. You can't see her now."

Holly sensed the sound of lies, lying words.

"I'd like to see her please, Mrs. Cody."

"I won't wake her."

"All right," Holly said. "I'll wait."

Zara Cody stared hard at her. "You can't wait here," she told Holly.

"I'll wait in my car."

"No."

"I don't think that Jasmine is taking a nap. Where is she?" Holly stepped closer, confronting the woman.

"She's sleeping in her room," Zara Cody stolidly insisted.

Holly looked toward the house. The woman blocked her path to the front door. There had to be a way inside at the back, she was thinking, and she started for it. Zara broke from her impassive stance and chased after Holly. She carried the hoe with her.

"You can't go in there," she warned Holly. "I won't have it. I won't have you in my house."

But Holly was already inside. She ran through the kitchen and down a dark hallway. She was throwing open doors as she went, but all the rooms behind them were empty. She could hear Zara Cody's pursuit. She opened the door of the last room. It was Jasmine's. She knew that it was. The doll that she had given her was lying on the small bed, but Jasmine was not there. Zara Cody had lied. Holly saw her come to the doorway of the room. She stood there with her hoe and Holly felt a wave of fear. She was trapped, but she couldn't let Zara Cody know that she was. She walked toward the woman and the door.

"Where is Jasmine?" she demanded to know.

"Never you mind where she is . . . where she is . . . is where she ought to be."

Holly stood directly in front of her, facing her.

"Where?" Holly asked.

"No," Zara Cody said in answer.

Holly stepped around her. She wanted to run down the hallway, but she did not. She walked slowly and deliberately out of Zara Cody's house. In the yard she stopped and called out.

"Jasmine! Jasmine!"

The searching cries of that name reminded her of something. Her calls were echoic. She remembered Mama or Lily crying into the desert for Jasmine to come home. Jasmine. Jasmine, her sister who had died. And Holly felt a cold dread that this Jasmine, too, might be dead or dying. She believed Zara Cody capable of killing.

"Jasmine! Jasmine!"

She heard how panicked and desperate she sounded, how afraid.

"Jasmine, where are you?" she asked quietly. "Jasmine. Jasmine," she whispered.

The fear was still there. Now it was low-pitched and gnawing.

"Here. Here I am."

Holly heard the child's voice. It was coming from somewhere nearby, but she couldn't see Jasmine anywhere. She scanned the sterile desert horizon for the little girl, but there was nothing.

"Where are you, Jasmine?" she asked.

"Here. Here."

Holly followed the sound to some planks on the ground a few yards away from the back porch.

"Jasmine?" she asked, no longer into nothingness.

"Here I am," she said.

Holly began tearing at the boards. She found Jasmine down in the hole and lifted her out. She was aware of Zara Cody watching. She untied Jasmine's hands. Her wrists were red and raw from the tight binding.

"Aunt Holly," Jasmine said.

"Yes, it's Aunt Holly. Are you all right?"

Jasmine looked off toward her grandmother. Zara Cody had returned to her garden. Still she clutched her hoe. Holly saw Jasmine's look.

"Don't be afraid of her. You can tell me, Jasmine. You're going to come with me. She's not going to hurt you anymore. You can tell me what she's done to you," she said. She took one of the child's abused hands. "I won't let her hurt you. Never again."

"Are we going now?" Jasmine asked.

"Yes, now."

"I want to take Snow," she said.

It took Holly only a moment to realize what the little girl was saying. Jasmine didn't want to leave her doll behind.

"All right," Holly said.

They walked together toward the house. Then Holly released her hand.

"You go on in and get Snow. Come right out." she directed the child.

Jasmine ran into the house. Holly went over to the garden. She wasn't going to blame Zara Cody. What the woman had done went beyond blame. She was to be damned, but Holly wouldn't damn her either. She said only, "I'm taking her. You can't stop me. I'm taking her with me right now."

"Take her then. I never wanted her. They brought her to me. Her and the dead boy. Take her from me. I never wanted her here."

Jasmine came from the house. She had Snow in her arms. She

went straight to the car, not once looking at her grandmother, not speaking a word to her.

"Take her away," Zara Cody intoned. She resumed hoeing her empty garden.

Holly left her there. She got into the car and started the engine.

"Jess died," Jasmine said quietly.

Holly knew she was speaking of the old blind dog.

"Grandma buried him yesterday."

Holly said nothing.

"She buried him in the garden," Jasmine went on.

Holly shuddered. She hoped that the dust rising up from the wheels of the car would settle quickly and there would be no trace left of them, no trail to follow.

During the drive to California Holly told Jasmine of the Calder sisters. In the telling to the child it became a simpler and sweeter story, one with beginning and end.

". . . Daddy built dams and he dreamed of making the desert a garden. Mama wanted a garden, but there was never time. We didn't stay long enough in one place. So Mama named all of us, all of the sisters, for flowers. She said she could carry her garden with her then, wherever we went. Her girls were her garden. There was Lily, Jasmine, Rose, Holly, Iris, and Poppy . . ."

"Jasmine, like me?" the little girl asked, recognizing her name.

"Yes. You were named for Jasmine. Jasmine died when she was very young. She was born in New Mexico and she . . ." Holly hesitated. "She was buried there."

Holly realized that within the simplicity she was creating for the child's understanding there was a meaning that had escaped her before, that had been hidden in the labyrinth of the remembered and the forgotten, but was now clear to her, revealed in her story told for the little girl.

"Lily is the oldest sister. She was born in Kansas and she lives there still. Lily has one daughter and the rest of her children are boys, big blond boys. They live on a farm," she concluded and left the Kansas home of Lily at that for Jasmine. She would try to leave it that way for herself also, she decided. She continued. "Rose is the sister of laughter. Through all her life she has tried to smile and find something bright or funny or good. She fell in love and married young. Rose is going to live in Nevada with her husband. We'll be driving through Nevada, Jasmine. Rose was born there." The story was taking shape as she told it. Holly's thoughts were traveling far ahead of her words. She could see the pattern now. It was very plain. "Iris was the most beautiful." She would omit the horrible end of that beauty, she decided. That she would not share with the child. "All of her life Iris was loved for her beauty. She was born in California where we're going, where you were born, Jasmine. Iris went too fast. One night she crashed and she died beneath a pine tree not far from the sea." Holly painted the death beautifully, knowing full well its horror. "And Poppy is the youngest. She's your mother, Jasmine. Do you remember her?" she asked.

"No," Jasmine answered.

"She loves you very much. And she didn't want to leave you, but she had to, Jasmine. She's so sorry. She had to leave, but she'll always love you. She lives in a place way up north. Maybe someday we can go and visit her there. Would you like that?"

"Is there snow there?"

"Sometimes there is."

"Could we see the snow and Mama, too?" Jasmine asked.

"I think that we could. She'd love to see you. She wants that so much," Holly told her.

"Why doesn't she come to see me?"

"She can't leave where she is, but we could go to her. We'd take a boat across the water and then go inside a house with tall walls and walk through lots and lots of doors to see her."

"Will she ever get to leave there?"

"No, Jasmine, she won't. She'll live in that house all of her life. She was born not far from it. All the sisters, all the flowers of Mama's garden went back to the places that they'd come from, all but one."

"Who didn't?"

"I didn't."

"Why didn't you?" the child asked.

It was so simple, Holly was thinking. "For a while it seemed that all that grew in Mama's garden were wildflowers. The sisters blew apart and scattered, but one by one they all returned to their root, their core, to Mama and the earth where they'd been seeds. All of them but one, the one true wildflower among them," she said.

"You," Jasmine said. "You didn't tell me about you, Aunt Holly. You told me all about the others."

"That's because I was telling the story. That's what I do. And that's what I am."

"You're the teller," the child said.

"Yes, I'm the teller," Holly confessed.

"Tell me more," Jasmine asked of her.

And Holly did, weaving the words like silken threads into a whole piece of cloth, all the long way home to the place she hoped to root, to make her fountainhead.

She parked the car up on the highway. They walked down a flight of weathered wooden stairs to the beach. The early morning early spring air was not drawing sunbathers, not even sweatered strollers. They were alone on the sand. Holly had purposely parked some distance from Paul's house. She wanted to go slowly to it, composing her thoughts, her words, her face, in advance of the meeting. She wanted, too, to see what she was coming upon before she was seen. She was about to embark on living her life, but there remained these last few moments of approach, of being the cautious observer.

Jasmine did not remember the ocean. She was wild to go into the water. Holly held her hand and told her.

"It's too cold now. When the summer comes you can go in the way you used to. You loved the water when you were a baby. I would carry you in and you would dangle your fingers in the waves and then lick them. You loved even the taste of the ocean. And we would build sand castles. Right here, Jasmine. On this beach. You don't remember?"

Jasmine was looking up at her.

"And we'd go to the pier. To the merry-go-round. You'd ride in front of me on the horse."

"The white one," Jasmine said.

"Yes, the white one with the purple reins painted on it. That was your favorite. You would cry if I took you on any other and point to the white one. You do remember."

Jasmine nodded her head. The happiness of her very early life was slowly returning to her. She was beginning to remember the feeling of it. She was beginning to feel it again.

Holly looked ahead. They were close to Paul's house now. Still there was no one in sight. The white cottage looked deserted. Her heart contracted. Paul was gone. He wasn't there. She'd waited too long to come back to him. Jasmine spoke, her low and clear, old voice coming incongruously from her.

"Cotton candy."

"What?" Holly asked, jarred from her thoughts.

"Cotton candy, Aunt Holly. It was pink, soft and pink, and it was sweet. Good. Cotton candy. You called it that. I remember," she said and the taste of it was on her tongue.

"Yes, Jasmine."

Holly was searching for the sight of him. They were in front of the house now. The bougainvillea she had planted was spilling over the low fence, its purple bracts bright against the white pickets, gorgeously untended and giving a look of splendid abandon to the place.

"Pretty," Jasmine said, looking at the house.

"Do you like it?" Holly asked. She didn't ask this time if the child remembered. She didn't want to prompt her. She hoped that Jasmine might recall it, as she had the cotton candy, on her own. Holly hoped she would recall this place and Paul who had ridden her piggyback on his shoulders into the waves. Holly remembered so well. All of it. Even the spiny and bloomless little plant that she had put into the ground, she remembered. And how it had grown, spreading in rampaging color, she thought.

"Yes," Jasmine said and she freed herself from Holly's holding hand, ran toward the house.

"Wait!" Holly called to her. "Wait! Don't Jasmine!" She had feared the house was empty and now she was more afraid that it was not. Jasmine might disturb the occupant and it might be a stranger, not Paul but a stranger, and she couldn't bear that, she knew. "Wait!"

"Pretty," the child shouted back to her. She pulled a handful of the flowers and came running, returning, to Holly with them. "Pretty," she said and presented them.

Holly took the flowers. The door of the house opened. Jasmine looked up at the sound. And so did Holly. Paul stepped out onto the terrace. He saw them. Jasmine, wary suddenly, hid herself at Holly's legs. Holly wished for a place to hide. Paul didn't smile. He didn't come down the steps to them. He stood and silently stared. Holly watched for any greeting from him, any response. It was Paul and not a stranger, but he might have grown into a stranger, grown as the bougainvillea had.

"Hello, Paul," she called up to him.

Then he started down the steps. She saw that he was wearing his father's coat, the one that they had made a bed of, made love upon, not so very long ago. Or was it longer than she realized, she wondered. Was it too long ago? He crossed the short stretch of sand and stopped before her. He still didn't speak, but kneeled down to Jasmine. He smiled and held out his hand to her. She took it. He lifted her up into his arms and stood.

"Paul, I . . . we've come home," Holly said.

Jasmine had easily put her arms around his neck. He held her to him with one arm. With his free hand he touched Holly's face.

"Welcome home," he said finally.

Without another word spoken they turned and walked toward the house, Holly releasing in a vivid and fluttering stream the flowers that had been picked for her by Jasmine.

Drusilla Campbell

BROKEN PROMISES

A terrible secret lies buried in the Hopewell past –
a mystery that haunts the dreams and hopes of
beautiful 18-year-old Suzannah Hopewell.

Born the daughter of a rigid New England mill-
owning family, Suzannah longs for a love that will
take her away from the cruelty and injustice that
surround her.

Though she finds tenderness in Travis Paine, a
brilliant young architect, a new passion sweeps her
into the arms of Roberto Monteleone, a sculptor
from far-distant Sicily.

But as she struggles with her deepest feelings, a
ruthless tyrant stands in her way, covering up an
unspeakable crime. He is the man she must call
"Father".

Here is a brilliant saga of shattering love, and a
young woman's conflict with destiny.